HACK

VOLUME TWO: DEATH BY SEQUEL

A
TIM SEELEY/STEFANO CASELLI
PRODUCTION

WRITER **TIM SEELEY**

ART **DAVE CROSLAND, TIM SEELEY, SKOTTIE YOUNG, MIKE NORTON
MARK ENGLERT, NATE BELLGARDE, STEFANO CASSELI, ANDY KUHN,
JOSH MEDORS, JOE LARGENT, SEAN DOVE**

COLORS **KATIE DESOUSA, ROALD MUNOZ, PETER SOFRONAS,
ANDREW DALHOUSE, CHRIS SUMMERS, MARK ENGLERT,
JOSH BLAYLOCK, DANIELE RUDONI**

LETTERERS **STEVE SEELEY, BRIAN J. CROWLEY**

REPRINT SERIES DESIGN & PRODUCTION **MONICA GARCIA**

REPRINT SERIES EDITOR **JAMES LOWDER**

IMAGE COMICS. INC.

ROBERT KIRKMAN CHIEF OPERATING OFFICER
ERIK LARSEN CHIEF FINANCIAL OFFICER
TODD MCFARLANE PRESIDENT
MARC SILVESTRI CHIEF EXECUTIVE OFFICER
JIM VALENTINO VICE-PRESIDENT

ERIC STEPHENSON PUBLISHER
TODD MARTINEZ SALES & LICENSING COORDINATOR
JENNIFER DE GUZMAN PR & MARKETING DIRECTOR
BRANWYN BIGGLESTONE ACCOUNTS MANAGER
EMILY MILLER ADMINISTRATIVE ASSISTANT
JAMIE PARRENO MARKETING ASSISTANT
SARAH DELAINE EVENTS COORDINATOR

KEVIN YUEN DIGITAL RIGHTS COORDINATOR
DREW GILL ART DIRECTOR
JONATHAN CHAN PRODUCTION MANAGER
MONICA GARCIA PRODUCTION ARTIST
VINCENT KUKUA PRODUCTION ARTIST
JANA COOK PRODUCTION ARTIST
WWW.IMAGECOMICS.COM

HACK/SLASH Vol. 2: DEATH BY SEQUEL
ISBN: 978-1-60706-606-4
First Printing

September 2012. Published by Image Comics, Inc. Office of publication: 2134 Allston Way, 2nd Floor, Berkeley, CA 94704. Copyright © 2012 Hack/Slash, Inc.
Originally published in single magazine form by Devil's Due Publishing as THE LAND OF LOST TOYS #1-3, TRAILERS #1, SLICE HARD PREQUEL, and SLICE HARD.
All rights reserved. HACK/SLASH™ (including all prominent characters featured herein), its logo and all character likenesses are trademarks of Hack/Slash,
Inc. unless otherwise noted. Image Comics® and its logos are registered trademarks of Image Comics, Inc. No part of this publication may be reproduced or
transmitted, in any form or by any means (except for short excerpts for review purposes) without the express written permission of Image Comics, Inc. All names,
characters, events and locales in this publication are entirely fictional. Any resemblance to actual persons (living or dead), events or places, without satiric intent,
is coincidental. All rights reserved. International Rights / Foreign Licensing -- foreignlicensing@imagecomics.com. For information regarding the CPSIA on this
printed material call: 203-595-3636 and provide reference # RICH – 454707.
PRINTED IN USA.

INTRO/TIFFANY SHEPIS

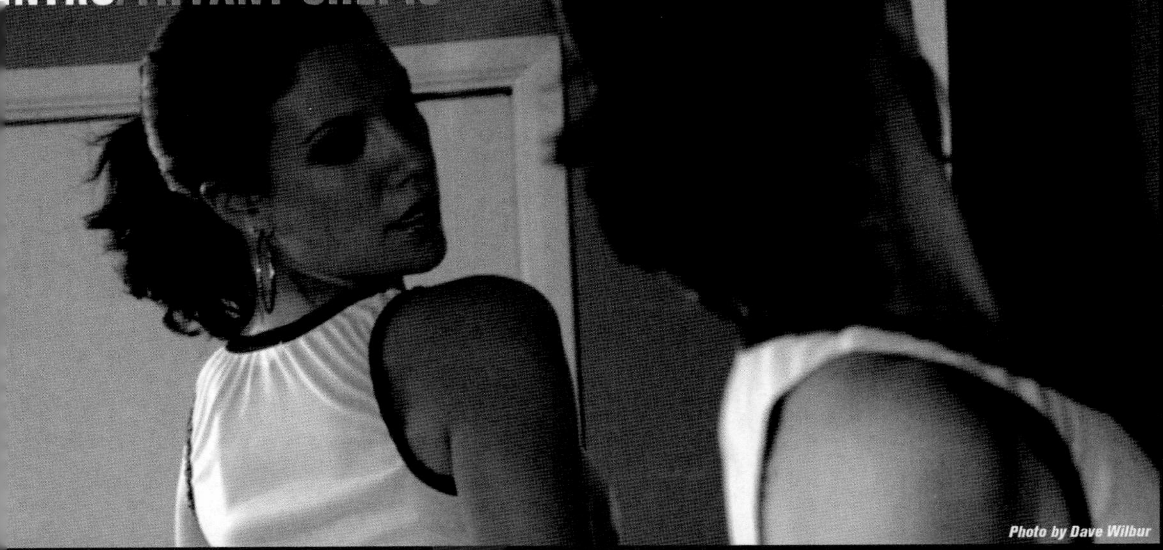

Photo by Dave Wilbur

Let's talk a bit about the man behind *Hack/Slash*: Mr. Tim Seeley. You know what makes Tim great? While most people steal identities with credit cards and Social Security numbers, crafty Tim steals them with comic books! Let me explain. You see, the man stole my likeness, my occupation, and my all-around badass-ness to create his Cassie character, but he was still nice enough to send me a copy of the comic, free of charge, after he did it. Classy!

So from here on out, we will be referring to him as *Tim Stealy*.

I finally got a chance to meet Tim at the Fangoria Convention in Burbank, California. I wish I could say some super-nice, great things about this talented guy, but all I really got out of the meeting was that he was kinda cute and he had a super-hot, obviously insane girlfriend. How do these geeks do it? I'll tell you how: they create a comic book based on me – instant popularity! I watched him float around the convention with that "I'm-too-good-for-everybody" look. All the while, you could (or at least I could) see the fear in his eyes . . . the fear that someone would catch on to his dirty little secret: Cassie is not a concoction made up by some genius comics creator. Cassie is more like Tim's secret stalker homage to me.

I should be flattered, I guess. After all, he's crossed over the line where sick and twisted meets fun and charming and he does it well. Now if he will only seal the deal: let me have my part as Cassie in the film version of *Hack/Slash*. The world would be a better place.

In the words of my dear friend Billy Jean: "FAIR IS FAIR!"

It's owed to me. Come on, kids. The only thing that he didn't do was put the spider tattoo over Cassie's ass crack.

So at the end of the day, my identity has been stolen to make some pretty kick-ass comic books. I guess it could be worse. At least Tim was gracious enough to allow me to write this lame-ass introduction to some pretty amazing books. It's great to see an obvious fan of the horror/slasher genre bring it to comics.

I really am a fan of Tim, and everything *Hack/Slash*, no matter how hard a time I give him. They say jealousy is the biggest compliment – I'M F*%KING JEALOUS! Thanks, Mr. Stealy, for keeping us gore/camp hounds entertained. Uh, I mean Seeley.

ENJOY.

–Tiffany "Cassie" Shepis

Tiffany Shepis is the star of *Scarecrow*, *Delta Delta Die!*, *The Hazing*, *Nightmare Man*, *Abominable*, and *Troma's Edge TV*

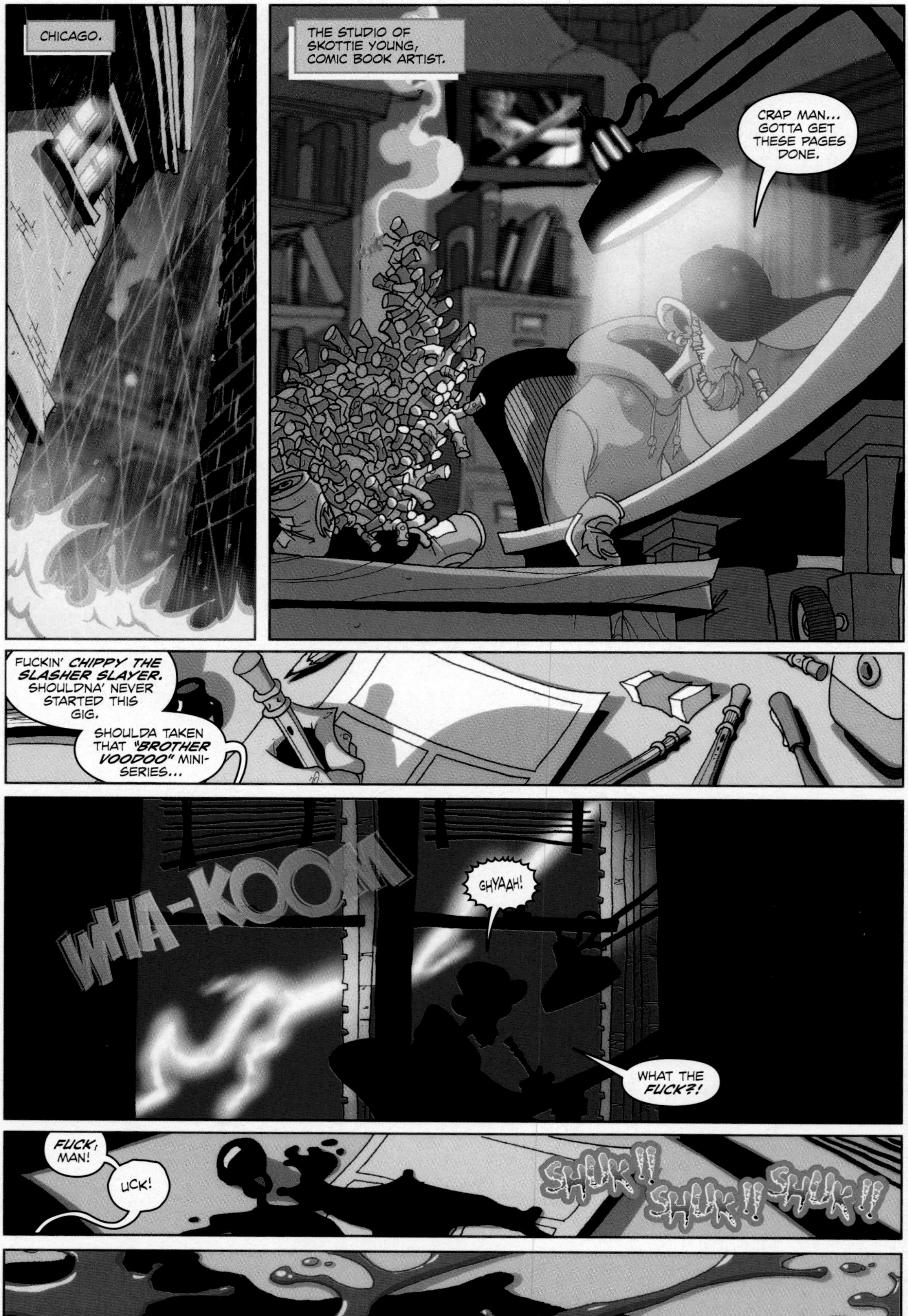
CHICAGO.
THE STUDIO OF SKOTTIE YOUNG, COMIC BOOK ARTIST.
CRAP MAN... GOTTA GET THESE PAGES DONE.
FUCKIN' *CHIPPY THE SLASHER SLAYER.* SHOULDNA' NEVER STARTED THIS GIG.
SHOULDA TAKEN THAT *"BROTHER VOODOO"* MINI-SERIES...
WHA-KOOM
GHYAAH!
WHAT THE *FUCK?!*
FUCK, MAN!
UCK!
SHUK!! SHUK!! SHUK!!

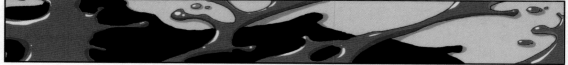

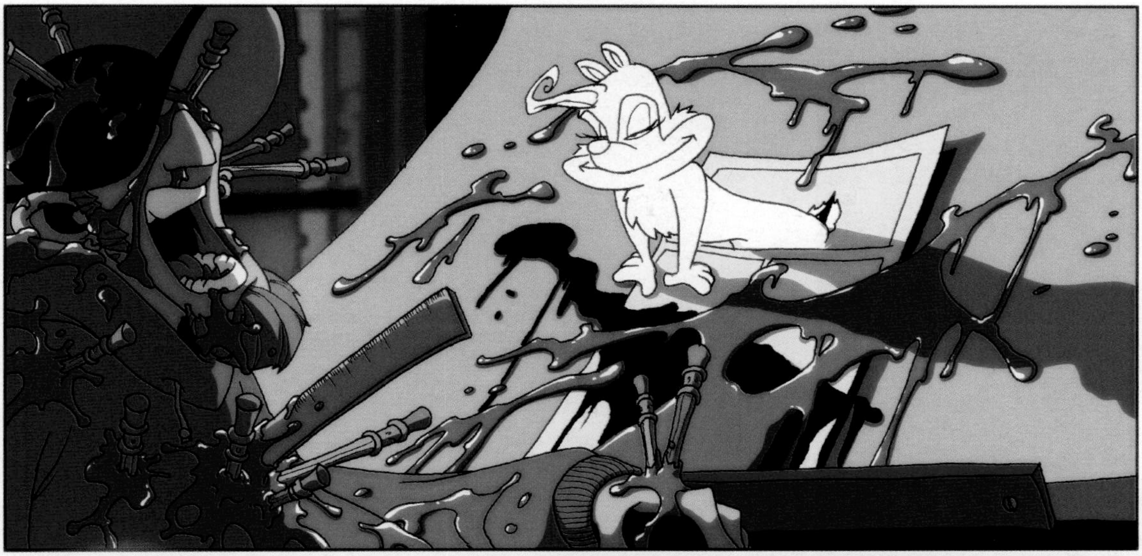

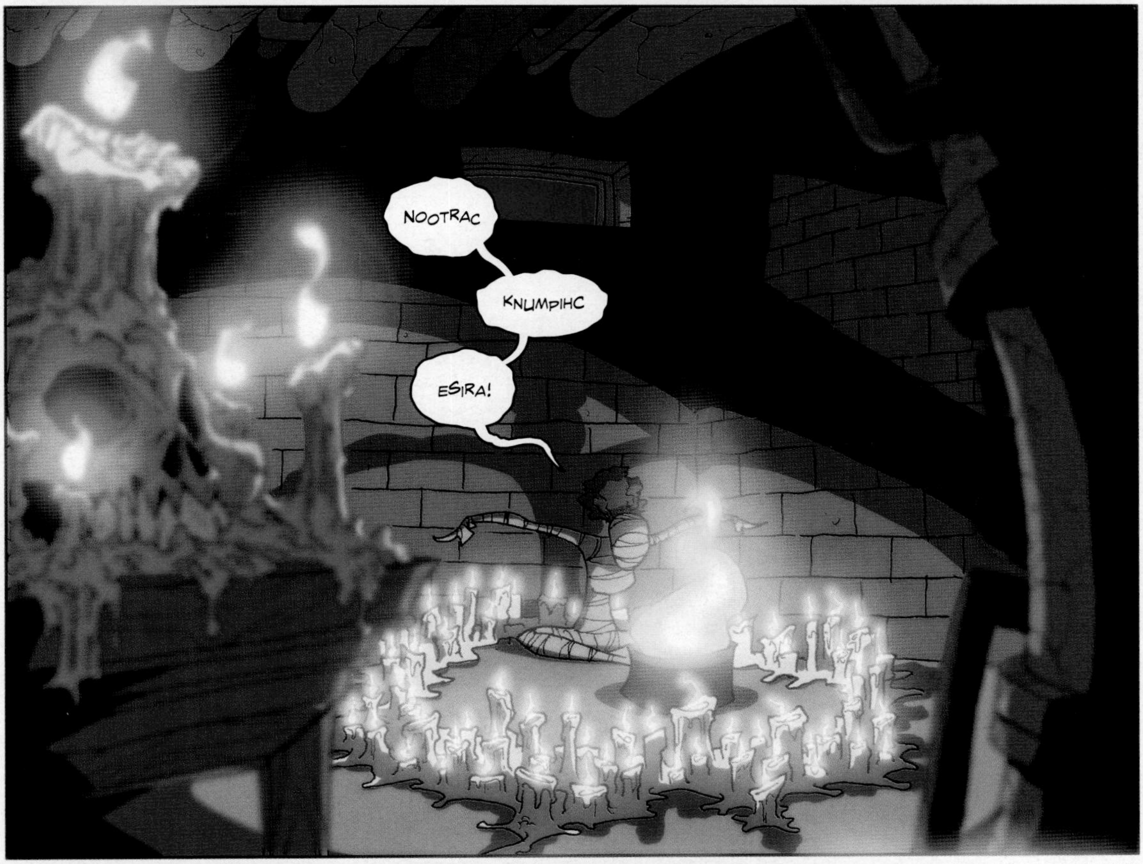
NOOTRAC
KNUMPIHC
ESIRA!

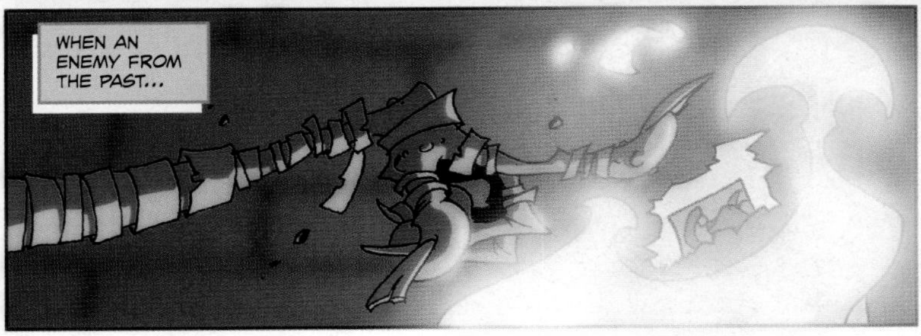
WHEN AN ENEMY FROM THE PAST...

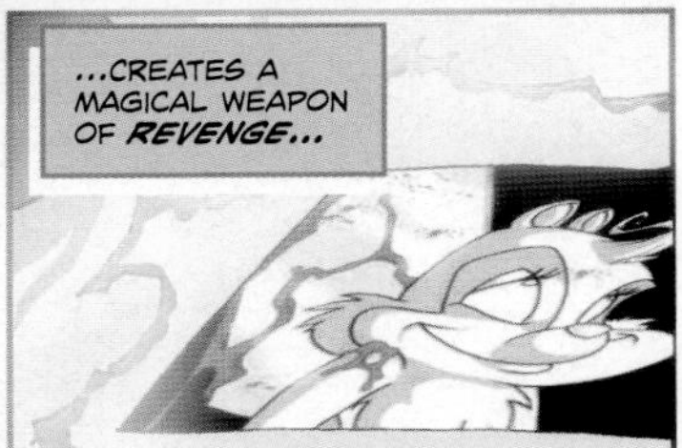
...CREATES A MAGICAL WEAPON OF ***REVENGE...***

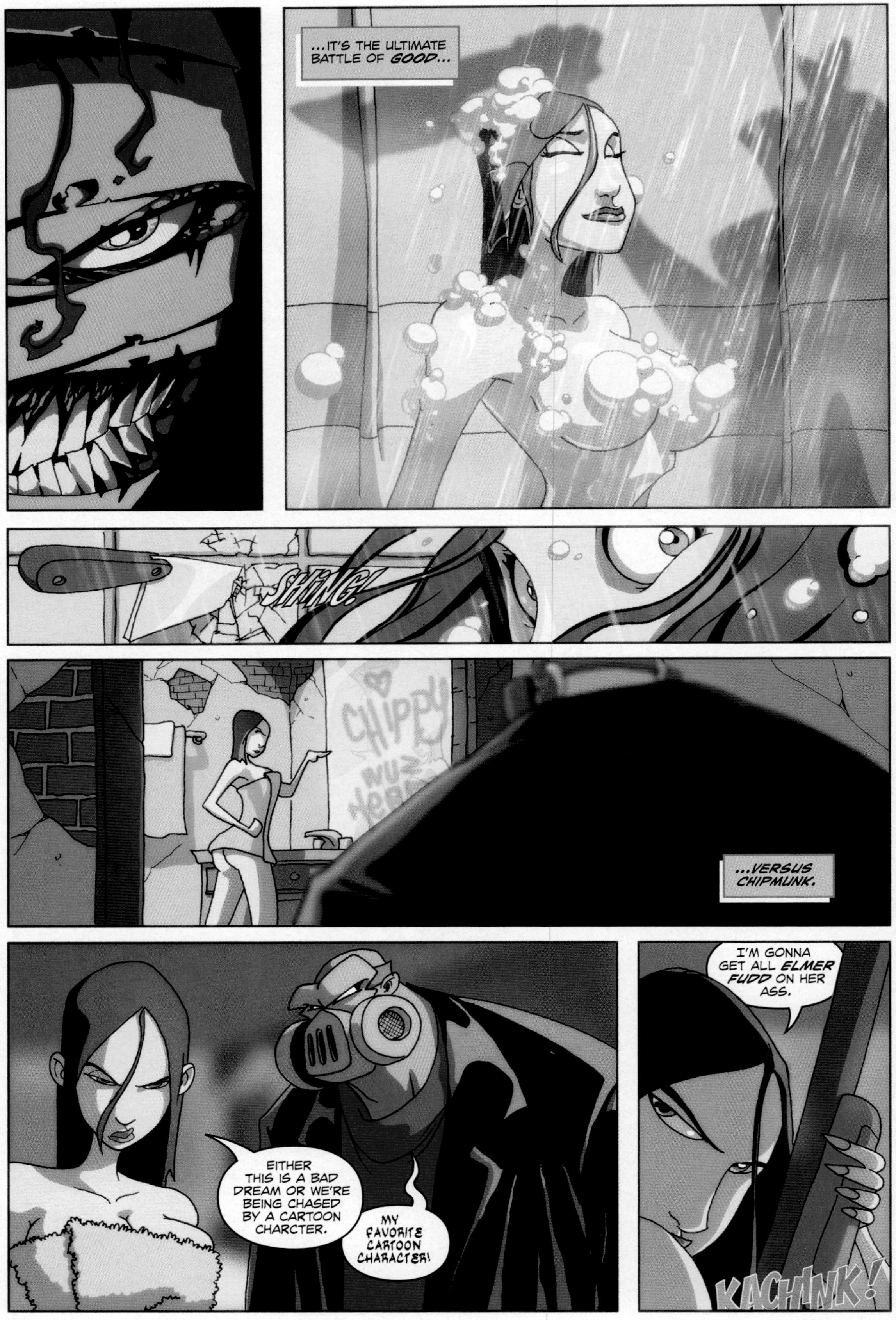

...IT'S THE ULTIMATE BATTLE OF *GOOD*...
SHING!
CHIPPY
...VERSUS CHIPMUNK.
EITHER THIS IS A BAD DREAM OR WE'RE BEING CHASED BY A CARTOON CHARCTER.
MY FAVORITE CARTOON CHARACTER!
I'M GONNA GET ALL *ELMER FUDD* ON HER ASS.
KACHINK!

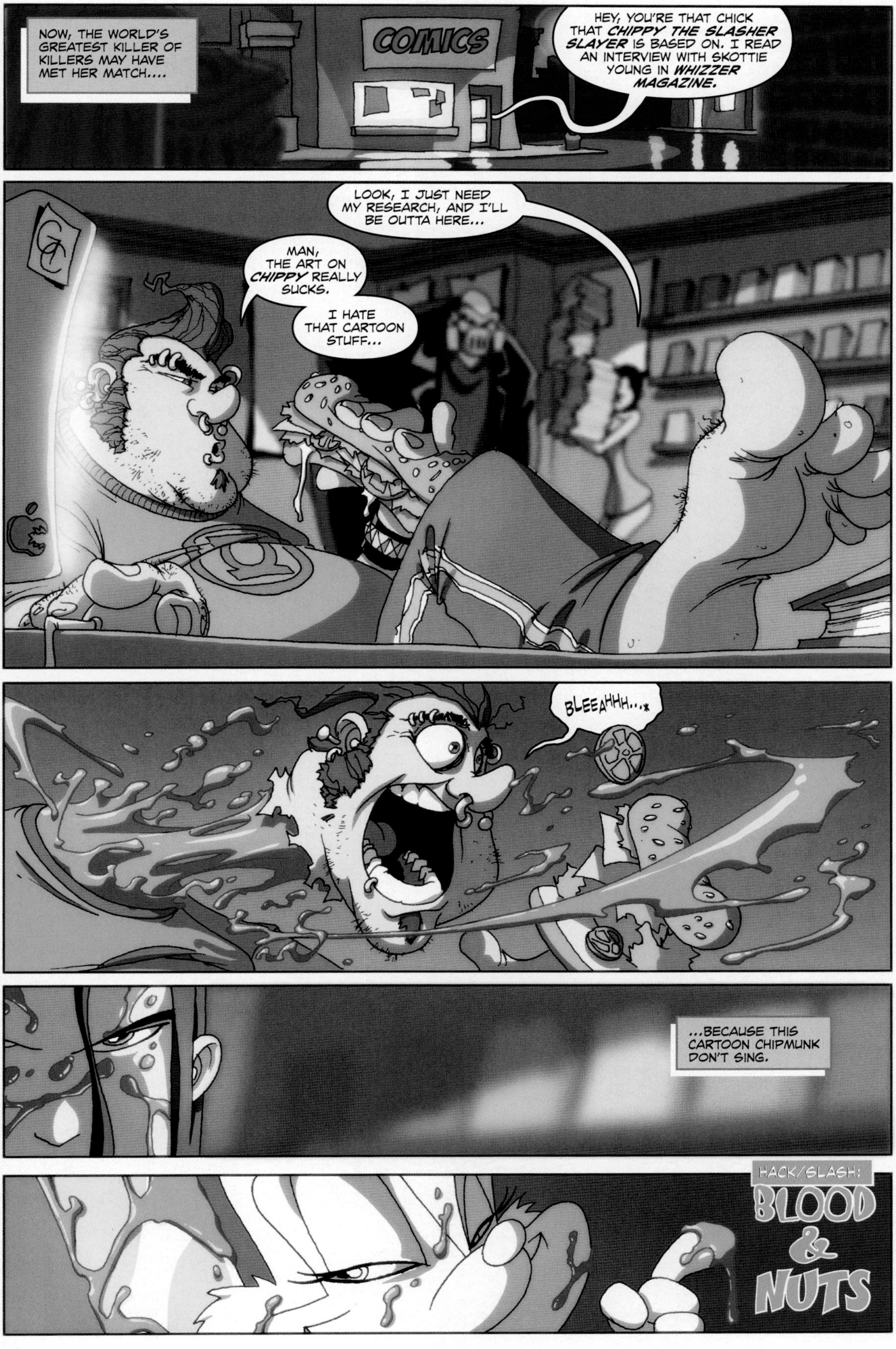
NOW, THE WORLD'S GREATEST KILLER OF KILLERS MAY HAVE MET HER MATCH....
COMICS
HEY, YOU'RE THAT CHICK THAT CHIPPY THE SLASHER SLAYER IS BASED ON. I READ AN INTERVIEW WITH SKOTTIE YOUNG IN WHIZZER MAGAZINE.
LOOK, I JUST NEED MY RESEARCH, AND I'LL BE OUTTA HERE...
MAN, THE ART ON CHIPPY REALLY SUCKS.
I HATE THAT CARTOON STUFF...
BLEEAHHH...*
...BECAUSE THIS CARTOON CHIPMUNK DON'T SING.
HACK/SLASH:
BLOOD & NUTS

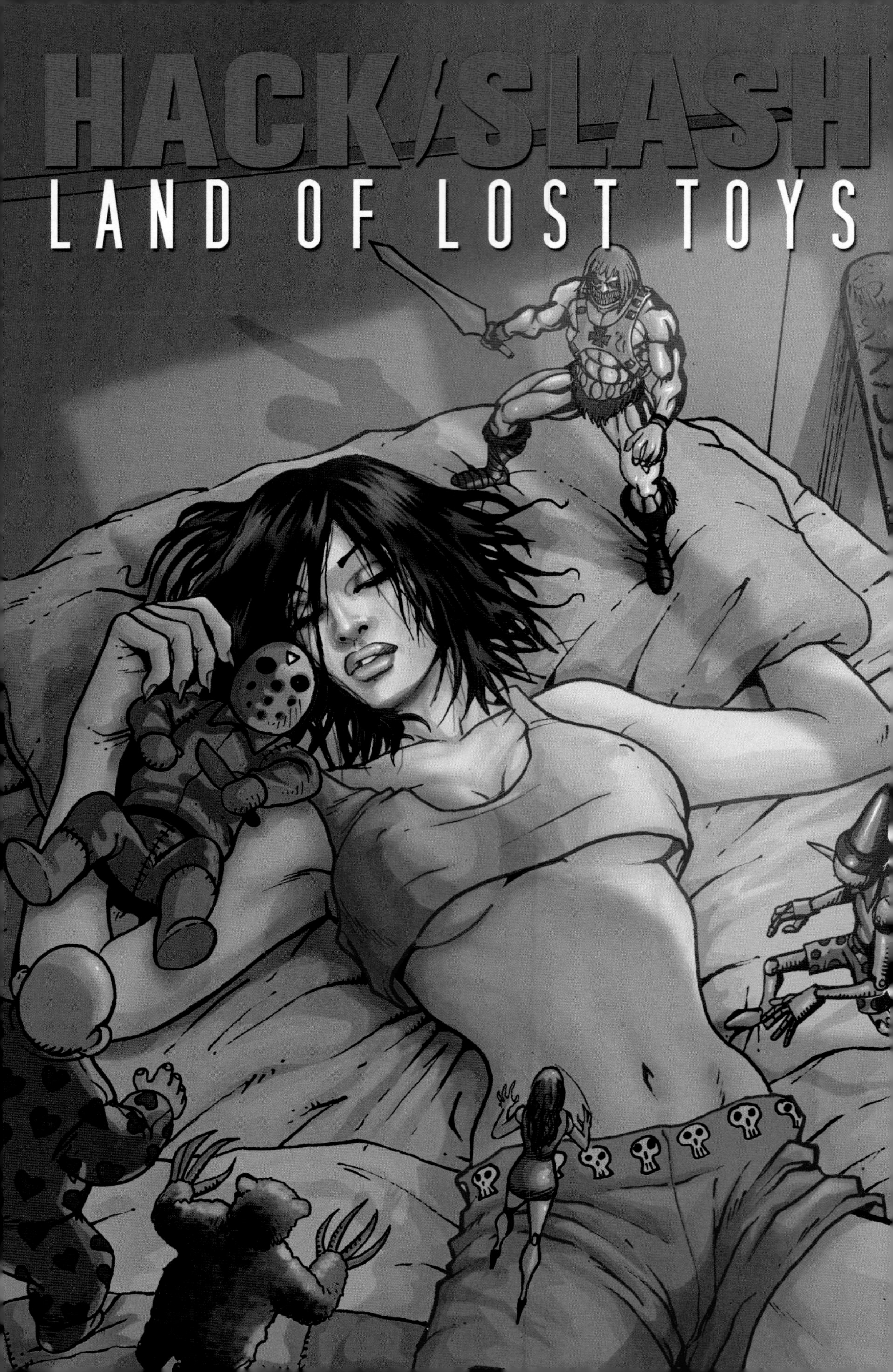
HACK/SLASH
LAND OF LOST TOYS

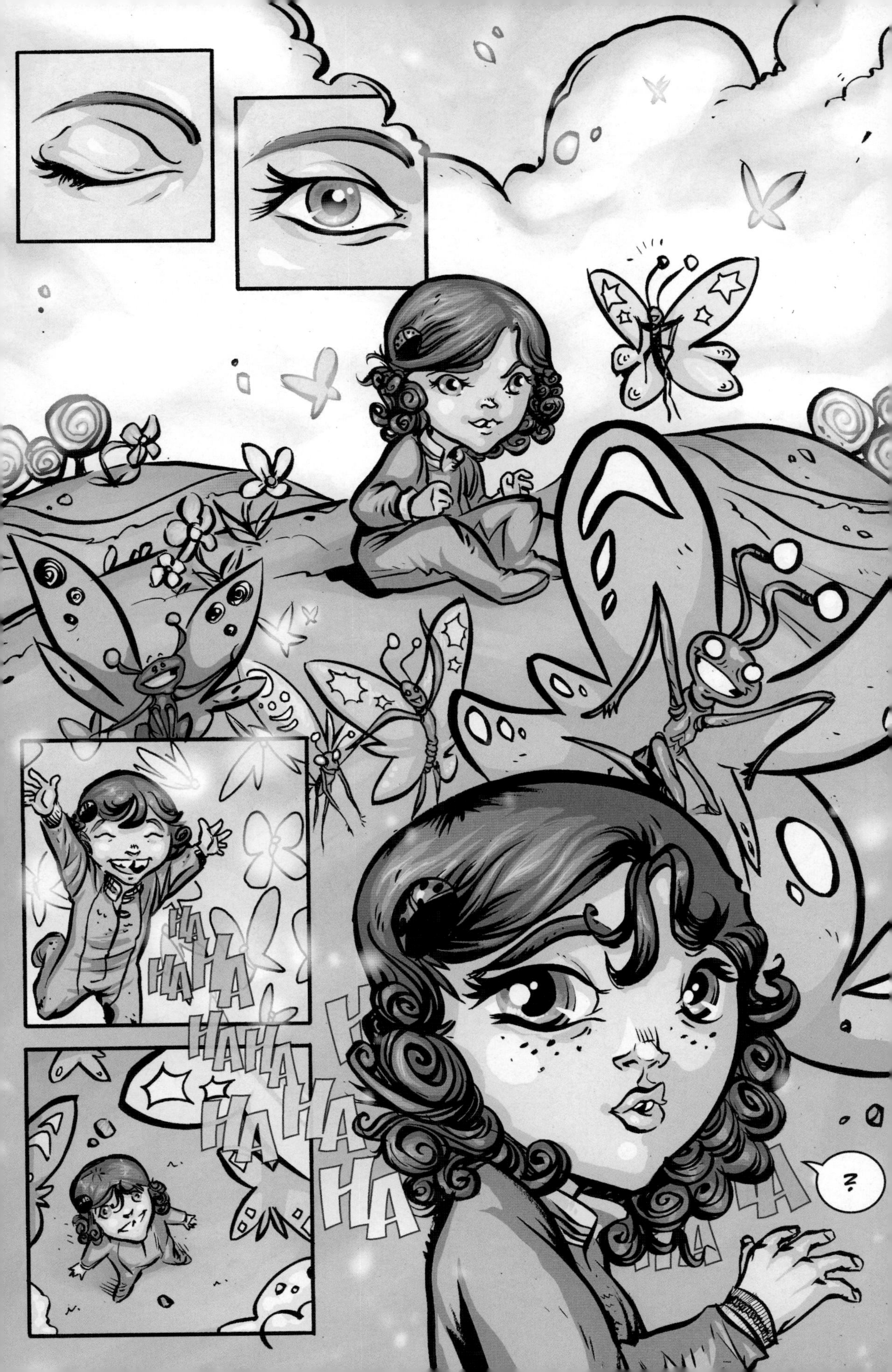
HA HA HA HA
HAHAHAHA HA HA HA
HA HA
?

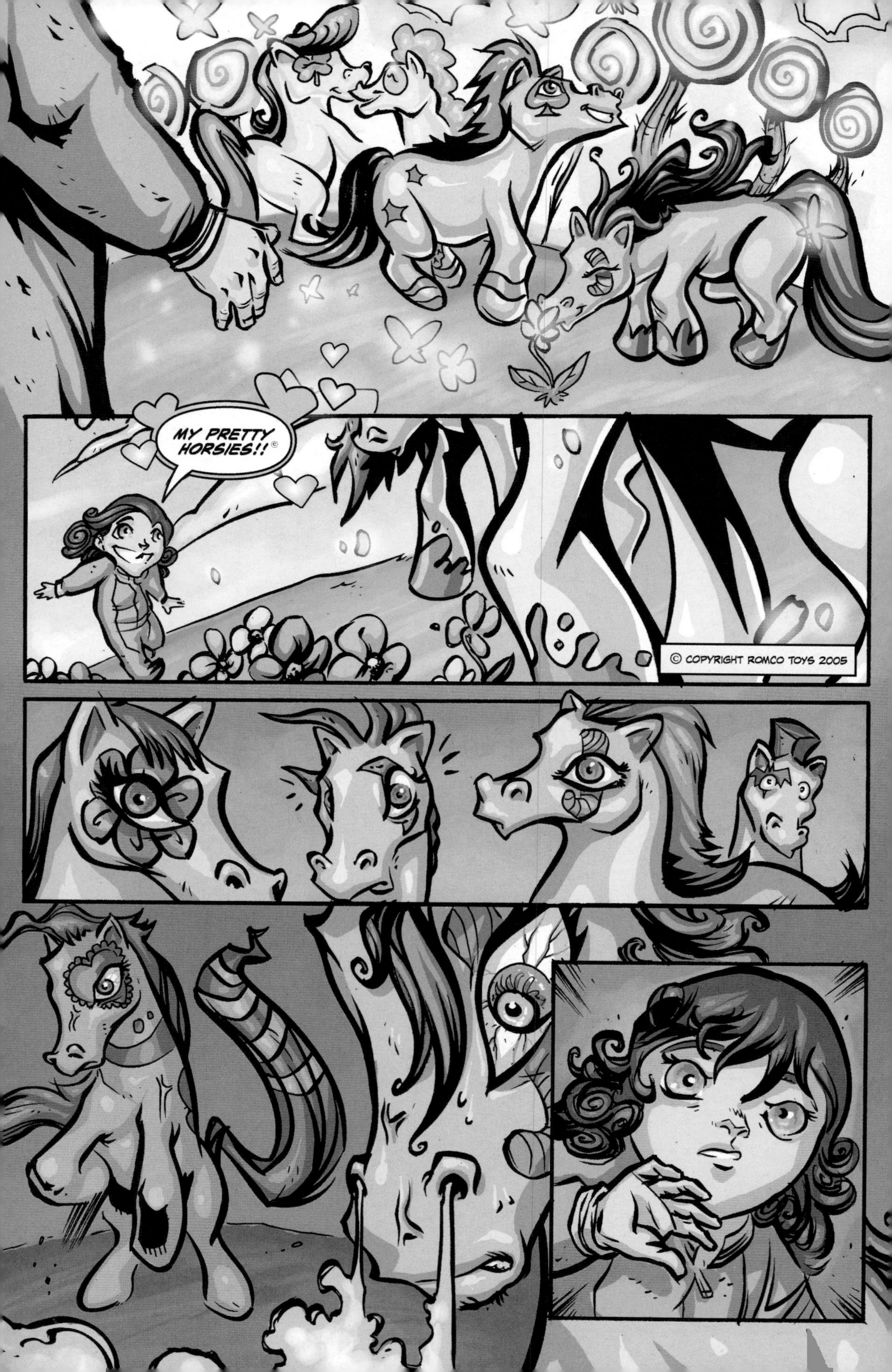
MY PRETTY HORSIES!! ©
© COPYRIGHT ROMCO TOYS 2005

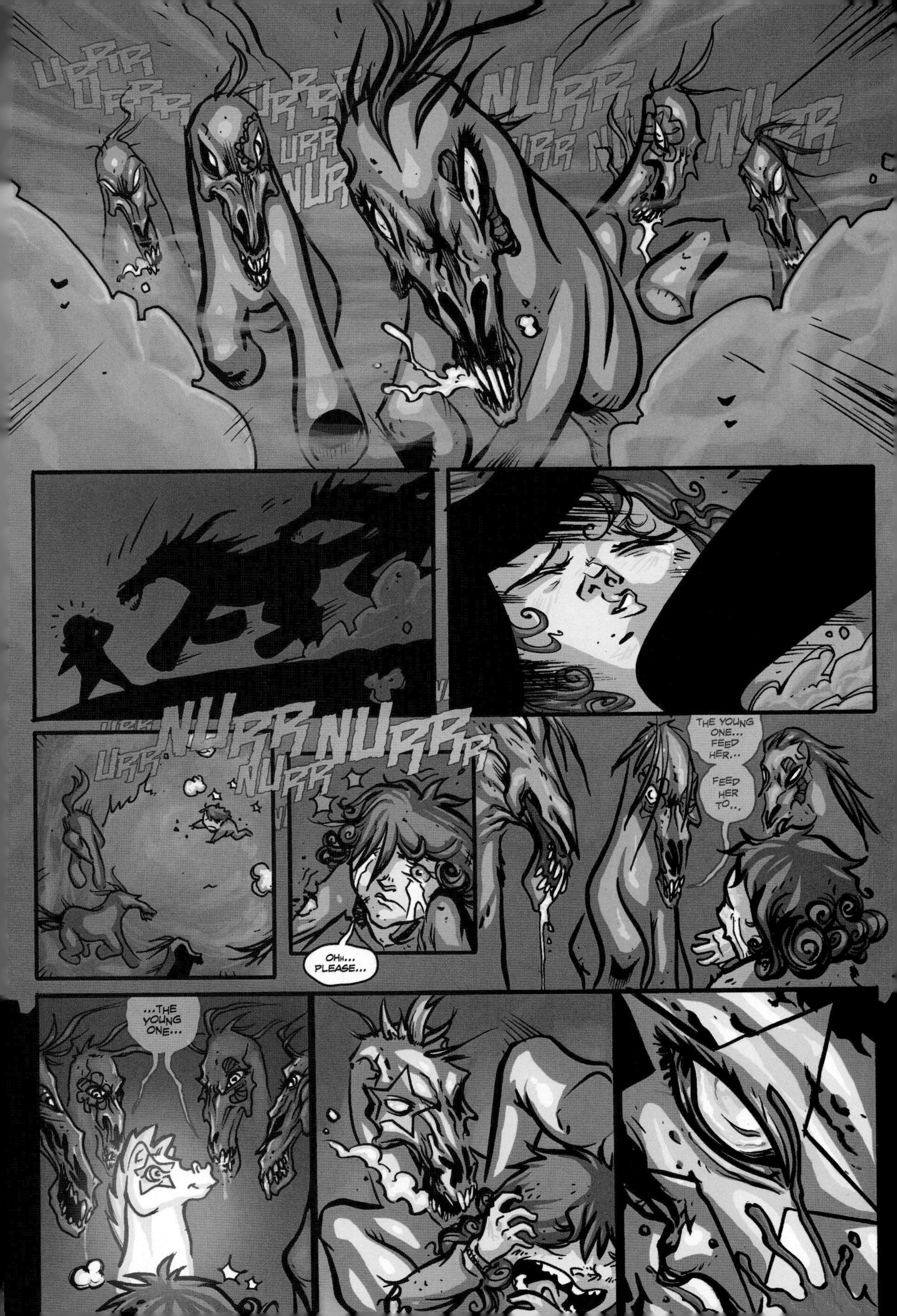
URRR URRR
NURRR
URRR
NURR
NURR
URRR NURR
NURR
URRR NURR NURRR
NURR
OHH... PLEASE...
THE YOUNG ONE... FEED HER...
FEED HER TO...
...THE YOUNG ONE...

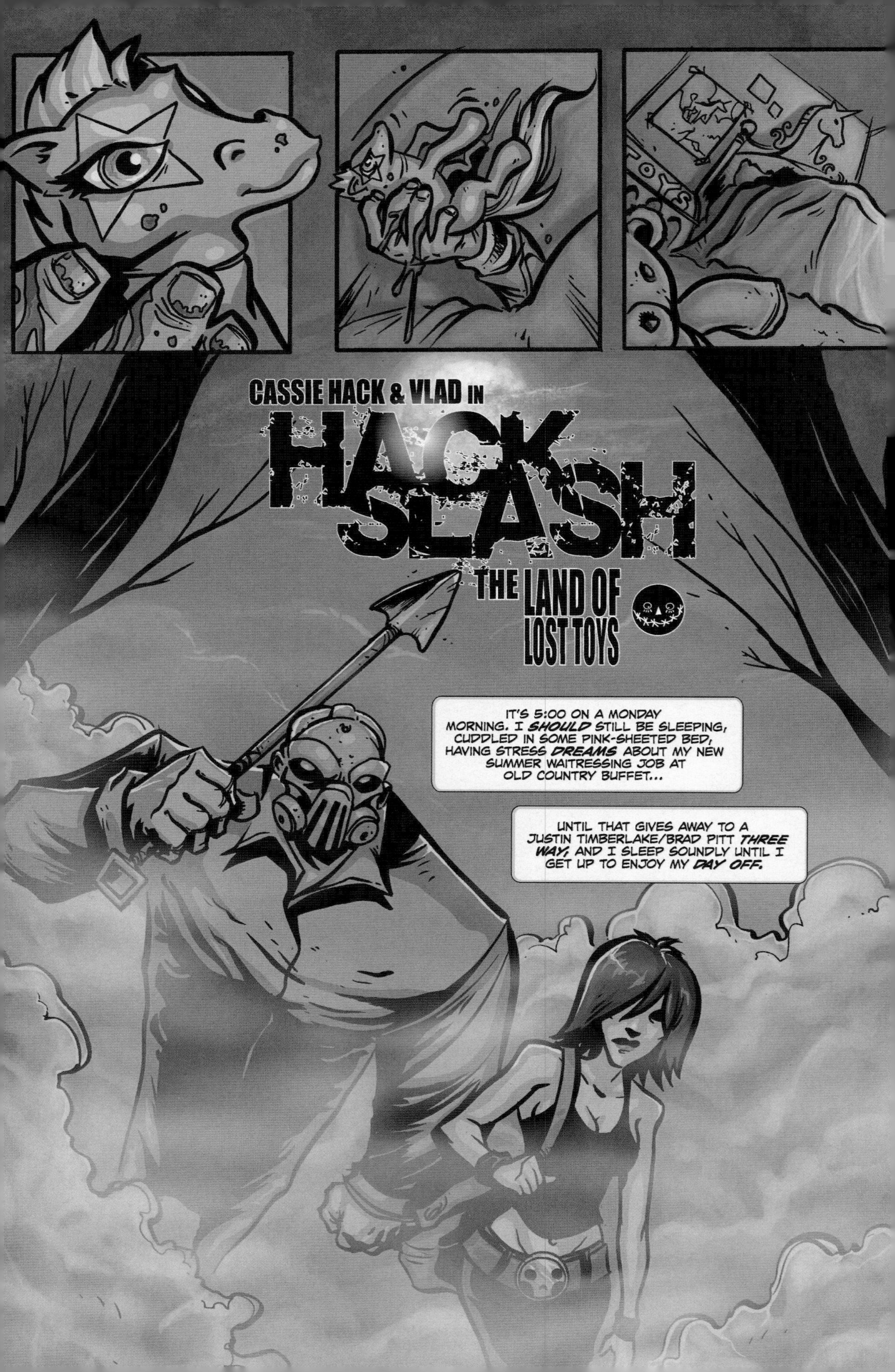
CASSIE HACK & VLAD IN
HACK SLASH
THE LAND OF LOST TOYS
IT'S 5:00 ON A MONDAY MORNING. I SHOULD STILL BE SLEEPING, CUDDLED IN SOME PINK-SHEETED BED, HAVING STRESS DREAMS ABOUT MY NEW SUMMER WAITRESSING JOB AT OLD COUNTRY BUFFET...
UNTIL THAT GIVES AWAY TO A JUSTIN TIMBERLAKE/BRAD PITT THREE WAY, AND I SLEEP SOUNDLY UNTIL I GET UP TO ENJOY MY DAY OFF.

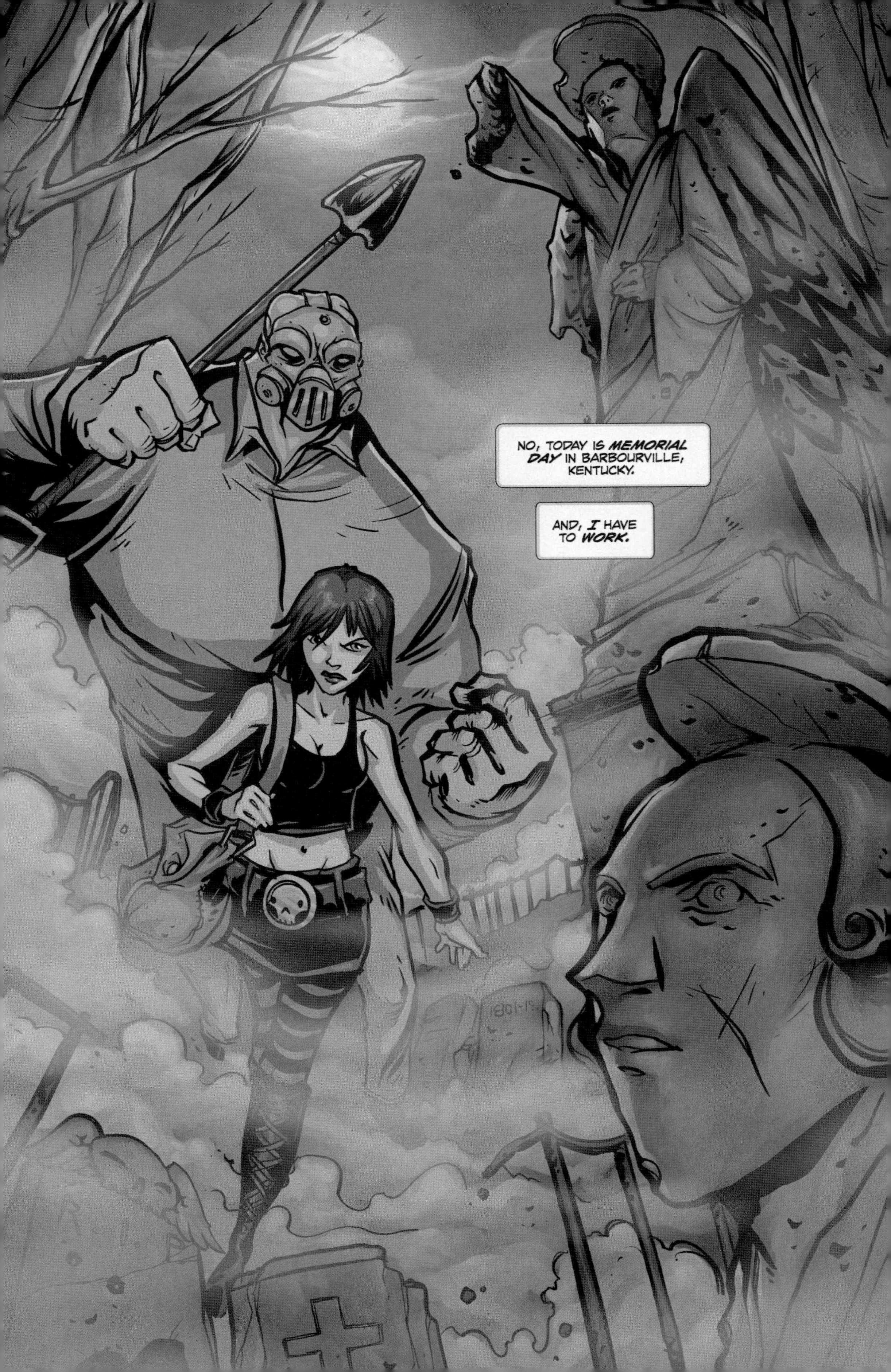
NO, TODAY IS MEMORIAL DAY IN BARBOURVILLE, KENTUCKY.
AND, I HAVE TO WORK.
1801-18

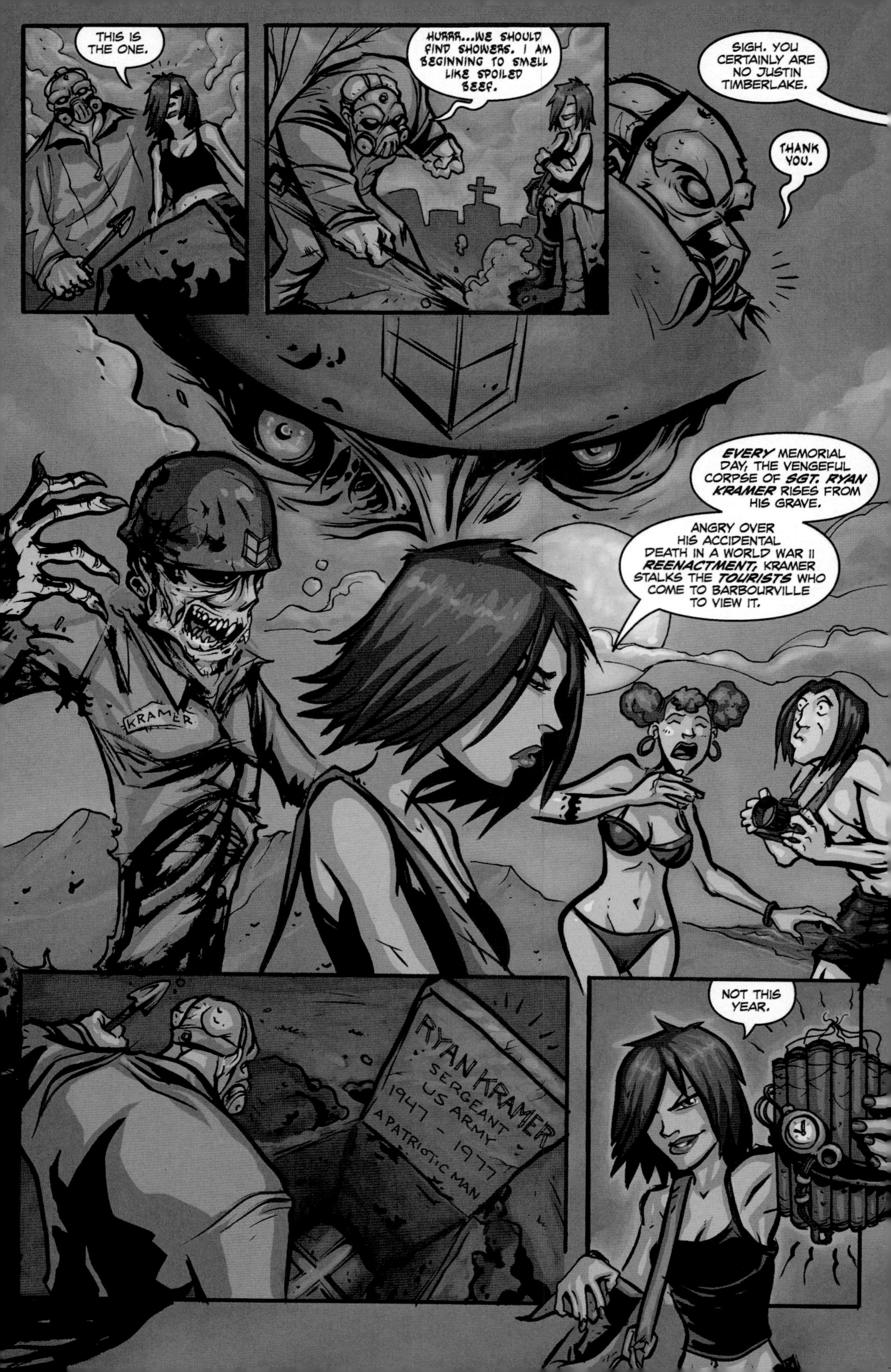
THIS IS THE ONE.
HURRR...WE SHOULD FIND SHOWERS. I AM BEGINNING TO SMELL LIKE SPOILED BEEF.
SIGH. YOU CERTAINLY ARE NO JUSTIN TIMBERLAKE.
THANK YOU.
EVERY MEMORIAL DAY, THE VENGEFUL CORPSE OF SGT. RYAN KRAMER RISES FROM HIS GRAVE.
ANGRY OVER HIS ACCIDENTAL DEATH IN A WORLD WAR II REENACTMENT, KRAMER STALKS THE TOURISTS WHO COME TO BARBOURVILLE TO VIEW IT.
KRAMER
RYAN KRAMER SERGEANT US ARMY 1947 - 1977 A PATRIOTIC MAN
NOT THIS YEAR.

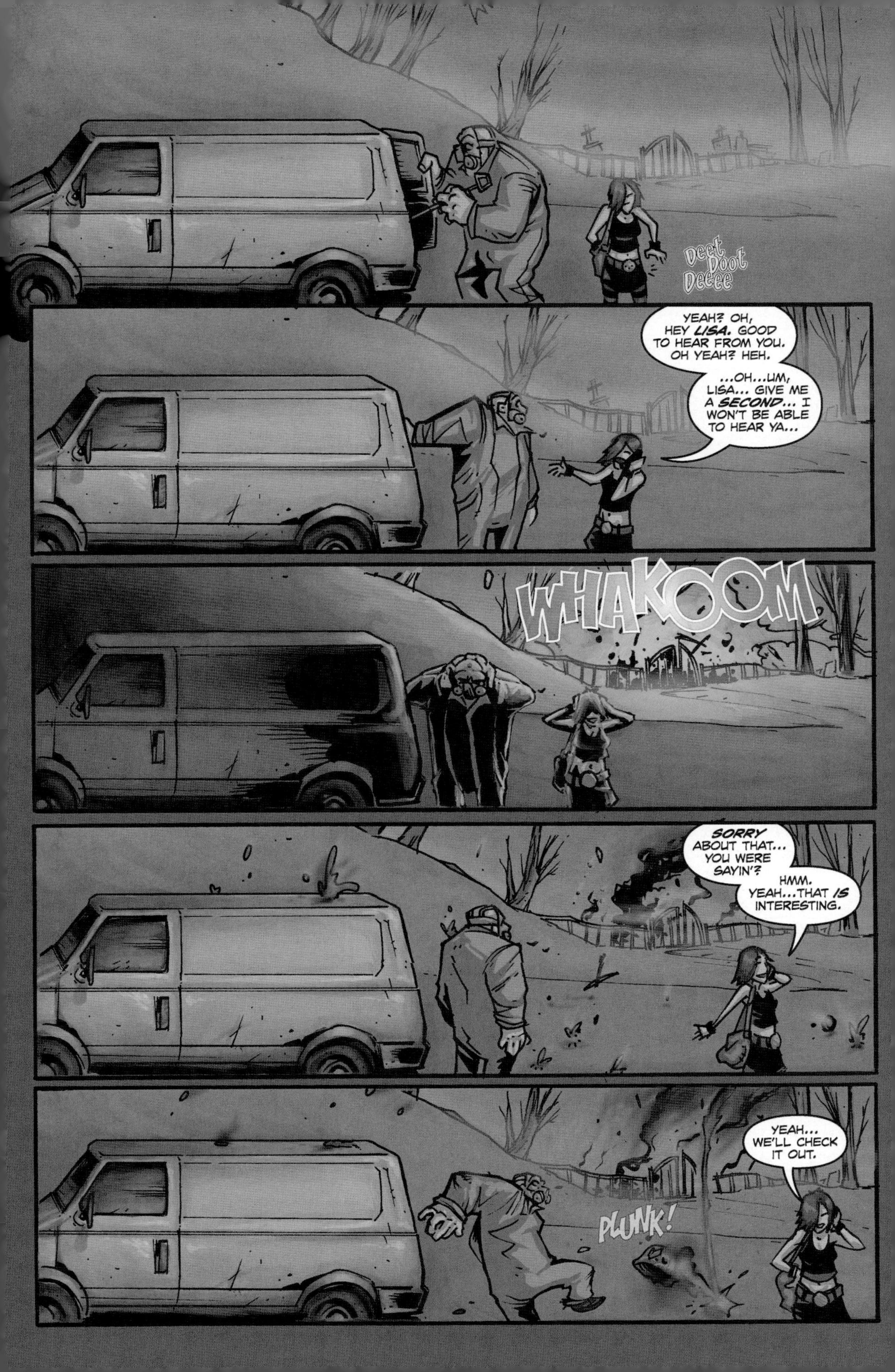
Deet Doot Deeee
YEAH? OH, HEY LISA. GOOD TO HEAR FROM YOU. OH YEAH? HEH.
...OH...UM, LISA... GIVE ME A SECOND... I WON'T BE ABLE TO HEAR YA...
WHAKOOM
SORRY ABOUT THAT... YOU WERE SAYIN'?
HMM. YEAH...THAT IS INTERESTING.
YEAH... WE'LL CHECK IT OUT.
PLUNK!

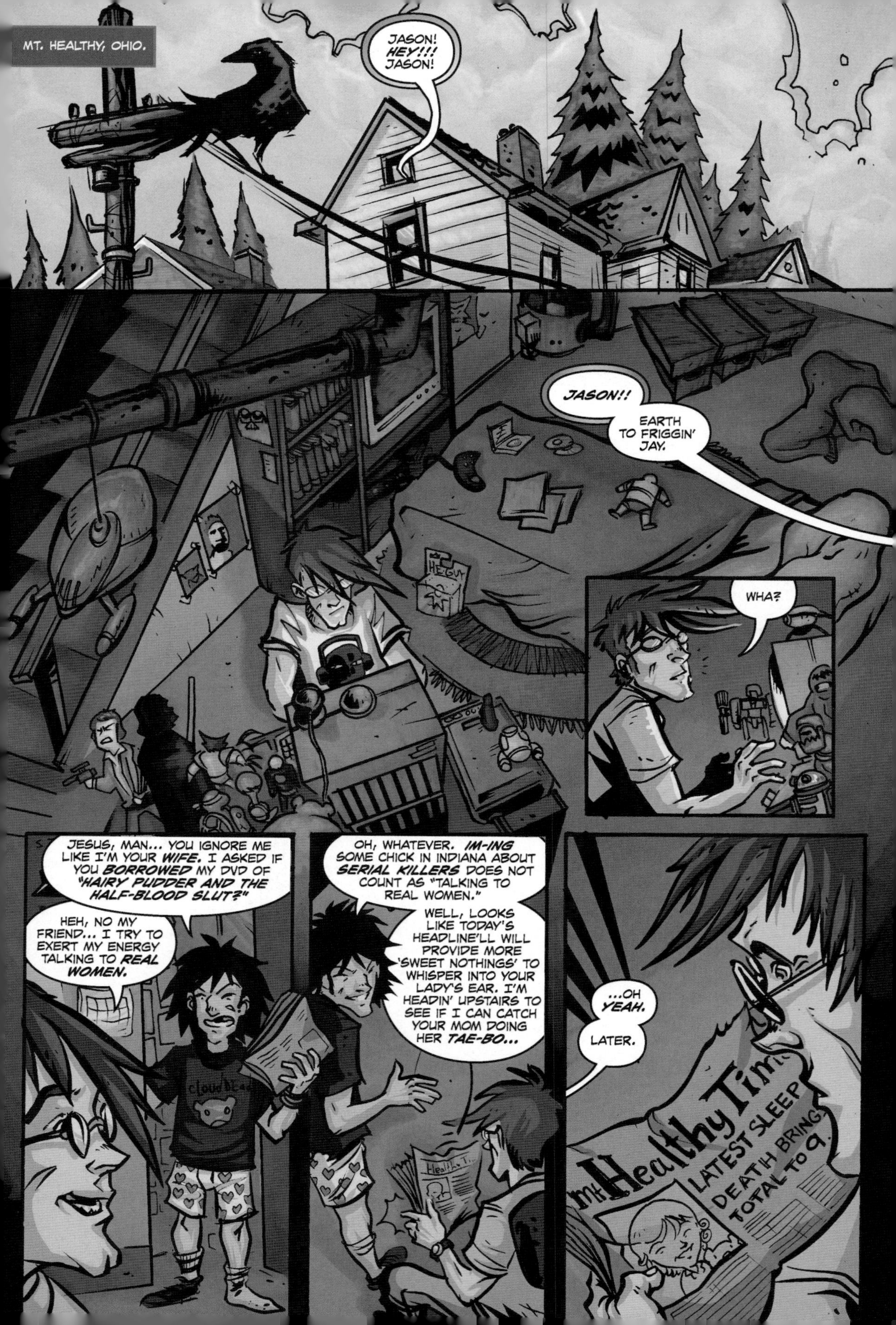
MT. HEALTHY, OHIO.
JASON! HEY!!! JASON!
JASON!!
EARTH TO FRIGGIN' JAY.
HE-GUY
WHA?
JESUS, MAN... YOU IGNORE ME LIKE I'M YOUR WIFE. I ASKED IF YOU BORROWED MY DVD OF "HAIRY PUDDER AND THE HALF-BLOOD SLUT?"
HEH, NO MY FRIEND... I TRY TO EXERT MY ENERGY TALKING TO REAL WOMEN.
OH, WHATEVER. IM-ING SOME CHICK IN INDIANA ABOUT SERIAL KILLERS DOES NOT COUNT AS "TALKING TO REAL WOMEN."
WELL, LOOKS LIKE TODAY'S HEADLINE'LL WILL PROVIDE MORE 'SWEET NOTHINGS' TO WHISPER INTO YOUR LADY'S EAR. I'M HEADIN' UPSTAIRS TO SEE IF I CAN CATCH YOUR MOM DOING HER TAE-BO...
...OH YEAH.
LATER.
mt. Healthy Tim
LATEST SLEEP DEATH BRINGS TOTAL TO 9.

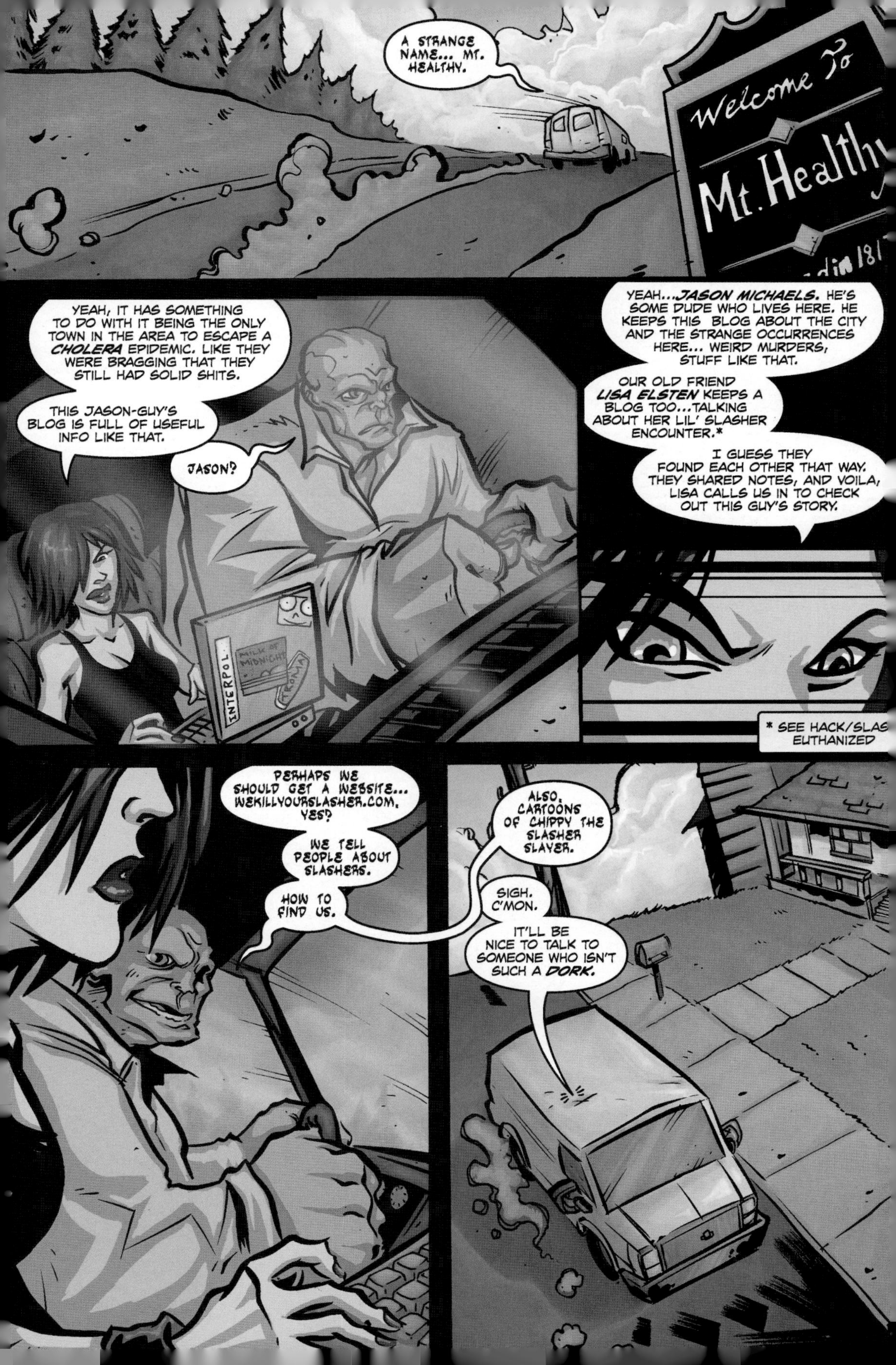
A STRANGE NAME... MT. HEALTHY.
Welcome To
Mt. Healthy
YEAH, IT HAS SOMETHING TO DO WITH IT BEING THE ONLY TOWN IN THE AREA TO ESCAPE A CHOLERA EPIDEMIC. LIKE THEY WERE BRAGGING THAT THEY STILL HAD SOLID SHITS.
THIS JASON-GUY'S BLOG IS FULL OF USEFUL INFO LIKE THAT.
JASON?
INTERPOL
MILK OF MIDNIGHT
TROMA
YEAH...JASON MICHAELS. HE'S SOME DUDE WHO LIVES HERE. HE KEEPS THIS BLOG ABOUT THE CITY AND THE STRANGE OCCURRENCES HERE... WEIRD MURDERS, STUFF LIKE THAT.
OUR OLD FRIEND LISA ELSTEN KEEPS A BLOG TOO...TALKING ABOUT HER LIL' SLASHER ENCOUNTER.*
I GUESS THEY FOUND EACH OTHER THAT WAY. THEY SHARED NOTES, AND VOILA, LISA CALLS US IN TO CHECK OUT THIS GUY'S STORY.
* SEE HACK/SLAS EUTHANIZED
PERHAPS WE SHOULD GET A WEBSITE... WEKILLYOURSLASHER.COM. YES?
WE TELL PEOPLE ABOUT SLASHERS.
HOW TO FIND US.
ALSO, CARTOONS OF CHIPPY THE SLASHER SLAYER.
SIGH. C'MON.
IT'LL BE NICE TO TALK TO SOMEONE WHO ISN'T SUCH A DORK.

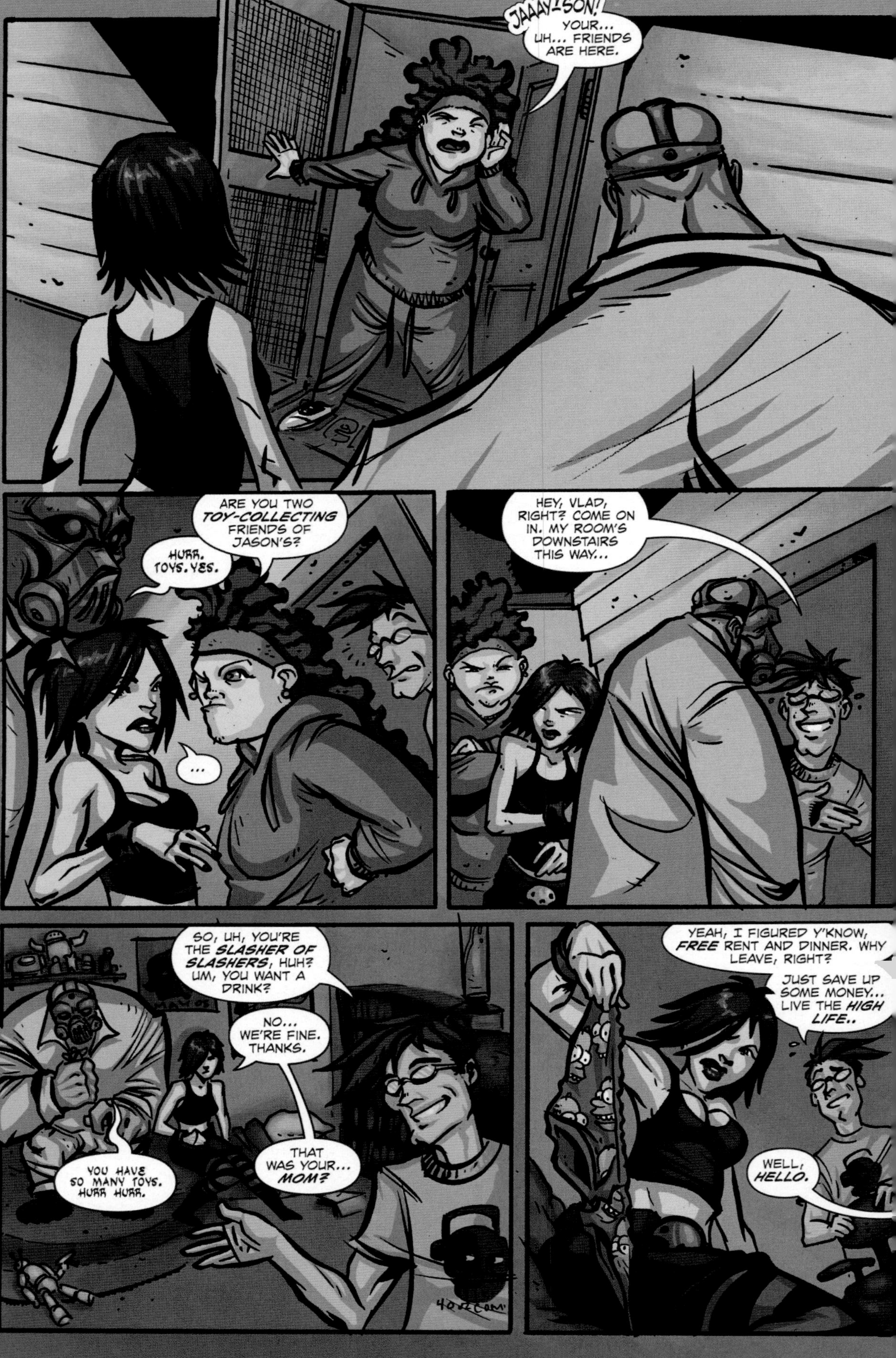
JAAAY-SON!
YOUR... UH... FRIENDS ARE HERE.
ARE YOU TWO *TOY-COLLECTING* FRIENDS OF JASON'S?
HURR. TOYS. YES.
...
HEY, VLAD, RIGHT? COME ON IN. MY ROOM'S DOWNSTAIRS THIS WAY...
SO, UH, YOU'RE THE ***SLASHER OF SLASHERS***, HUH? UM, YOU WANT A DRINK?
NO... WE'RE FINE. THANKS.
YOU HAVE SO MANY TOYS. HURR HURR.
THAT WAS YOUR... ***MOM?***
YEAH, I FIGURED Y'KNOW, ***FREE*** RENT AND DINNER. WHY LEAVE, RIGHT?
JUST SAVE UP SOME MONEY... LIVE THE ***HIGH LIFE***..
WELL, ***HELLO***.

YOU TAKING SOME INTERNET BUDDIES OVER TO *CINCINASTY*? WHY DIDN'T YOU SAY SO?

I KNOW THE PERFECT CLUB FOR THIS PRETTY LADY...

CHRIS. HERE. GO.

YOU DICK... YOU *DID HAVE* IT.

SORRY... HE DOESN'T SEE A LOT OF WOMEN.

ANYWAY, I'VE BEEN SORT OF *UNEMPLOYED* LATELY; SO I'VE BEEN WORKING ON A *PASSION* OF MINE...

I'M A DETECTIVE, I GUESS YOU COULD SAY... I RESEARCH THINGS THAT FALL BETWEEN THE *CRACKS*... AND MAKE CONNECTIONS.

THESE CONNECTIONS CAN LEAD TO *UNEXPECTED* PLACES. *UNNATURAL PLACES.* I THINK THERE'S SOMETHING GOING ON HERE THAT NEEDS YOUR *SPECIAL* ATTENTION.

HM... WELL... SAYS HERE, THESE *NINE* KIDS DIED IN THEIR *SLEEP*, ANEURYSMS?...

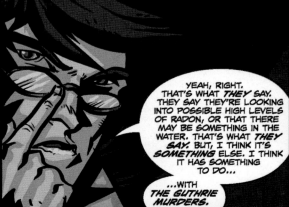

YEAH, RIGHT. THAT'S WHAT *THEY* SAY. THEY SAY THEY'RE LOOKING INTO POSSIBLE HIGH LEVELS OF RADON, OR THAT THERE MAY BE SOMETHING IN THE WATER. THAT'S WHAT *THEY* SAY. BUT, I THINK IT'S *SOMETHING* ELSE. I THINK IT HAS SOMETHING TO DO...

...WITH *THE GUTHRIE MURDERS.*

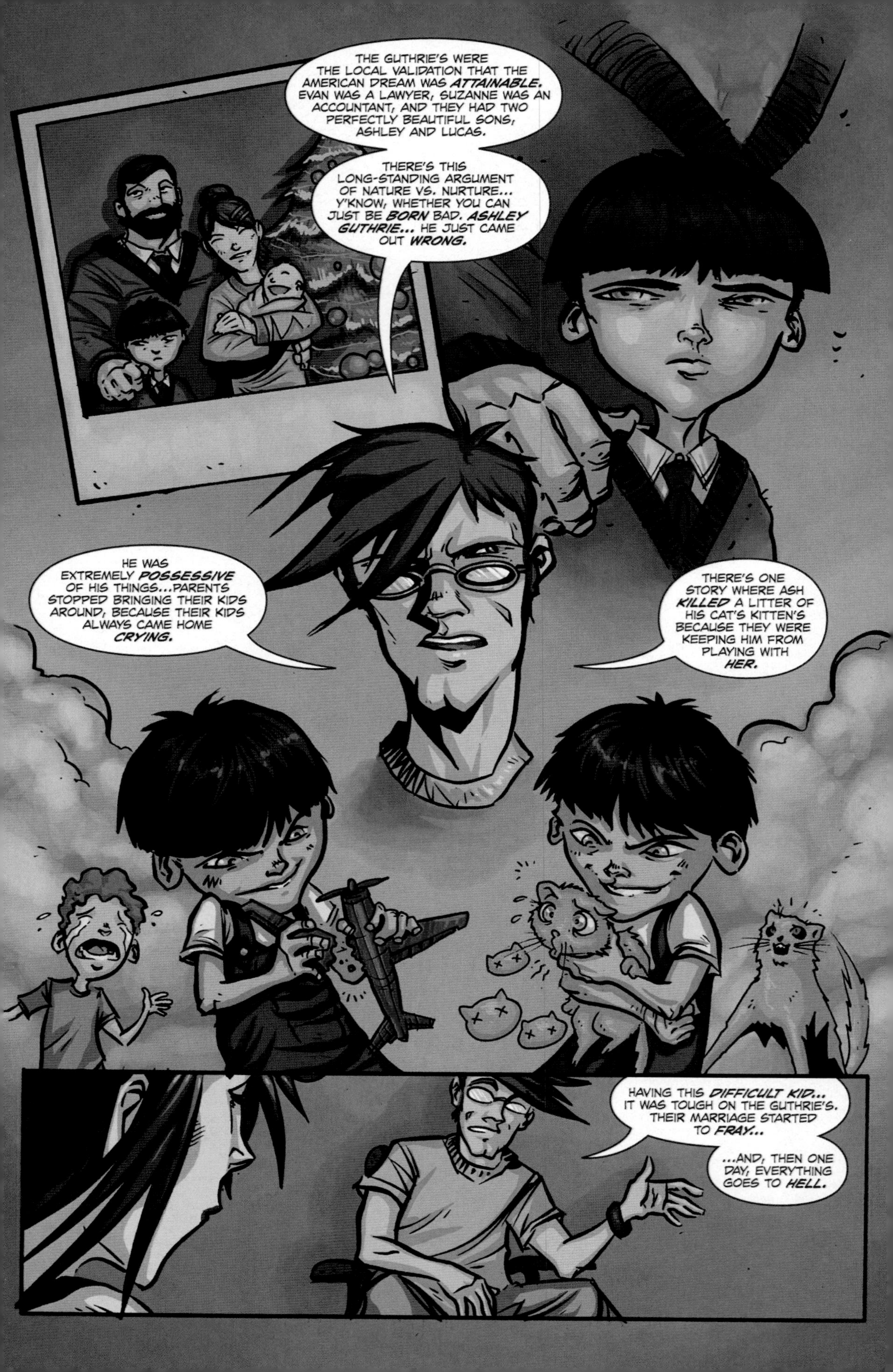
THE GUTHRIE'S WERE THE LOCAL VALIDATION THAT THE AMERICAN DREAM WAS ATTAINABLE. EVAN WAS A LAWYER, SUZANNE WAS AN ACCOUNTANT, AND THEY HAD TWO PERFECTLY BEAUTIFUL SONS, ASHLEY AND LUCAS.
THERE'S THIS LONG-STANDING ARGUMENT OF NATURE VS. NURTURE... Y'KNOW, WHETHER YOU CAN JUST BE BORN BAD. ASHLEY GUTHRIE... HE JUST CAME OUT WRONG.
HE WAS EXTREMELY POSSESSIVE OF HIS THINGS...PARENTS STOPPED BRINGING THEIR KIDS AROUND, BECAUSE THEIR KIDS ALWAYS CAME HOME CRYING.
THERE'S ONE STORY WHERE ASH KILLED A LITTER OF HIS CAT'S KITTEN'S BECAUSE THEY WERE KEEPING HIM FROM PLAYING WITH HER.
HAVING THIS DIFFICULT KID... IT WAS TOUGH ON THE GUTHRIE'S. THEIR MARRIAGE STARTED TO FRAY...
...AND, THEN ONE DAY, EVERYTHING GOES TO HELL.

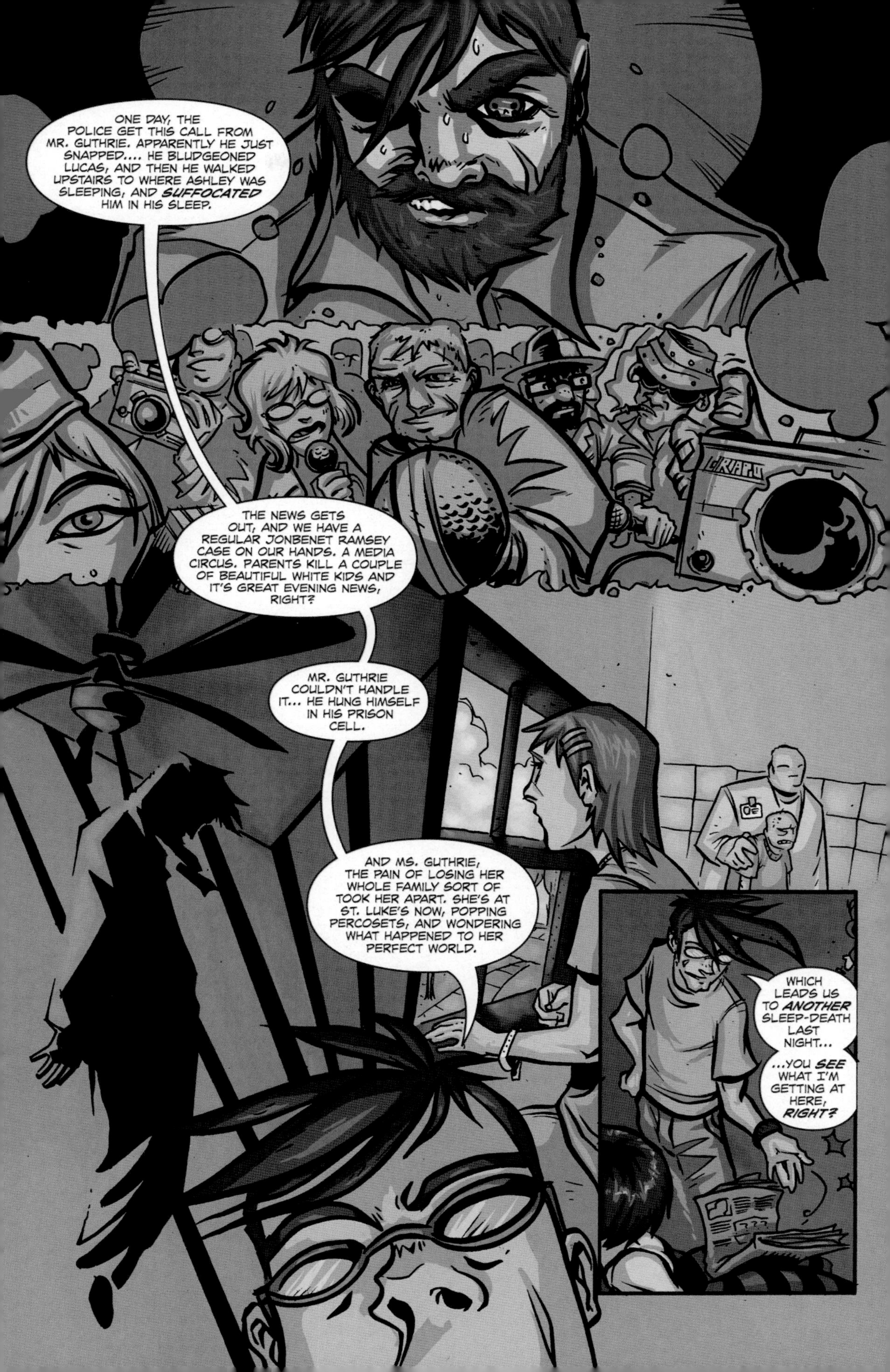
ONE DAY, THE POLICE GET THIS CALL FROM MR. GUTHRIE. APPARENTLY HE JUST SNAPPED.... HE BLUDGEONED LUCAS, AND THEN HE WALKED UPSTAIRS TO WHERE ASHLEY WAS SLEEPING, AND SUFFOCATED HIM IN HIS SLEEP.
THE NEWS GETS OUT, AND WE HAVE A REGULAR JONBENET RAMSEY CASE ON OUR HANDS. A MEDIA CIRCUS. PARENTS KILL A COUPLE OF BEAUTIFUL WHITE KIDS AND IT'S GREAT EVENING NEWS, RIGHT?
MR. GUTHRIE COULDN'T HANDLE IT... HE HUNG HIMSELF IN HIS PRISON CELL.
AND MS. GUTHRIE, THE PAIN OF LOSING HER WHOLE FAMILY SORT OF TOOK HER APART. SHE'S AT ST. LUKE'S NOW, POPPING PERCOSETS, AND WONDERING WHAT HAPPENED TO HER PERFECT WORLD.
WHICH LEADS US TO ANOTHER SLEEP-DEATH LAST NIGHT...
...YOU SEE WHAT I'M GETTING AT HERE, RIGHT?

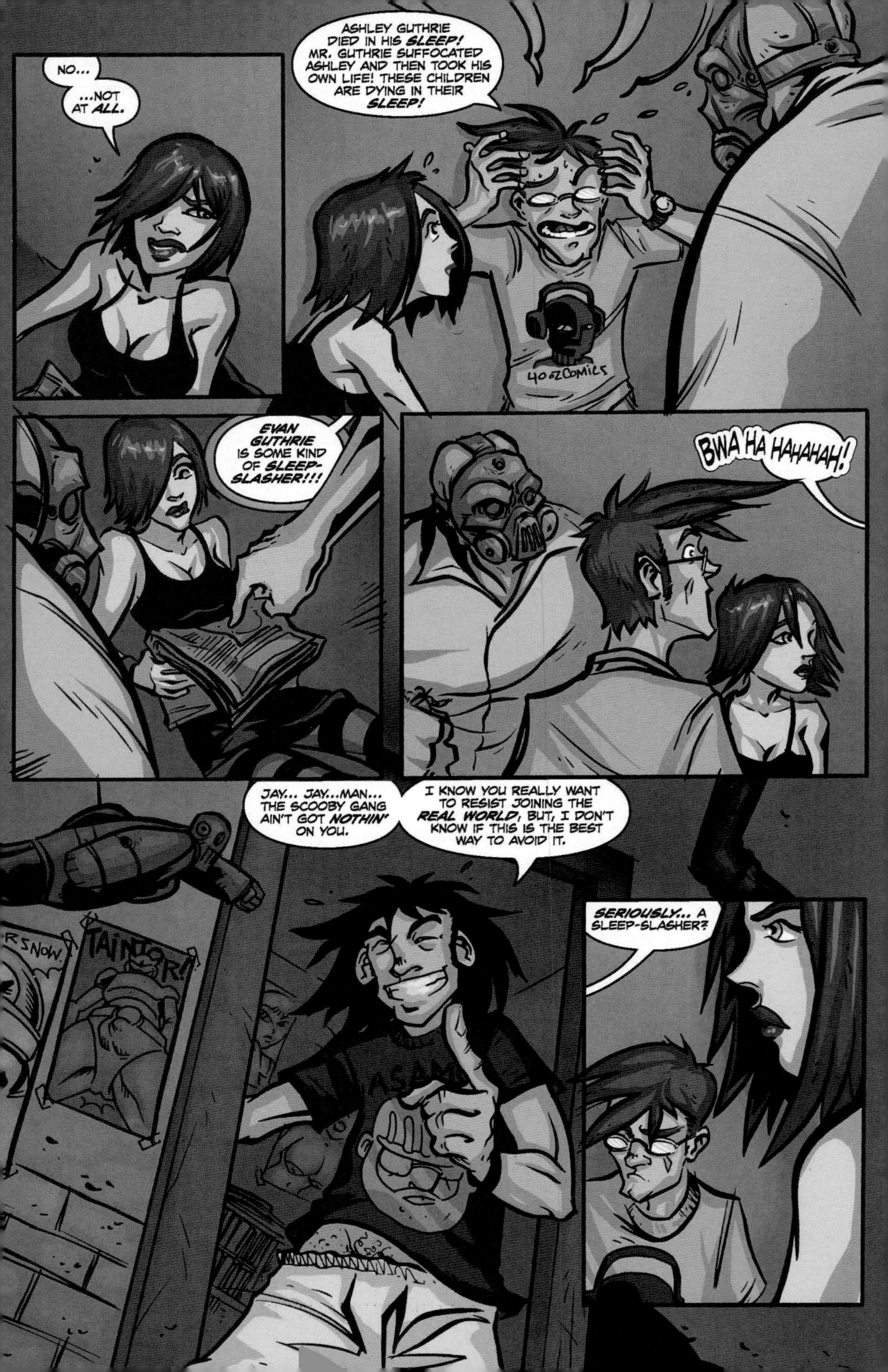
NO...
...NOT AT ALL.
ASHLEY GUTHRIE DIED IN HIS SLEEP! MR. GUTHRIE SUFFOCATED ASHLEY AND THEN TOOK HIS OWN LIFE! THESE CHILDREN ARE DYING IN THEIR SLEEP!
40oz COMICS
EVAN GUTHRIE IS SOME KIND OF SLEEP-SLASHER!!!
BWA HA HAHAHAH!
JAY... JAY...MAN... THE SCOOBY GANG AIN'T GOT NOTHIN' ON YOU.
I KNOW YOU REALLY WANT TO RESIST JOINING THE REAL WORLD, BUT, I DON'T KNOW IF THIS IS THE BEST WAY TO AVOID IT.
TAINTOR!
SERIOUSLY... A SLEEP-SLASHER?

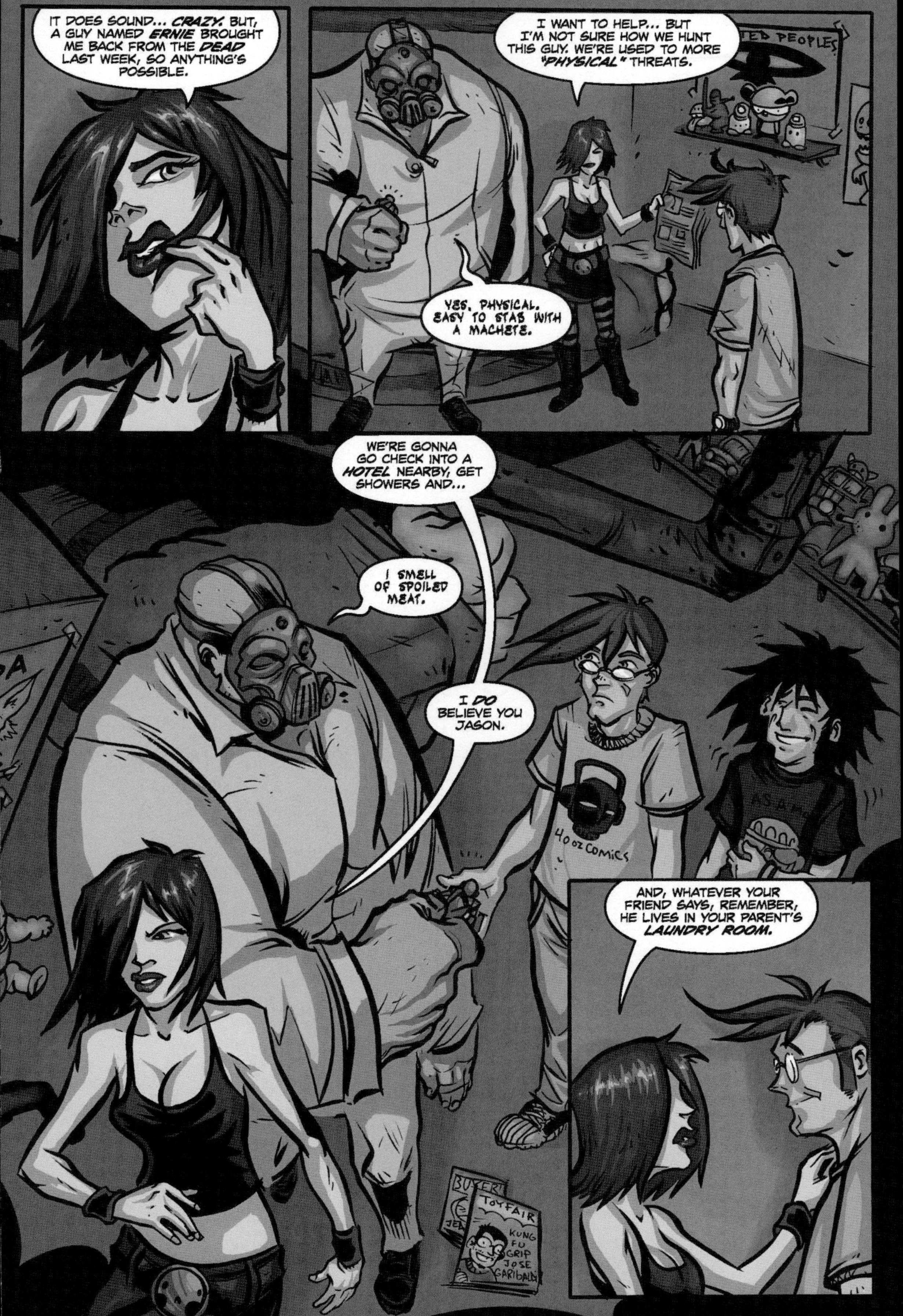
IT DOES SOUND... CRAZY. BUT, A GUY NAMED ERNIE BROUGHT ME BACK FROM THE DEAD LAST WEEK, SO ANYTHING'S POSSIBLE.
I WANT TO HELP... BUT I'M NOT SURE HOW WE HUNT THIS GUY. WE'RE USED TO MORE "PHYSICAL" THREATS.
YES. PHYSICAL. EASY TO STAB WITH A MACHETE.
WE'RE GONNA GO CHECK INTO A HOTEL NEARBY, GET SHOWERS AND...
I SMELL OF SPOILED MEAT.
I DO BELIEVE YOU JASON.
40 oz COMICS
AND, WHATEVER YOUR FRIEND SAYS, REMEMBER, HE LIVES IN YOUR PARENT'S LAUNDRY ROOM.
TOYFAIR
KUNG FU GRIP JOSE GARIBALDI

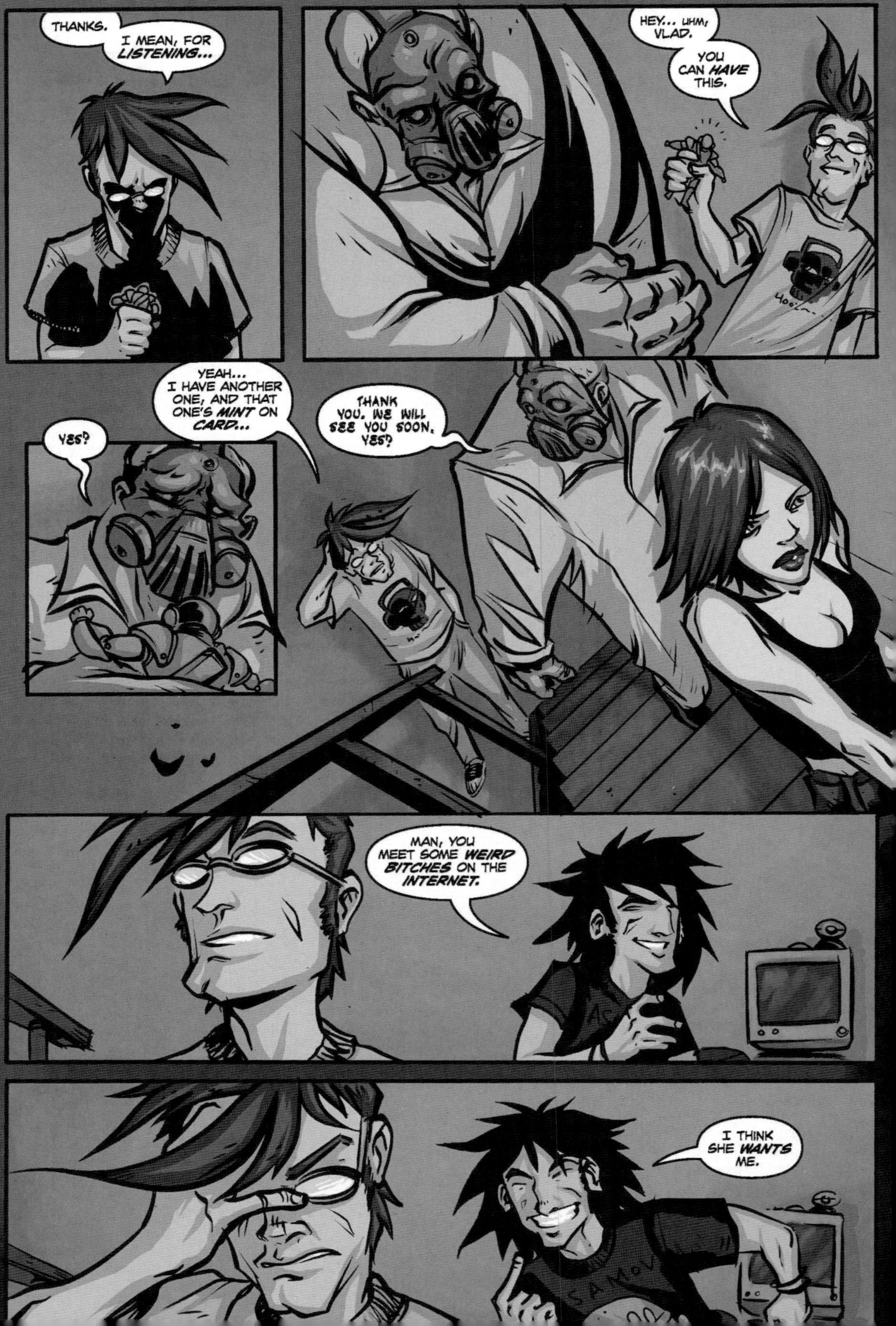
THANKS.
I MEAN, FOR LISTENING...
HEY... UHM, VLAD.
YOU CAN HAVE THIS.
YES?
YEAH... I HAVE ANOTHER ONE, AND THAT ONE'S MINT ON CARD...
THANK YOU. WE WILL SEE YOU SOON. YES?
MAN, YOU MEET SOME WEIRD BITCHES ON THE INTERNET.
I THINK SHE WANTS ME.

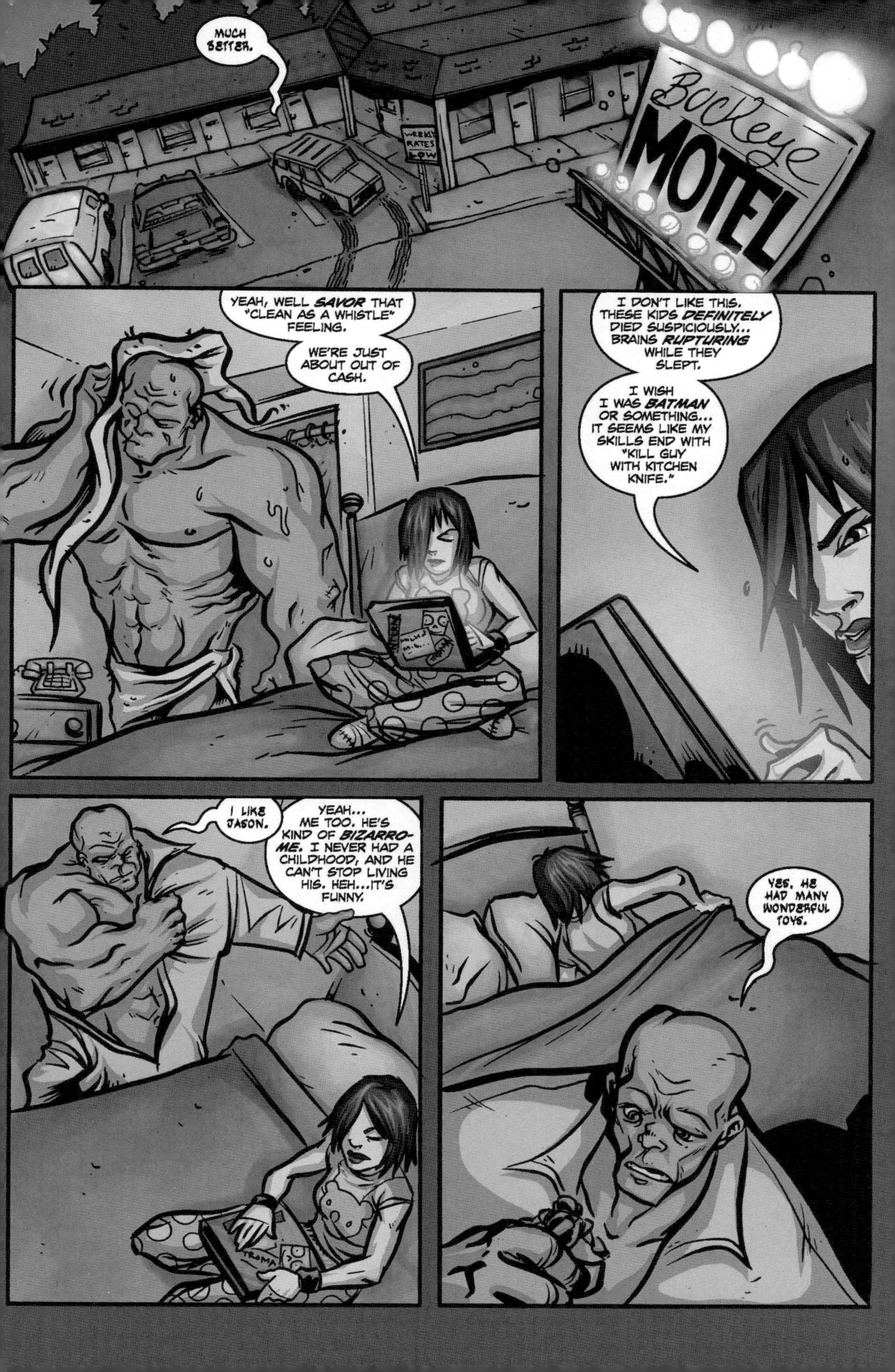
MUCH BETTER.
Buckeye MOTEL
WEEKLY RATES LOW
YEAH, WELL SAVOR THAT "CLEAN AS A WHISTLE" FEELING.
WE'RE JUST ABOUT OUT OF CASH.
I DON'T LIKE THIS. THESE KIDS DEFINITELY DIED SUSPICIOUSLY... BRAINS RUPTURING WHILE THEY SLEPT.
I WISH I WAS BATMAN OR SOMETHING... IT SEEMS LIKE MY SKILLS END WITH "KILL GUY WITH KITCHEN KNIFE."
I LIKE JASON.
YEAH... ME TOO. HE'S KIND OF BIZARRO-ME. I NEVER HAD A CHILDHOOD, AND HE CAN'T STOP LIVING HIS. HEH...IT'S FUNNY.
YES. HE HAD MANY WONDERFUL TOYS.

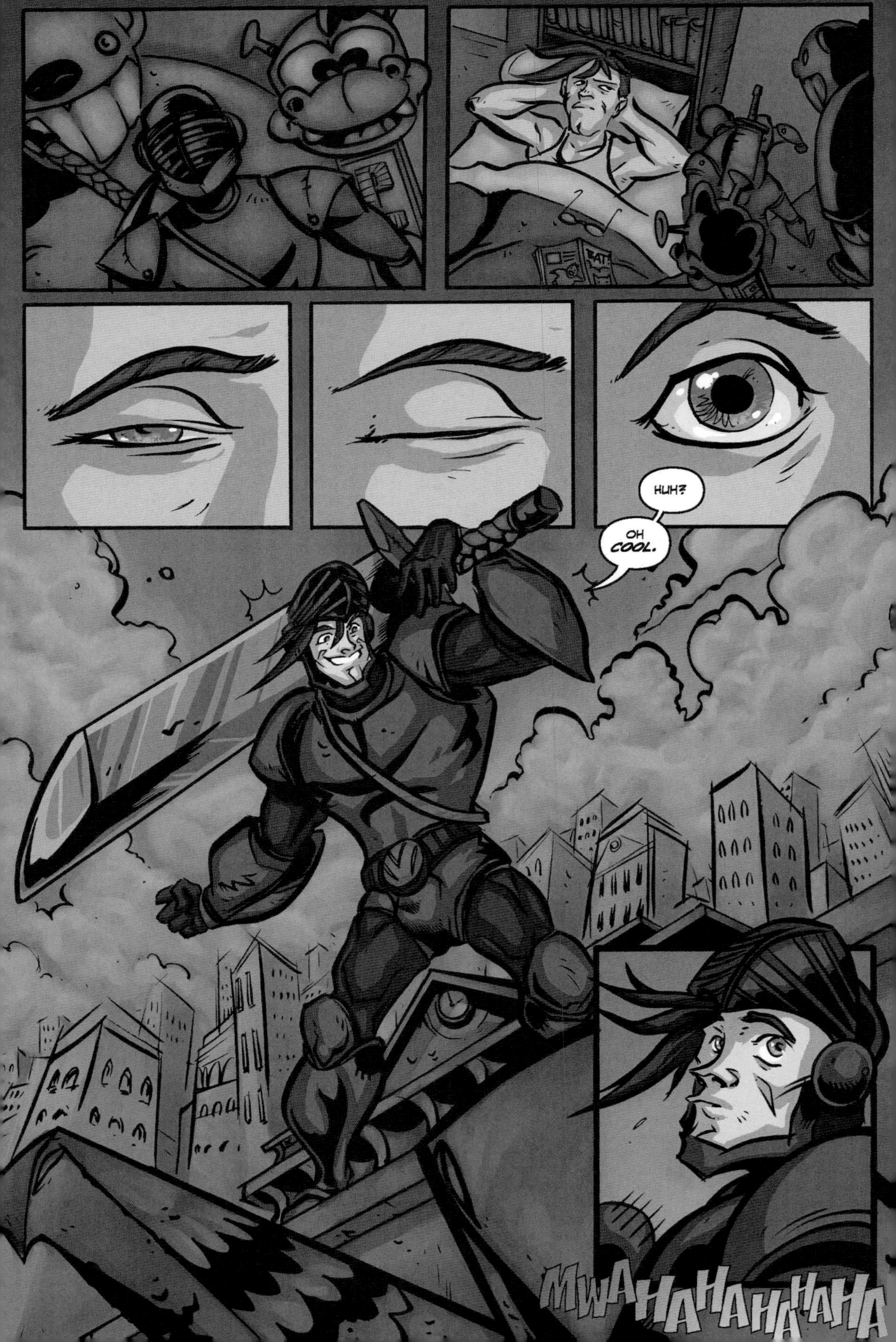

HUH?
OH COOL.
MWAHAHAHAHAHAHA

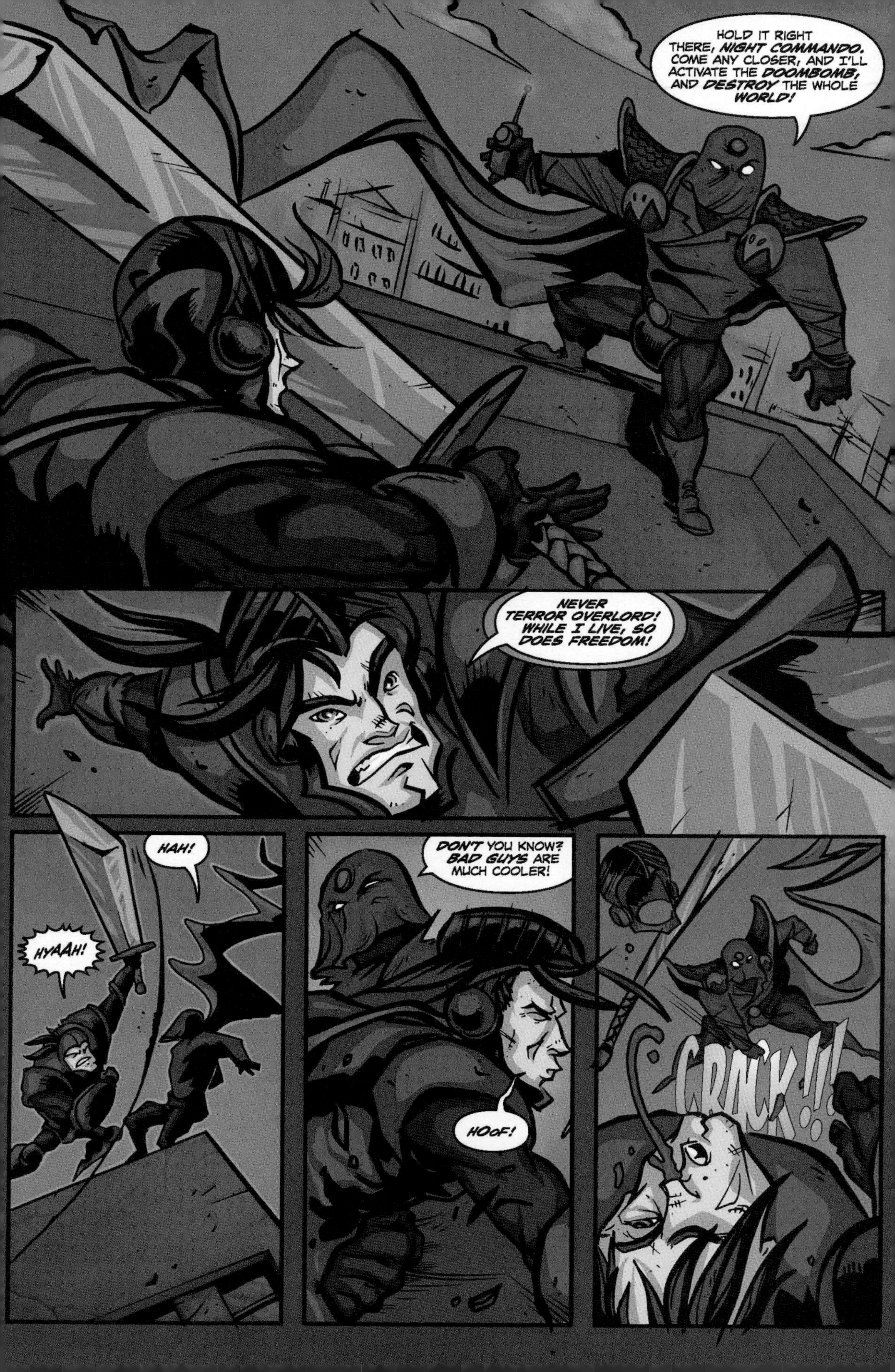
HOLD IT RIGHT THERE, NIGHT COMMANDO. COME ANY CLOSER, AND I'LL ACTIVATE THE DOOMBOMB, AND DESTROY THE WHOLE WORLD!
NEVER TERROR OVERLORD! WHILE I LIVE, SO DOES FREEDOM!
HAH!
HYAAH!
DON'T YOU KNOW? BAD GUYS ARE MUCH COOLER!
HOOF!
CRACK!!!

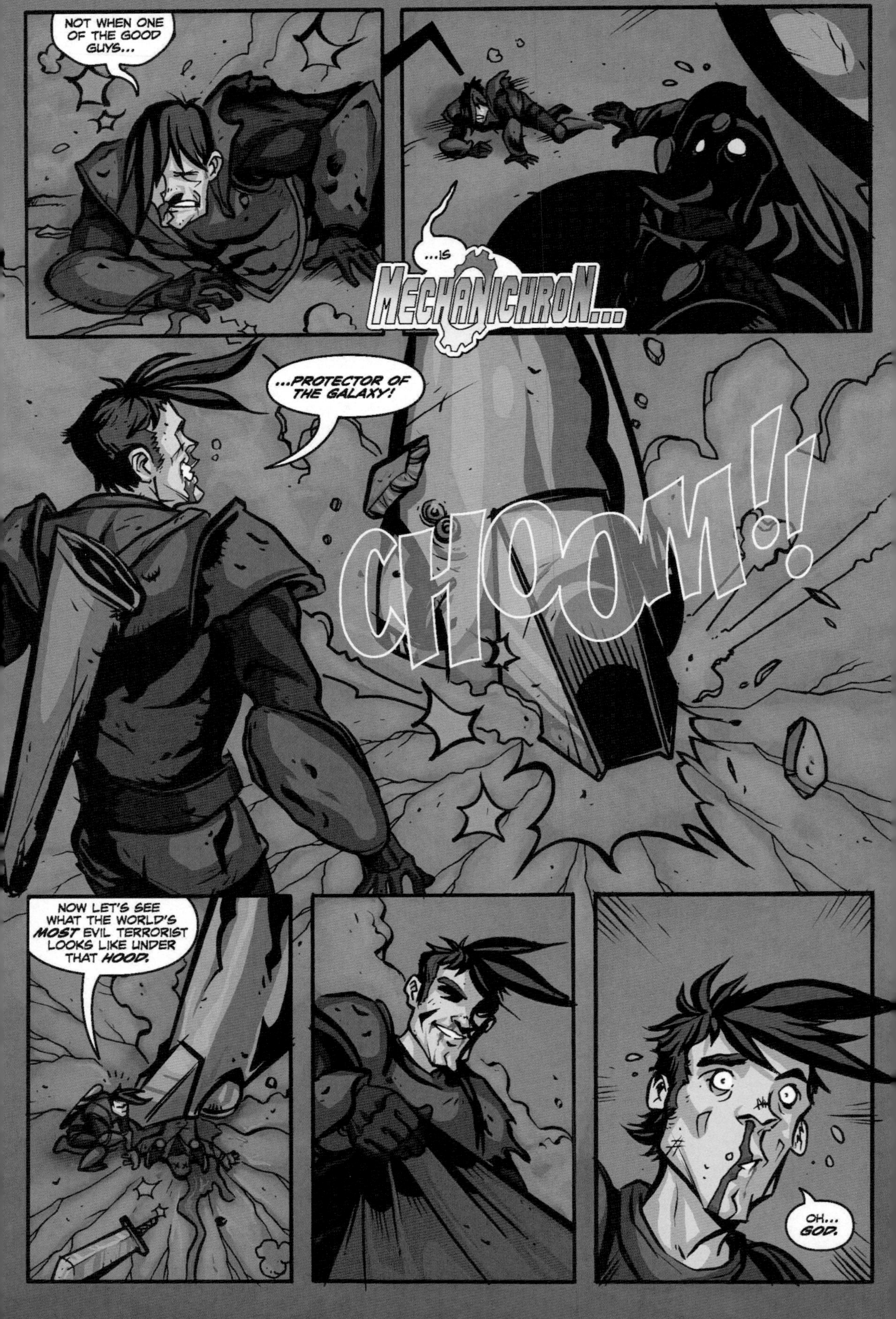
NOT WHEN ONE OF THE GOOD GUYS...
...IS
MECHANICHRON...
...PROTECTOR OF THE GALAXY!
CHOOM!!
NOW LET'S SEE WHAT THE WORLD'S *MOST* EVIL TERRORIST LOOKS LIKE UNDER THAT *HOOD.*
OH... *GOD.*

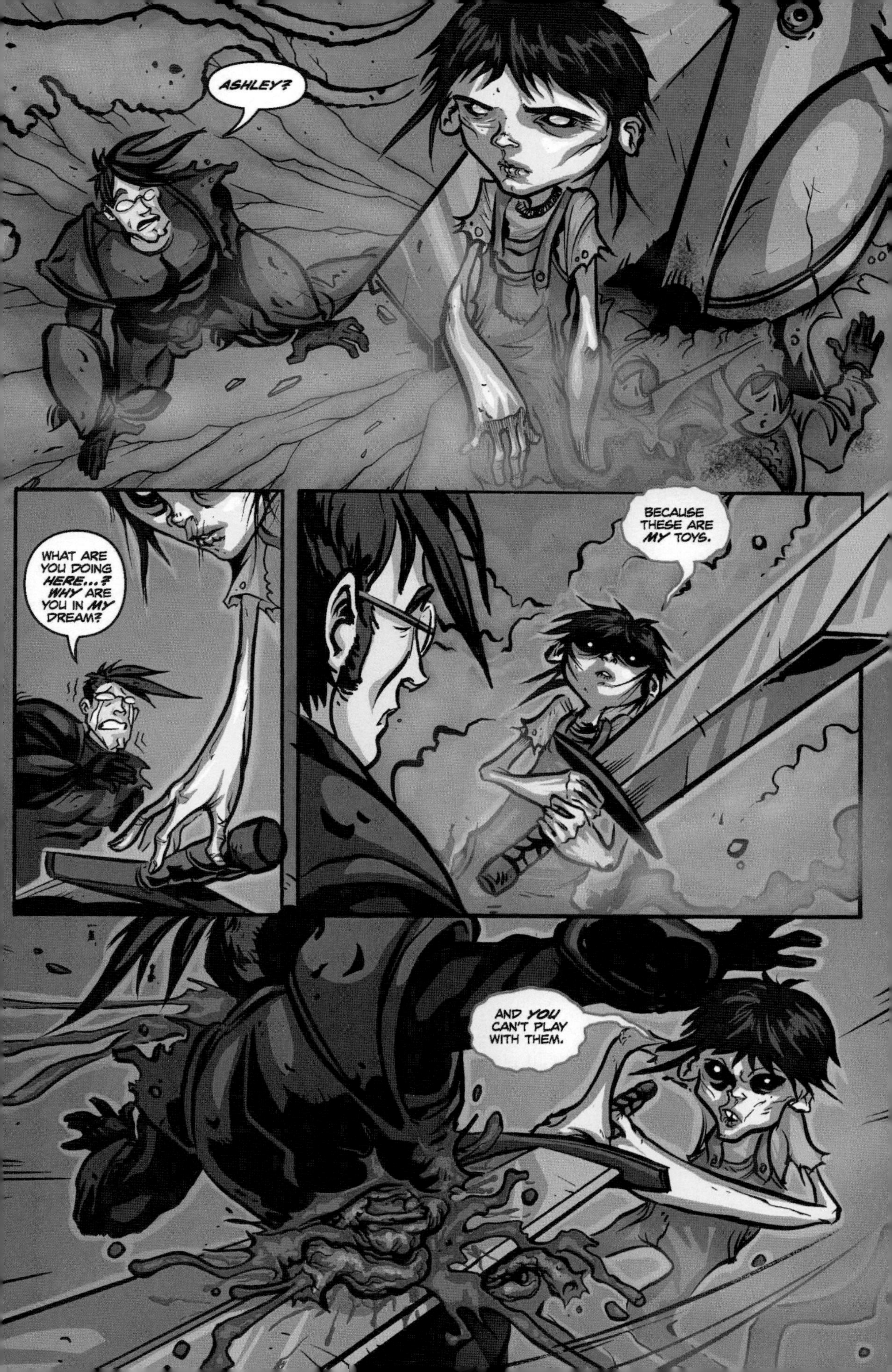
ASHLEY?
WHAT ARE YOU DOING HERE...? WHY ARE YOU IN MY DREAM?
BECAUSE THESE ARE MY TOYS.
AND YOU CAN'T PLAY WITH THEM.

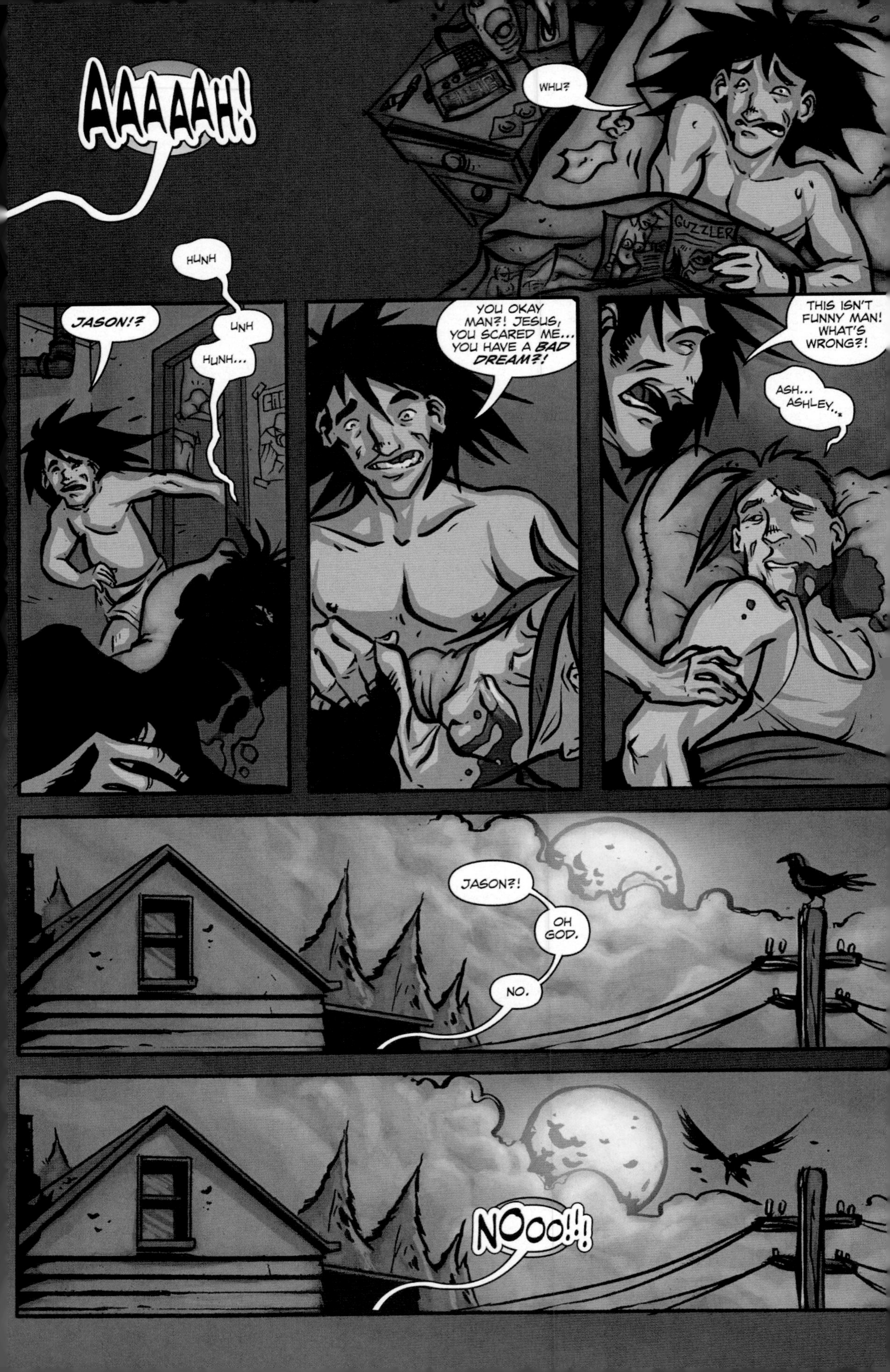
AAAAAH!
WHU?
HUNH
JASON!?
UNH
HUNH...
YOU OKAY MAN?! JESUS, YOU SCARED ME... YOU HAVE A BAD DREAM?!
THIS ISN'T FUNNY MAN! WHAT'S WRONG?!
ASH... ASHLEY...
JASON?!
OH GOD.
NO.
NOOO!!!

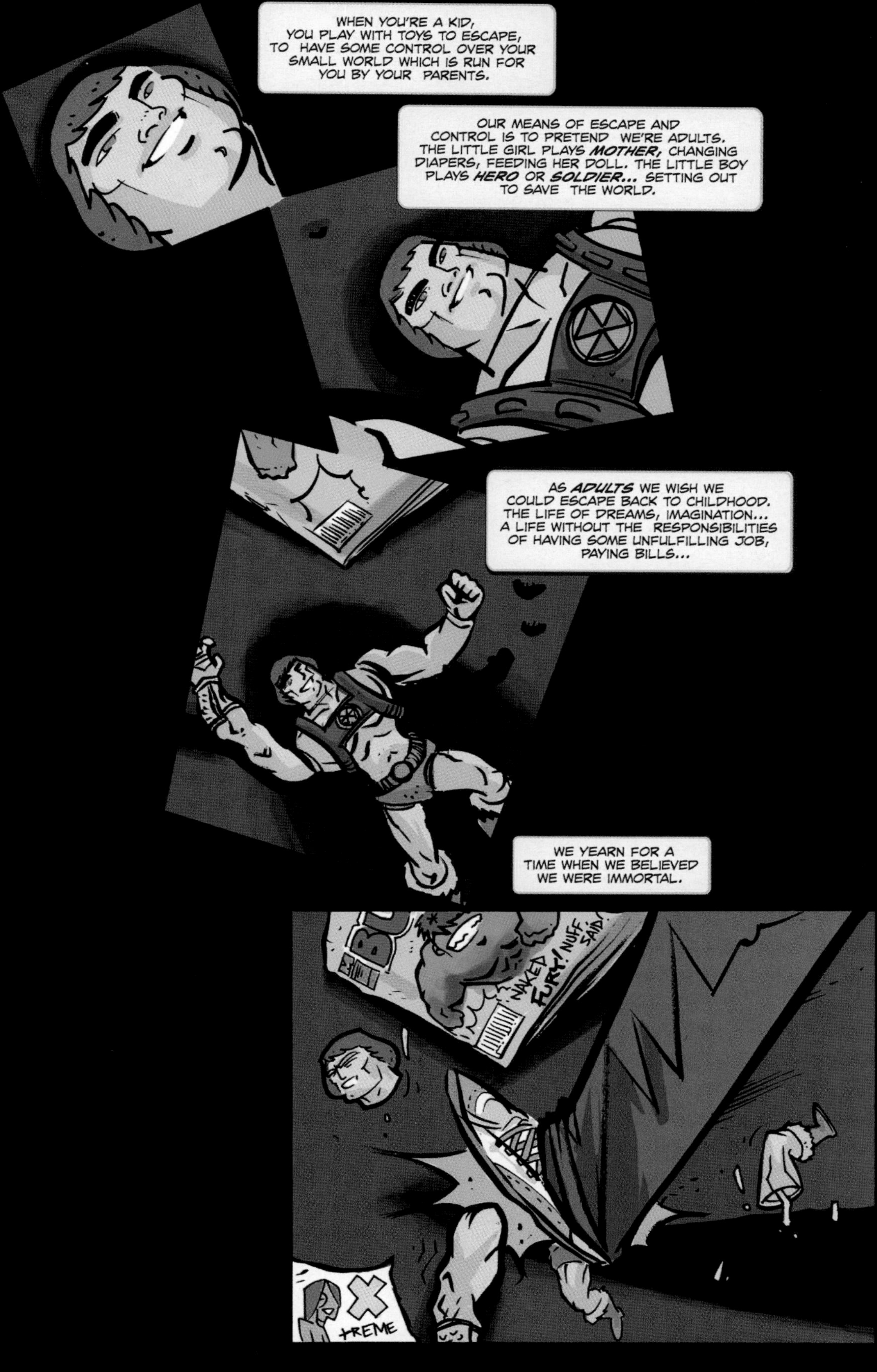
WHEN YOU'RE A KID, YOU PLAY WITH TOYS TO ESCAPE, TO HAVE SOME CONTROL OVER YOUR SMALL WORLD WHICH IS RUN FOR YOU BY YOUR PARENTS.
OUR MEANS OF ESCAPE AND CONTROL IS TO PRETEND WE'RE ADULTS. THE LITTLE GIRL PLAYS *MOTHER,* CHANGING DIAPERS, FEEDING HER DOLL. THE LITTLE BOY PLAYS *HERO* OR *SOLDIER...* SETTING OUT TO SAVE THE WORLD.
AS *ADULTS* WE WISH WE COULD ESCAPE BACK TO CHILDHOOD. THE LIFE OF DREAMS, IMAGINATION... A LIFE WITHOUT THE RESPONSIBILITIES OF HAVING SOME UNFULFILLING JOB, PAYING BILLS...
WE YEARN FOR A TIME WHEN WE BELIEVED WE WERE IMMORTAL.
NAKED FURY! NUFF SAID!

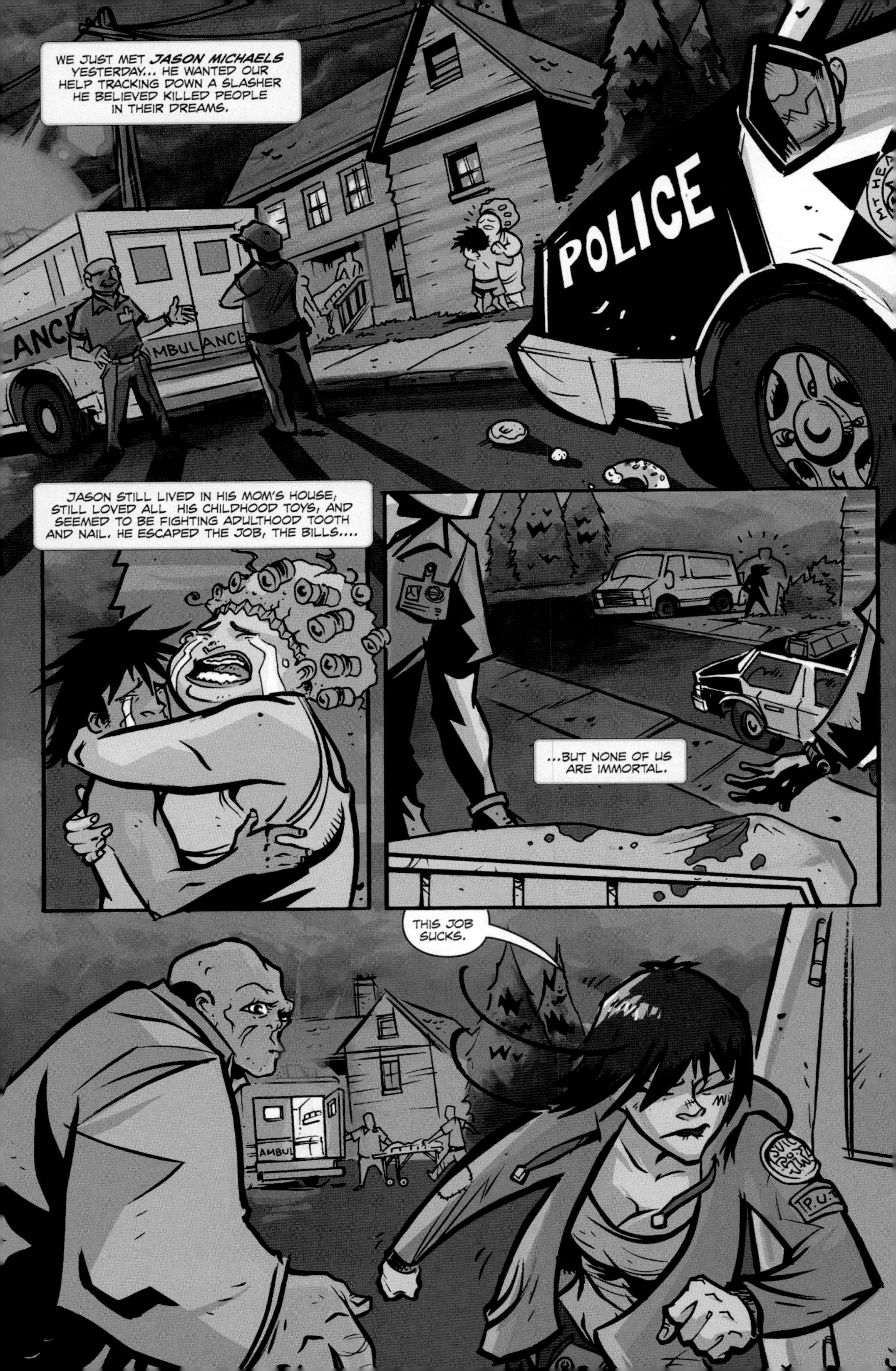

WE JUST MET JASON MICHAELS YESTERDAY... HE WANTED OUR HELP TRACKING DOWN A SLASHER HE BELIEVED KILLED PEOPLE IN THEIR DREAMS.
POLICE
AMBULANCE
JASON STILL LIVED IN HIS MOM'S HOUSE, STILL LOVED ALL HIS CHILDHOOD TOYS, AND SEEMED TO BE FIGHTING ADULTHOOD TOOTH AND NAIL. HE ESCAPED THE JOB, THE BILLS....
...BUT NONE OF US ARE IMMORTAL.
THIS JOB SUCKS.

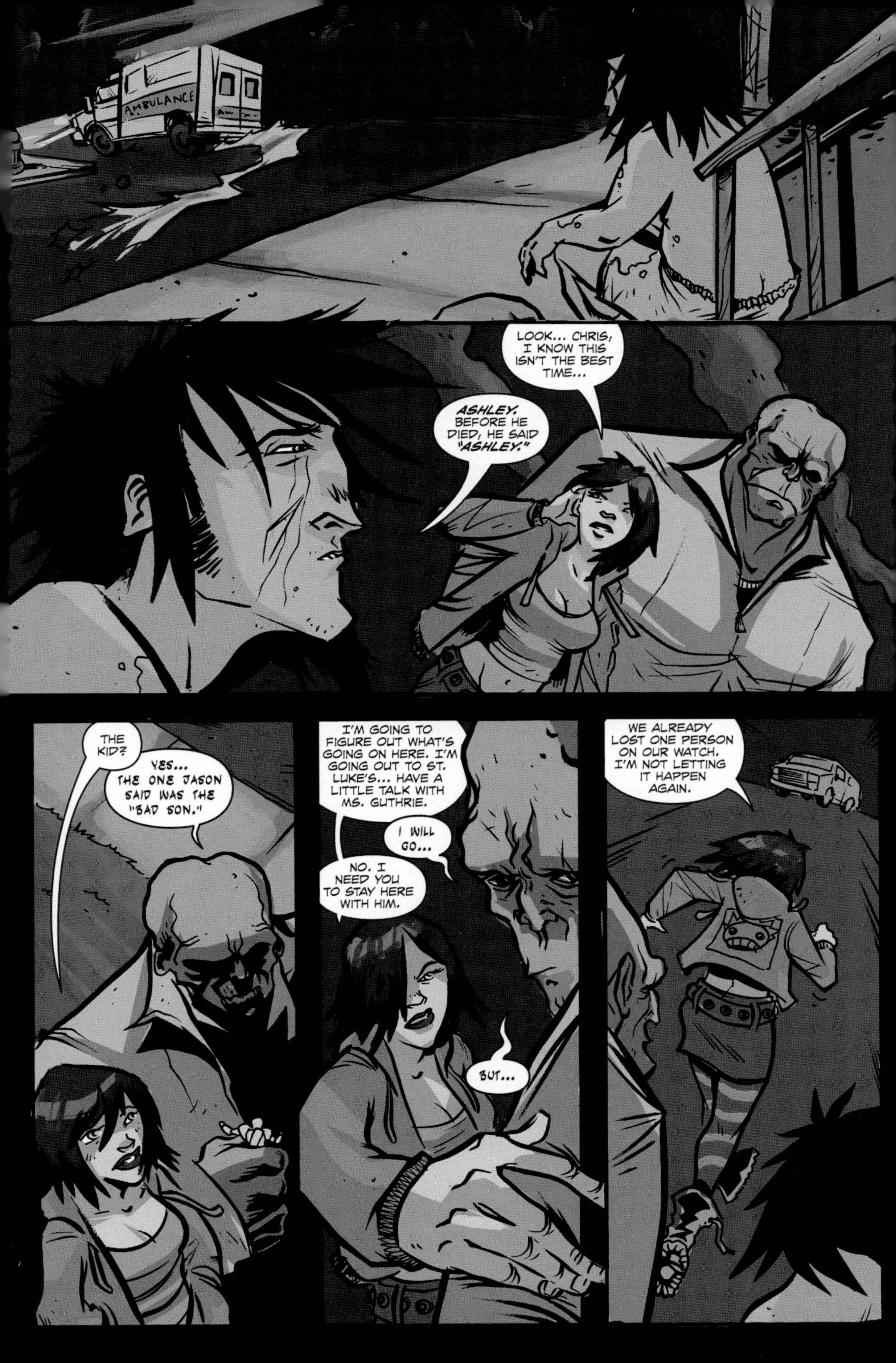
AMBULANCE
LOOK... CHRIS, I KNOW THIS ISN'T THE BEST TIME...
ASHLEY. BEFORE HE DIED, HE SAID "ASHLEY."
THE KID?
YES... THE ONE JASON SAID WAS THE "BAD SON."
I'M GOING TO FIGURE OUT WHAT'S GOING ON HERE. I'M GOING OUT TO ST. LUKE'S... HAVE A LITTLE TALK WITH MS. GUTHRIE.
I WILL GO...
NO. I NEED YOU TO STAY HERE WITH HIM.
BUT...
WE ALREADY LOST ONE PERSON ON OUR WATCH. I'M NOT LETTING IT HAPPEN AGAIN.

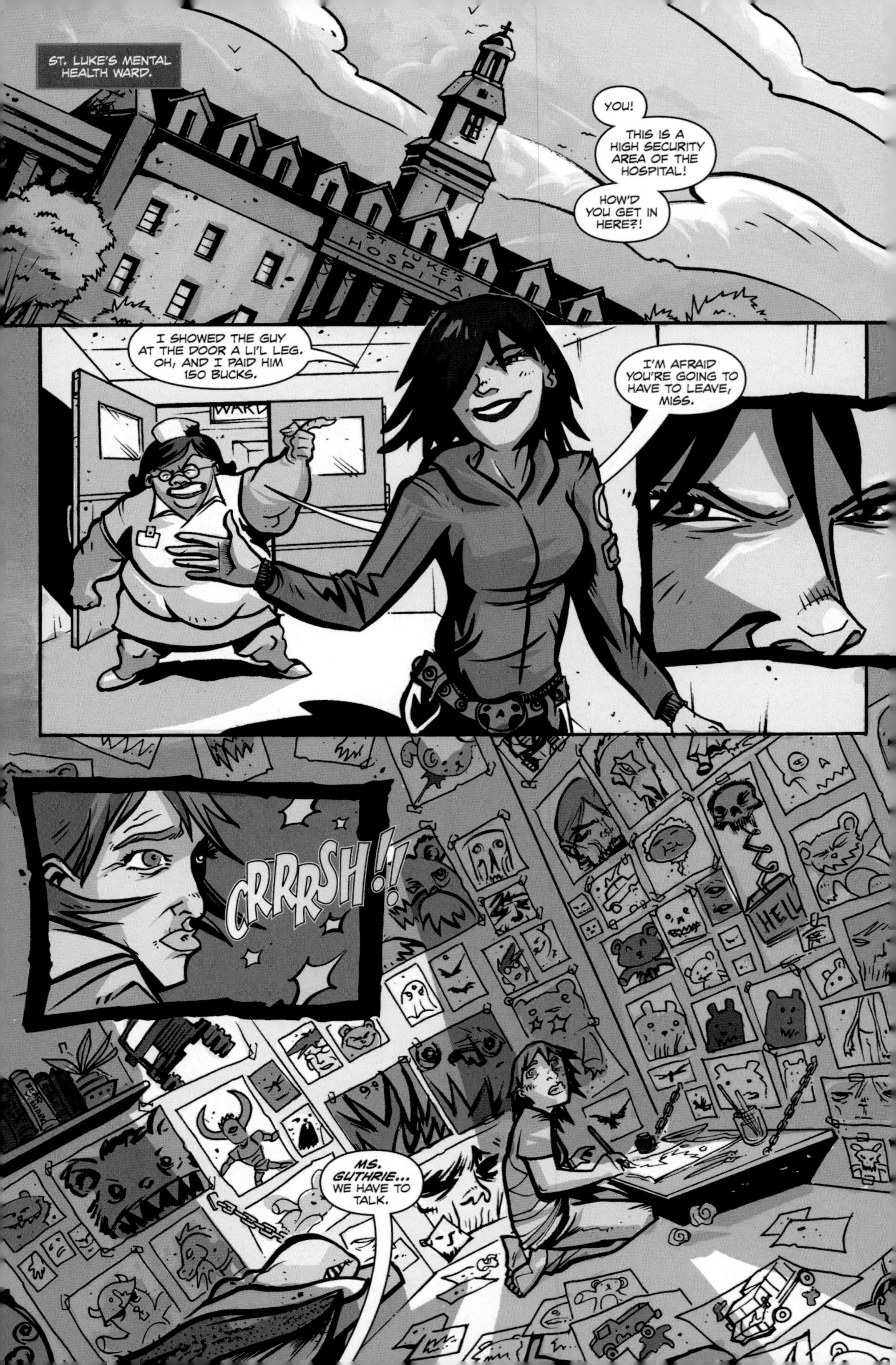
ST. LUKE'S MENTAL HEALTH WARD.
YOU!
THIS IS A HIGH SECURITY AREA OF THE HOSPITAL!
HOW'D YOU GET IN HERE?!
ST. LUKE'S HOSPITAL
I SHOWED THE GUY AT THE DOOR A LI'L LEG. OH, AND I PAID HIM 150 BUCKS.
WARD
I'M AFRAID YOU'RE GOING TO HAVE TO LEAVE, MISS.
CRRRSH!!
HELL
MS. GUTHRIE... WE HAVE TO TALK.

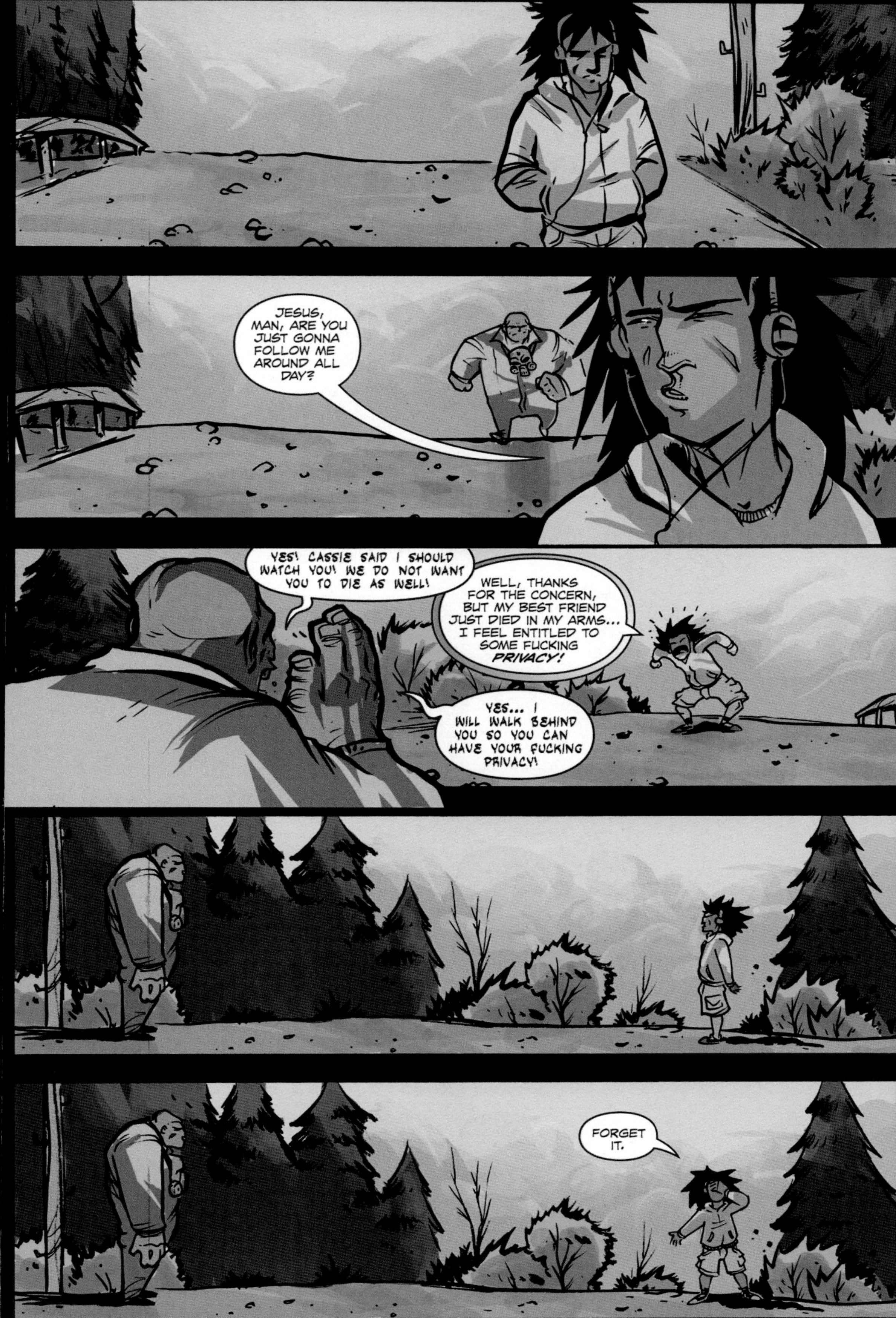
JESUS, MAN, ARE YOU JUST GONNA FOLLOW ME AROUND ALL DAY?
YES! CASSIE SAID I SHOULD WATCH YOU! WE DO NOT WANT YOU TO DIE AS WELL!
WELL, THANKS FOR THE CONCERN, BUT MY BEST FRIEND JUST DIED IN MY ARMS... I FEEL ENTITLED TO SOME FUCKING *PRIVACY!*
YES... I WILL WALK BEHIND YOU SO YOU CAN HAVE YOUR FUCKING PRIVACY!
FORGET IT.

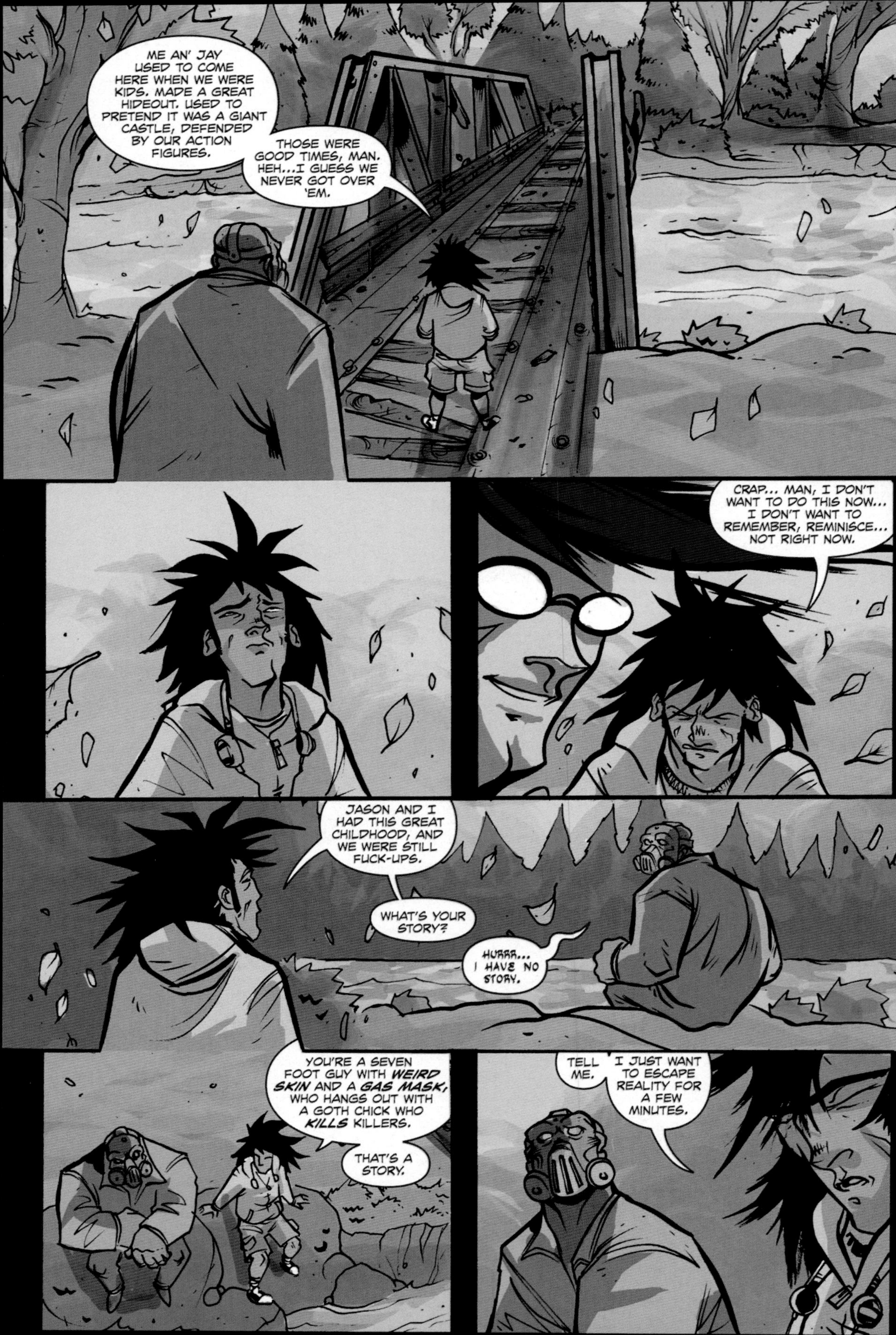
ME AN' JAY USED TO COME HERE WHEN WE WERE KIDS. MADE A GREAT HIDEOUT. USED TO PRETEND IT WAS A GIANT CASTLE, DEFENDED BY OUR ACTION FIGURES.
THOSE WERE GOOD TIMES, MAN. HEH...I GUESS WE NEVER GOT OVER 'EM.
CRAP... MAN, I DON'T WANT TO DO THIS NOW... I DON'T WANT TO REMEMBER, REMINISCE... NOT RIGHT NOW.
JASON AND I HAD THIS GREAT CHILDHOOD, AND WE WERE STILL FUCK-UPS.
WHAT'S YOUR STORY?
HURRR... I HAVE NO STORY.
YOU'RE A SEVEN FOOT GUY WITH WEIRD SKIN AND A GAS MASK, WHO HANGS OUT WITH A GOTH CHICK WHO KILLS KILLERS.
THAT'S A STORY.
TELL ME.
I JUST WANT TO ESCAPE REALITY FOR A FEW MINUTES.

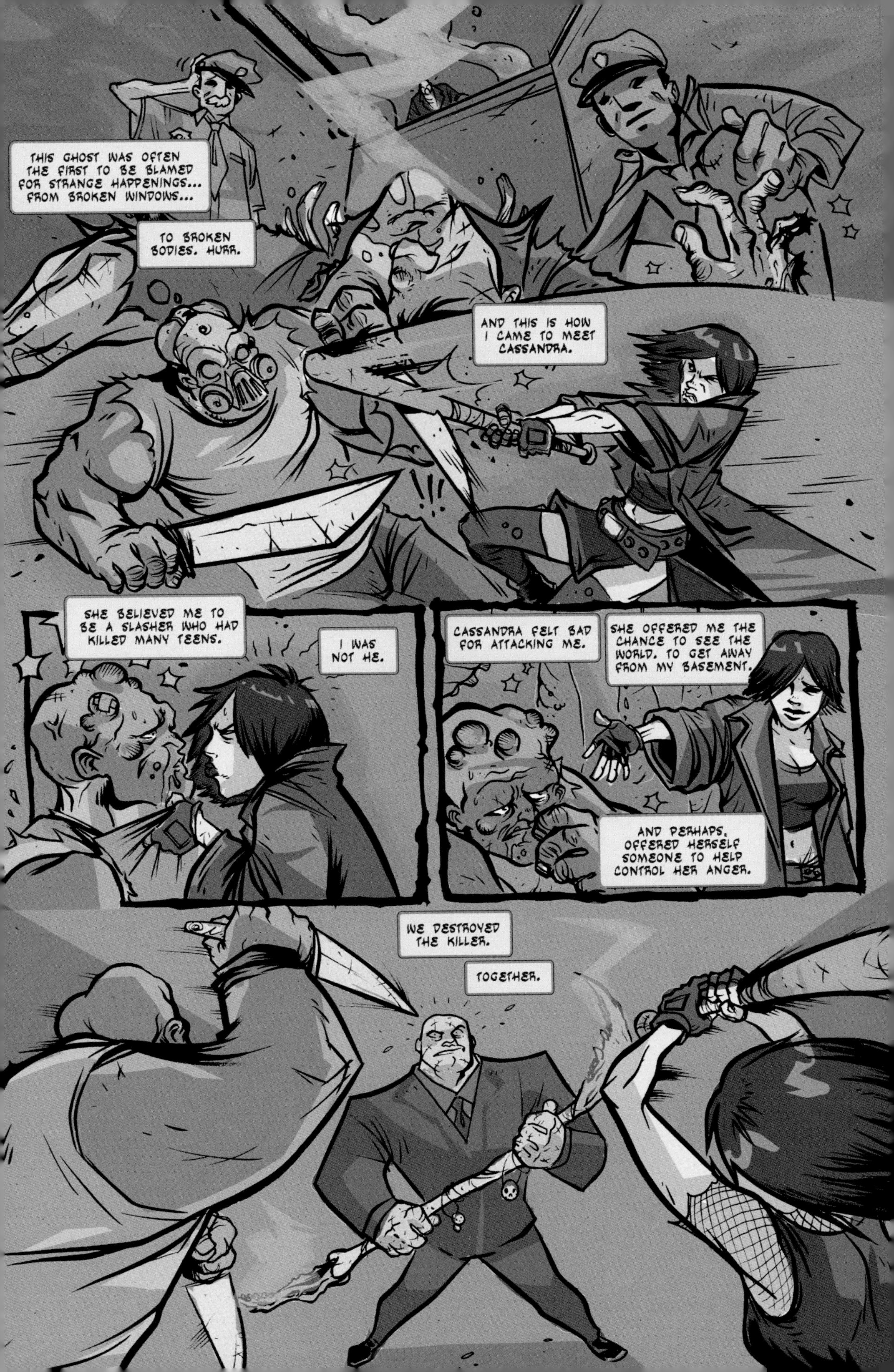
THIS GHOST WAS OFTEN THE FIRST TO BE BLAMED FOR STRANGE HAPPENINGS... FROM BROKEN WINDOWS...
TO BROKEN BODIES. HURR.
AND THIS IS HOW I CAME TO MEET CASSANDRA.
SHE BELIEVED ME TO BE A SLASHER WHO HAD KILLED MANY TEENS.
I WAS NOT HE.
CASSANDRA FELT BAD FOR ATTACKING ME.
SHE OFFERED ME THE CHANCE TO SEE THE WORLD. TO GET AWAY FROM MY BASEMENT.
AND PERHAPS, OFFERED HERSELF SOMEONE TO HELP CONTROL HER ANGER.
WE DESTROYED THE KILLER.
TOGETHER.

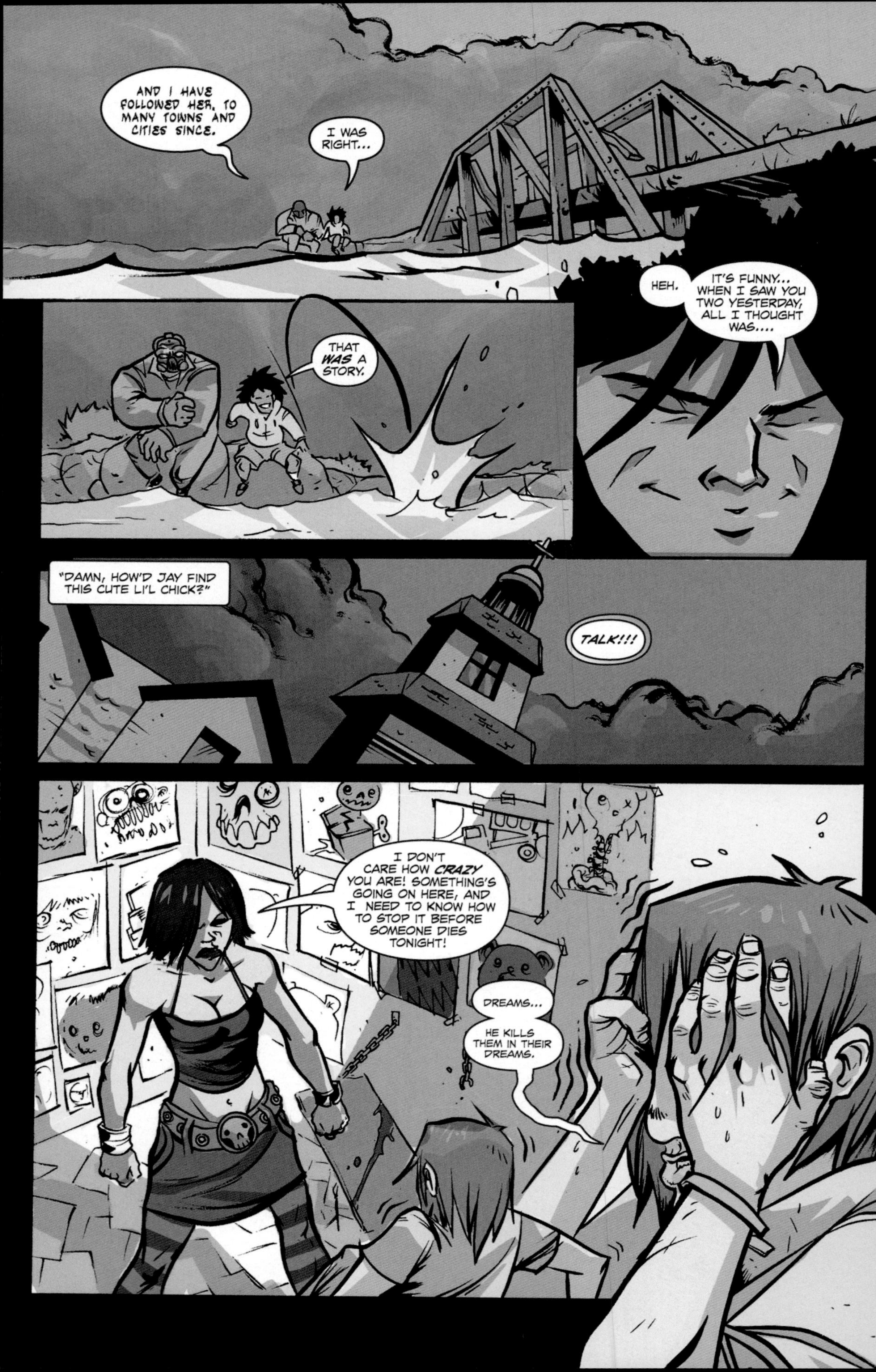
AND I HAVE FOLLOWED HER, TO MANY TOWNS AND CITIES SINCE.
I WAS RIGHT...
THAT WAS A STORY.
HEH.
IT'S FUNNY... WHEN I SAW YOU TWO YESTERDAY, ALL I THOUGHT WAS....
"DAMN, HOW'D JAY FIND THIS CUTE LI'L CHICK?"
TALK!!!
I DON'T CARE HOW CRAZY YOU ARE! SOMETHING'S GOING ON HERE, AND I NEED TO KNOW HOW TO STOP IT BEFORE SOMEONE DIES TONIGHT!
DREAMS...
HE KILLS THEM IN THEIR DREAMS.

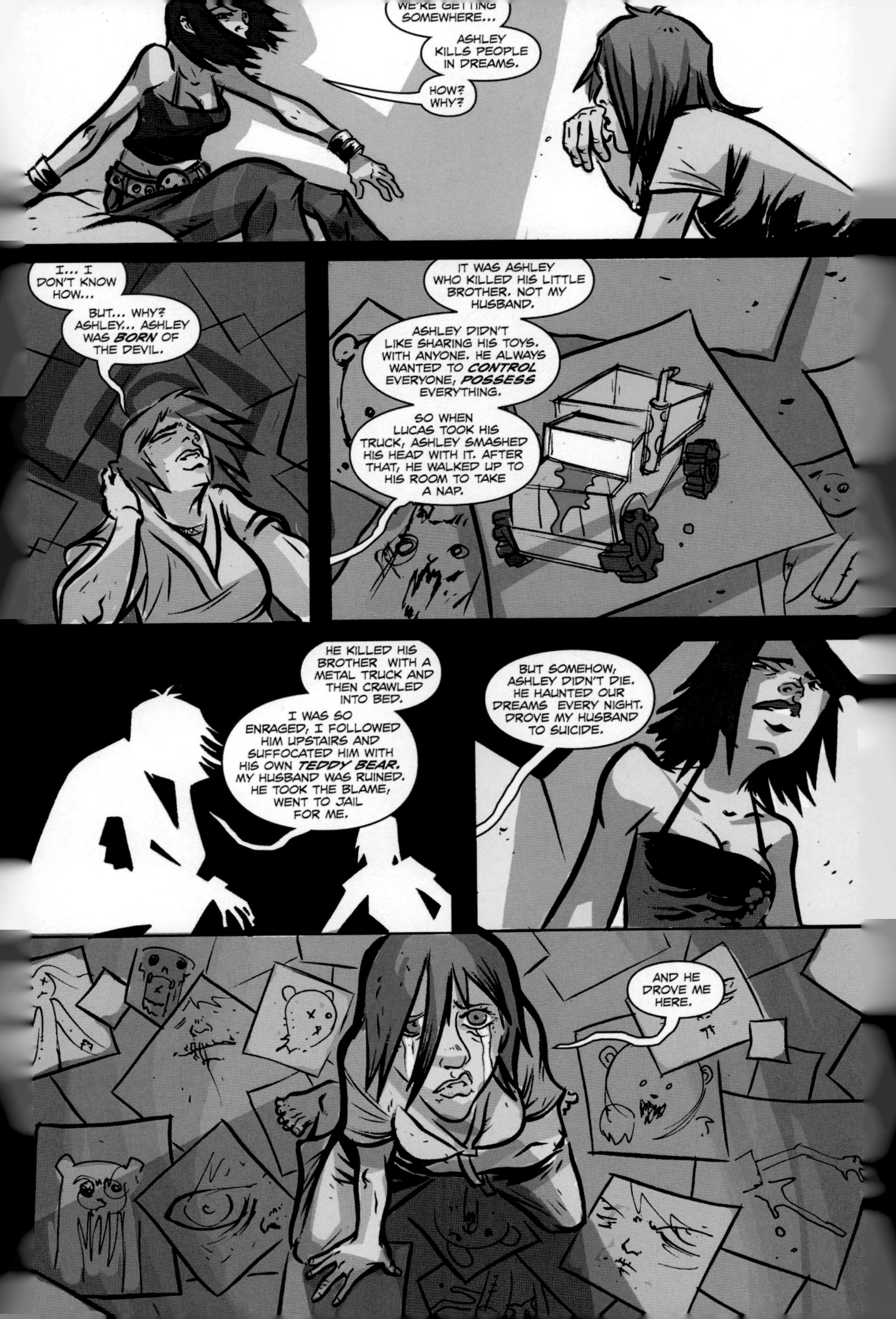
WE'RE GETTING SOMEWHERE...
ASHLEY KILLS PEOPLE IN DREAMS.
HOW? WHY?
I... I DON'T KNOW HOW...
BUT... WHY? ASHLEY... ASHLEY WAS BORN OF THE DEVIL.
IT WAS ASHLEY WHO KILLED HIS LITTLE BROTHER. NOT MY HUSBAND.
ASHLEY DIDN'T LIKE SHARING HIS TOYS. WITH ANYONE. HE ALWAYS WANTED TO CONTROL EVERYONE, POSSESS EVERYTHING.
SO WHEN LUCAS TOOK HIS TRUCK, ASHLEY SMASHED HIS HEAD WITH IT. AFTER THAT, HE WALKED UP TO HIS ROOM TO TAKE A NAP.
HE KILLED HIS BROTHER WITH A METAL TRUCK AND THEN CRAWLED INTO BED.
I WAS SO ENRAGED, I FOLLOWED HIM UPSTAIRS AND SUFFOCATED HIM WITH HIS OWN TEDDY BEAR. MY HUSBAND WAS RUINED. HE TOOK THE BLAME, WENT TO JAIL FOR ME.
BUT SOMEHOW, ASHLEY DIDN'T DIE. HE HAUNTED OUR DREAMS EVERY NIGHT. DROVE MY HUSBAND TO SUICIDE.
AND HE DROVE ME HERE.

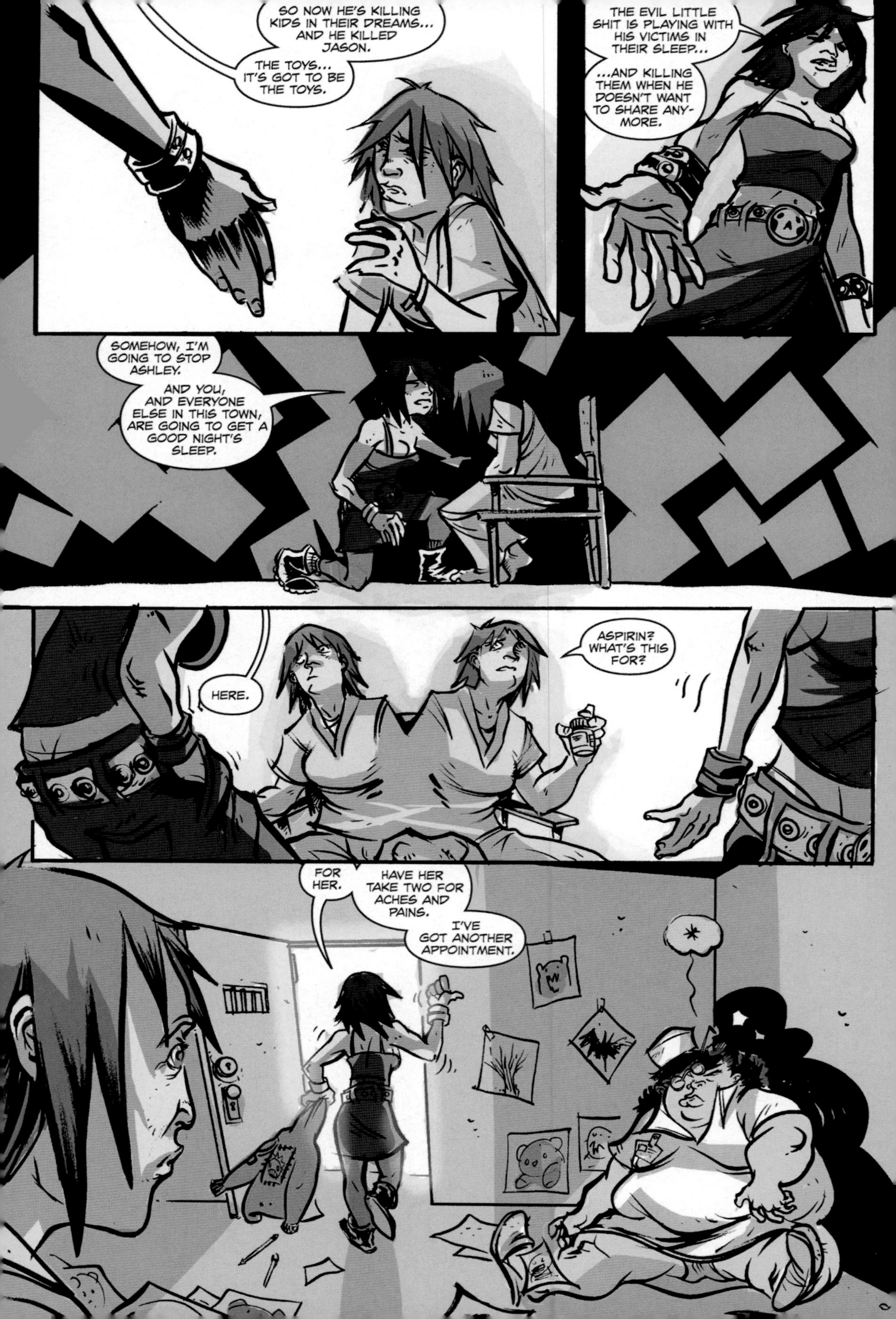
SO NOW HE'S KILLING KIDS IN THEIR DREAMS... AND HE KILLED JASON.
THE TOYS... IT'S GOT TO BE THE TOYS.
THE EVIL LITTLE SHIT IS PLAYING WITH HIS VICTIMS IN THEIR SLEEP...
...AND KILLING THEM WHEN HE DOESN'T WANT TO SHARE ANY-MORE.
SOMEHOW, I'M GOING TO STOP ASHLEY.
AND YOU, AND EVERYONE ELSE IN THIS TOWN, ARE GOING TO GET A GOOD NIGHT'S SLEEP.
HERE.
ASPIRIN? WHAT'S THIS FOR?
FOR HER.
HAVE HER TAKE TWO FOR ACHES AND PAINS.
I'VE GOT ANOTHER APPOINTMENT.
*

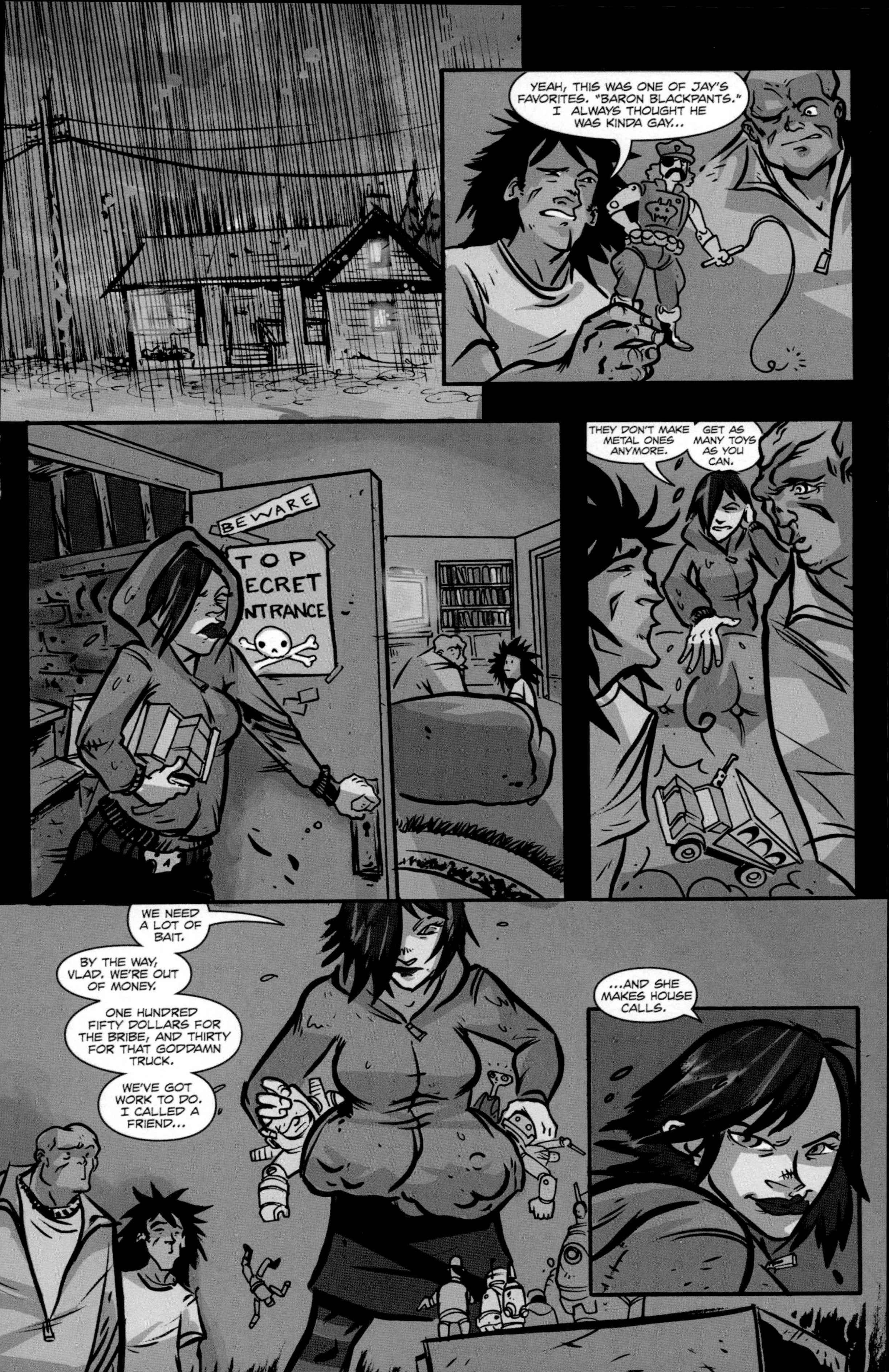
YEAH, THIS WAS ONE OF JAY'S FAVORITES. "BARON BLACKPANTS." I ALWAYS THOUGHT HE WAS KINDA GAY...
BEWARE
TOP SECRET ENTRANCE
THEY DON'T MAKE METAL ONES ANYMORE.
GET AS MANY TOYS AS YOU CAN.
WE NEED A LOT OF BAIT.
BY THE WAY, VLAD. WE'RE OUT OF MONEY.
ONE HUNDRED FIFTY DOLLARS FOR THE BRIBE, AND THIRTY FOR THAT GODDAMN TRUCK.
WE'VE GOT WORK TO DO. I CALLED A FRIEND...
...AND SHE MAKES HOUSE CALLS.

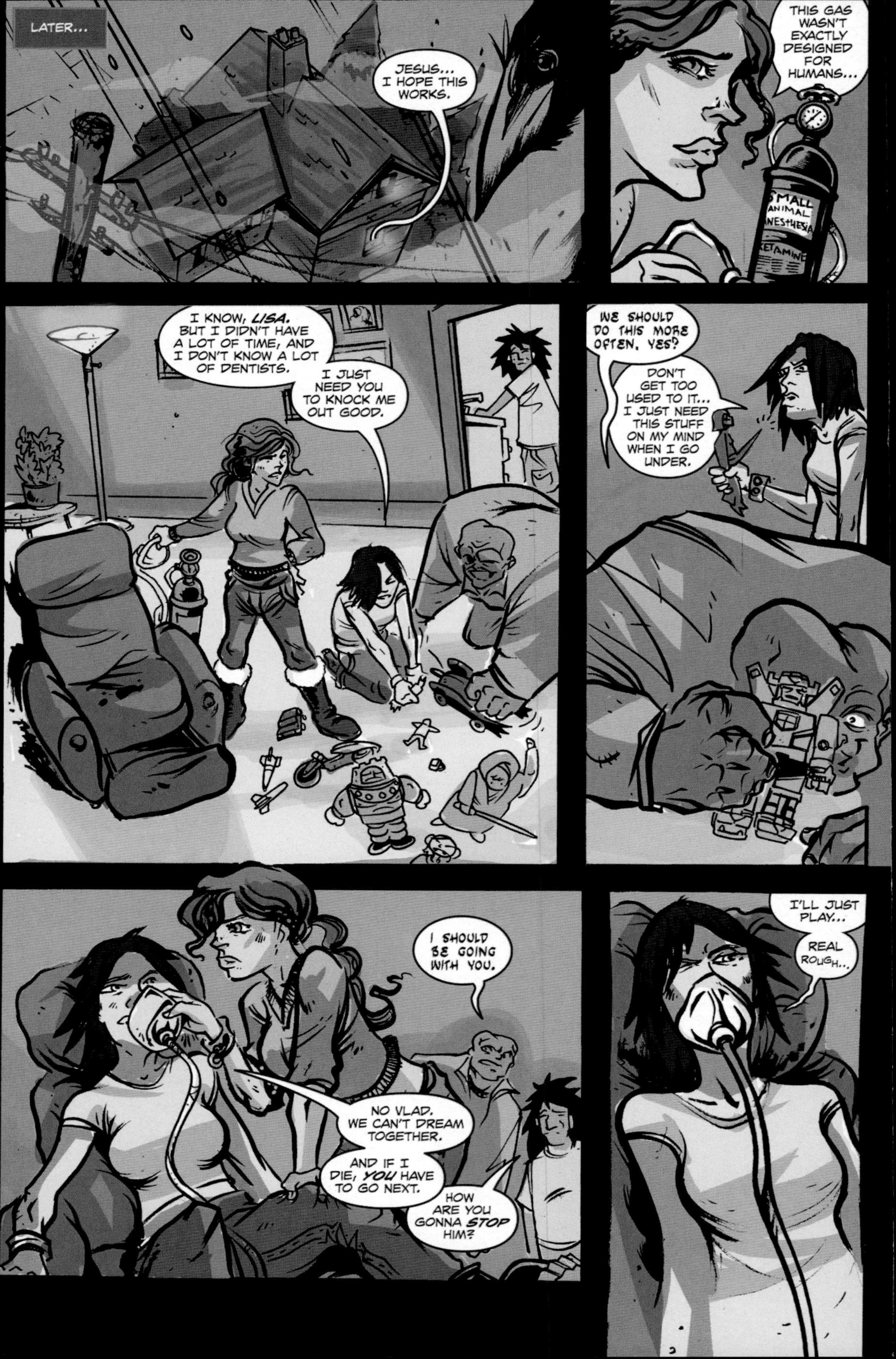
LATER...
JESUS... I HOPE THIS WORKS.
THIS GAS WASN'T EXACTLY DESIGNED FOR HUMANS...
SMALL ANIMAL ANESTHESIA
KETAMINE
I KNOW, LISA. BUT I DIDN'T HAVE A LOT OF TIME, AND I DON'T KNOW A LOT OF DENTISTS.
I JUST NEED YOU TO KNOCK ME OUT GOOD.
WE SHOULD DO THIS MORE OFTEN, YES?
DON'T GET TOO USED TO IT... I JUST NEED THIS STUFF ON MY MIND WHEN I GO UNDER.
I SHOULD BE GOING WITH YOU.
NO VLAD. WE CAN'T DREAM TOGETHER.
AND IF I DIE, YOU HAVE TO GO NEXT.
HOW ARE YOU GONNA STOP HIM?
I'LL JUST PLAY...
REAL ROUGH...

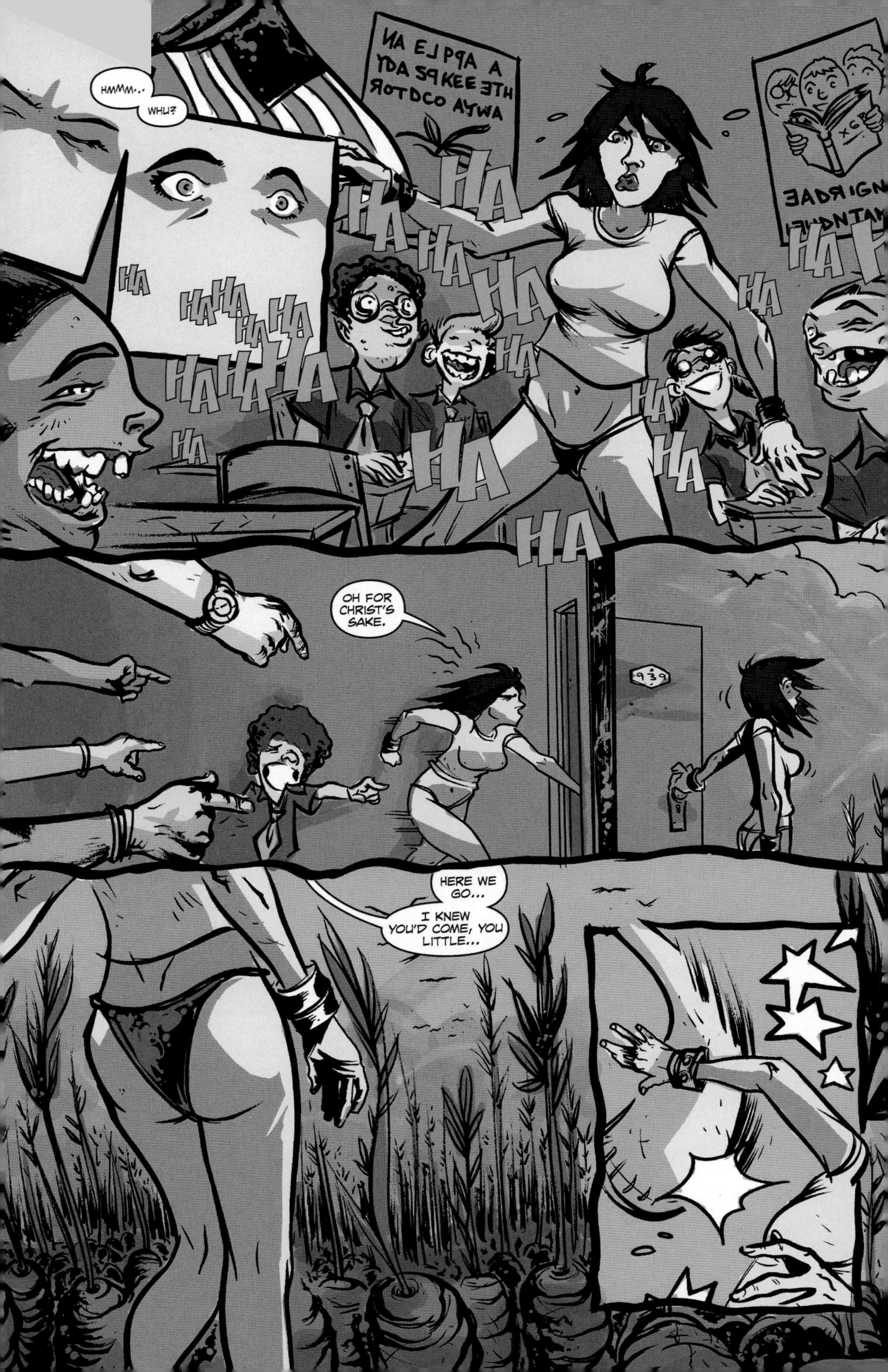
HMMM...
WHU?
HA HA HA
OH FOR CHRIST'S SAKE.
HERE WE GO...
I KNEW YOU'D COME, YOU LITTLE...

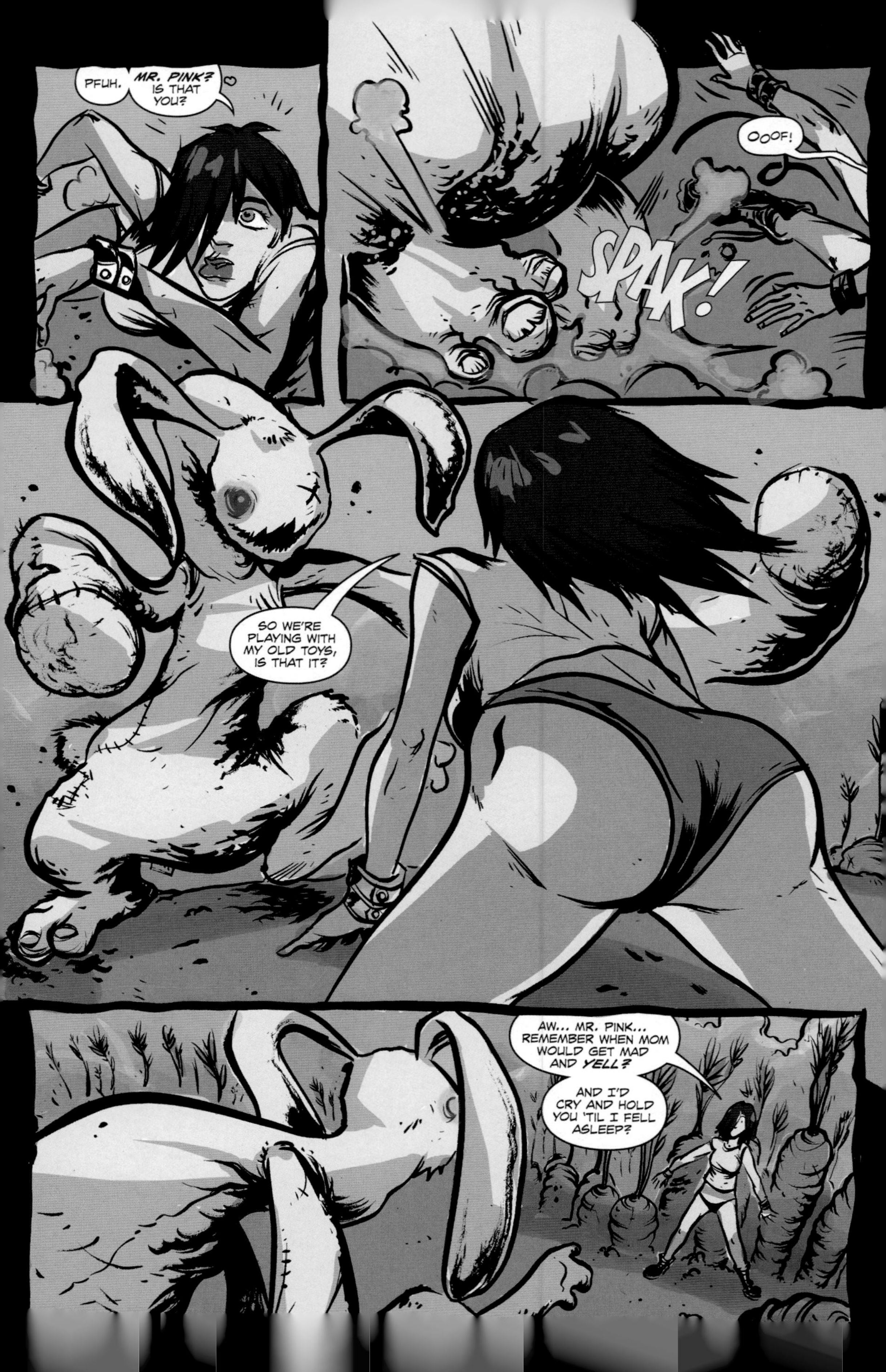
PFUH.
MR. PINK? IS THAT YOU?
OOOF!
SPAK!
SO WE'RE PLAYING WITH MY OLD TOYS, IS THAT IT?
AW... MR. PINK... REMEMBER WHEN MOM WOULD GET MAD AND YELL?
AND I'D CRY AND HOLD YOU 'TIL I FELL ASLEEP?

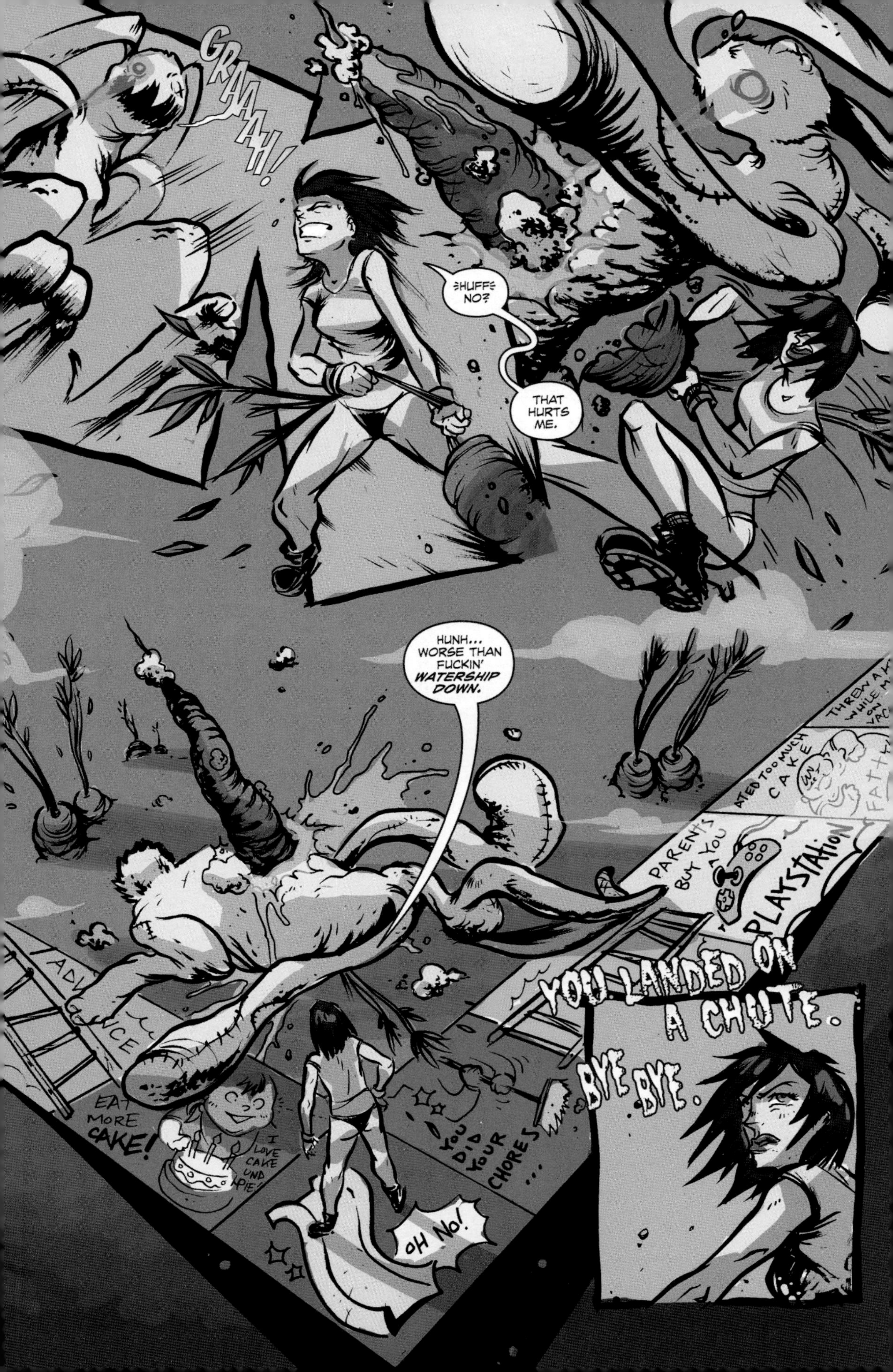
GRAAAAH!
HUFF
NO?
THAT HURTS ME.
HUNH... WORSE THAN FUCKIN' WATERSHIP DOWN.
ATED TOO MUCH CAKE
PARENTS BUY YOU
PLAYSTATION
EAT MORE CAKE!
I LOVE CAKE UND PIE!
YOU DID YOUR CHORES...
OH NO!
YOU LANDED ON A CHUTE.
BYE BYE.

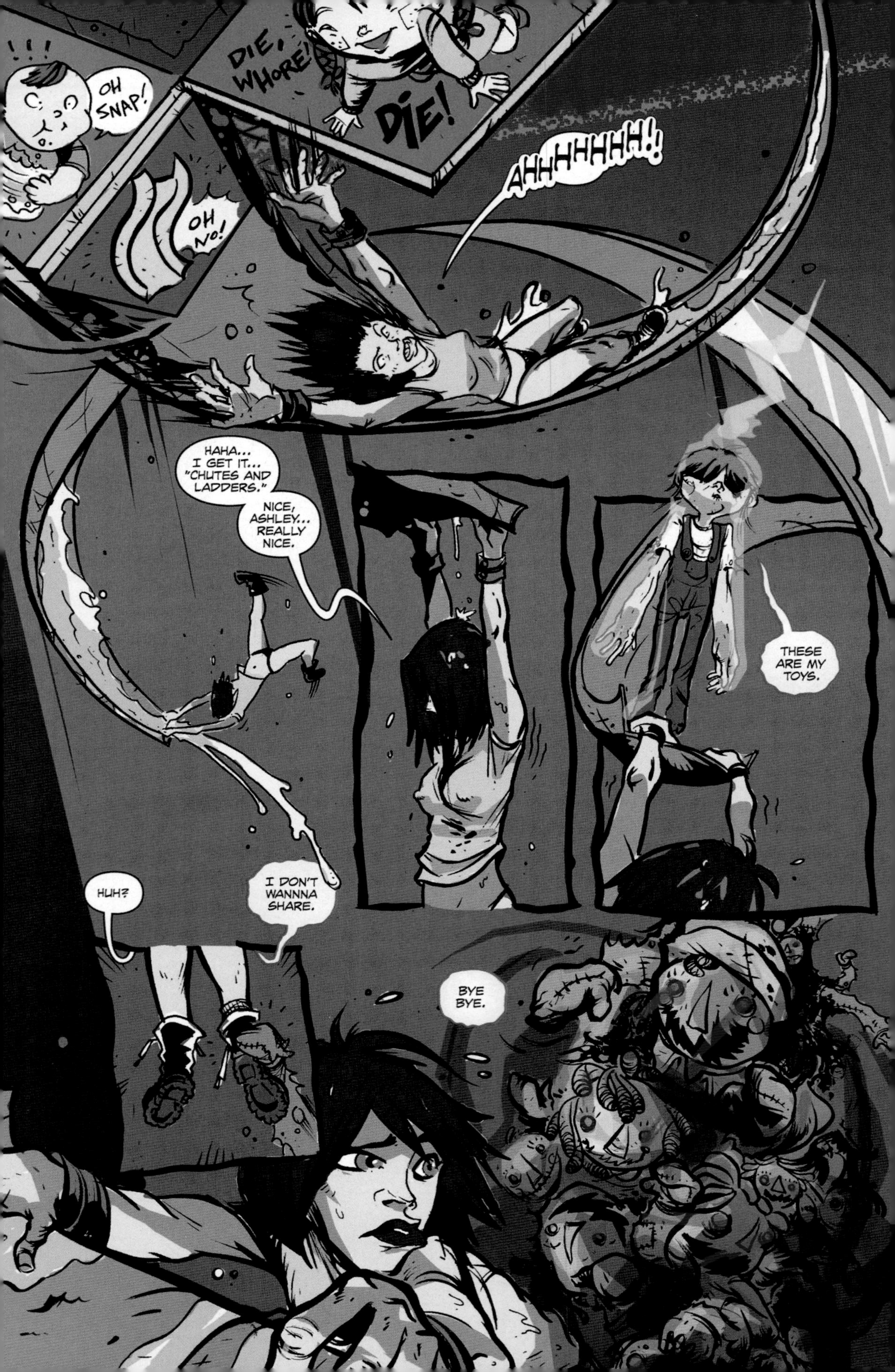

OH SNAP!
DIE, WHORE!
DIE!
OH NO!
AHHHHHHH!!
HAHA... I GET IT... "CHUTES AND LADDERS."
NICE, ASHLEY... REALLY NICE.
THESE ARE MY TOYS.
HUH?
I DON'T WANNNA SHARE.
BYE BYE.

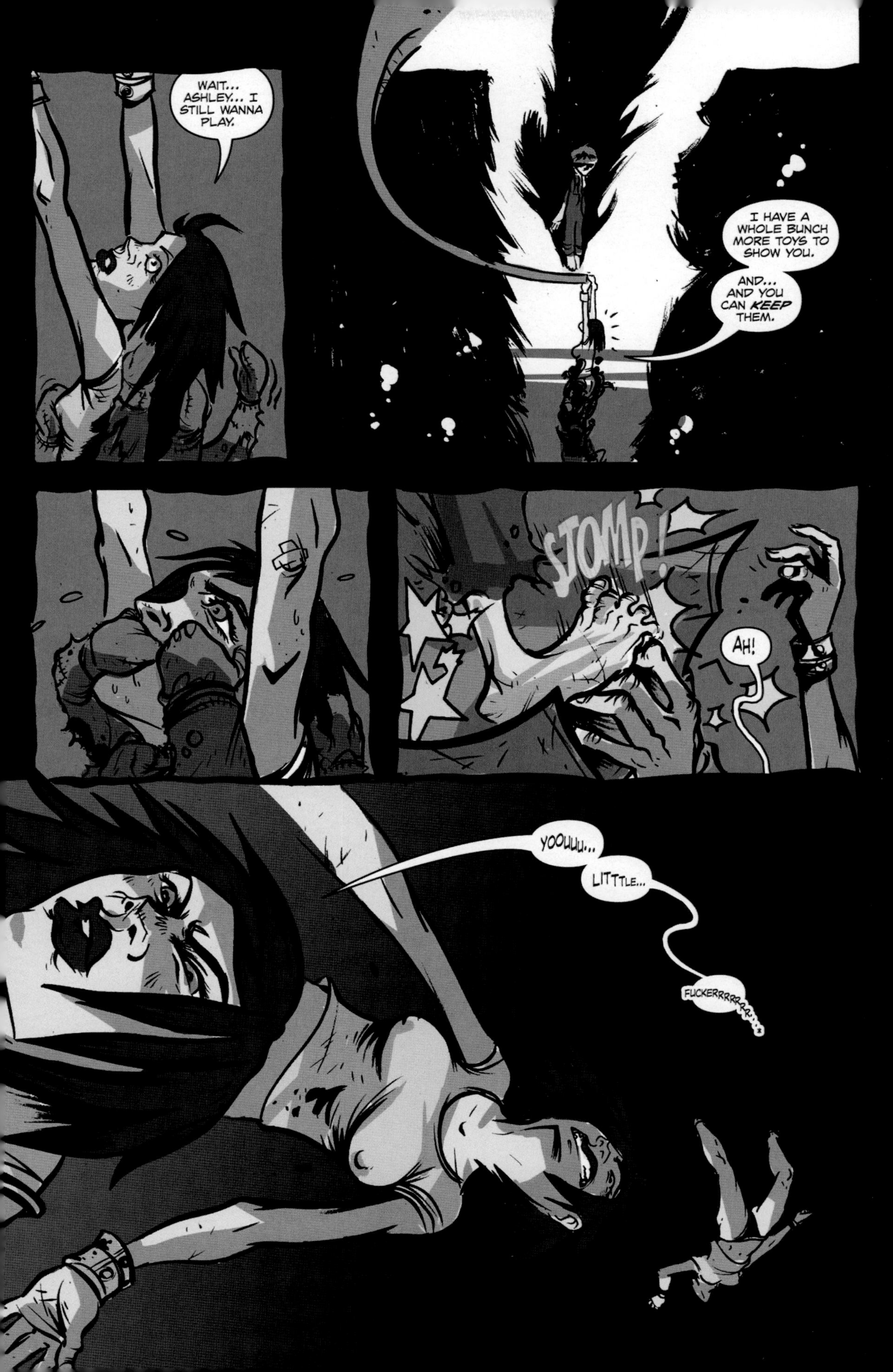
WAIT... ASHLEY... I STILL WANNA PLAY.
I HAVE A WHOLE BUNCH MORE TOYS TO SHOW YOU.
AND... AND YOU CAN KEEP THEM.
STOMP!
AH!
YOOuuu...
LITTTLE...
FUCKERRRRRR...

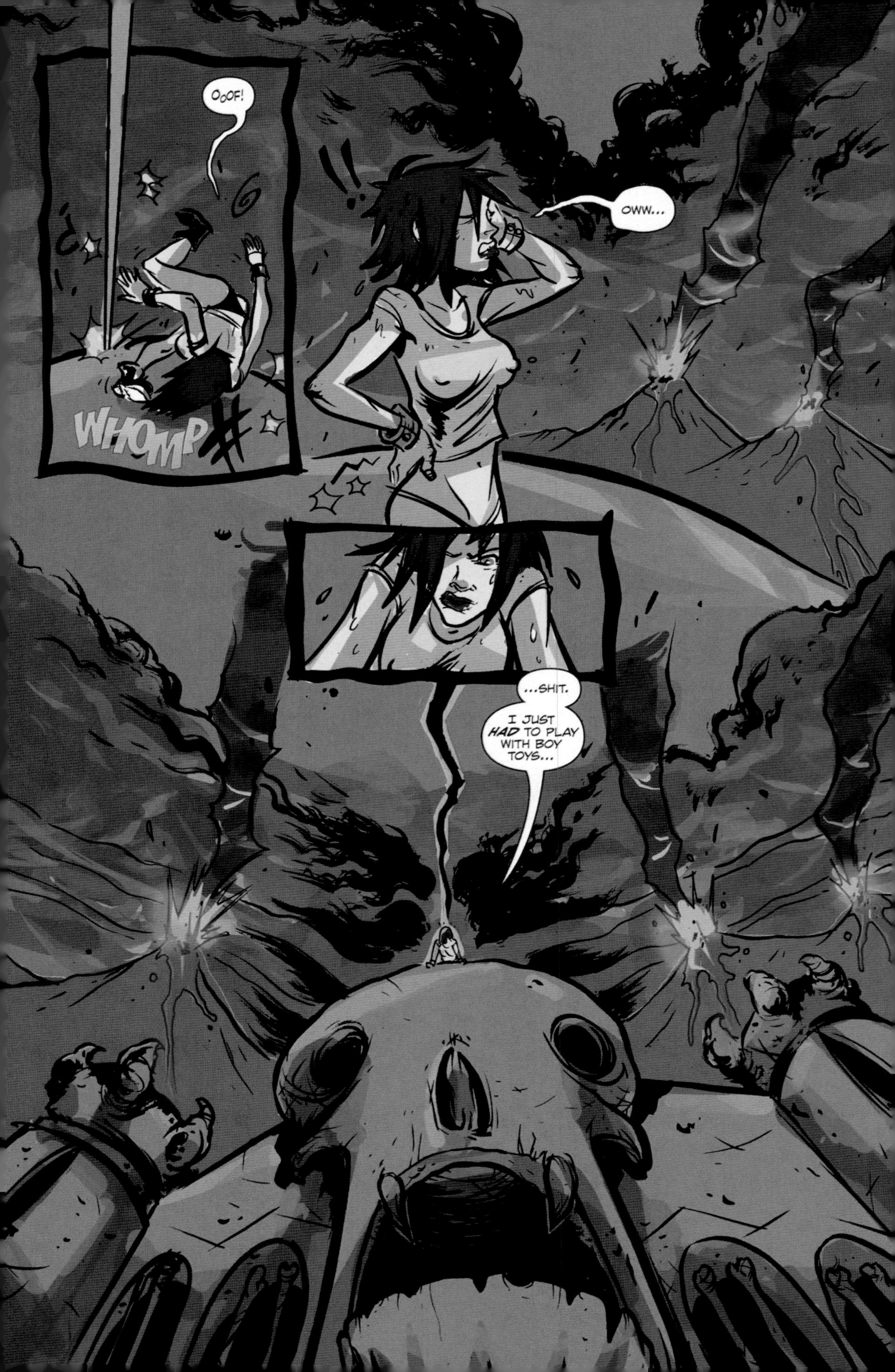
OOOF!
WHOMP
OWW...
...SHIT.
I JUST HAD TO PLAY WITH BOY TOYS...

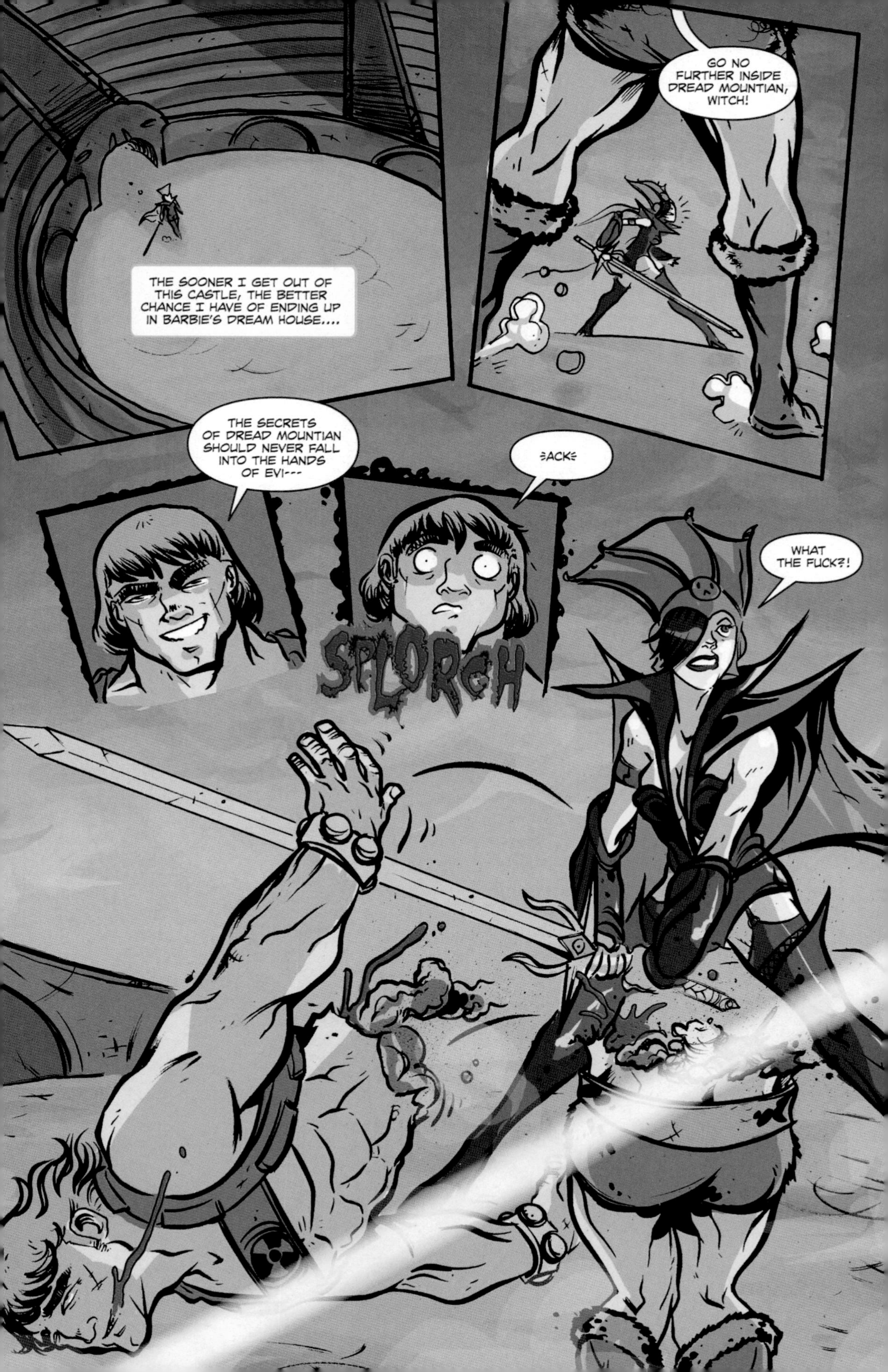
THE SOONER I GET OUT OF THIS CASTLE, THE BETTER CHANCE I HAVE OF ENDING UP IN BARBIE'S DREAM HOUSE....
GO NO FURTHER INSIDE DREAD MOUNTIAN, WITCH!
THE SECRETS OF DREAD MOUNTIAN SHOULD NEVER FALL INTO THE HANDS OF EVI---
ACK
SPLORGH
WHAT THE FUCK?!

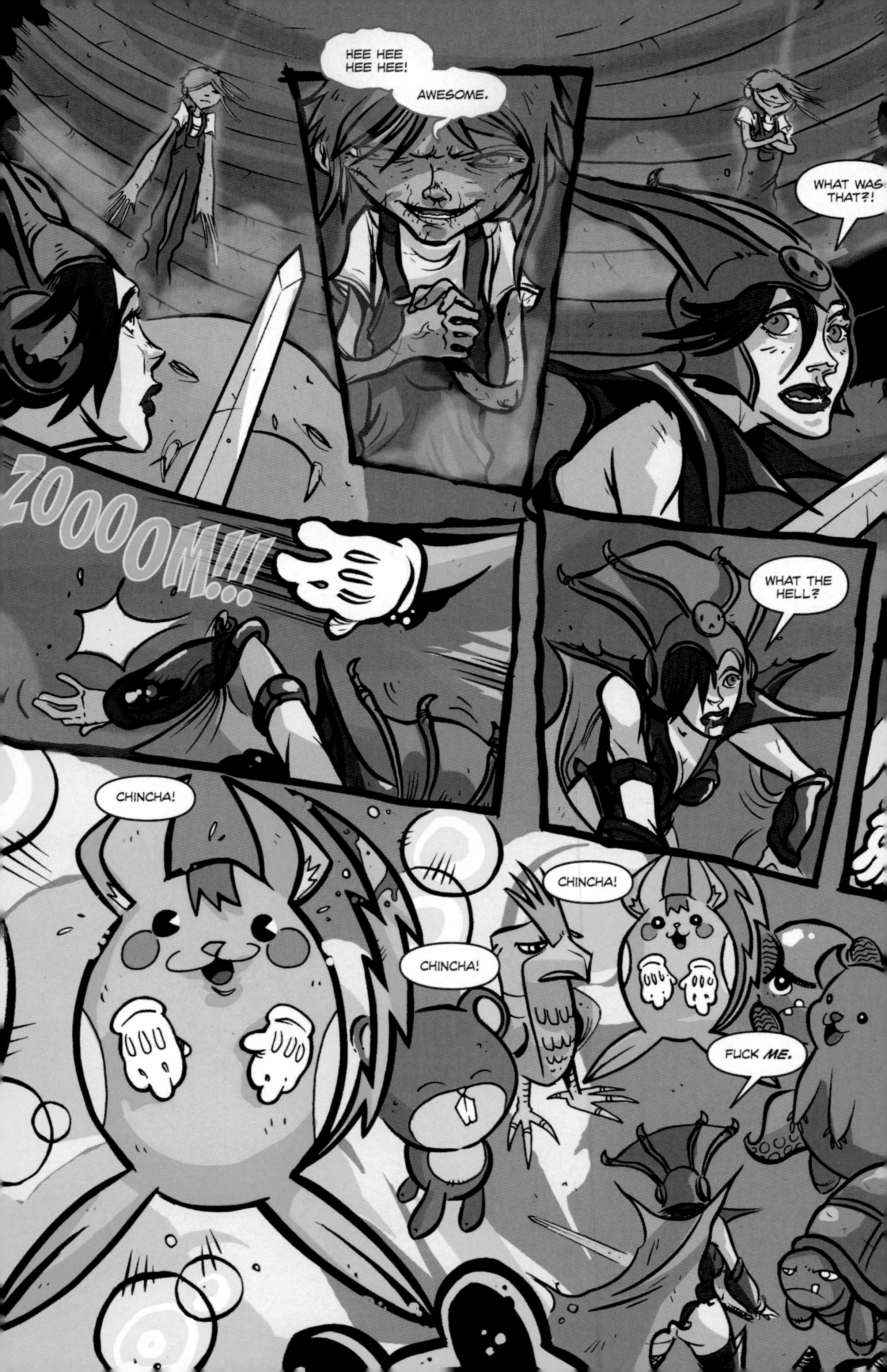
HEE HEE
HEE HEE!
AWESOME.
WHAT WAS THAT?!
ZOOOOM!!!
WHAT THE HELL?
CHINCHA!
CHINCHA!
CHINCHA!
FUCK *ME.*

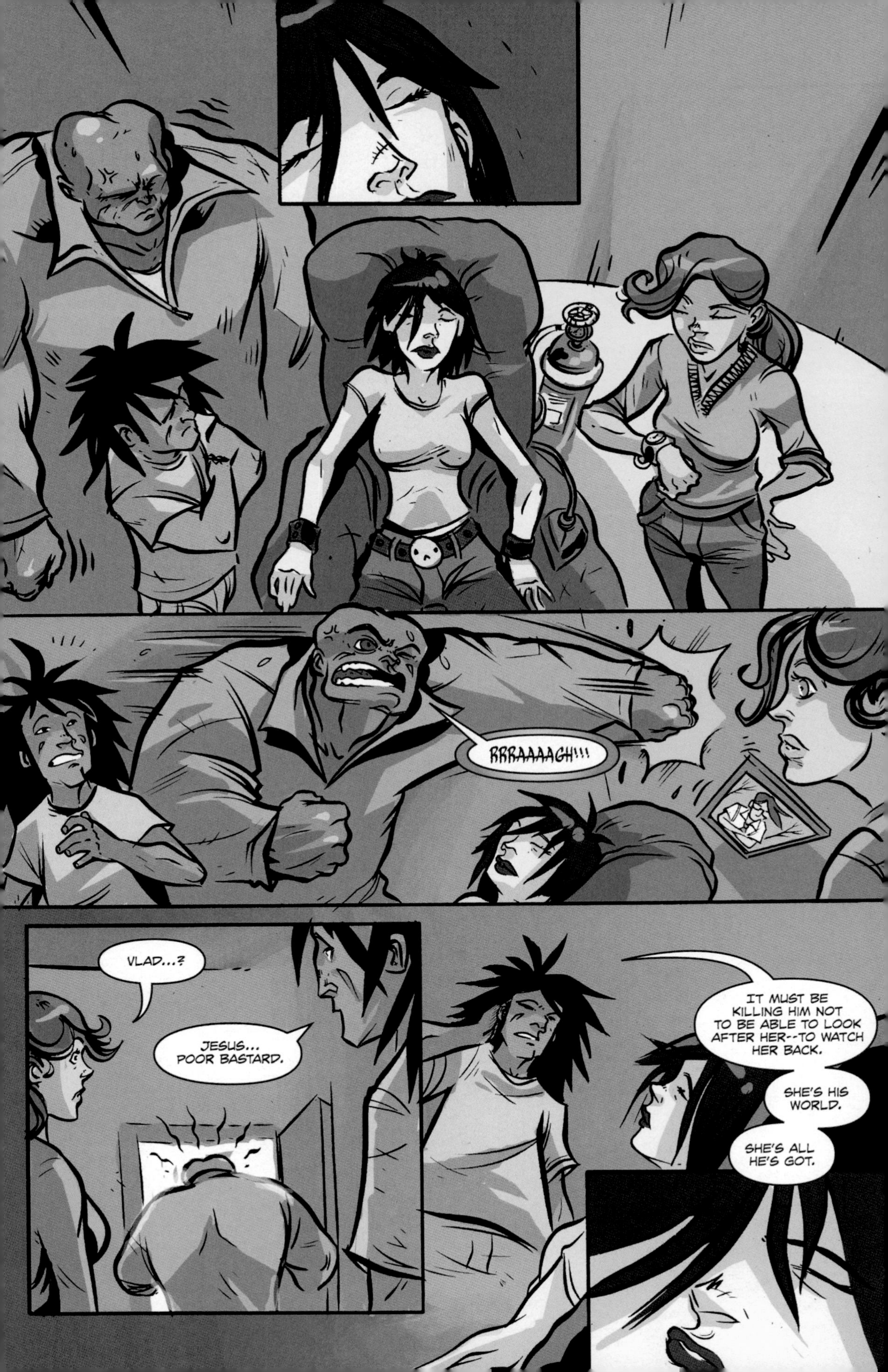
RRRAAAAGH!!!
VLAD...?
JESUS... POOR BASTARD.
IT MUST BE KILLING HIM NOT TO BE ABLE TO LOOK AFTER HER--TO WATCH HER BACK.
SHE'S HIS WORLD.
SHE'S ALL HE'S GOT.

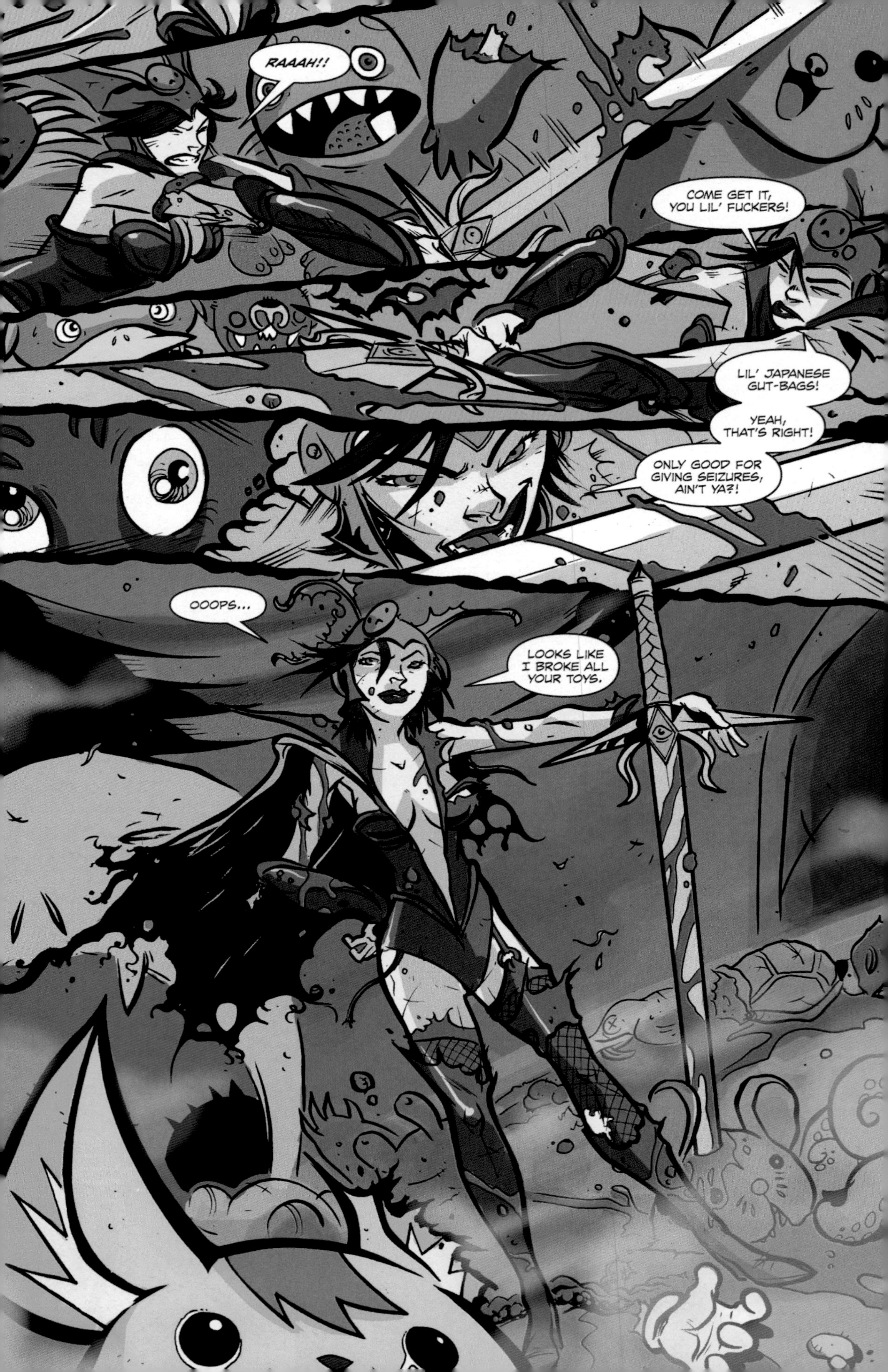
RAAAH!!
COME GET IT, YOU LIL' FUCKERS!
LIL' JAPANESE GUT-BAGS!
YEAH, THAT'S RIGHT!
ONLY GOOD FOR GIVING SEIZURES, AIN'T YA?!
OOOPS...
LOOKS LIKE I BROKE ALL YOUR TOYS.

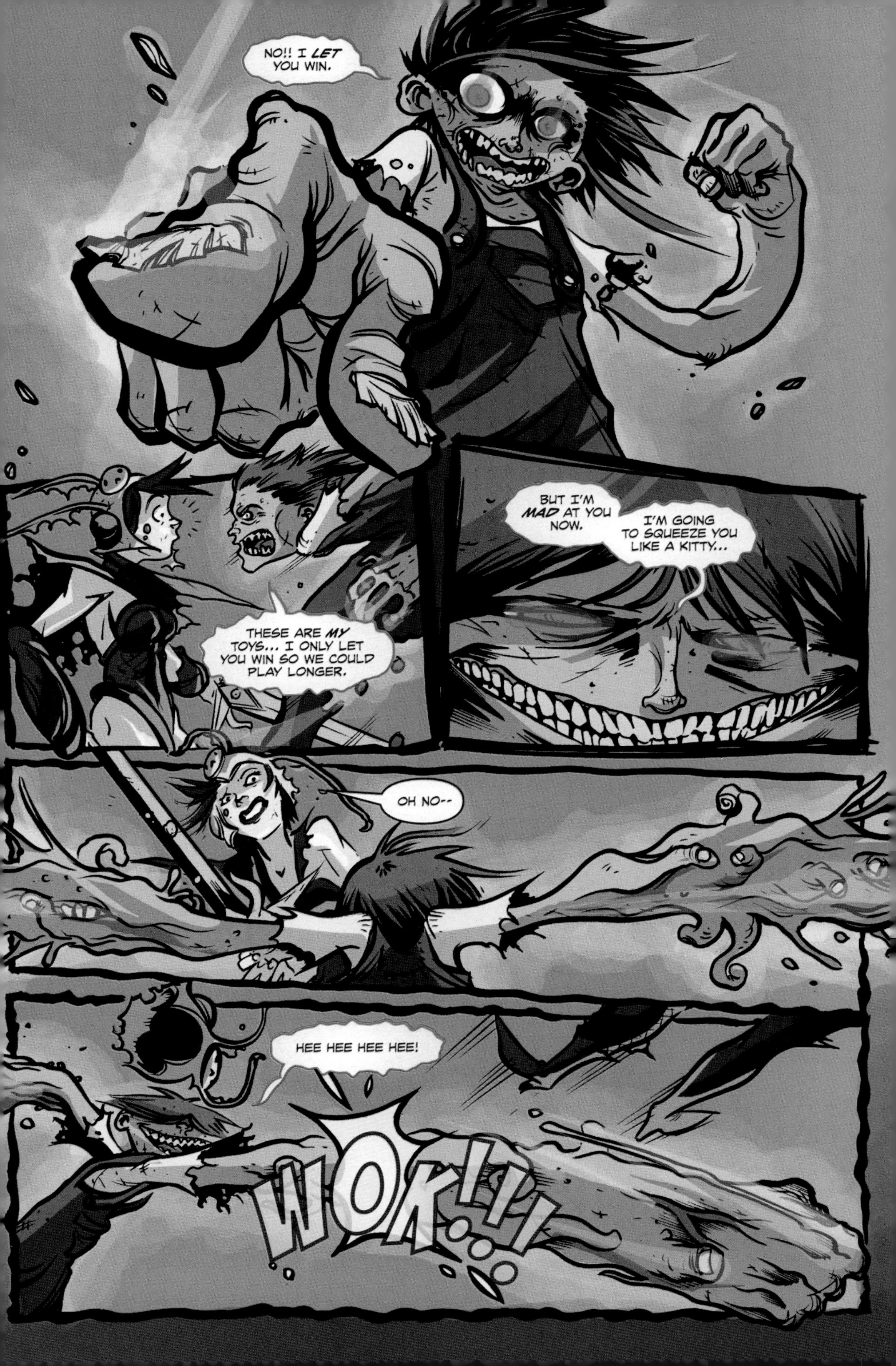
NO!! I LET YOU WIN.
THESE ARE MY TOYS... I ONLY LET YOU WIN SO WE COULD PLAY LONGER.
BUT I'M MAD AT YOU NOW.
I'M GOING TO SQUEEZE YOU LIKE A KITTY...
OH NO--
HEE HEE HEE HEE!
WOK!!!

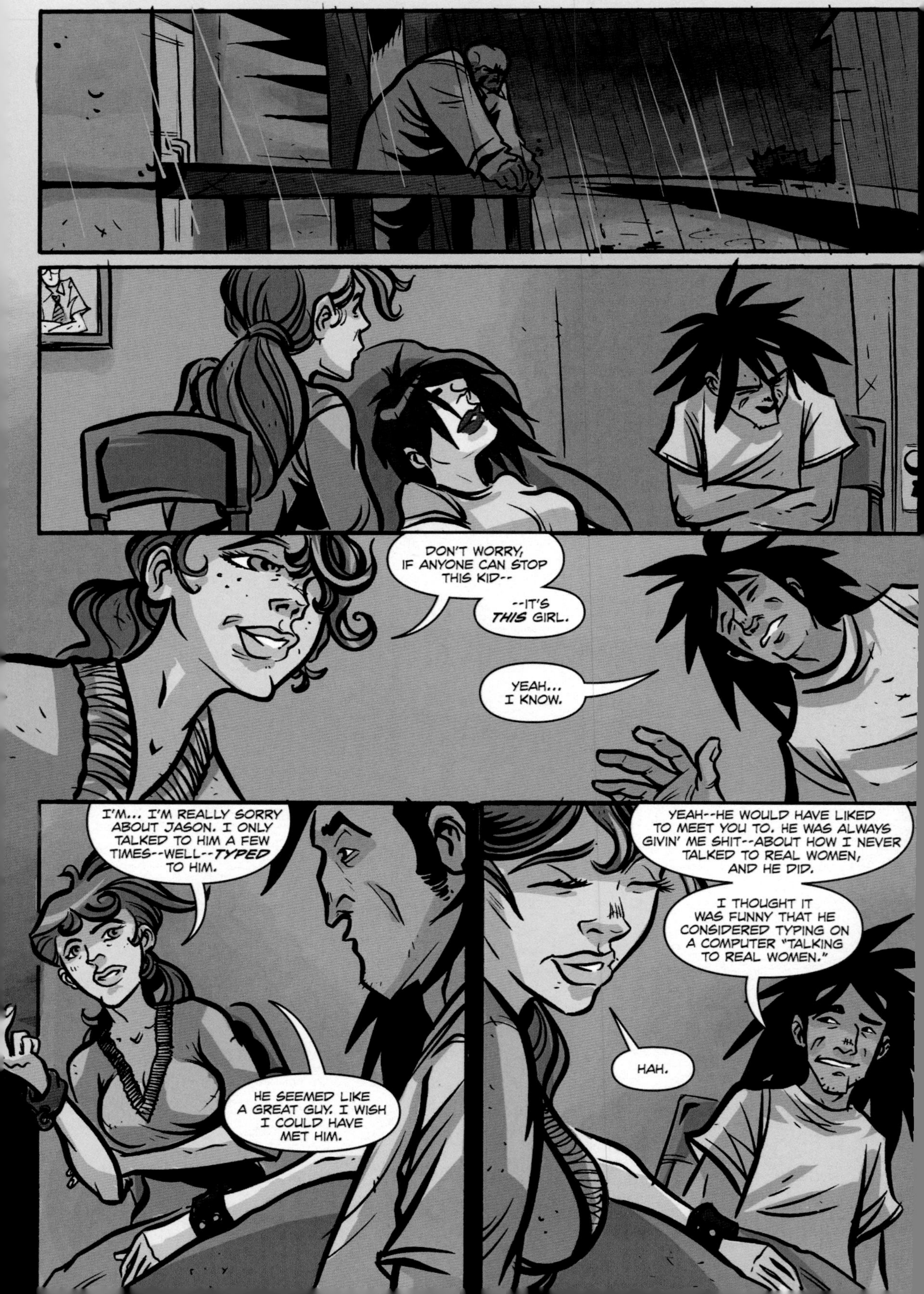
DON'T WORRY, IF ANYONE CAN STOP THIS KID--
--IT'S *THIS* GIRL.
YEAH... I KNOW.
I'M... I'M REALLY SORRY ABOUT JASON. I ONLY TALKED TO HIM A FEW TIMES--WELL--*TYPED* TO HIM.
HE SEEMED LIKE A GREAT GUY. I WISH I COULD HAVE MET HIM.
YEAH--HE WOULD HAVE LIKED TO MEET YOU TO. HE WAS ALWAYS GIVIN' ME SHIT--ABOUT HOW I NEVER TALKED TO REAL WOMEN, AND HE DID.
I THOUGHT IT WAS FUNNY THAT HE CONSIDERED TYPING ON A COMPUTER "TALKING TO REAL WOMEN."
HAH.

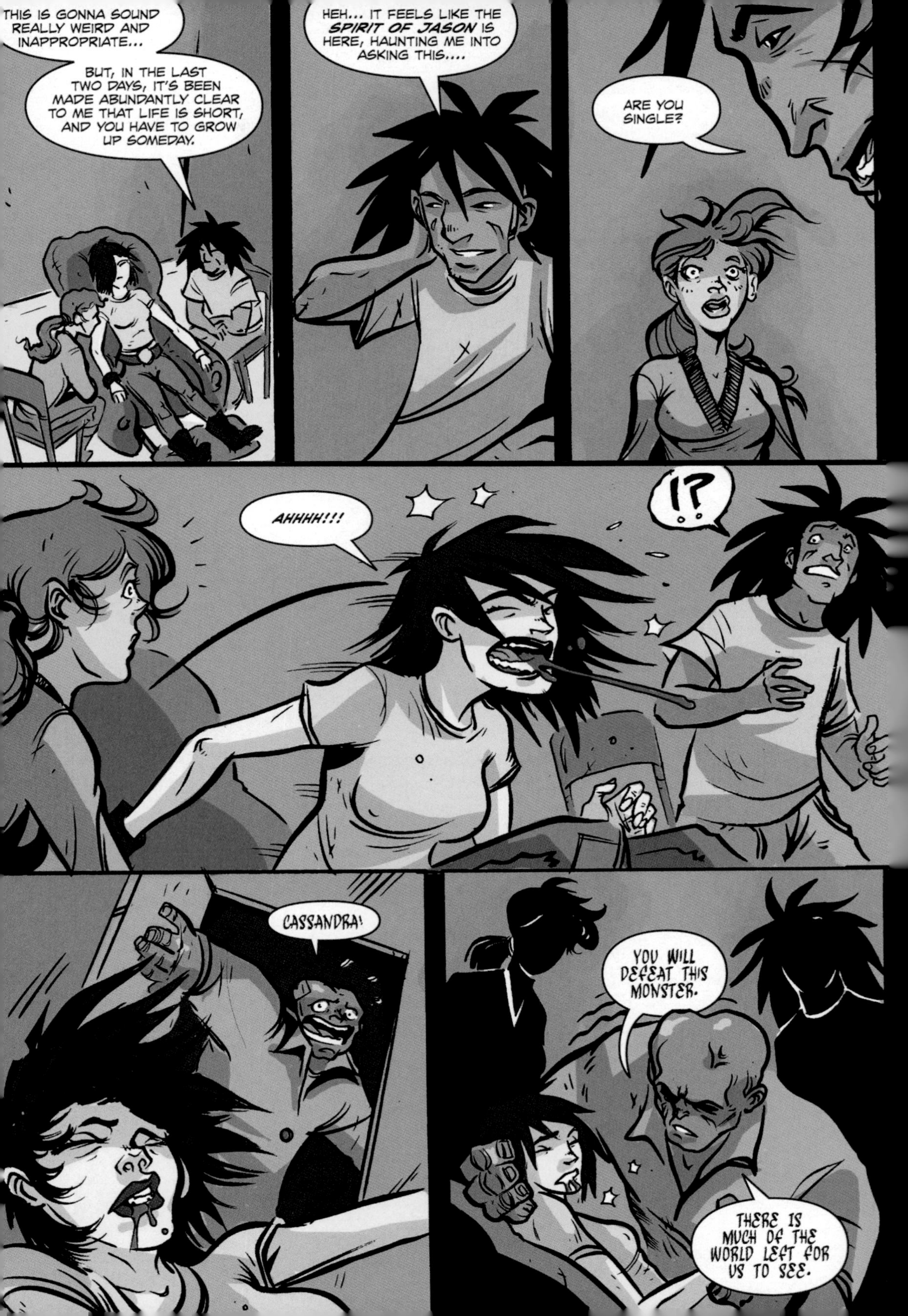
THIS IS GONNA SOUND REALLY WEIRD AND INAPPROPRIATE...
BUT, IN THE LAST TWO DAYS, IT'S BEEN MADE ABUNDANTLY CLEAR TO ME THAT LIFE IS SHORT, AND YOU HAVE TO GROW UP SOMEDAY.
HEH... IT FEELS LIKE THE SPIRIT OF JASON IS HERE, HAUNTING ME INTO ASKING THIS....
ARE YOU SINGLE?
AHHHH!!!
!?
CASSANDRA!
YOU WILL DEFEAT THIS MONSTER.
THERE IS MUCH OF THE WORLD LEFT FOR US TO SEE.

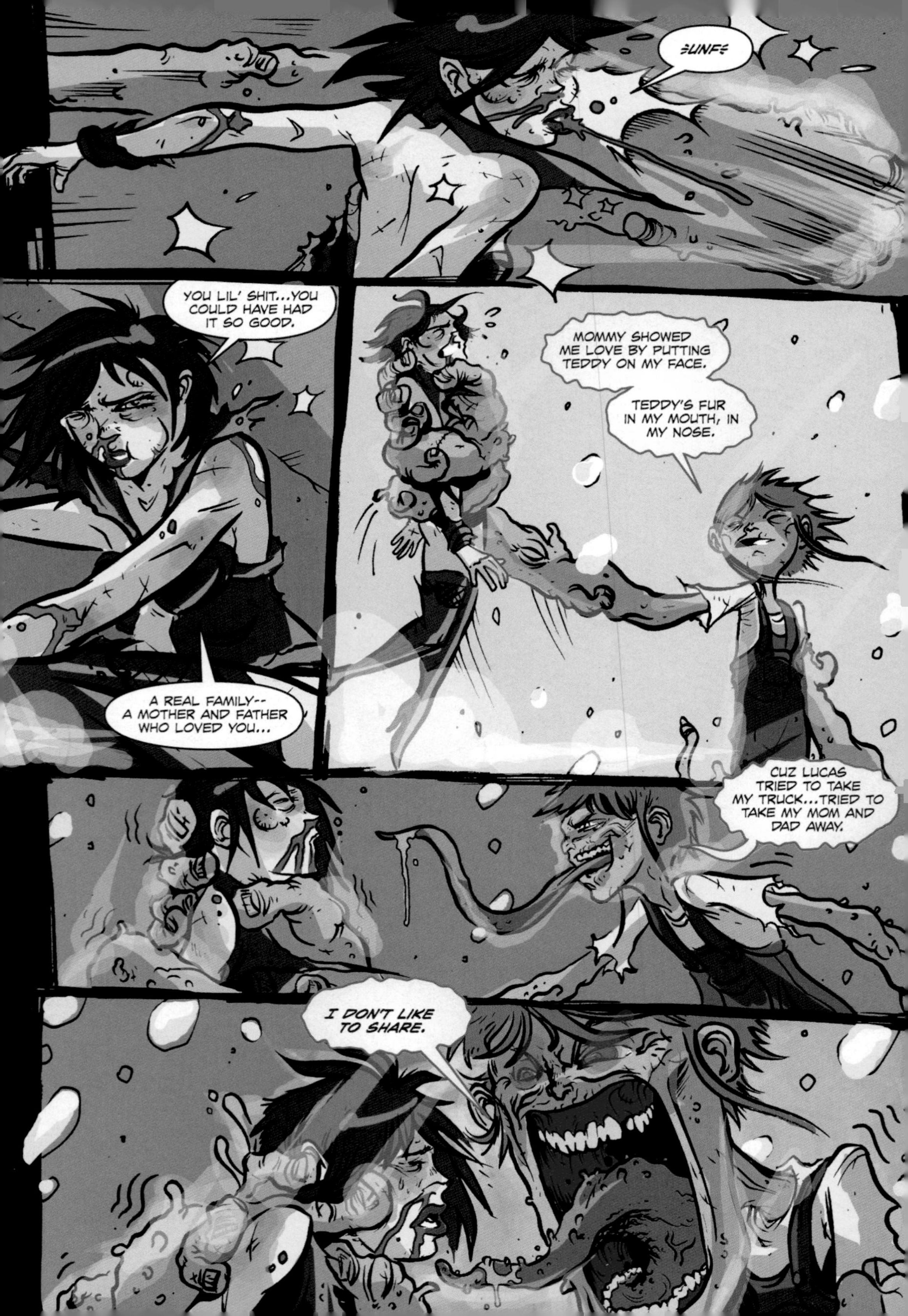
=UNF=
YOU LIL' SHIT...YOU COULD HAVE HAD IT SO GOOD.
A REAL FAMILY-- A MOTHER AND FATHER WHO LOVED YOU...
MOMMY SHOWED ME LOVE BY PUTTING TEDDY ON MY FACE.
TEDDY'S FUR IN MY MOUTH, IN MY NOSE.
CUZ LUCAS TRIED TO TAKE MY TRUCK...TRIED TO TAKE MY MOM AND DAD AWAY.
I DON'T LIKE TO SHARE.

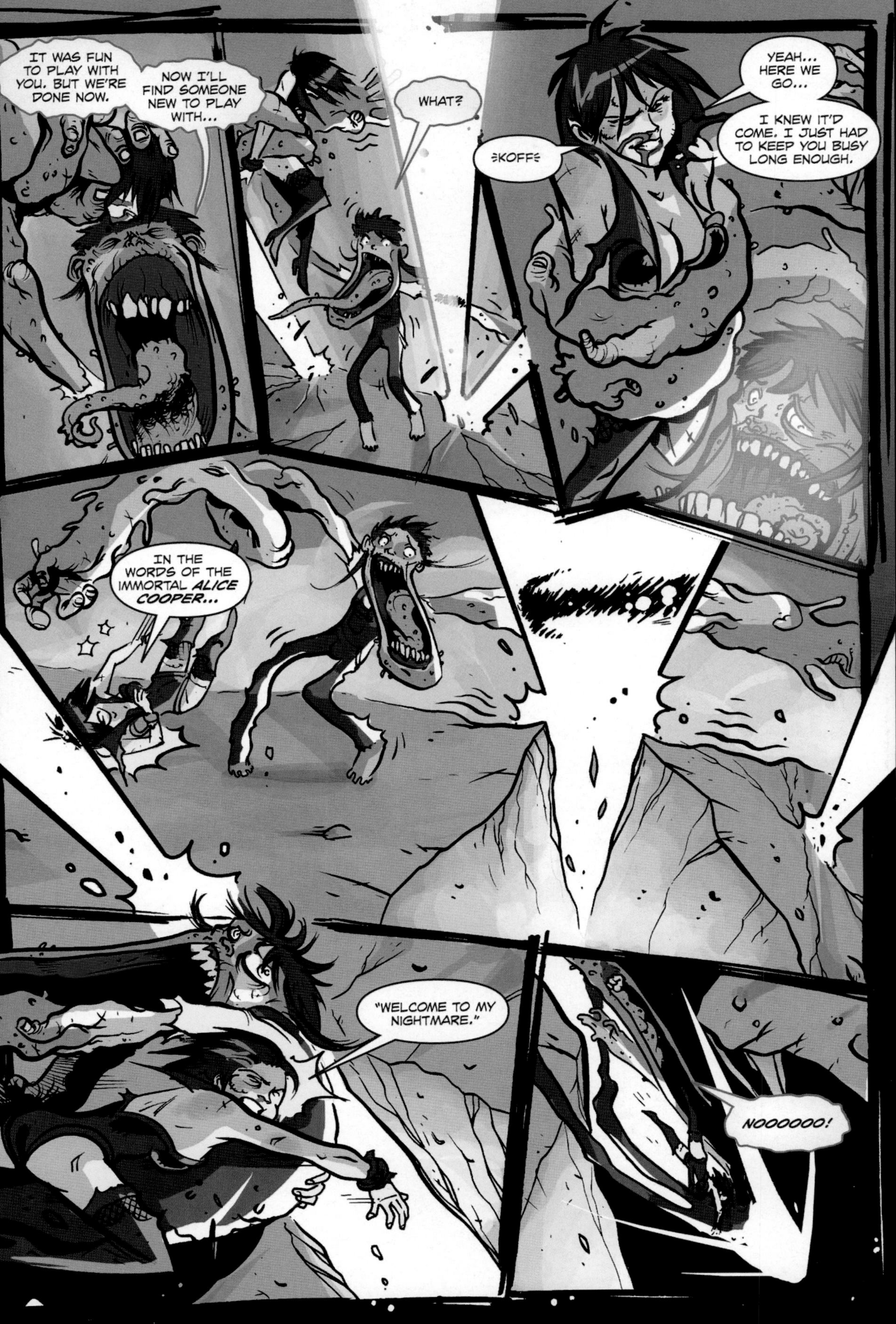
IT WAS FUN TO PLAY WITH YOU. BUT WE'RE DONE NOW.
NOW I'LL FIND SOMEONE NEW TO PLAY WITH...
WHAT?
YEAH... HERE WE GO...
KOFF
I KNEW IT'D COME. I JUST HAD TO KEEP YOU BUSY LONG ENOUGH.
IN THE WORDS OF THE IMMORTAL ALICE COOPER...
"WELCOME TO MY NIGHTMARE."
NOOOOOO!

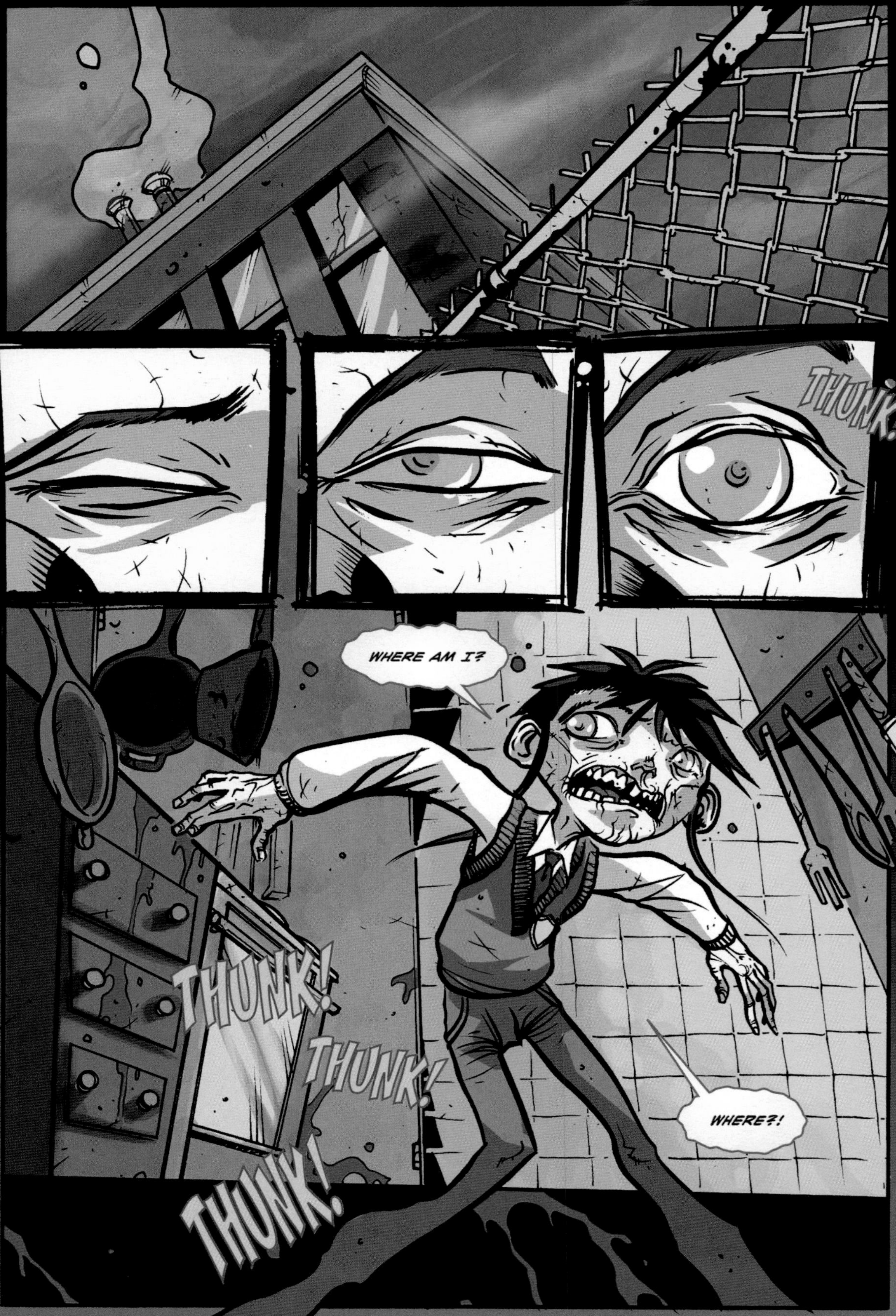
THUNK!
WHERE AM I?
THUNK!
THUNK!
THUNK!
WHERE?!

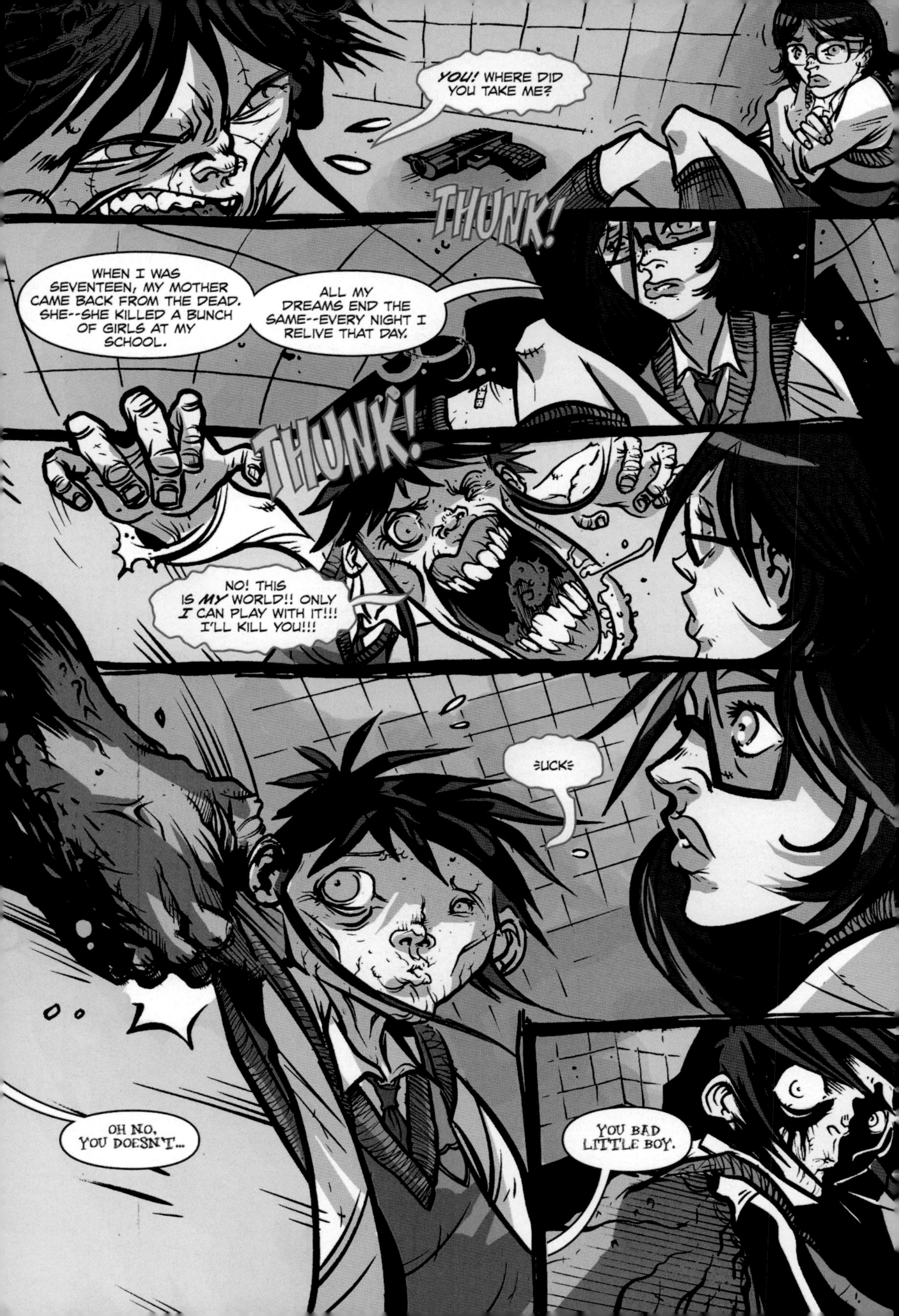

YOU! WHERE DID YOU TAKE ME?
THUNK!
WHEN I WAS SEVENTEEN, MY MOTHER CAME BACK FROM THE DEAD. SHE--SHE KILLED A BUNCH OF GIRLS AT MY SCHOOL.
ALL MY DREAMS END THE SAME--EVERY NIGHT I RELIVE THAT DAY.
THUNK!
NO! THIS IS MY WORLD!! ONLY I CAN PLAY WITH IT!!! I'LL KILL YOU!!!
UCK
OH NO, YOU DOESN'T...
YOU BAD LITTLE BOY.

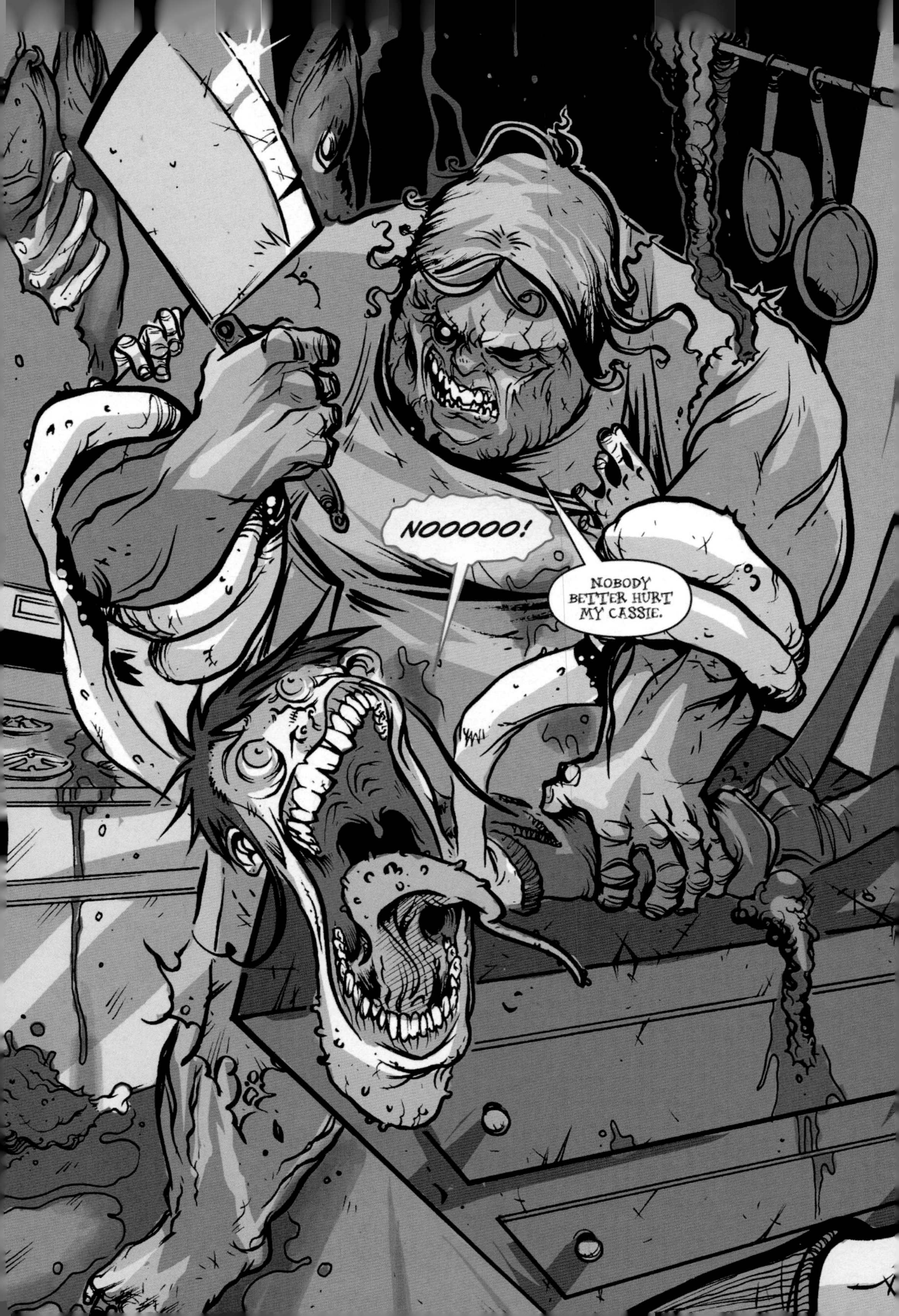
NOOOOO!
NOBODY BETTER HURT MY CASSIE.

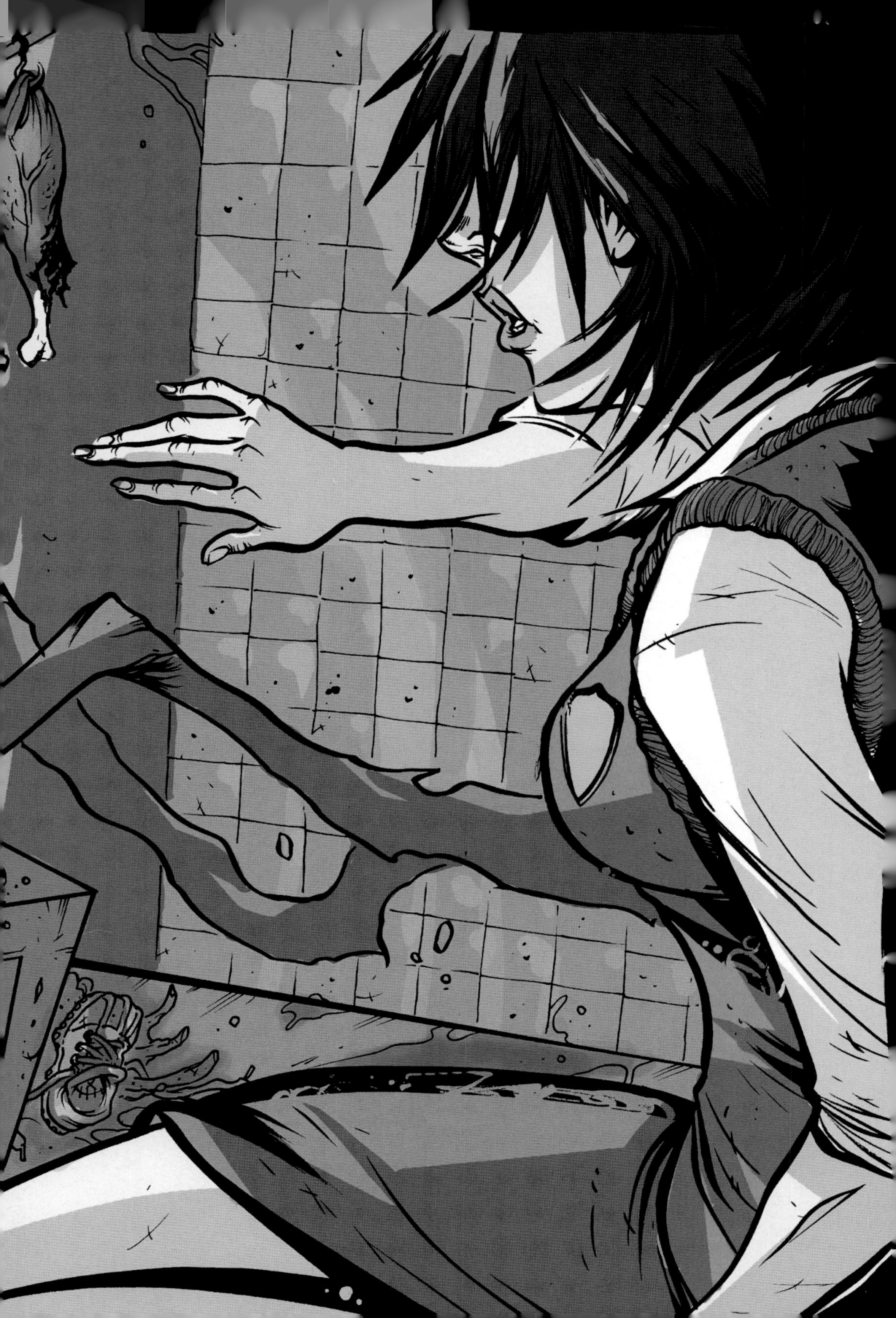

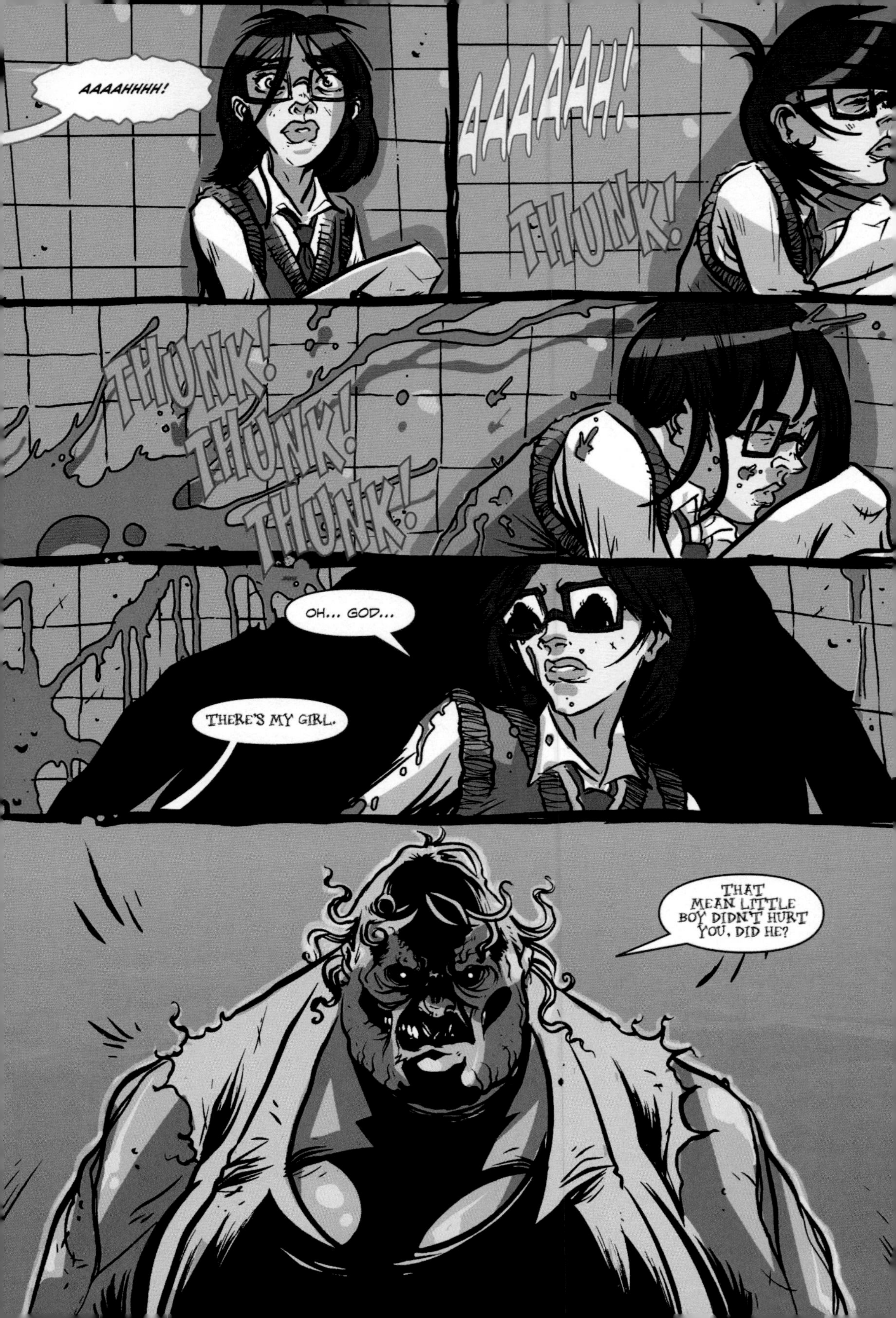
AAAAHHHH!
AAAAAH!
THUNK!
THUNK!
THUNK!
THUNK!
OH... GOD...
THERE'S MY GIRL.
THAT MEAN LITTLE BOY DIDN'T HURT YOU, DID HE?

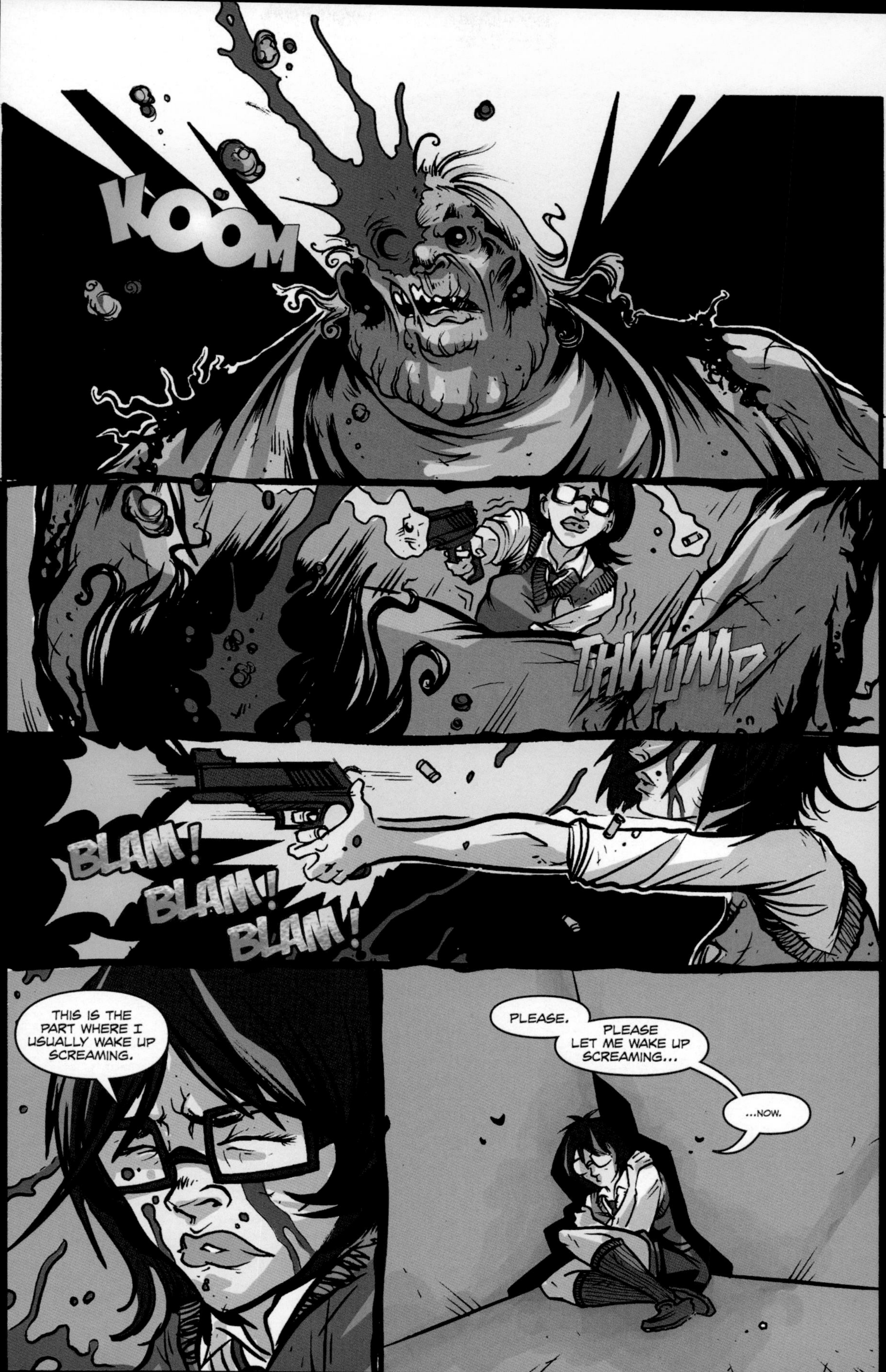
KOOM
THWUMP
BLAM!
BLAM!
BLAM!
THIS IS THE PART WHERE I USUALLY WAKE UP SCREAMING.
PLEASE.
PLEASE LET ME WAKE UP SCREAMING...
...NOW.

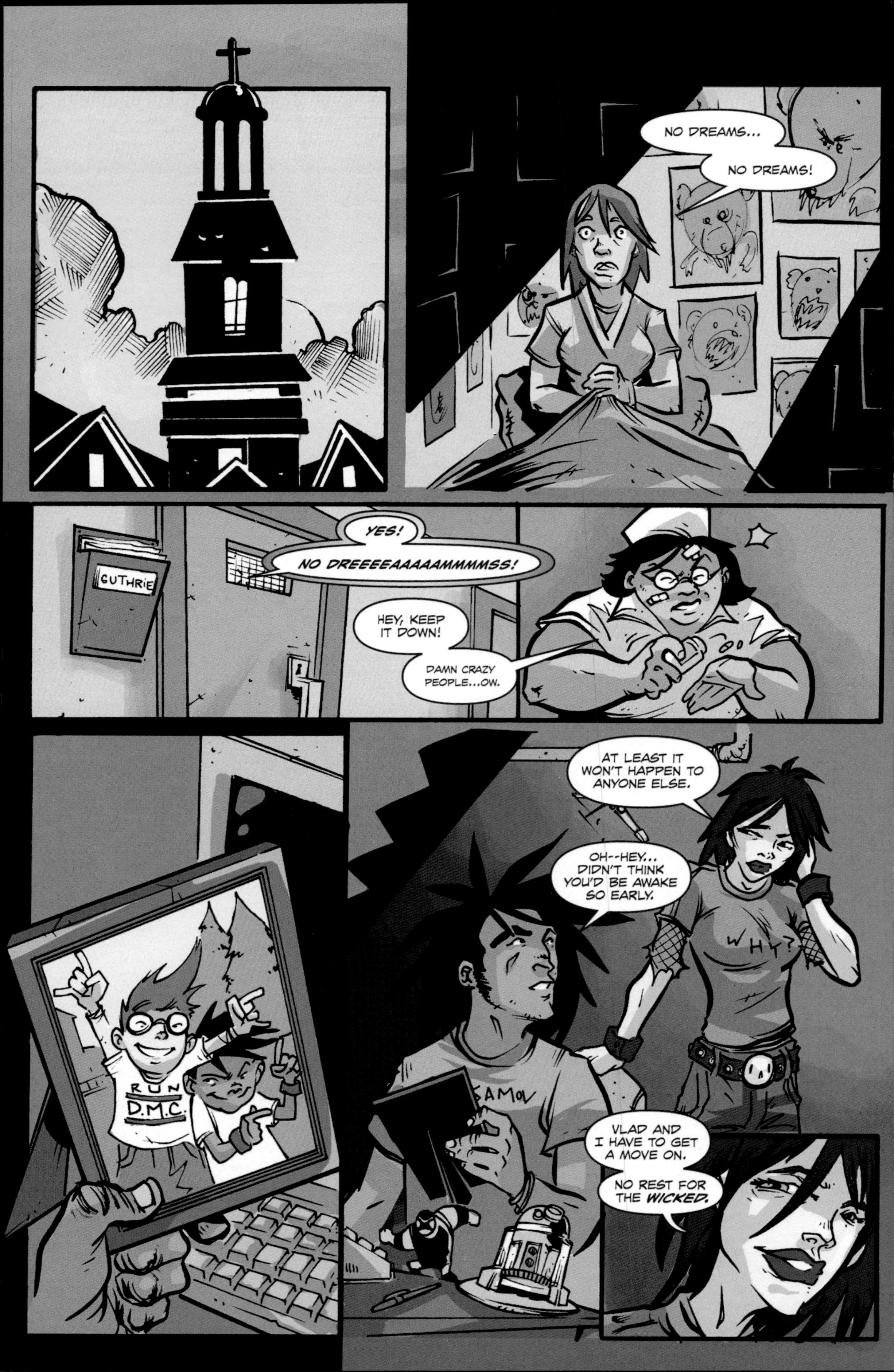

NO DREAMS...
NO DREAMS!
YES!
NO DREEEEAAAAAMMMMSS!
GUTHRIE
HEY, KEEP IT DOWN!
DAMN CRAZY PEOPLE...OW.
AT LEAST IT WON'T HAPPEN TO ANYONE ELSE.
OH--HEY... DIDN'T THINK YOU'D BE AWAKE SO EARLY.
WHY?
RUN D.M.C.
VLAD AND I HAVE TO GET A MOVE ON.
NO REST FOR THE *WICKED.*

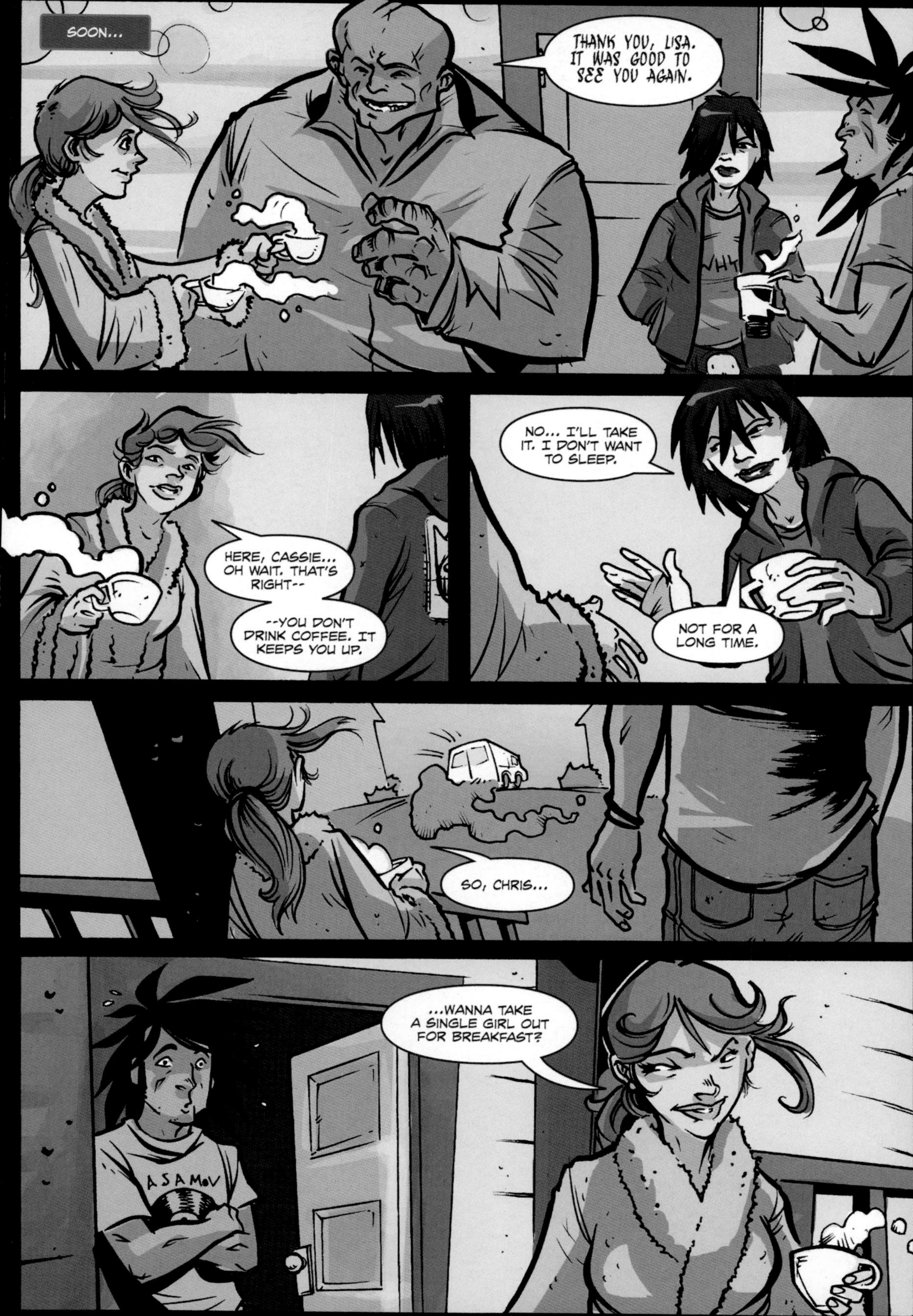
SOON...
THANK YOU, LISA. IT WAS GOOD TO SEE YOU AGAIN.
HERE, CASSIE... OH WAIT. THAT'S RIGHT--
--YOU DON'T DRINK COFFEE. IT KEEPS YOU UP.
NO... I'LL TAKE IT. I DON'T WANT TO SLEEP.
NOT FOR A LONG TIME.
SO, CHRIS...
...WANNA TAKE A SINGLE GIRL OUT FOR BREAKFAST?

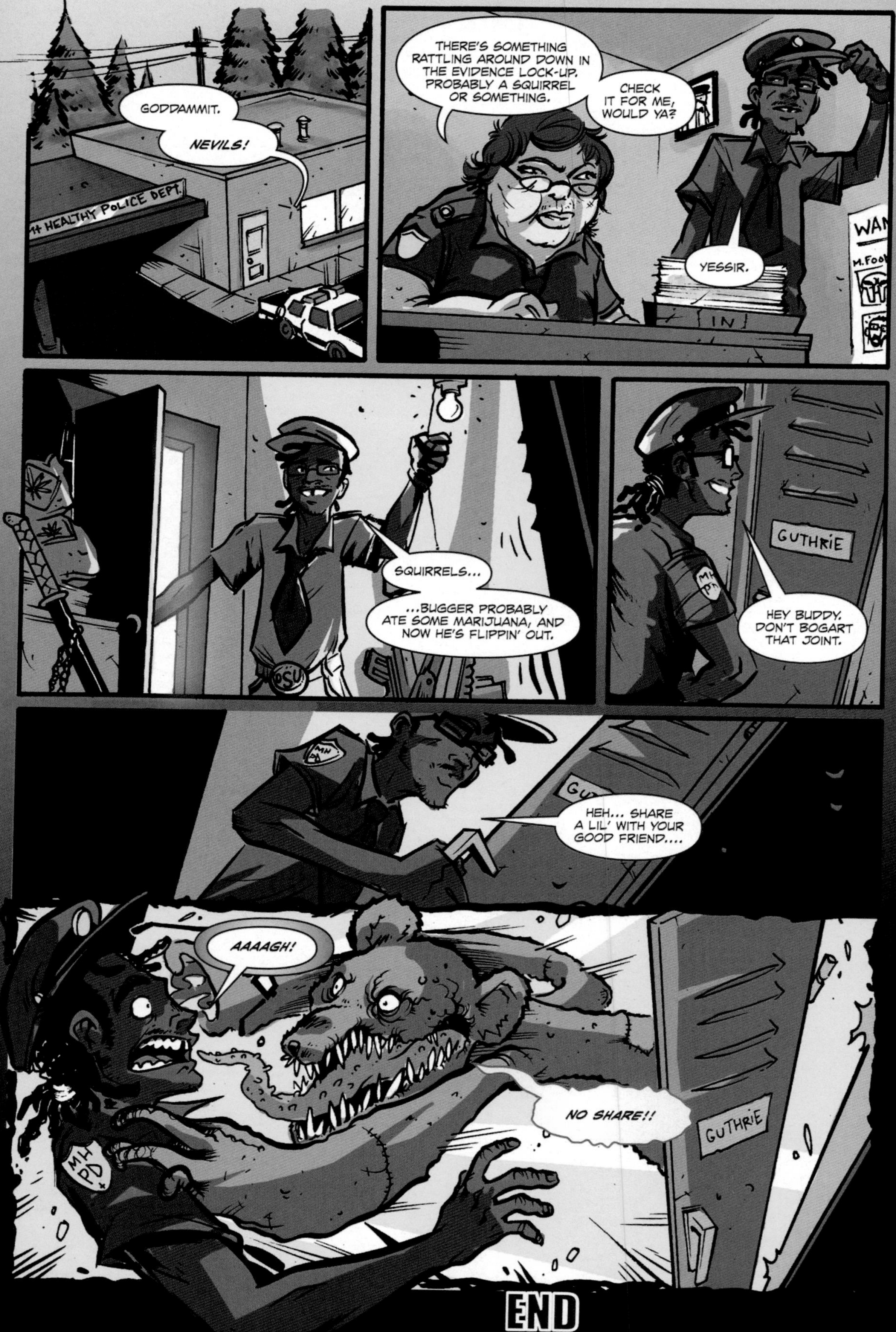
HEALTHY POLICE DEPT.
GODDAMMIT.
NEVILS!
THERE'S SOMETHING RATTLING AROUND DOWN IN THE EVIDENCE LOCK-UP. PROBABLY A SQUIRREL OR SOMETHING.
CHECK IT FOR ME, WOULD YA?
YESSIR.
IN
SQUIRRELS...
...BUGGER PROBABLY ATE SOME MARIJUANA, AND NOW HE'S FLIPPIN' OUT.
GUTHRIE
HEY BUDDY. DON'T BOGART THAT JOINT.
HEH... SHARE A LIL' WITH YOUR GOOD FRIEND....
AAAAGH!
NO SHARE!!
GUTHRIE
END

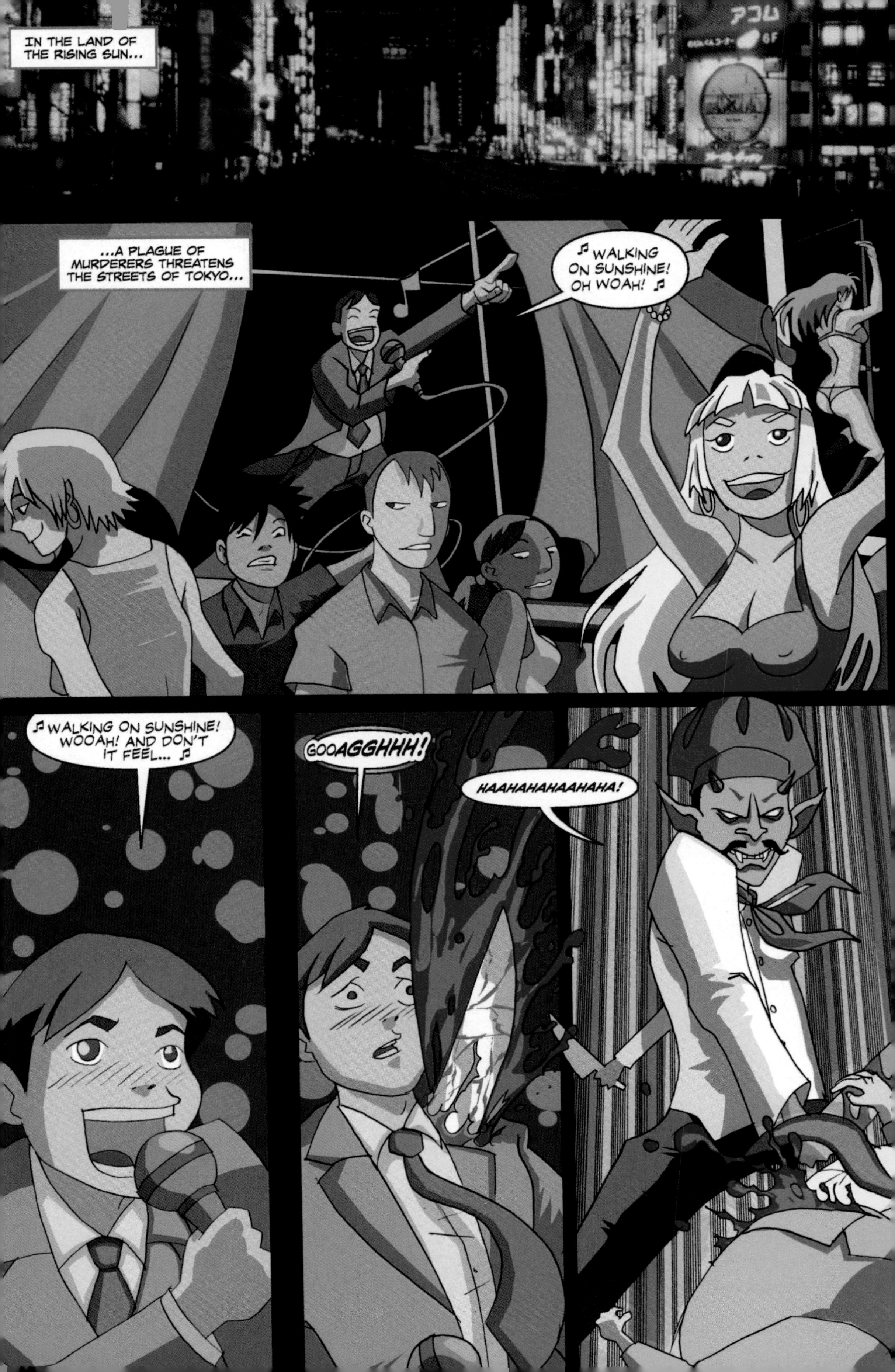
IN THE LAND OF THE RISING SUN...
...A PLAGUE OF MURDERERS THREATENS THE STREETS OF TOKYO...
♫ WALKING ON SUNSHINE! OH WOAH! ♫
♫ WALKING ON SUNSHINE! WOOAH! AND DON'T IT FEEL... ♫
GOOAGGHHH!
HAAHAHAHAAHAHA!

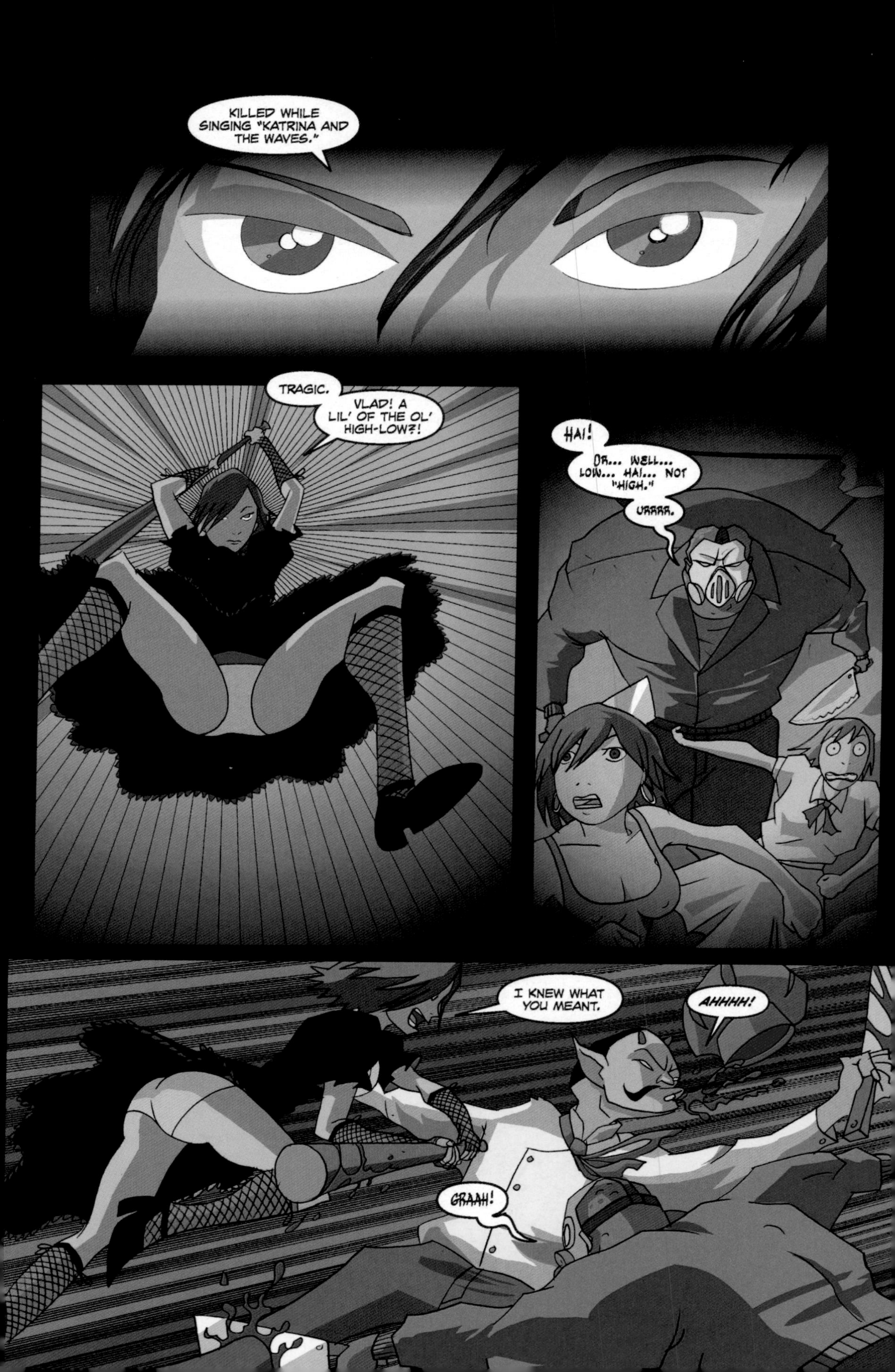
KILLED WHILE SINGING "KATRINA AND THE WAVES."
TRAGIC.
VLAD! A LIL' OF THE OL' HIGH-LOW?!
HAI!
OR... WELL... LOW... HAI... NOT "HIGH."
URRRR.
I KNEW WHAT YOU MEANT.
AHHHH!
GRAAH!

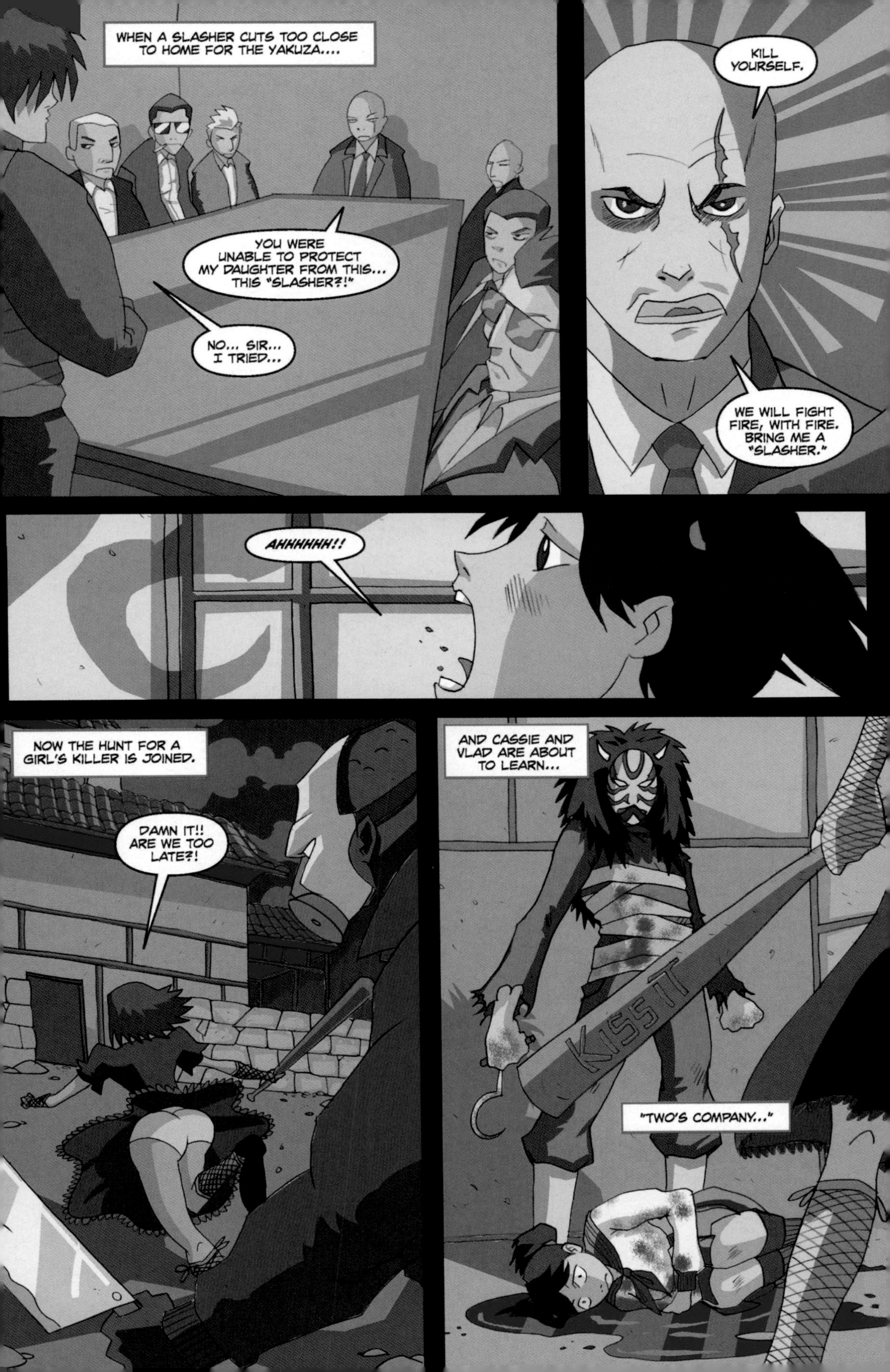
WHEN A SLASHER CUTS TOO CLOSE TO HOME FOR THE YAKUZA....
YOU WERE UNABLE TO PROTECT MY DAUGHTER FROM THIS... THIS "SLASHER?!"
NO... SIR... I TRIED...
KILL YOURSELF.
WE WILL FIGHT FIRE, WITH FIRE. BRING ME A "SLASHER."
AHHHHHH!!
NOW THE HUNT FOR A GIRL'S KILLER IS JOINED.
DAMN IT!! ARE WE TOO LATE?!
AND CASSIE AND VLAD ARE ABOUT TO LEARN...
KISS IT
"TWO'S COMPANY..."

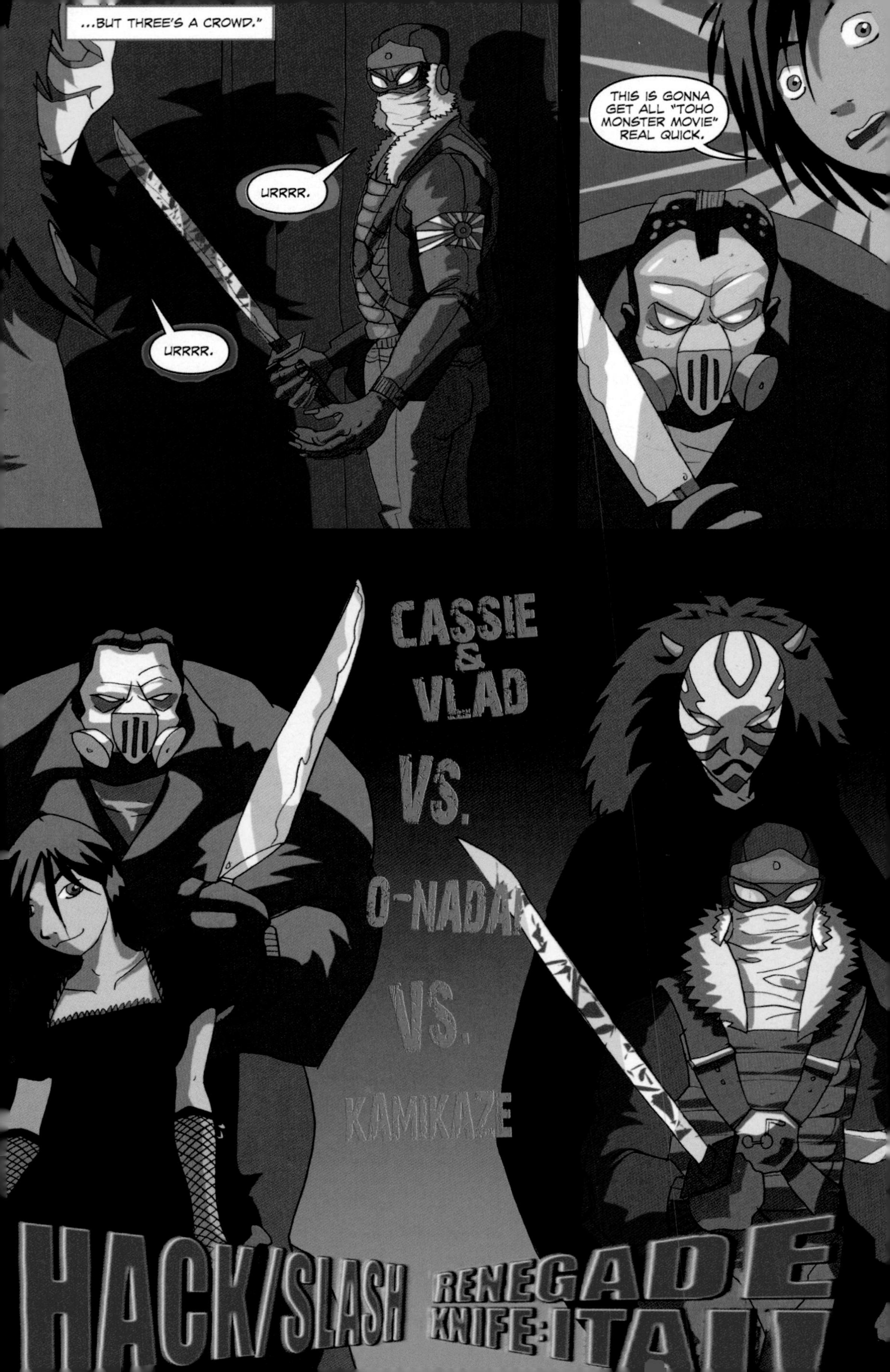
...BUT THREE'S A CROWD."
URRRR.
URRRR.
THIS IS GONNA GET ALL "TOHO MONSTER MOVIE" REAL QUICK.
CASSIE & VLAD
VS.
O-NADA
VS.
KAMIKAZE
HACK/SLASH RENEGADE KNIFE: ITALY

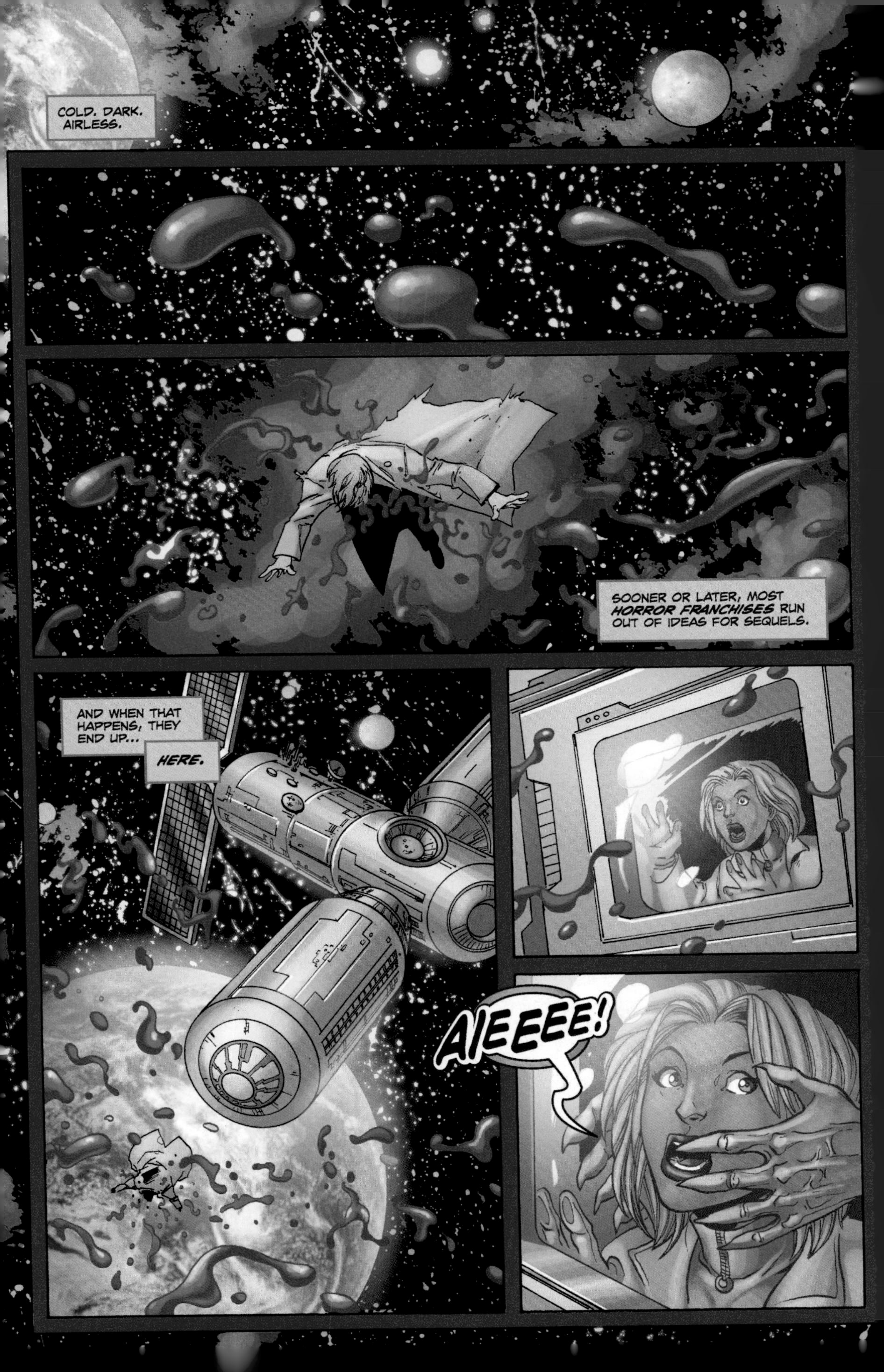
COLD. DARK. AIRLESS.
SOONER OR LATER, MOST HORROR FRANCHISES RUN OUT OF IDEAS FOR SEQUELS.
AND WHEN THAT HAPPENS, THEY END UP...
HERE.
AIEEEE!

WHAT BEGAN AS AN EXPERIMENT...

BY FREEZING THESE FELONS WE'RE ABLE TO TEST THE HUMAN BODY'S REACTION TO CRYOGENIC STASIS FOR DEEP SPACE TRAVEL.

AREN'T THESE ALL MURDERERS?

ALL THE BETTER TO BE OUR GUINEA PIGS.

BECAME A NIGHTMARE.

...AND THE PRISONERS HAVE TAKEN OVER THE SATELLITES.

I BRAKE FOR NOTHING!

WASH ME

BIG STORE

SUPERMARKET

WISCONSIN 143 HUB

BUT...THE PRISONERS... THEY'VE CHANGED. THEY'RE NOT... ALIVE.

THEY HAD NO CHOICE BUT TO TURN...

TO AN EXPERT.

LEMME GET THIS STRAIGHT.

YOU WANT US TO GO TO SPACE?

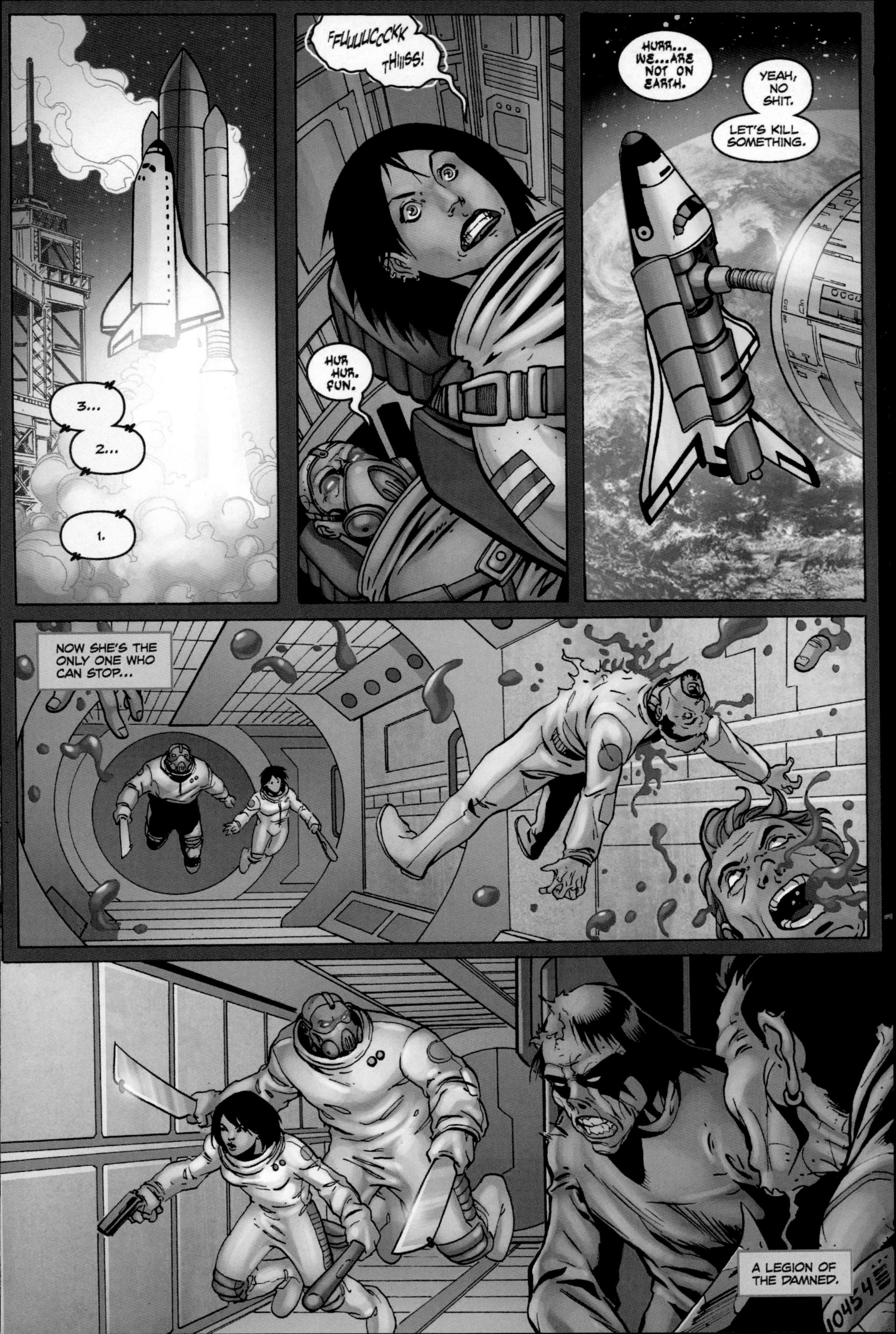
3...
2...
1.
FFUUUUCCCCKK THIIISS!
HUR HUR. FUN.
HURR... WE...ARE NOT ON EARTH.
YEAH, NO SHIT.
LET'S KILL SOMETHING.
NOW SHE'S THE ONLY ONE WHO CAN STOP...
A LEGION OF THE DAMNED.

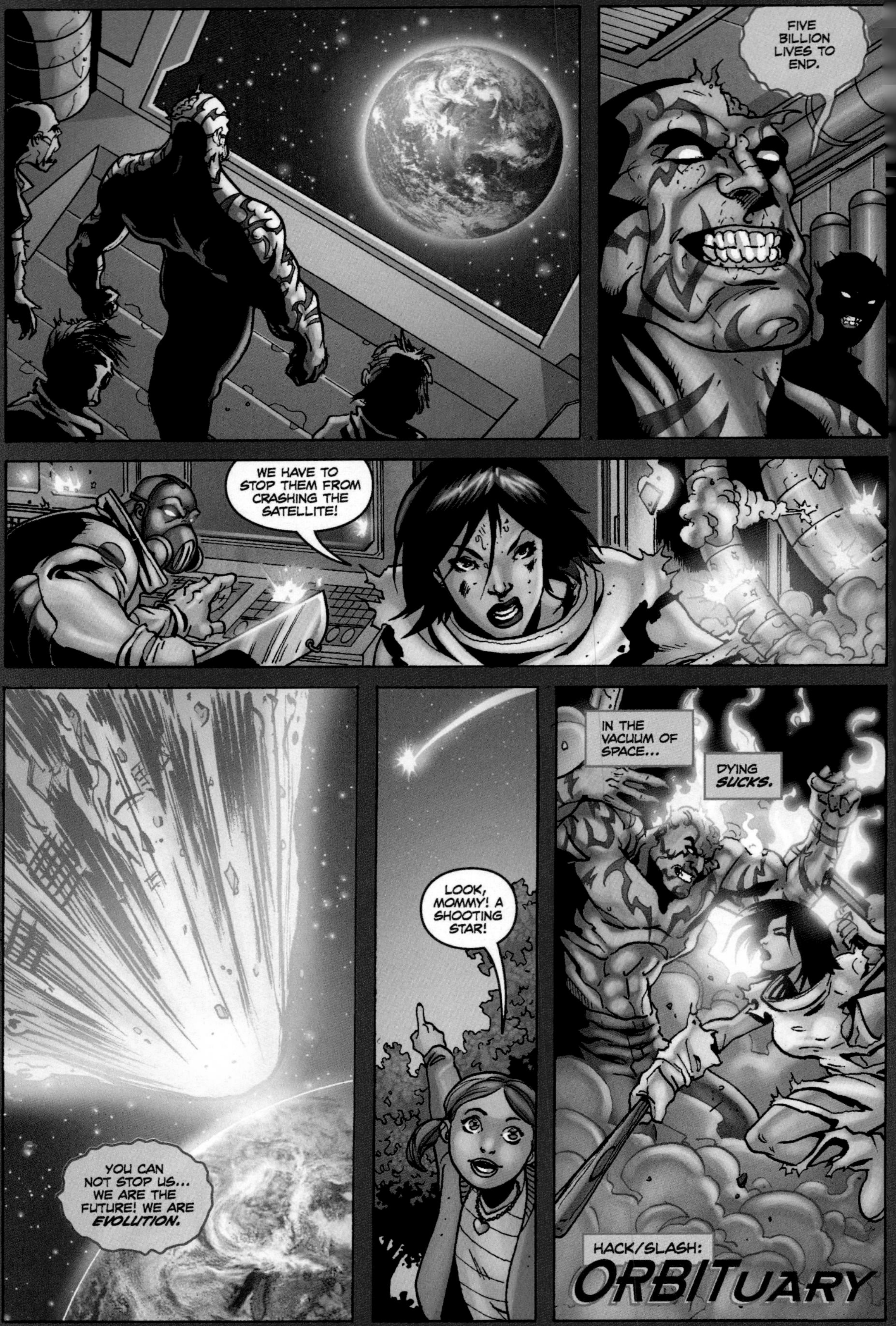
FIVE BILLION LIVES TO END.
WE HAVE TO STOP THEM FROM CRASHING THE SATELLITE!
YOU CAN NOT STOP US... WE ARE THE FUTURE! WE ARE EVOLUTION.
LOOK, MOMMY! A SHOOTING STAR!
IN THE VACUUM OF SPACE...
DYING SUCKS.
HACK/SLASH:
ORBITUARY

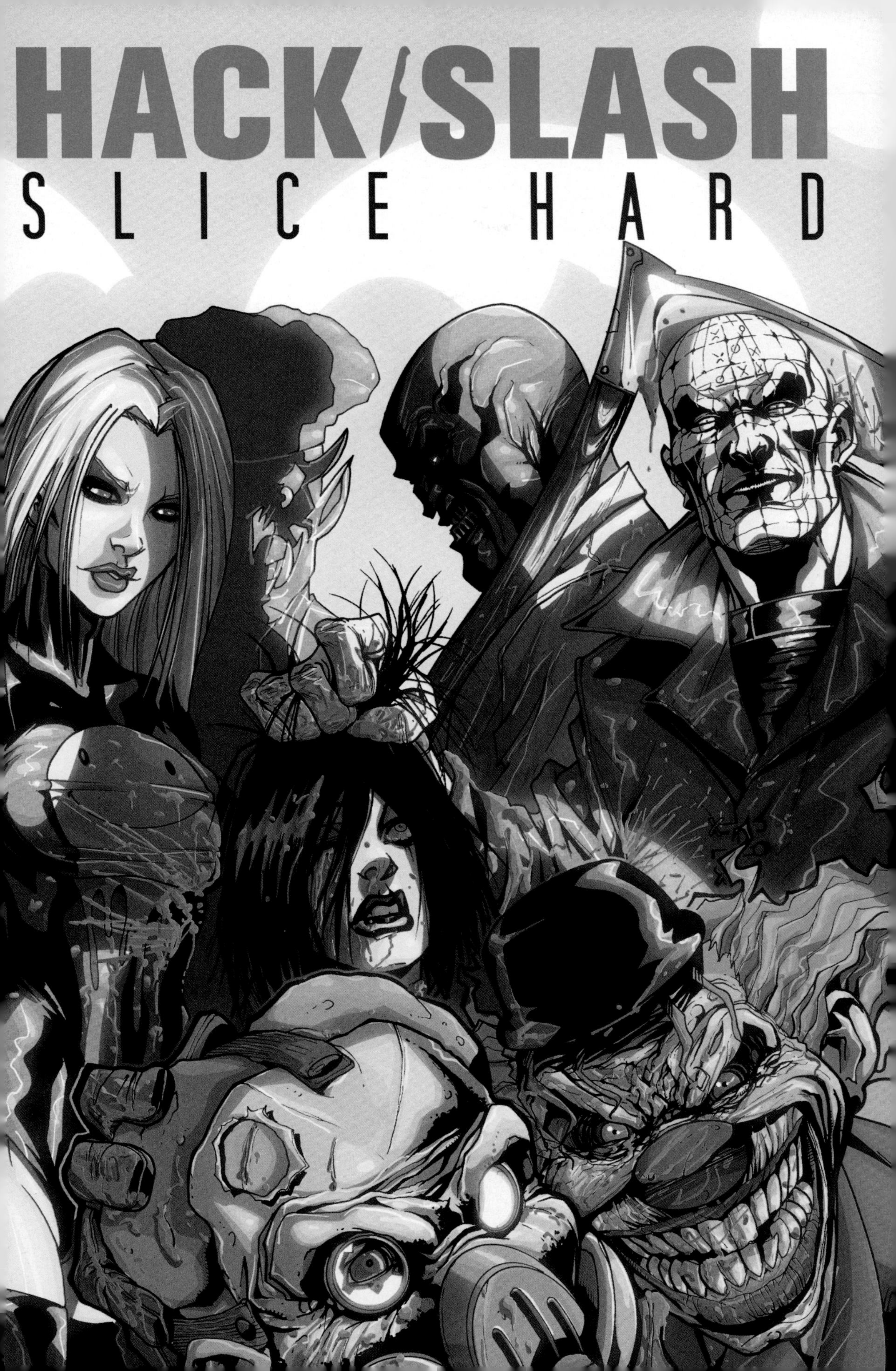
HACK/SLASH
SLICE HARD

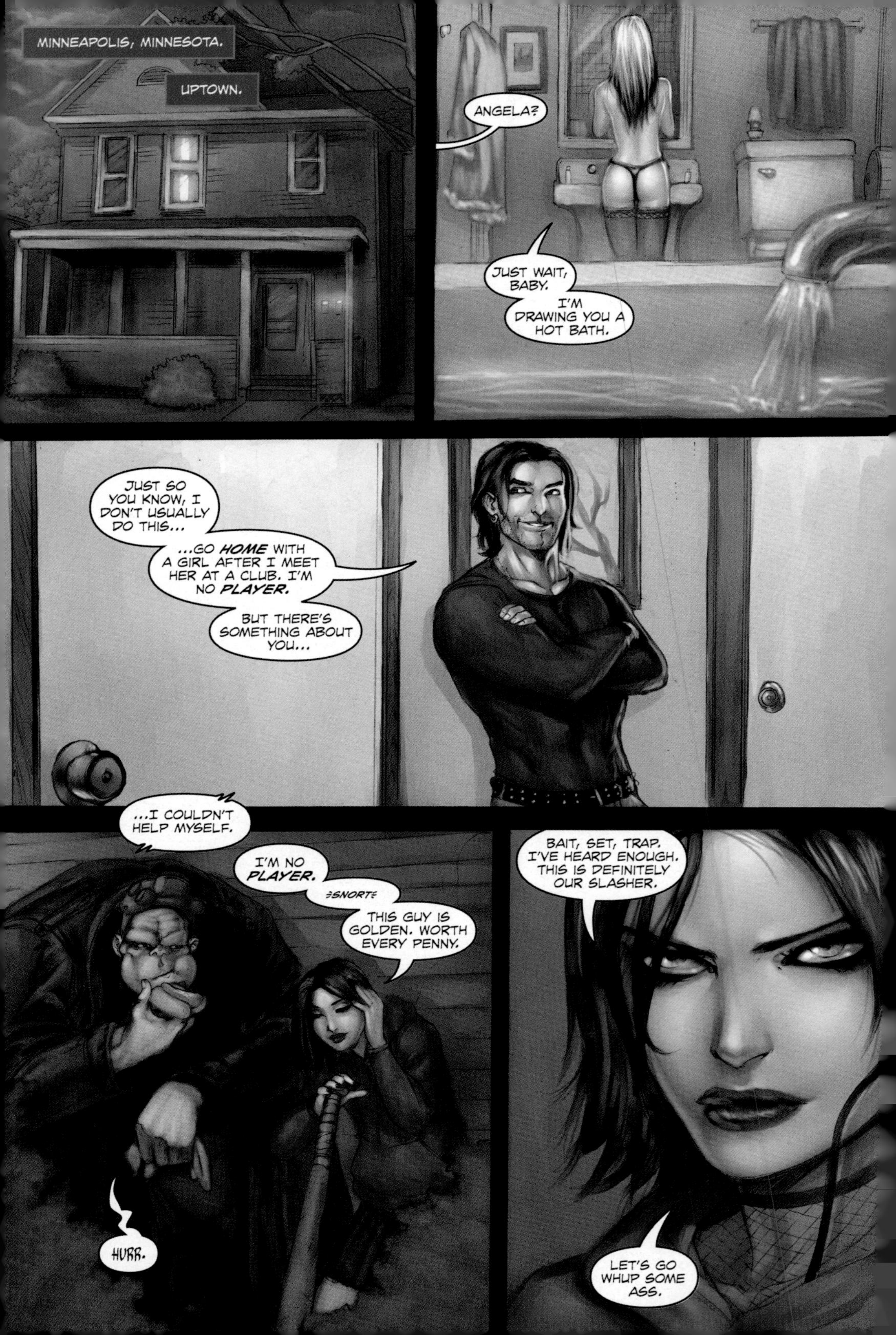
MINNEAPOLIS, MINNESOTA.
UPTOWN.
ANGELA?
JUST WAIT, BABY.
I'M DRAWING YOU A HOT BATH.
JUST SO YOU KNOW, I DON'T USUALLY DO THIS...
...GO HOME WITH A GIRL AFTER I MEET HER AT A CLUB. I'M NO PLAYER.
BUT THERE'S SOMETHING ABOUT YOU...
...I COULDN'T HELP MYSELF.
I'M NO PLAYER.
SNORT
THIS GUY IS GOLDEN. WORTH EVERY PENNY.
HURR.
BAIT, SET, TRAP. I'VE HEARD ENOUGH. THIS IS DEFINITELY OUR SLASHER.
LET'S GO WHUP SOME ASS.

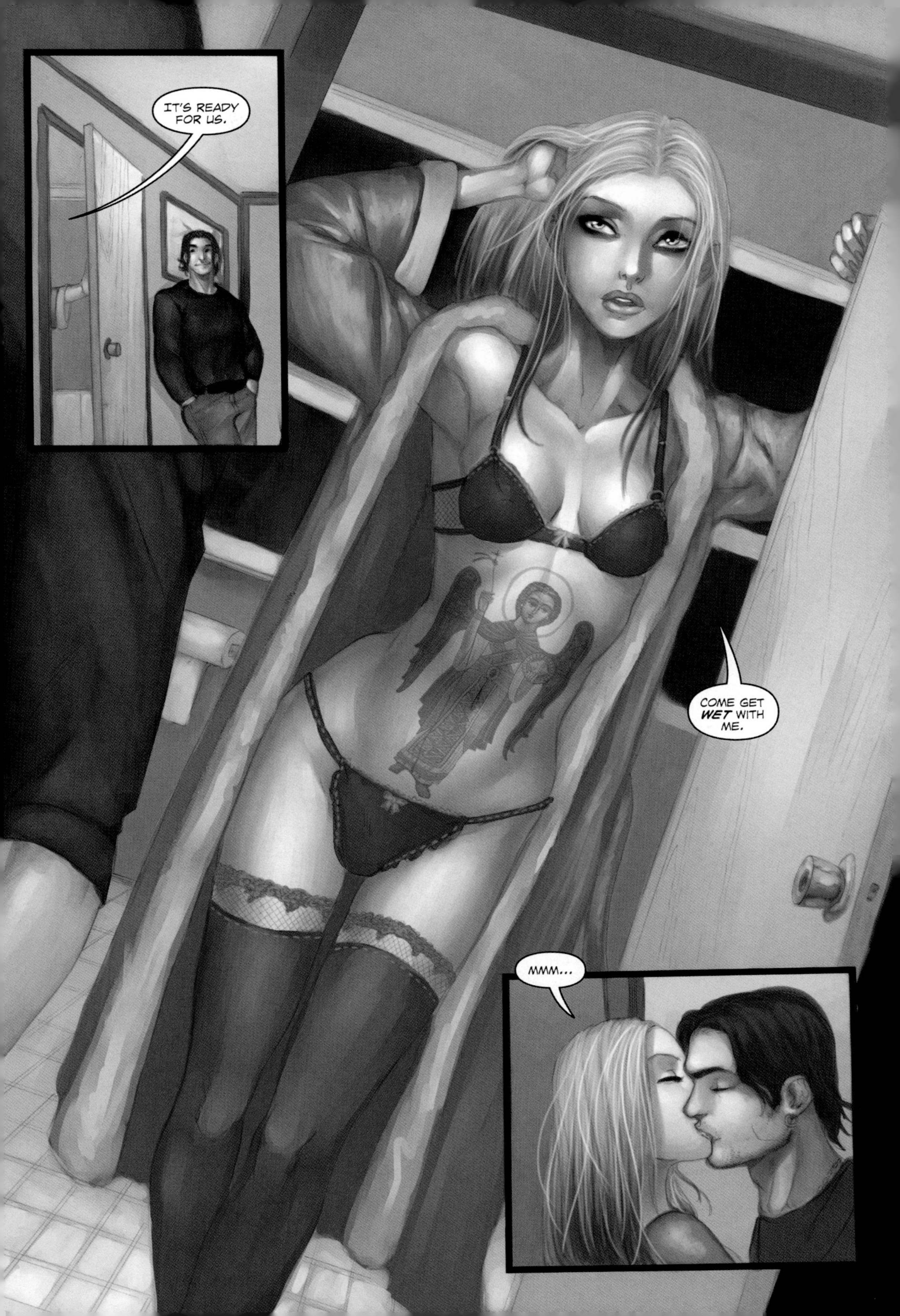
IT'S READY FOR US.
COME GET *WET* WITH ME.
MMM...

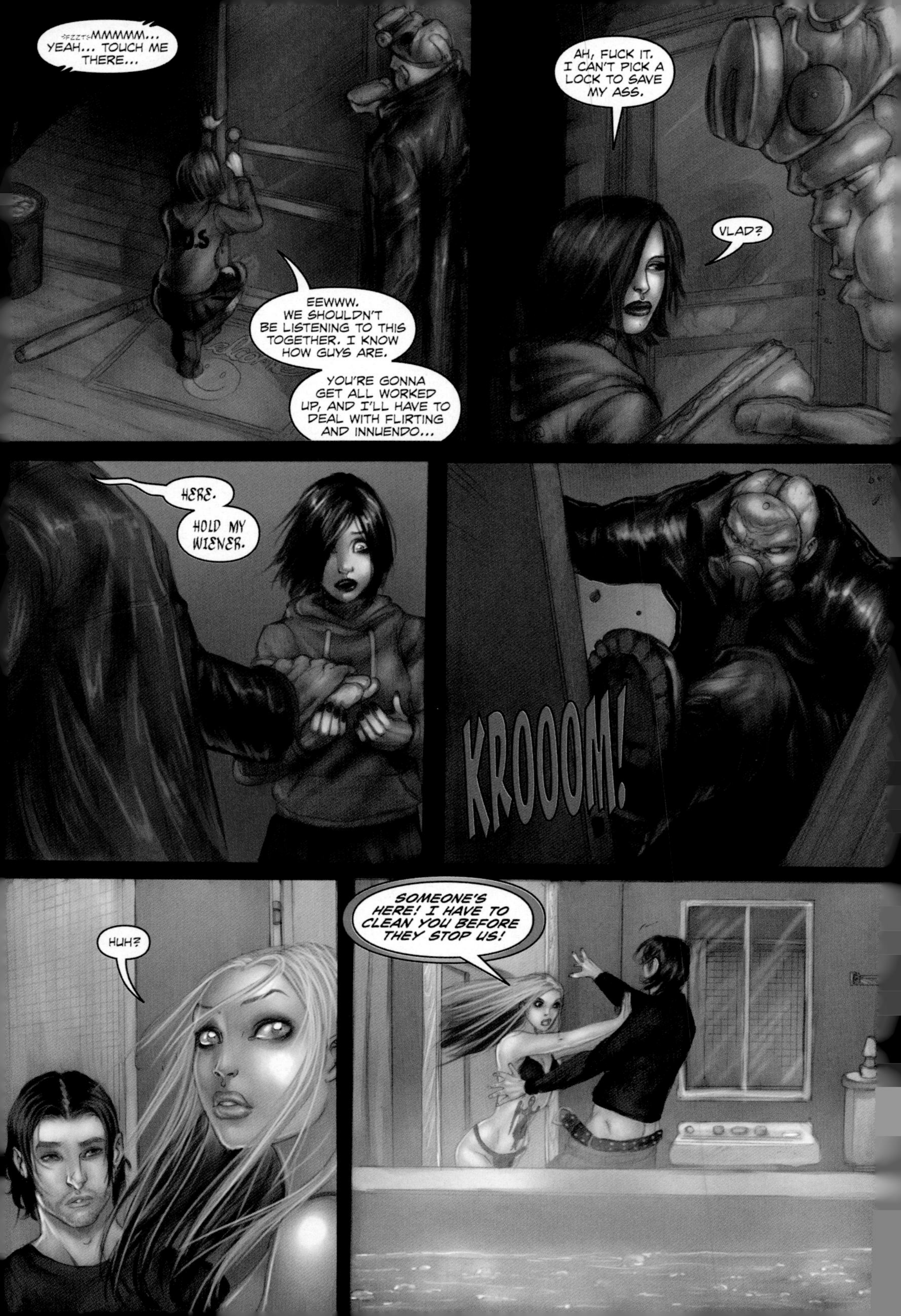

FZZT MMMMM... YEAH... TOUCH ME THERE...
EEWWW. WE SHOULDN'T BE LISTENING TO THIS TOGETHER. I KNOW HOW GUYS ARE.
YOU'RE GONNA GET ALL WORKED UP, AND I'LL HAVE TO DEAL WITH FLIRTING AND INNUENDO...
AH, FUCK IT. I CAN'T PICK A LOCK TO SAVE MY ASS.
VLAD?
HERE.
HOLD MY WIENER.
KROOOM!
HUH?
SOMEONE'S HERE! I HAVE TO CLEAN YOU BEFORE THEY STOP US!

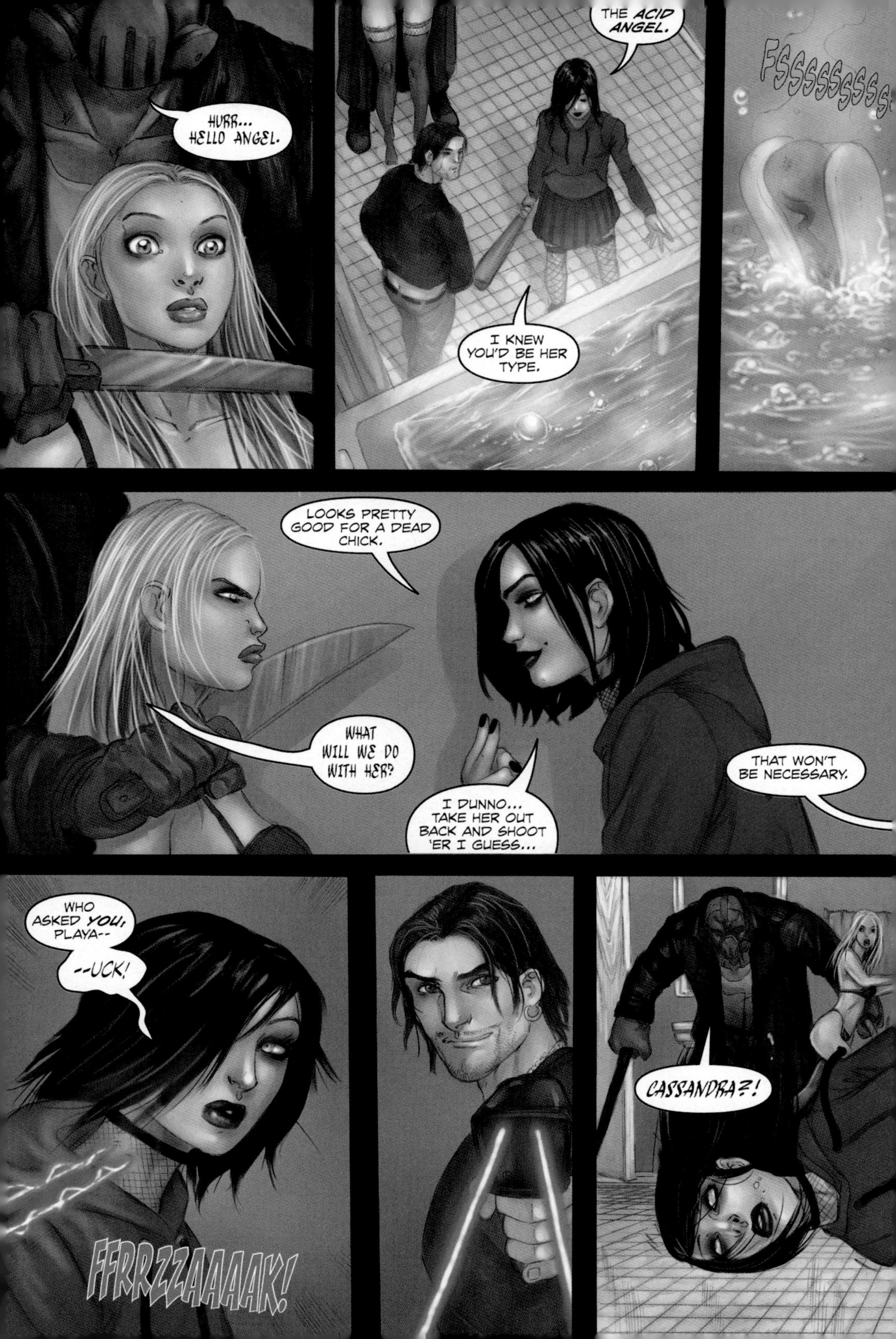
HURR... HELLO ANGEL.
THE ACID ANGEL.
I KNEW YOU'D BE HER TYPE.
FSSSSSSSSS
LOOKS PRETTY GOOD FOR A DEAD CHICK.
WHAT WILL WE DO WITH HER?
I DUNNO... TAKE HER OUT BACK AND SHOOT 'ER I GUESS...
THAT WON'T BE NECESSARY.
WHO ASKED YOU, PLAYA--
--UCK!
FFRRZZAAAAK!
CASSANDRA?!

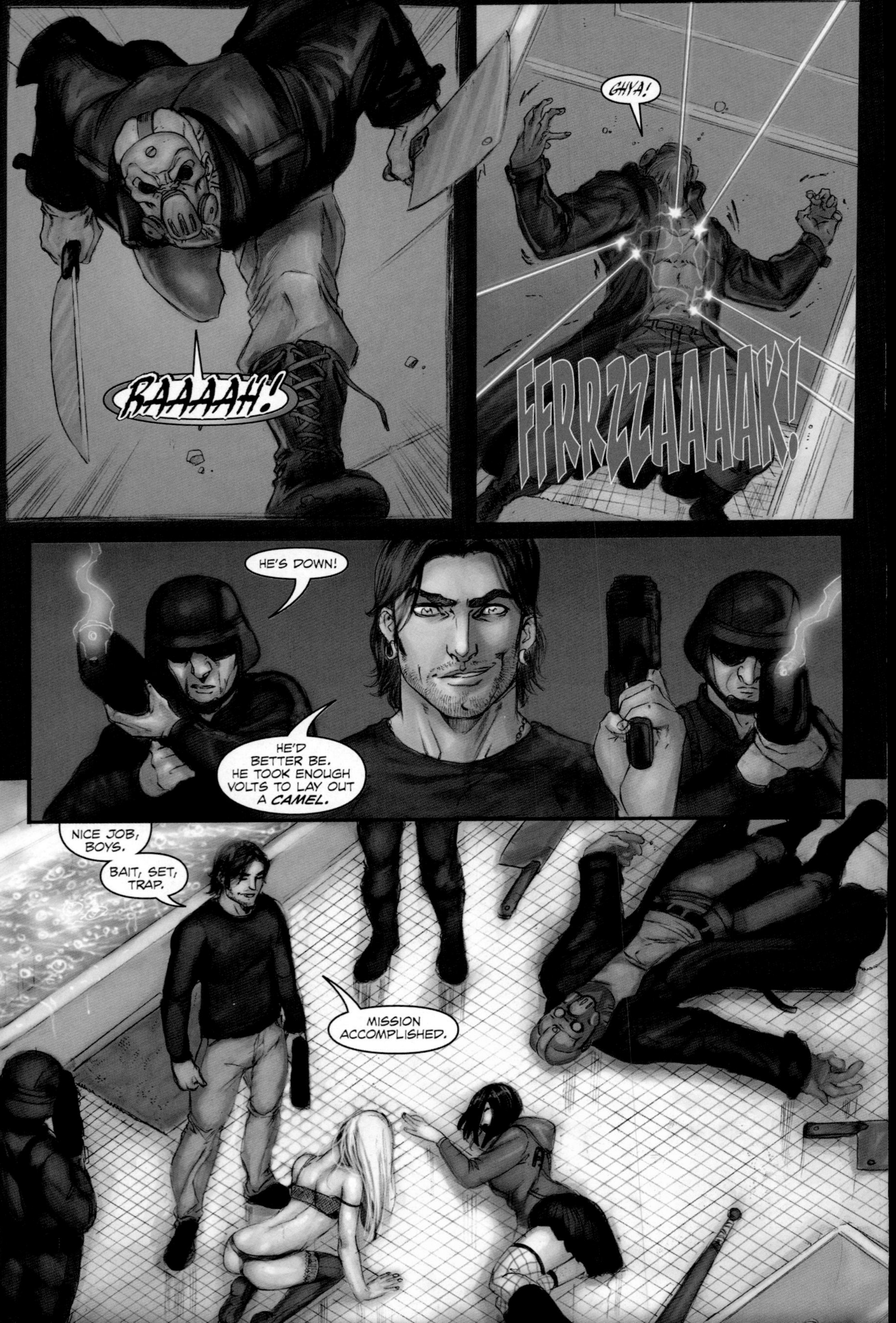
RAAAAH!
GHYA!
FFRRZZAAAAK!
HE'S DOWN!
HE'D BETTER BE. HE TOOK ENOUGH VOLTS TO LAY OUT A CAMEL.
NICE JOB, BOYS.
BAIT, SET, TRAP.
MISSION ACCOMPLISHED.

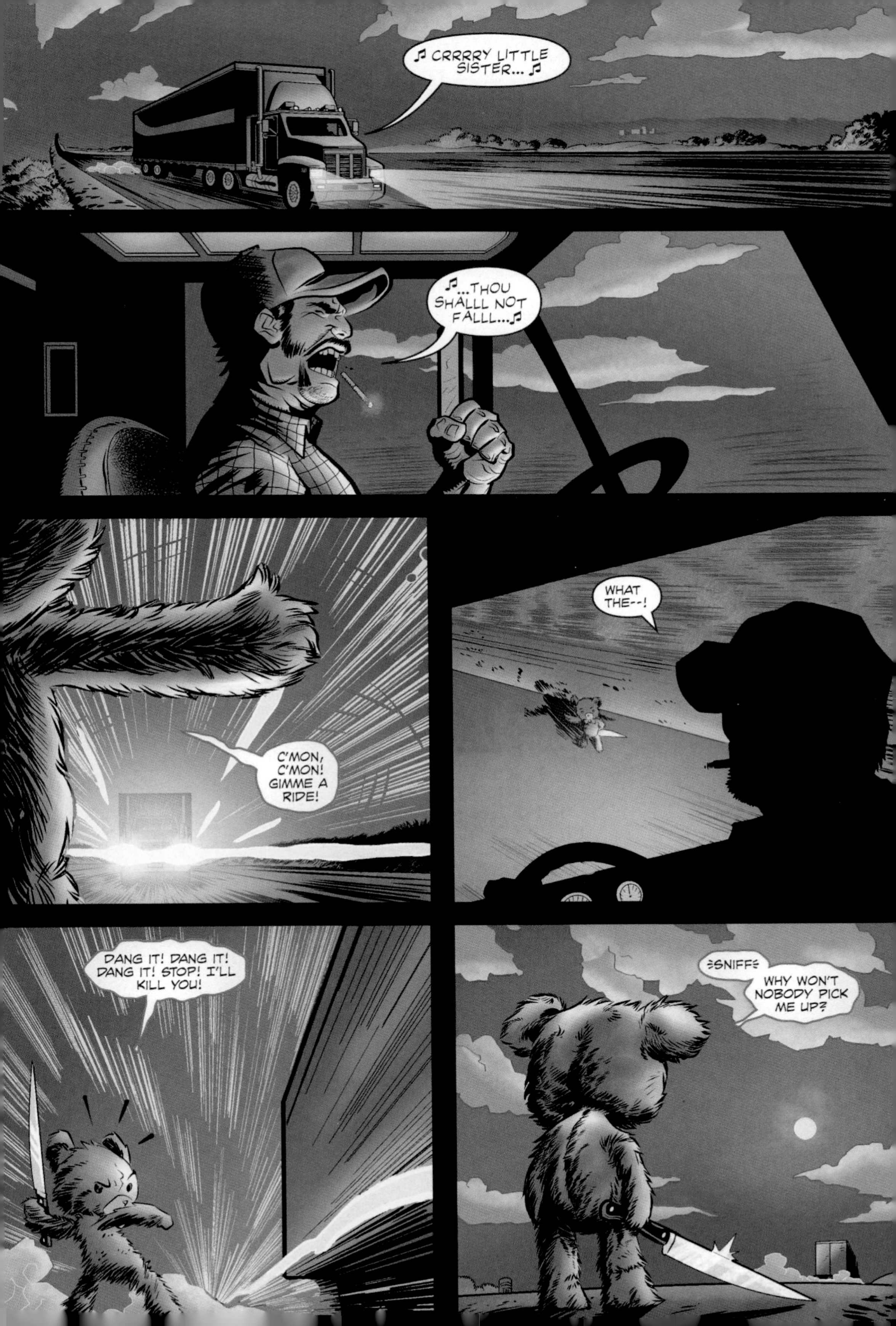
♫ CRRRRY LITTLE SISTER... ♫
♫ ...THOU SHALLL NOT FALLL... ♫
C'MON, C'MON! GIMME A RIDE!
WHAT THE--!
DANG IT! DANG IT! DANG IT! STOP! I'LL KILL YOU!
≈SNIFF≈
WHY WON'T NOBODY PICK ME UP?

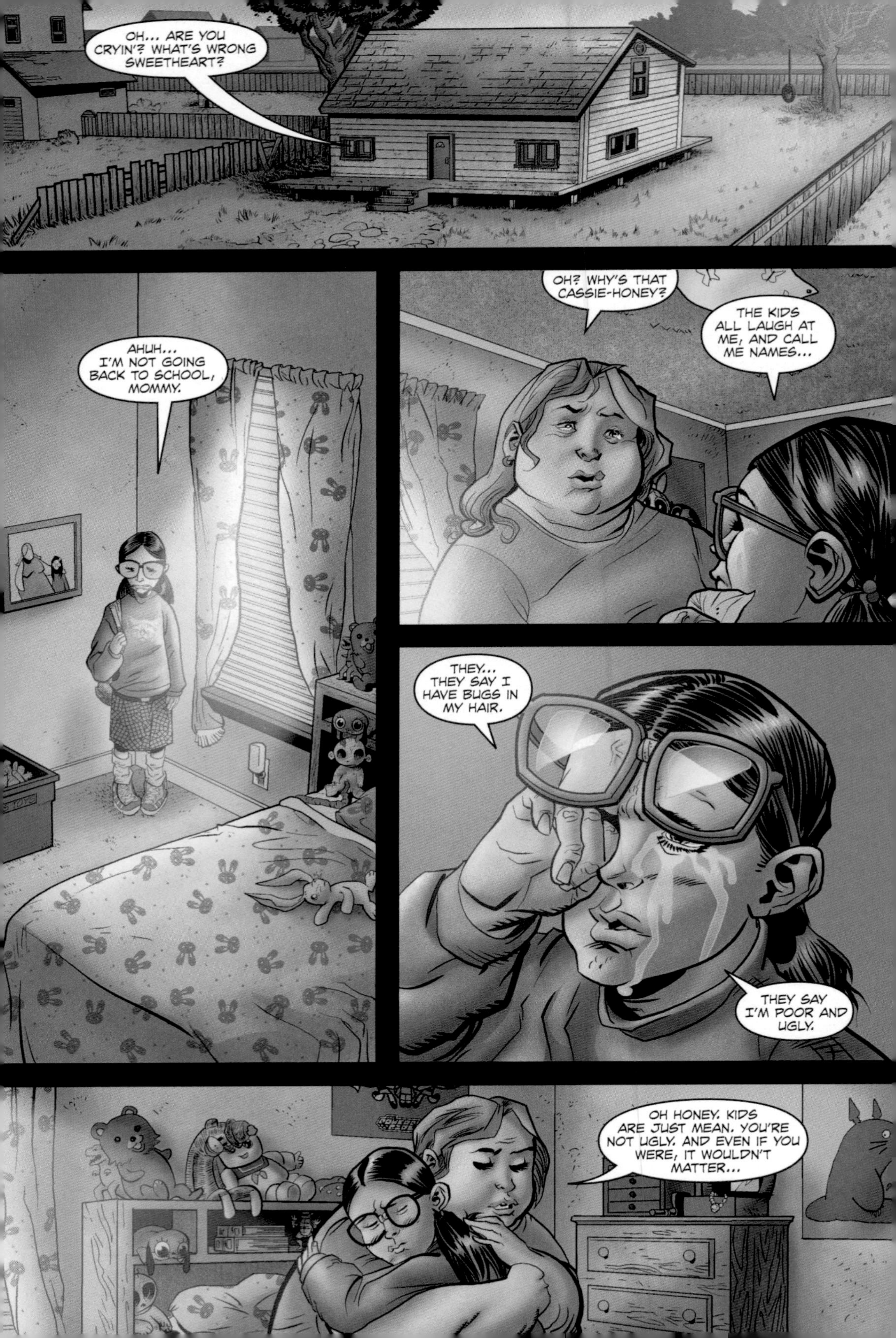
OH... ARE YOU CRYIN'? WHAT'S WRONG SWEETHEART?
AHUH... I'M NOT GOING BACK TO SCHOOL, MOMMY.
OH? WHY'S THAT CASSIE-HONEY?
THE KIDS ALL LAUGH AT ME, AND CALL ME NAMES...
THEY... THEY SAY I HAVE BUGS IN MY HAIR.
THEY SAY I'M POOR AND UGLY.
OH HONEY. KIDS ARE JUST MEAN. YOU'RE NOT UGLY. AND EVEN IF YOU WERE, IT WOULDN'T MATTER...

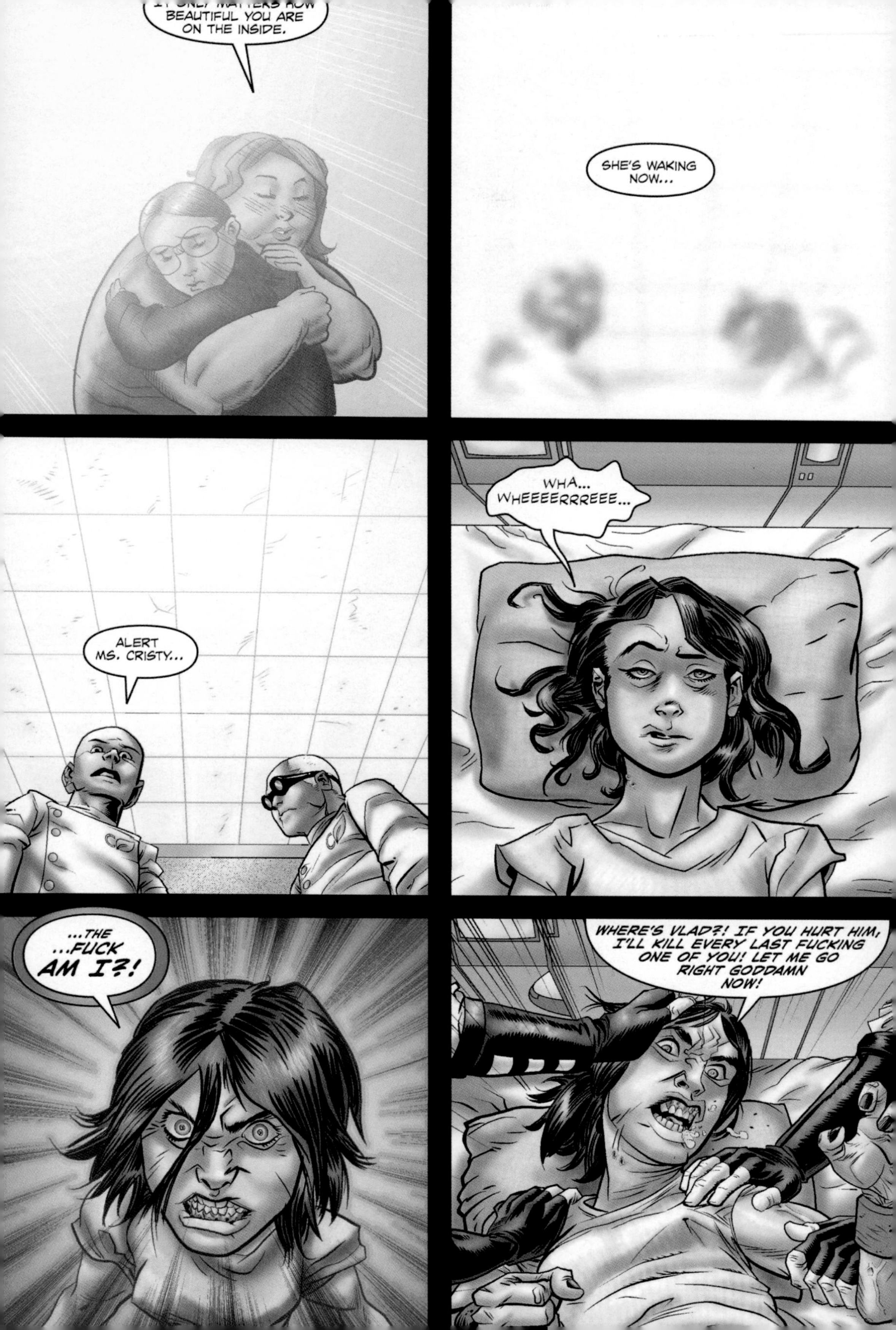
BEAUTIFUL YOU ARE ON THE INSIDE.
SHE'S WAKING NOW...
ALERT MS. CRISTY...
WHA... WHEEEERRREEE...
...THE ...FUCK AM I?!
WHERE'S VLAD?! IF YOU HURT HIM, I'LL KILL EVERY LAST FUCKING ONE OF YOU! LET ME GO RIGHT GODDAMN NOW!

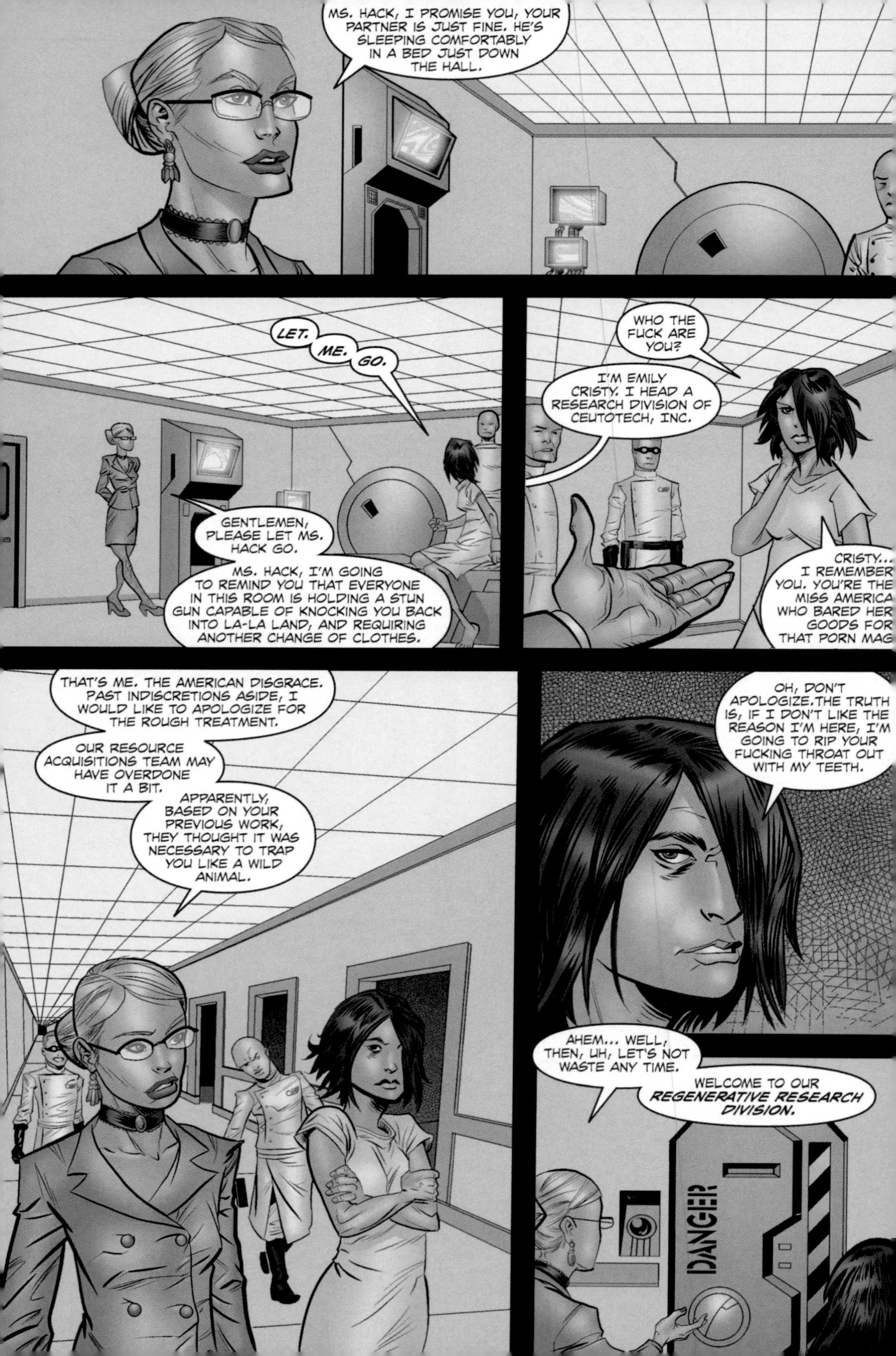
MS. HACK, I PROMISE YOU, YOUR PARTNER IS JUST FINE. HE'S SLEEPING COMFORTABLY IN A BED JUST DOWN THE HALL.
LET. ME. GO.
GENTLEMEN, PLEASE LET MS. HACK GO.
MS. HACK, I'M GOING TO REMIND YOU THAT EVERYONE IN THIS ROOM IS HOLDING A STUN GUN CAPABLE OF KNOCKING YOU BACK INTO LA-LA LAND, AND REQUIRING ANOTHER CHANGE OF CLOTHES.
WHO THE FUCK ARE YOU?
I'M EMILY CRISTY. I HEAD A RESEARCH DIVISION OF CEUTOTECH, INC.
CRISTY... I REMEMBER YOU. YOU'RE THE MISS AMERICA WHO BARED HER GOODS FOR THAT PORN MAG
THAT'S ME. THE AMERICAN DISGRACE. PAST INDISCRETIONS ASIDE, I WOULD LIKE TO APOLOGIZE FOR THE ROUGH TREATMENT.
OUR RESOURCE ACQUISITIONS TEAM MAY HAVE OVERDONE IT A BIT.
APPARENTLY, BASED ON YOUR PREVIOUS WORK, THEY THOUGHT IT WAS NECESSARY TO TRAP YOU LIKE A WILD ANIMAL.
OH, DON'T APOLOGIZE. THE TRUTH IS, IF I DON'T LIKE THE REASON I'M HERE, I'M GOING TO RIP YOUR FUCKING THROAT OUT WITH MY TEETH.
AHEM... WELL, THEN, UH, LET'S NOT WASTE ANY TIME.
WELCOME TO OUR REGENERATIVE RESEARCH DIVISION.
DANGER

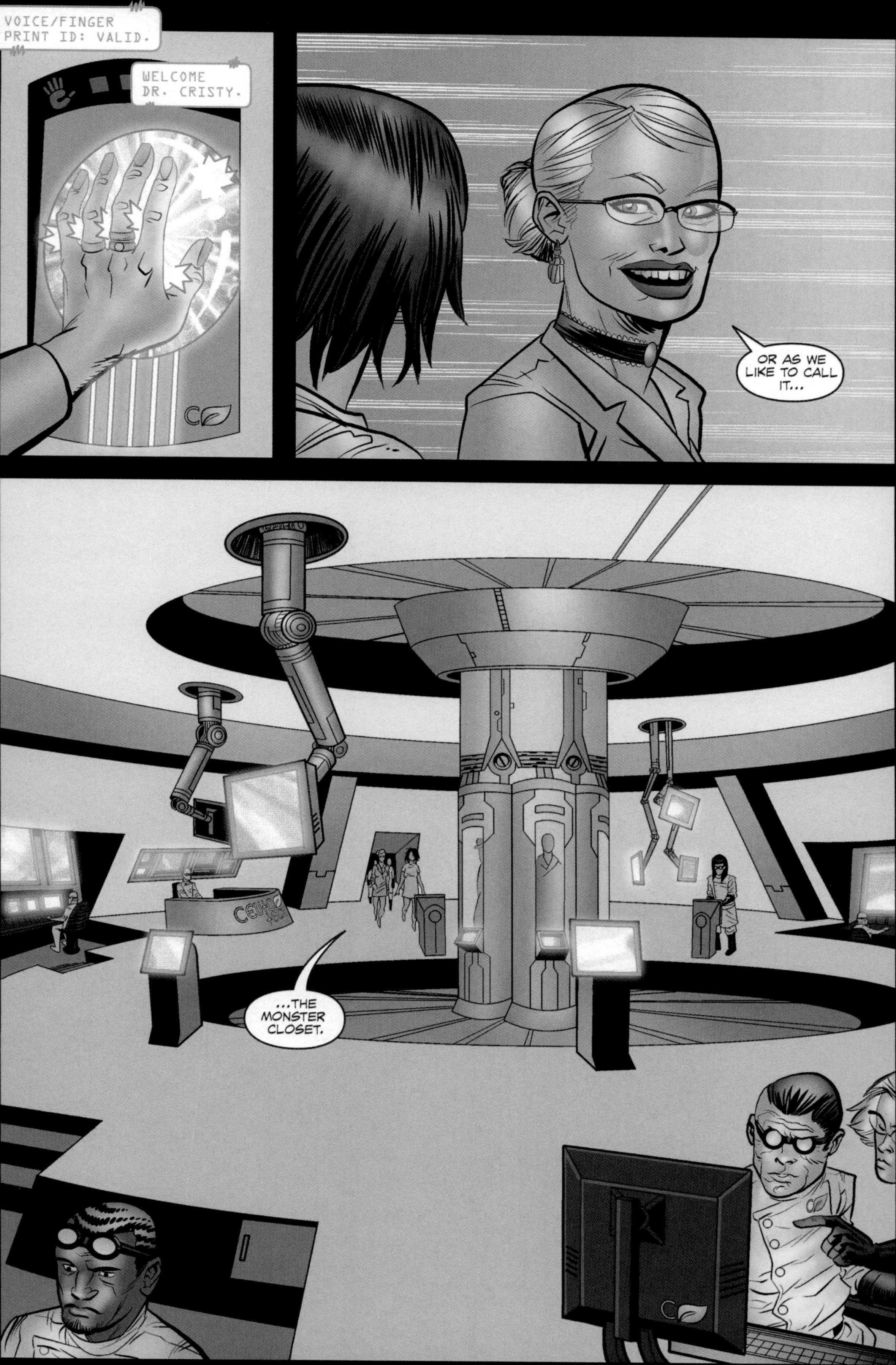

VOICE/FINGER
PRINT ID: VALID.
WELCOME
DR. CRISTY.
OR AS WE LIKE TO CALL IT...
...THE MONSTER CLOSET.

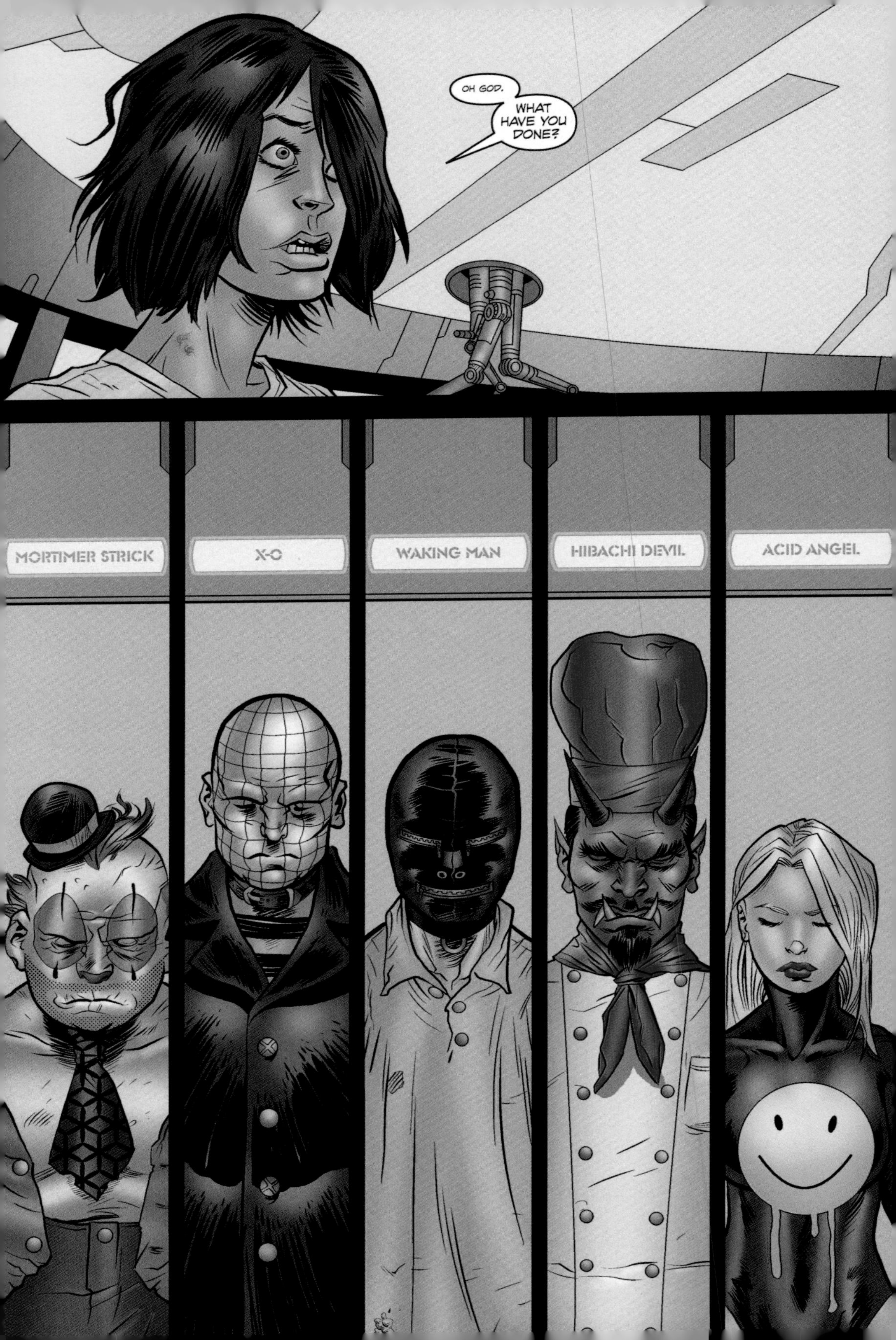

OH GOD.
WHAT HAVE YOU DONE?
MORTIMER STRICK
X-O
WAKING MAN
HIBACHI DEVIL
ACID ANGEL

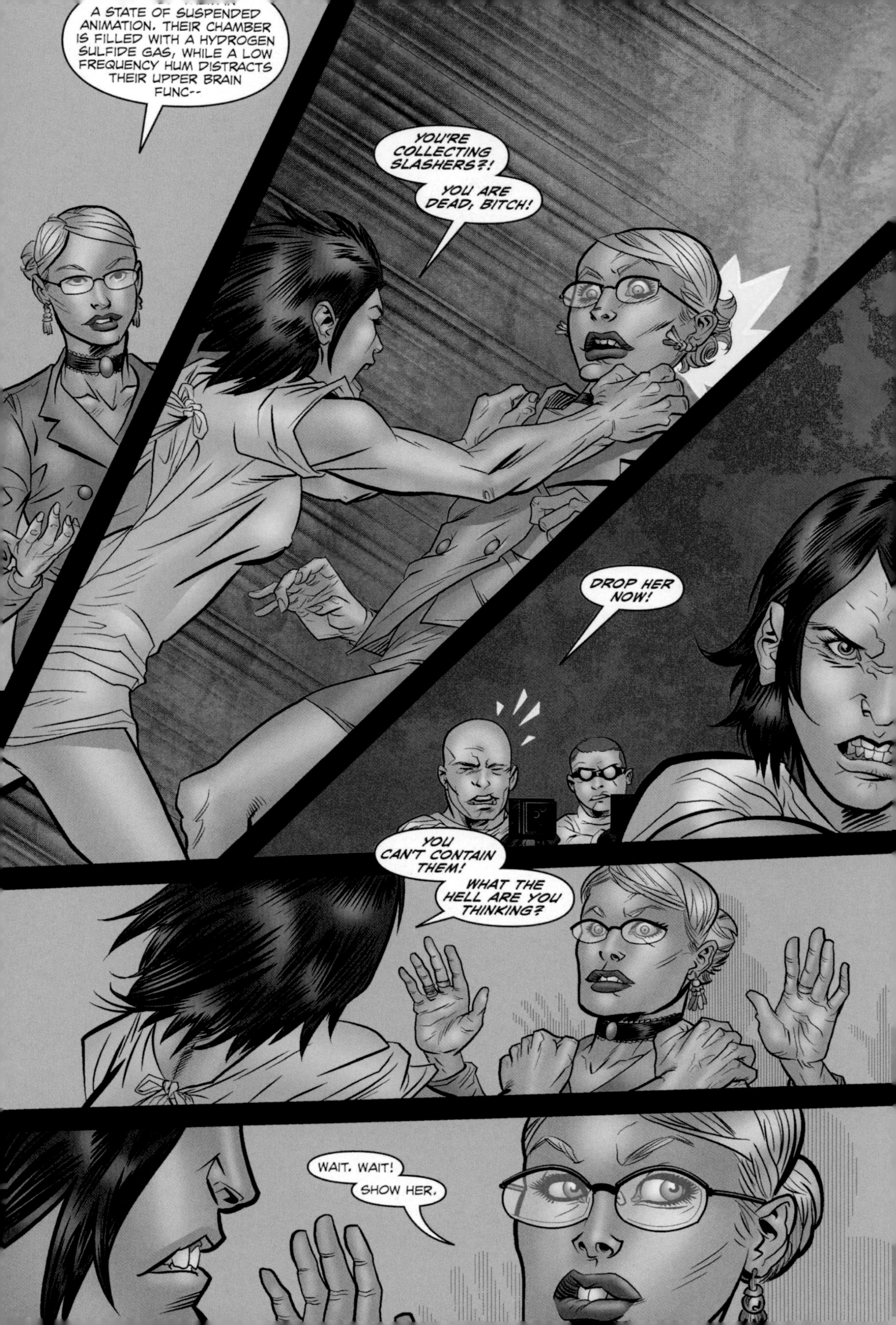
A STATE OF SUSPENDED ANIMATION. THEIR CHAMBER IS FILLED WITH A HYDROGEN SULFIDE GAS, WHILE A LOW FREQUENCY HUM DISTRACTS THEIR UPPER BRAIN FUNC--
YOU'RE COLLECTING SLASHERS?!
YOU ARE DEAD, BITCH!
DROP HER NOW!
YOU CAN'T CONTAIN THEM!
WHAT THE HELL ARE YOU THINKING?
WAIT. WAIT!
SHOW HER.

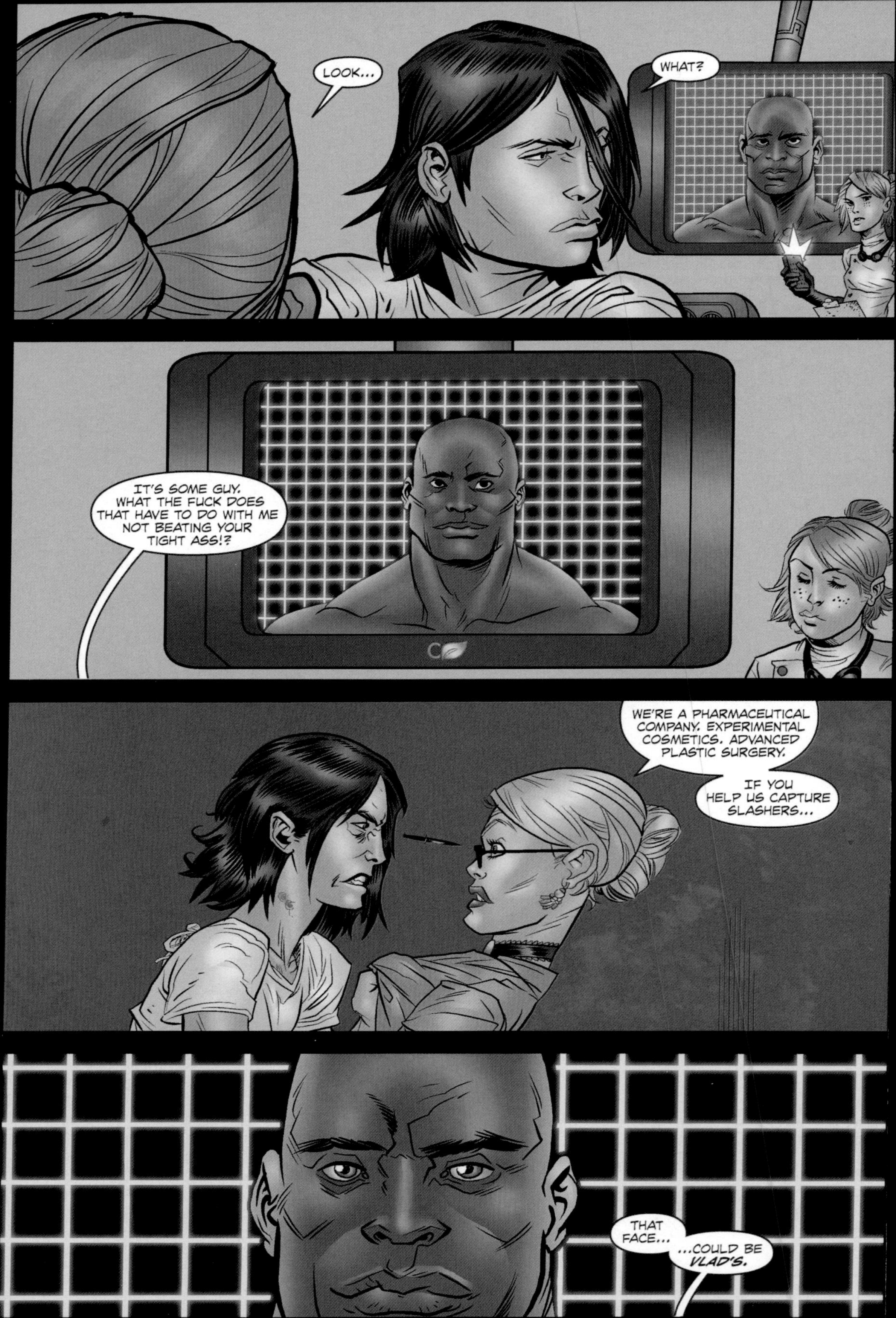
LOOK...
WHAT?
IT'S SOME GUY. WHAT THE FUCK DOES THAT HAVE TO DO WITH ME NOT BEATING YOUR TIGHT ASS!?
WE'RE A PHARMACEUTICAL COMPANY. EXPERIMENTAL COSMETICS. ADVANCED PLASTIC SURGERY.
IF YOU HELP US CAPTURE SLASHERS...
THAT FACE...
...COULD BE *VLAD'S.*

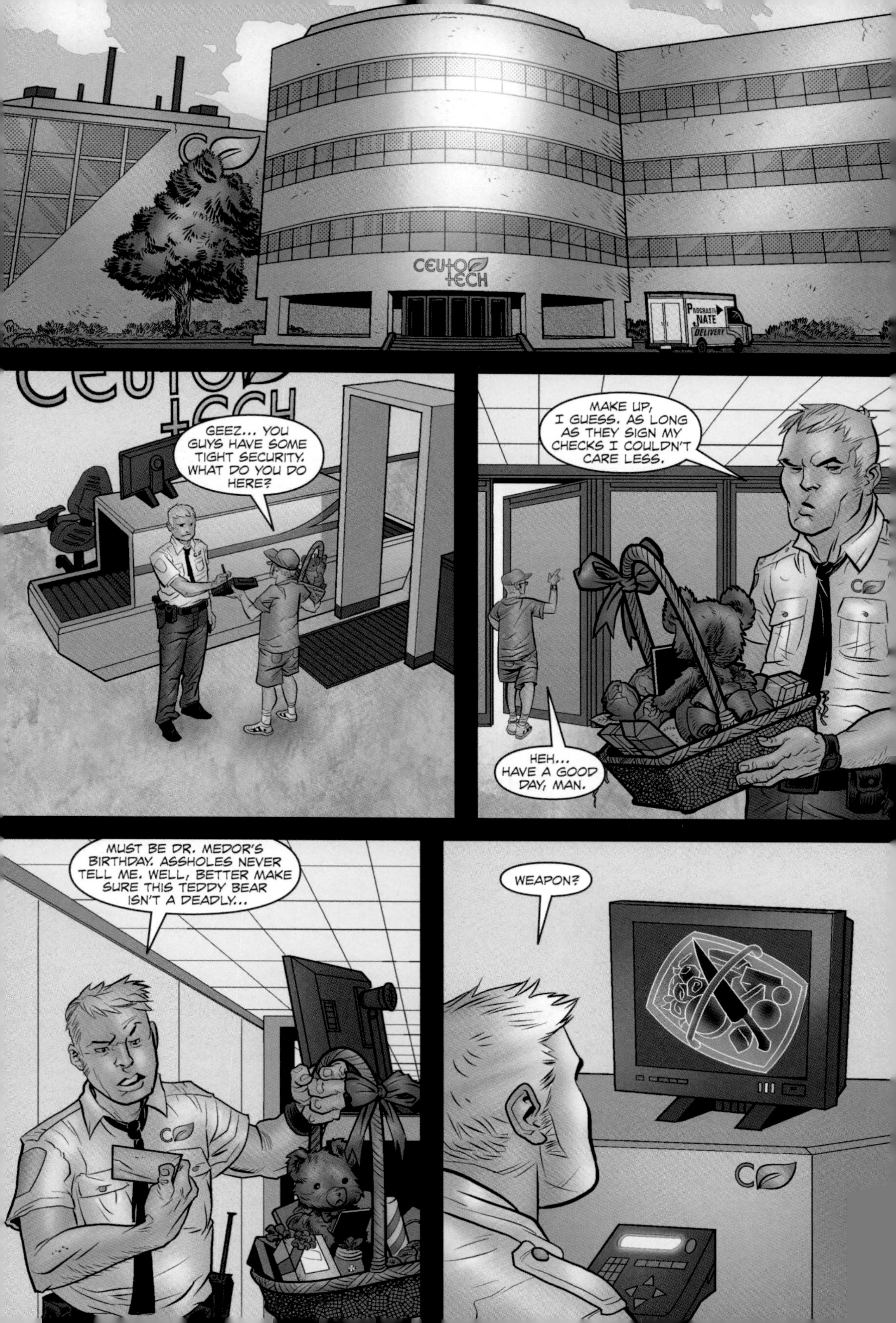
CEUTO TECH
PROCRASTI NATE DELIVERY
GEEZ... YOU GUYS HAVE SOME TIGHT SECURITY. WHAT DO YOU DO HERE?
MAKE UP, I GUESS. AS LONG AS THEY SIGN MY CHECKS I COULDN'T CARE LESS.
HEH... HAVE A GOOD DAY, MAN.
MUST BE DR. MEDOR'S BIRTHDAY. ASSHOLES NEVER TELL ME. WELL, BETTER MAKE SURE THIS TEDDY BEAR ISN'T A DEADLY...
WEAPON?

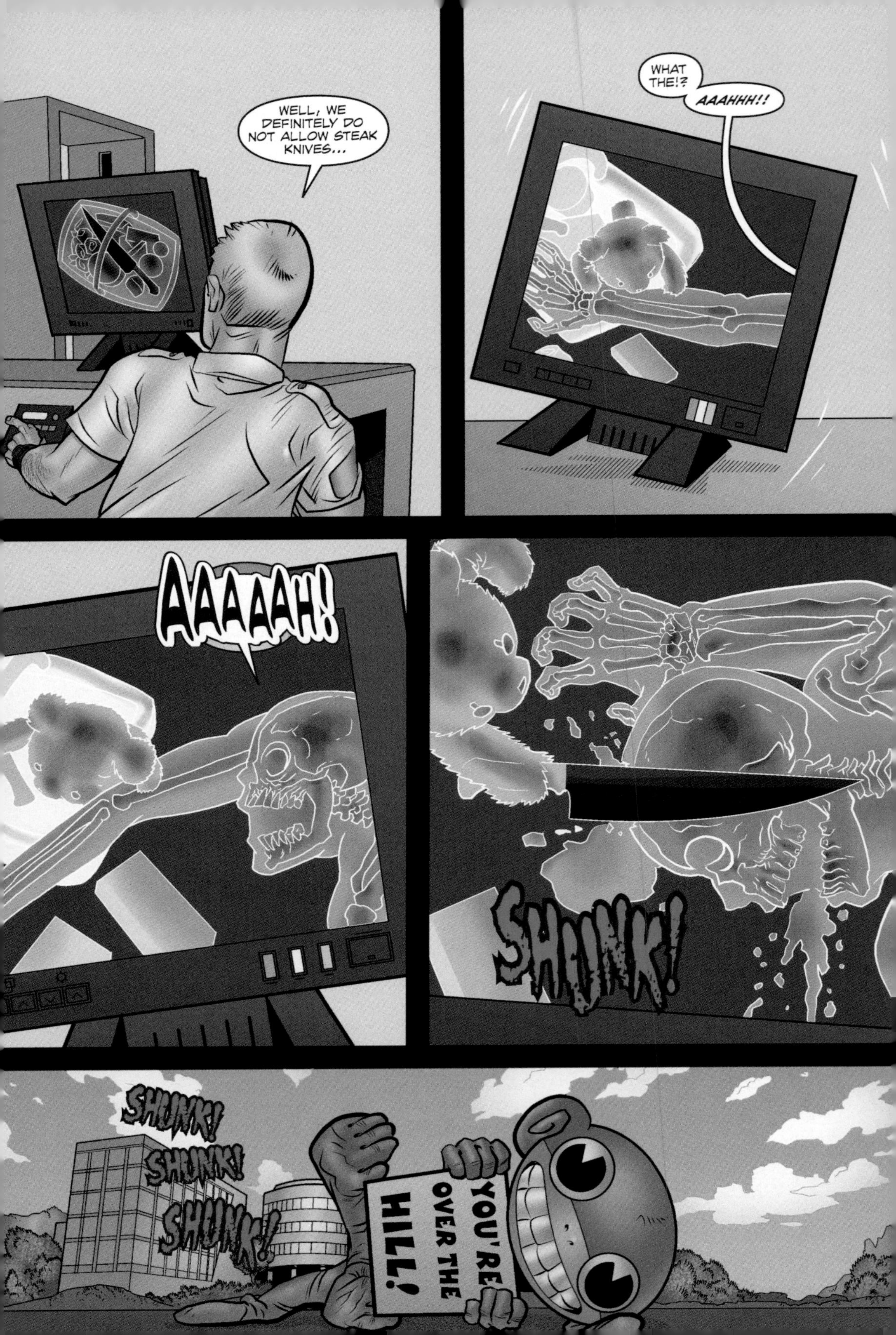
WELL, WE DEFINITELY DO NOT ALLOW STEAK KNIVES...
WHAT THE!?
AAAHHH!!
AAAAAH!
SHUNK!
SHUNK!
SHUNK!
SHUNK!
YOU'RE OVER THE HILL!

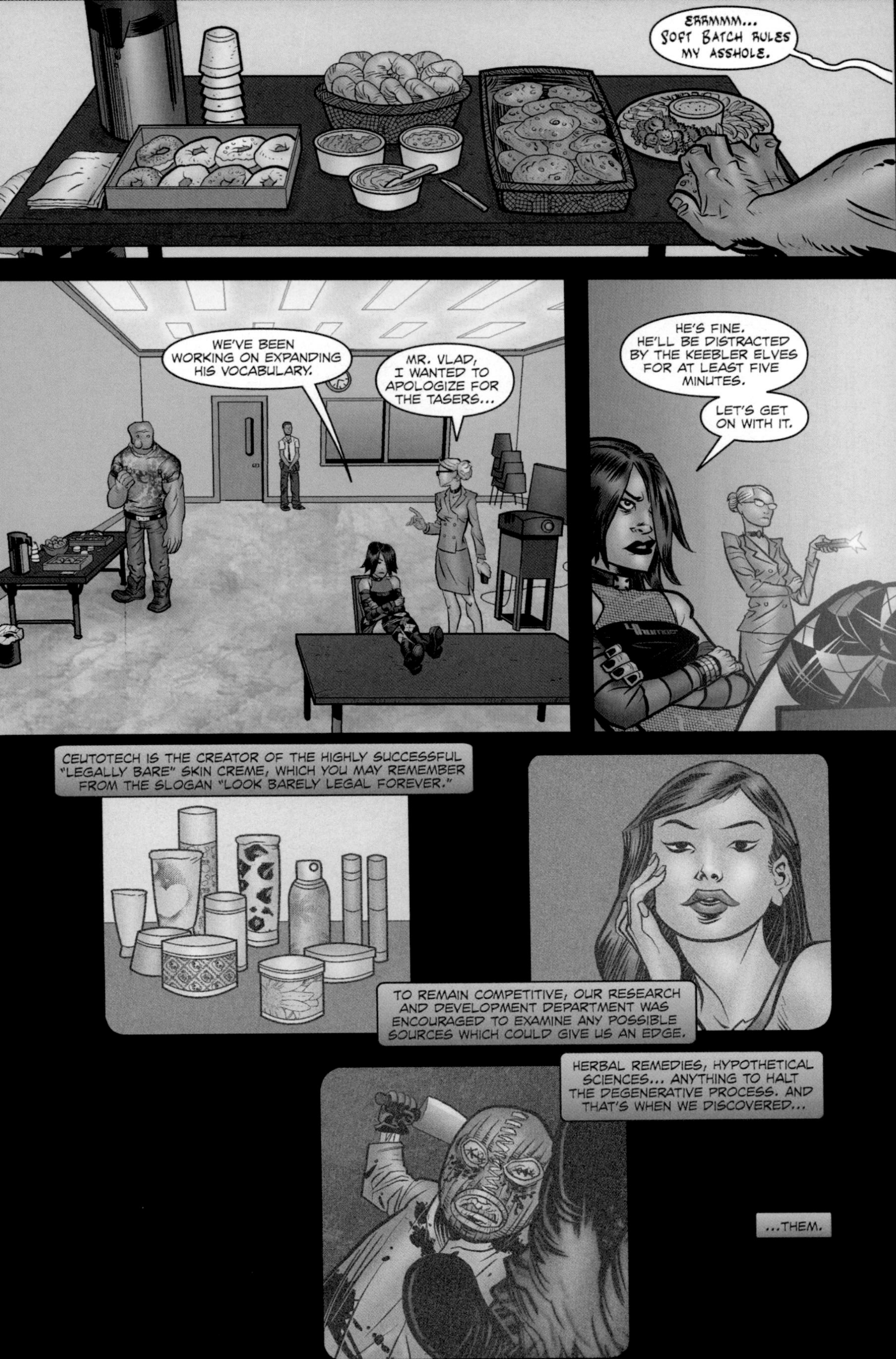
ERRMMM... SOFT BATCH RULES MY ASSHOLE.
WE'VE BEEN WORKING ON EXPANDING HIS VOCABULARY.
MR. VLAD, I WANTED TO APOLOGIZE FOR THE TASERS...
HE'S FINE. HE'LL BE DISTRACTED BY THE KEEBLER ELVES FOR AT LEAST FIVE MINUTES.
LET'S GET ON WITH IT.
CELLTOTECH IS THE CREATOR OF THE HIGHLY SUCCESSFUL "LEGALLY BARE" SKIN CREME, WHICH YOU MAY REMEMBER FROM THE SLOGAN "LOOK BARELY LEGAL FOREVER."
TO REMAIN COMPETITIVE, OUR RESEARCH AND DEVELOPMENT DEPARTMENT WAS ENCOURAGED TO EXAMINE ANY POSSIBLE SOURCES WHICH COULD GIVE US AN EDGE.
HERBAL REMEDIES, HYPOTHETICAL SCIENCES... ANYTHING TO HALT THE DEGENERATIVE PROCESS. AND THAT'S WHEN WE DISCOVERED...
...THEM.

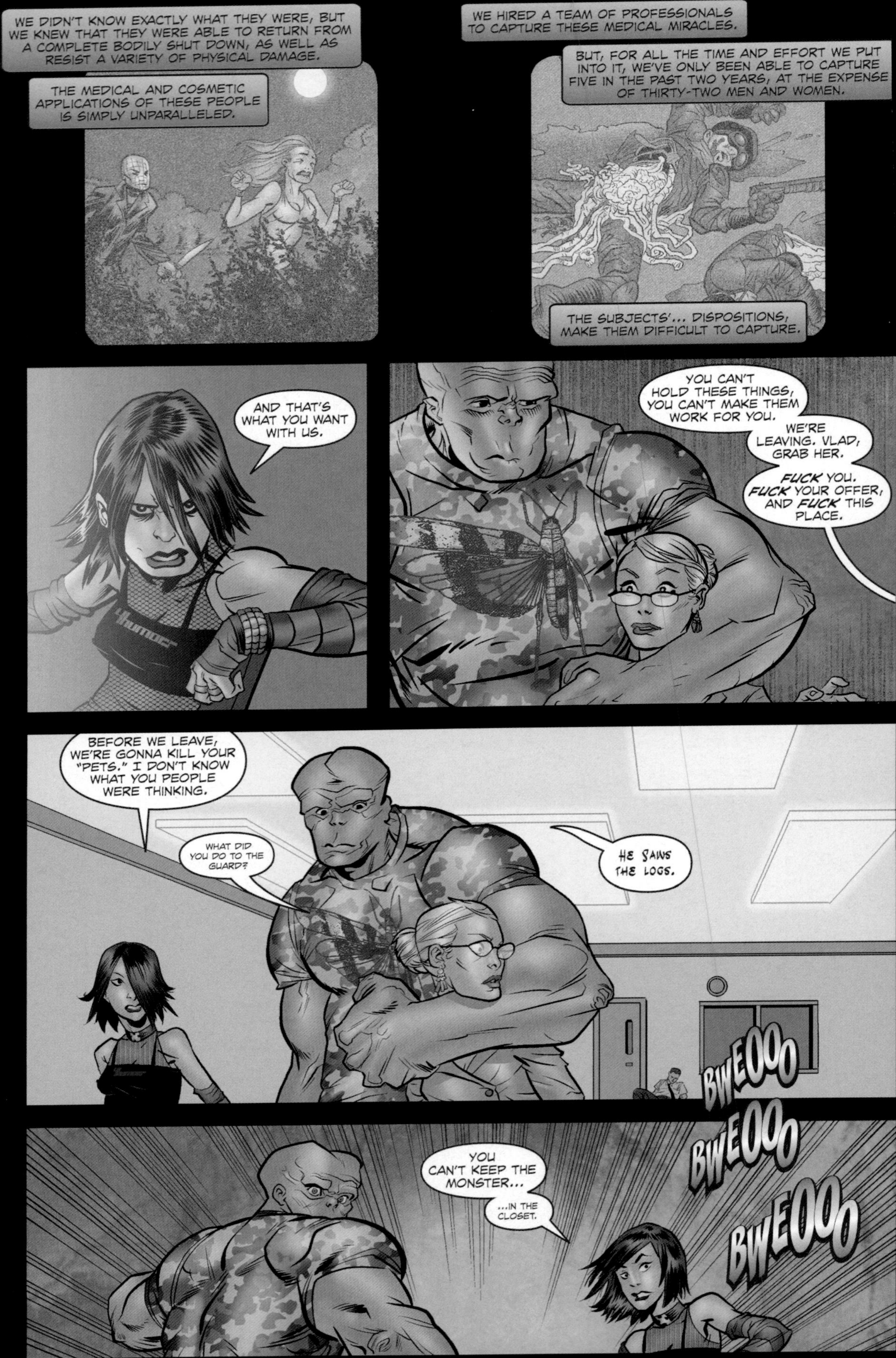
WE DIDN'T KNOW EXACTLY WHAT THEY WERE, BUT WE KNEW THAT THEY WERE ABLE TO RETURN FROM A COMPLETE BODILY SHUT DOWN, AS WELL AS RESIST A VARIETY OF PHYSICAL DAMAGE.
THE MEDICAL AND COSMETIC APPLICATIONS OF THESE PEOPLE IS SIMPLY UNPARALLELED.
WE HIRED A TEAM OF PROFESSIONALS TO CAPTURE THESE MEDICAL MIRACLES.
BUT, FOR ALL THE TIME AND EFFORT WE PUT INTO IT, WE'VE ONLY BEEN ABLE TO CAPTURE FIVE IN THE PAST TWO YEARS, AT THE EXPENSE OF THIRTY-TWO MEN AND WOMEN.
THE SUBJECTS'... DISPOSITIONS, MAKE THEM DIFFICULT TO CAPTURE.
AND THAT'S WHAT YOU WANT WITH US.
YOU CAN'T HOLD THESE THINGS, YOU CAN'T MAKE THEM WORK FOR YOU.
WE'RE LEAVING. VLAD, GRAB HER.
FUCK YOU. FUCK YOUR OFFER, AND FUCK THIS PLACE.
BEFORE WE LEAVE, WE'RE GONNA KILL YOUR "PETS." I DON'T KNOW WHAT YOU PEOPLE WERE THINKING.
WHAT DID YOU DO TO THE GUARD?
HE SAWS THE LOGS.
BWEOOO
BWEOOO
YOU CAN'T KEEP THE MONSTER...
...IN THE CLOSET.
BWEOOO

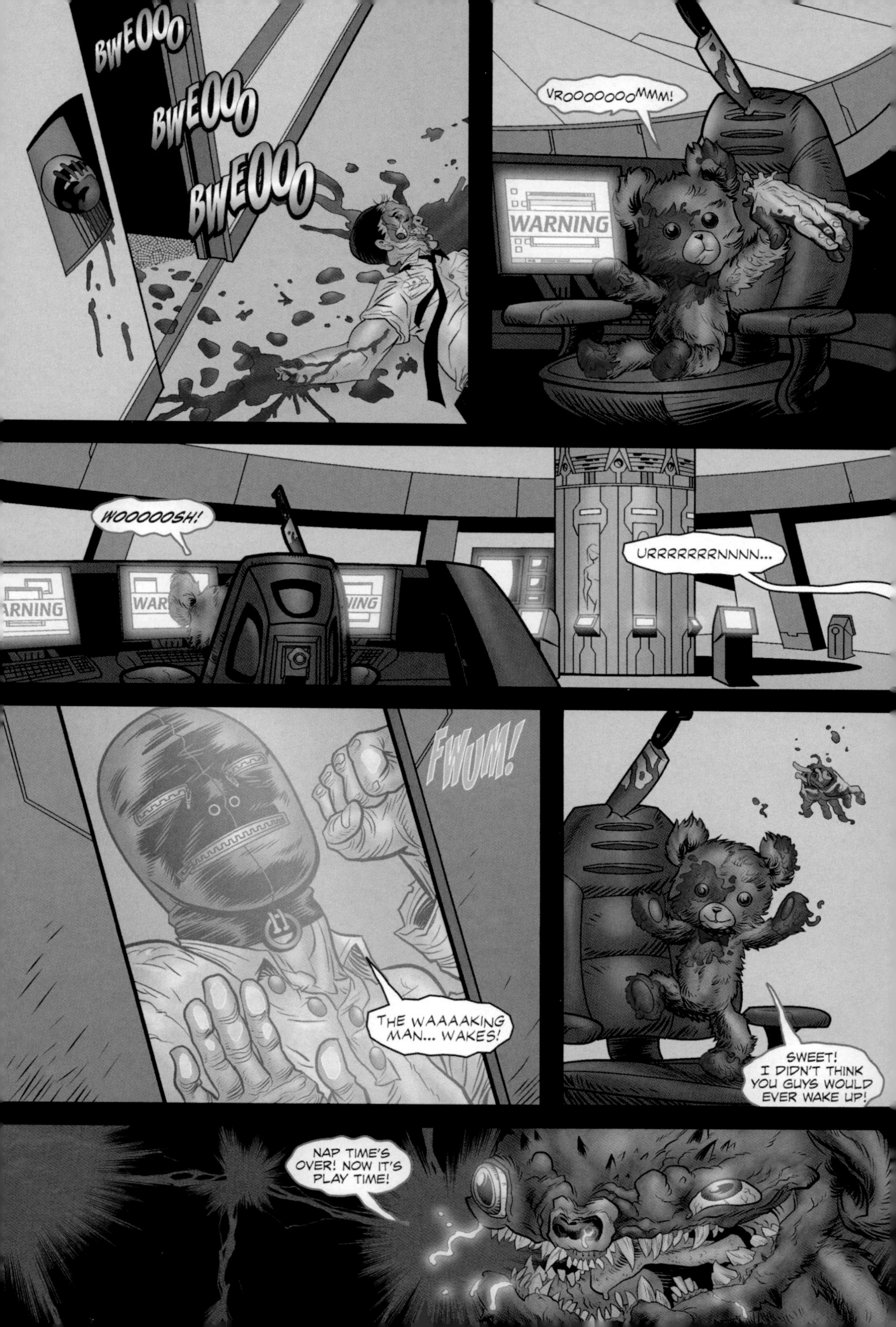
BWEOOO
BWEOOO
BWEOOO
VROOOOOOOMMM!
WARNING
WOOOOOSH!
WARNING
URRRRRRNNNN...
FWUM!
THE WAAAAKING MAN... WAKES!
SWEET! I DIDN'T THINK YOU GUYS WOULD EVER WAKE UP!
NAP TIME'S OVER! NOW IT'S PLAY TIME!

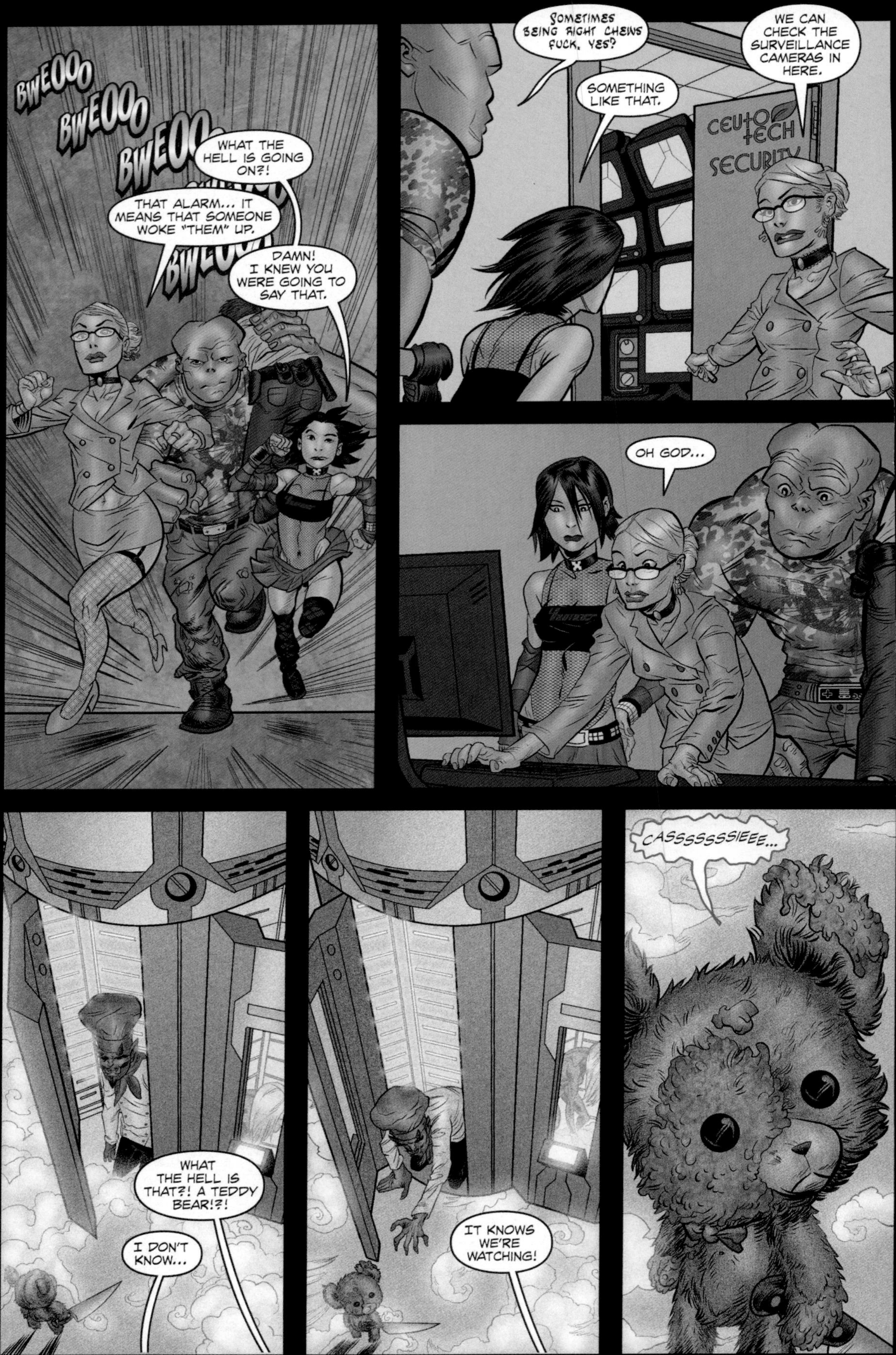
BWEOOO
BWEOOO
BWEOO
WHAT THE HELL IS GOING ON?!
THAT ALARM... IT MEANS THAT SOMEONE WOKE "THEM" UP.
DAMN! I KNEW YOU WERE GOING TO SAY THAT.
SOMETIMES BEING RIGHT CHEWS FUCK, YES?
SOMETHING LIKE THAT.
WE CAN CHECK THE SURVEILLANCE CAMERAS IN HERE.
CEUTO TECH SECURITY
OH GOD...
WHAT THE HELL IS THAT?! A TEDDY BEAR!?!
I DON'T KNOW...
IT KNOWS WE'RE WATCHING!
CASSSSSSSIEEE...

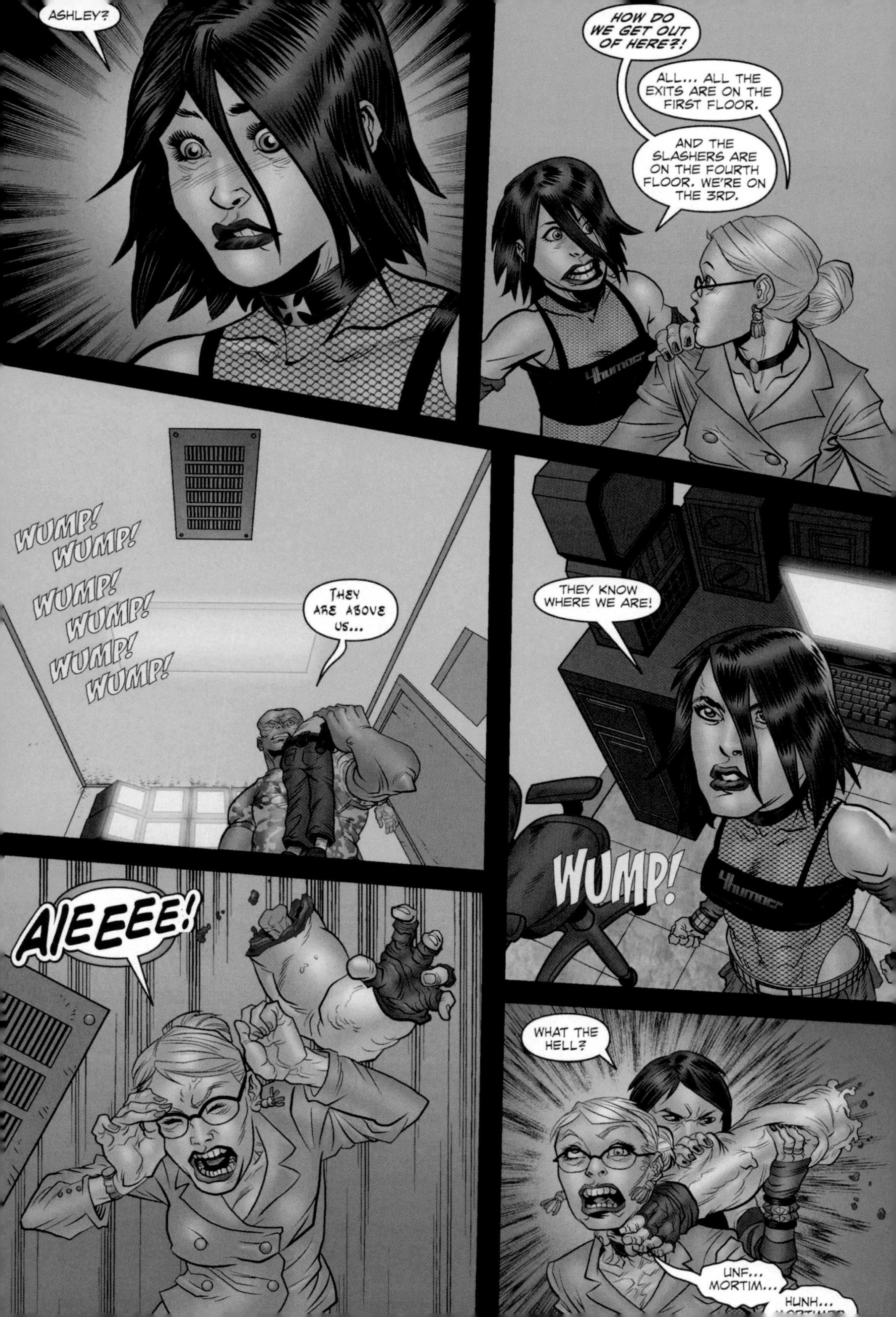
ASHLEY?
HOW DO WE GET OUT OF HERE?!
ALL... ALL THE EXITS ARE ON THE FIRST FLOOR.
AND THE SLASHERS ARE ON THE FOURTH FLOOR. WE'RE ON THE 3RD.
WUMP!
WUMP!
WUMP!
WUMP!
WUMP!
WUMP!
THEY ARE ABOVE US...
THEY KNOW WHERE WE ARE!
WUMP!
AIEEEE!
WHAT THE HELL?
UNF... MORTIM...
HUNH...

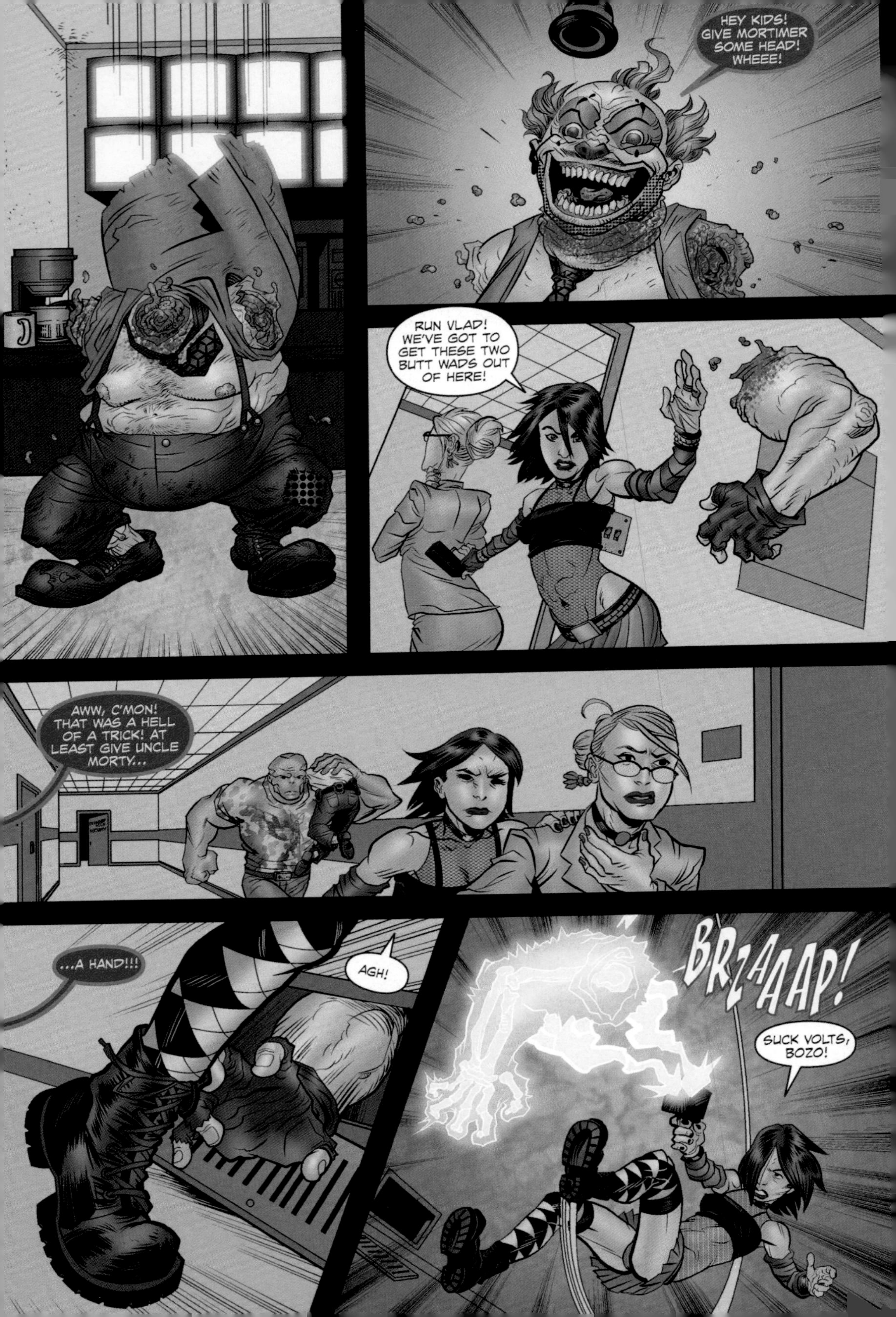
HEY KIDS! GIVE MORTIMER SOME HEAD! WHEEE!
RUN VLAD! WE'VE GOT TO GET THESE TWO BUTT WADS OUT OF HERE!
AWW, C'MON! THAT WAS A HELL OF A TRICK! AT LEAST GIVE UNCLE MORTY...
...A HAND!!!
AGH!
BRZAAAP!
SUCK VOLTS, BOZO!

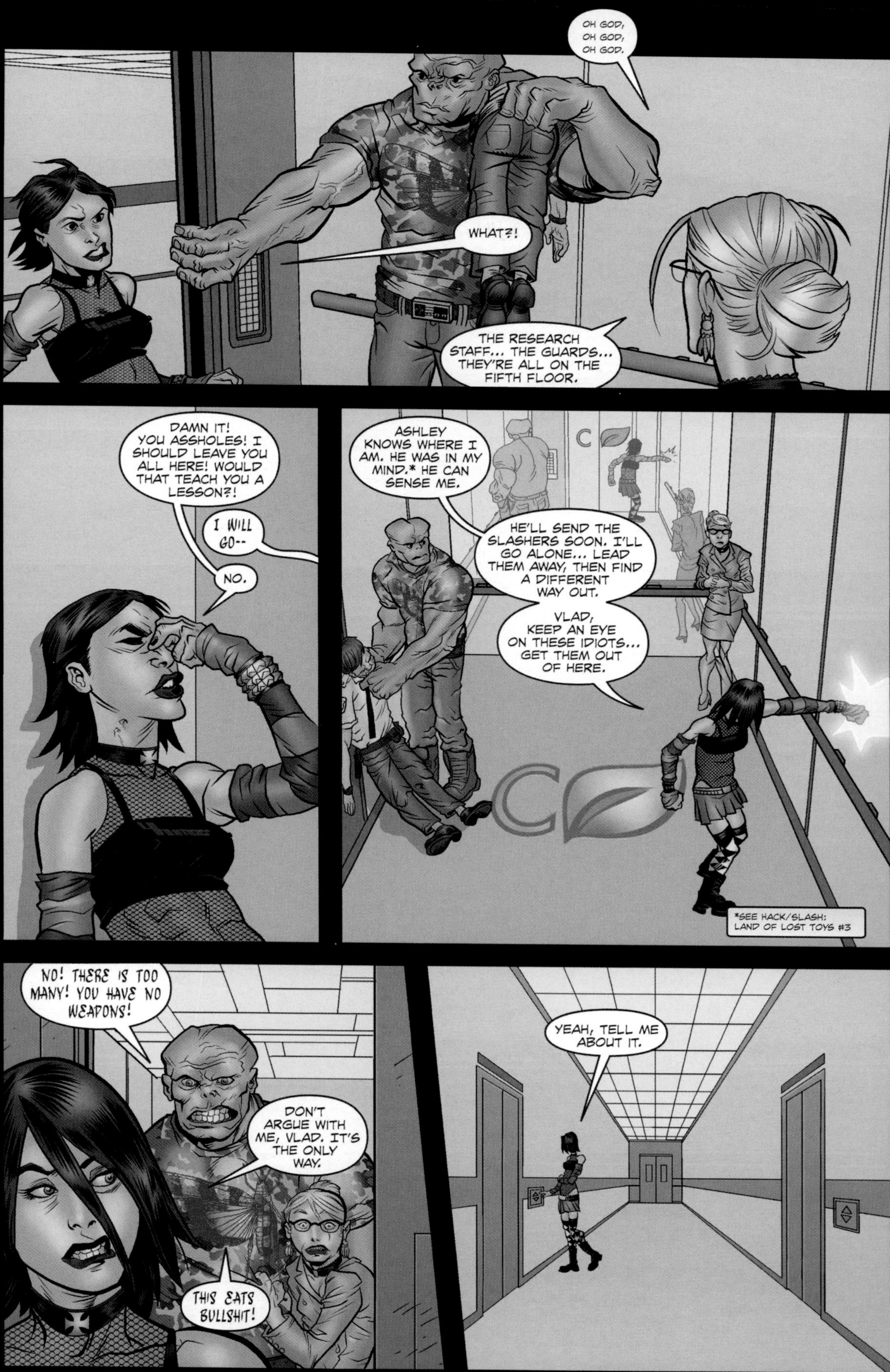
OH GOD, OH GOD, OH GOD.
WHAT?!
THE RESEARCH STAFF... THE GUARDS... THEY'RE ALL ON THE FIFTH FLOOR.
DAMN IT! YOU ASSHOLES! I SHOULD LEAVE YOU ALL HERE! WOULD THAT TEACH YOU A LESSON?!
I WILL GO--
NO.
ASHLEY KNOWS WHERE I AM. HE WAS IN MY MIND.* HE CAN SENSE ME.
HE'LL SEND THE SLASHERS SOON. I'LL GO ALONE... LEAD THEM AWAY, THEN FIND A DIFFERENT WAY OUT.
VLAD, KEEP AN EYE ON THESE IDIOTS... GET THEM OUT OF HERE.
*SEE HACK/SLASH: LAND OF LOST TOYS #3
NO! THERE IS TOO MANY! YOU HAVE NO WEAPONS!
DON'T ARGUE WITH ME, VLAD. IT'S THE ONLY WAY.
THIS EATS BULLSHIT!
YEAH, TELL ME ABOUT IT.

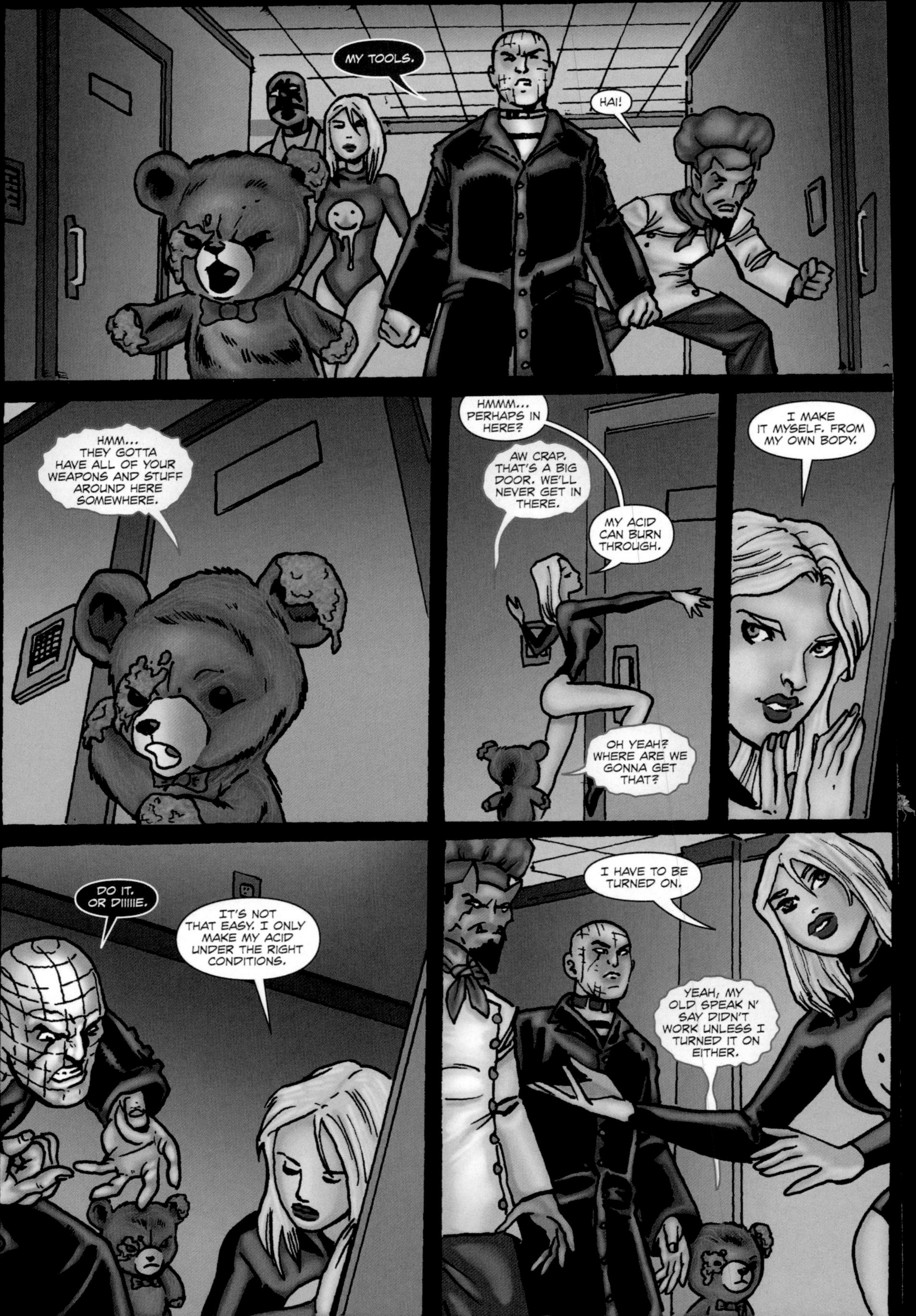
MY TOOLS.
HAI!
HMM... THEY GOTTA HAVE ALL OF YOUR WEAPONS AND STUFF AROUND HERE SOMEWHERE.
HMMM... PERHAPS IN HERE?
AW CRAP. THAT'S A BIG DOOR. WE'LL NEVER GET IN THERE.
MY ACID CAN BURN THROUGH.
OH YEAH? WHERE ARE WE GONNA GET THAT?
I MAKE IT MYSELF. FROM MY OWN BODY.
DO IT. OR DIIIIIE.
IT'S NOT THAT EASY. I ONLY MAKE MY ACID UNDER THE RIGHT CONDITIONS.
I HAVE TO BE TURNED ON.
YEAH, MY OLD SPEAK N' SAY DIDN'T WORK UNLESS I TURNED IT ON EITHER.

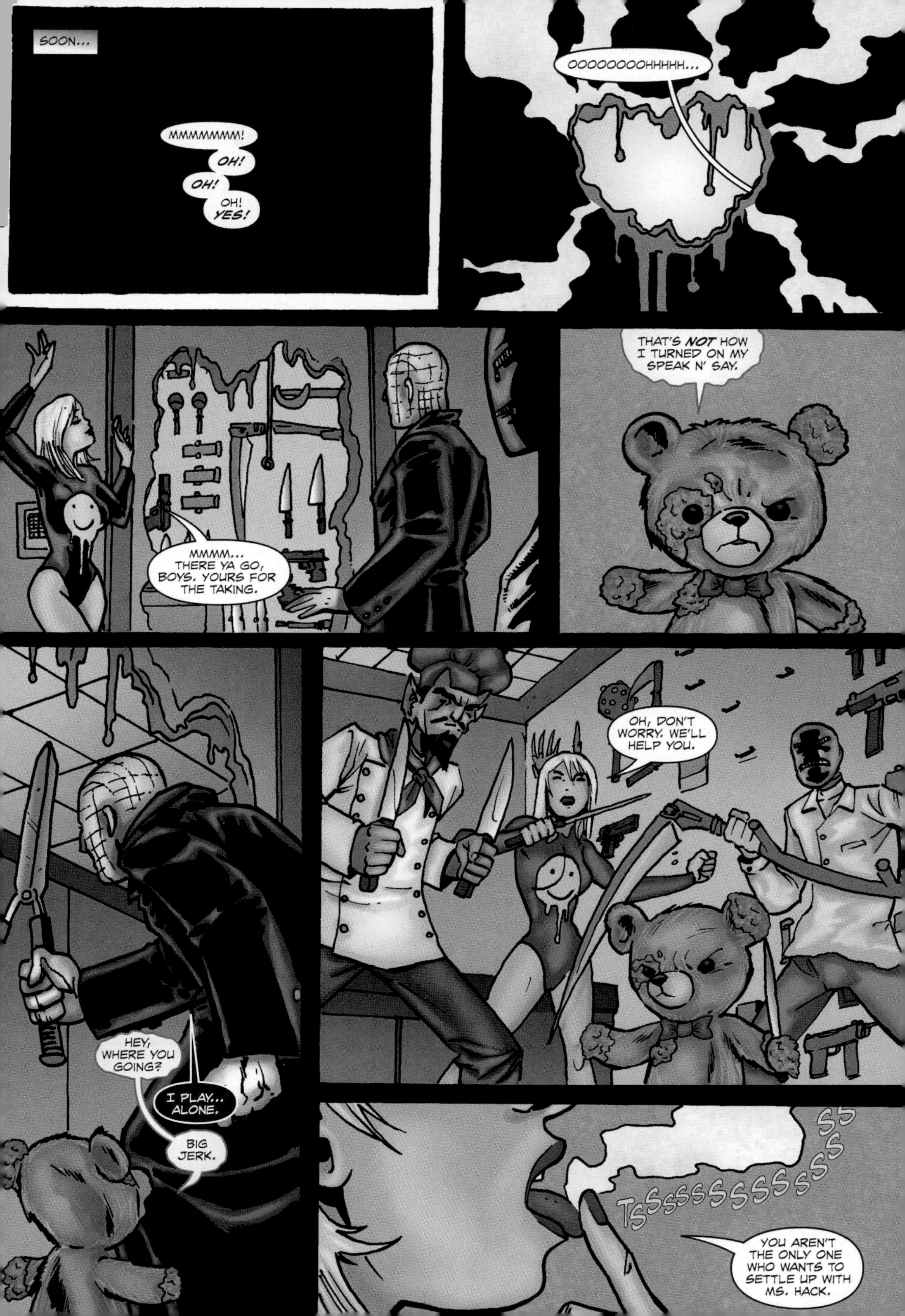
SOON...
MMMMMMMM!
OH!
OH!
OH! YES!
OOOOOOOOHHHHH...
MMMM... THERE YA GO, BOYS. YOURS FOR THE TAKING.
THAT'S **NOT** HOW I TURNED ON MY SPEAK N' SAY.
OH, DON'T WORRY. WE'LL HELP YOU.
HEY, WHERE YOU GOING?
I PLAY... ALONE.
BIG JERK.
TSSSSSSSSSSSSSSSS
YOU AREN'T THE ONLY ONE WHO WANTS TO SETTLE UP WITH MS. HACK.

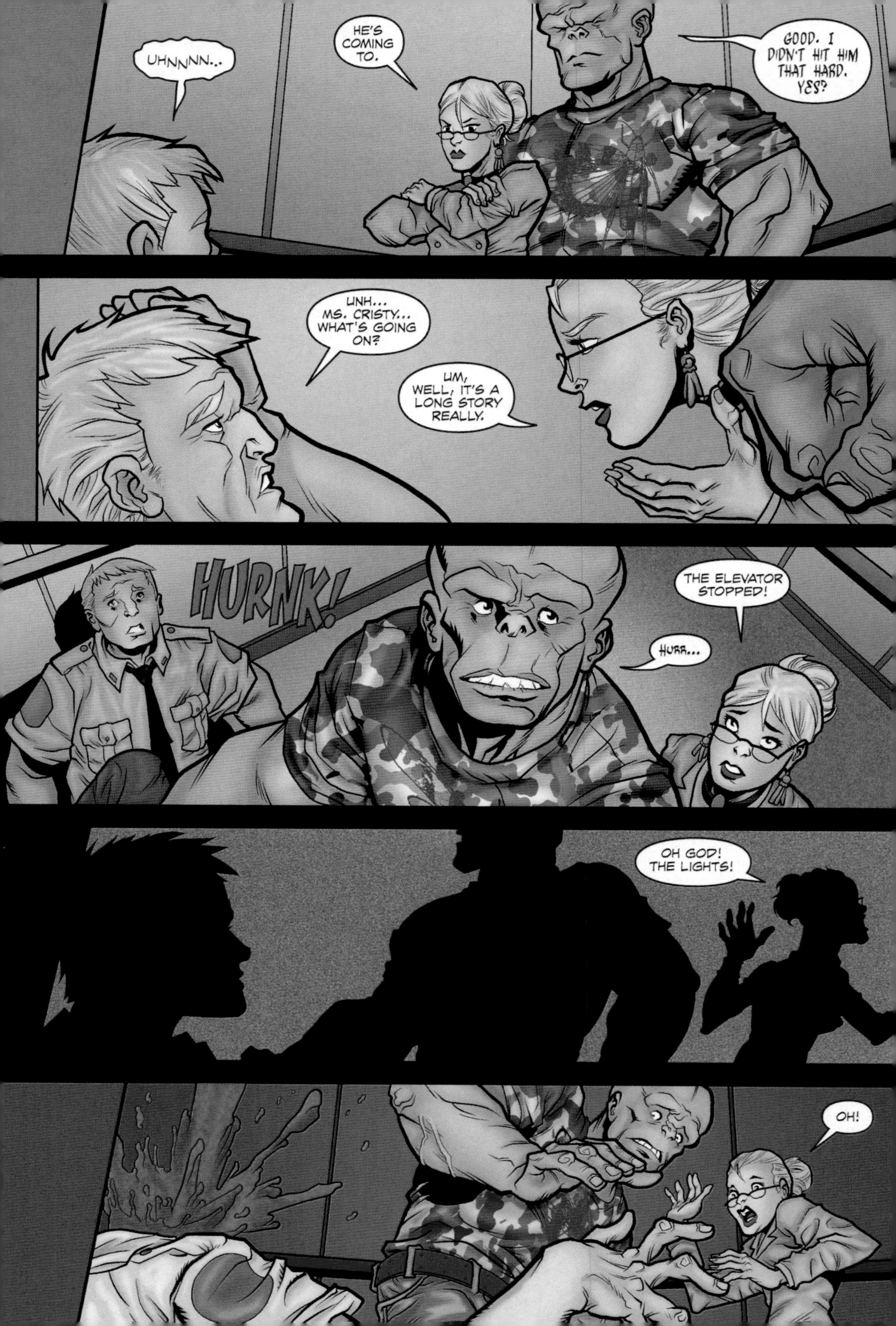
UHNNNN..
HE'S COMING TO.
GOOD. I DIDN'T HIT HIM THAT HARD. YES?
UNH... MS. CRISTY... WHAT'S GOING ON?
UM, WELL, IT'S A LONG STORY REALLY.
HURNK!
THE ELEVATOR STOPPED!
HURR...
OH GOD! THE LIGHTS!
OH!

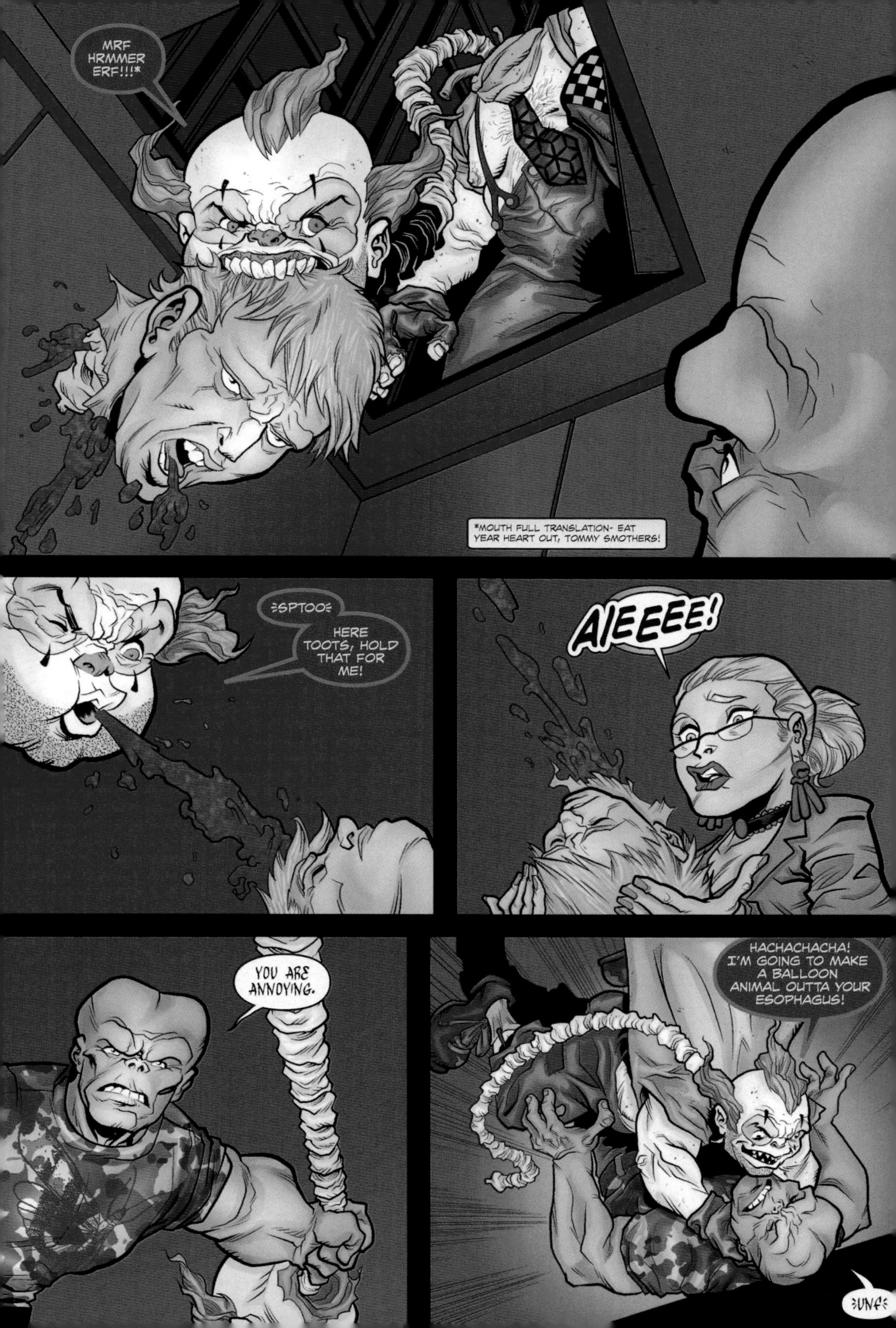
MRF HRMMER ERF!!!*
*MOUTH FULL TRANSLATION- EAT YEAR HEART OUT, TOMMY SMOTHERS!
SPTOO
HERE TOOTS, HOLD THAT FOR ME!
AIEEEE!
YOU ARE ANNOYING.
HACHACHACHA! I'M GOING TO MAKE A BALLOON ANIMAL OUTTA YOUR ESOPHAGUS!
UNF

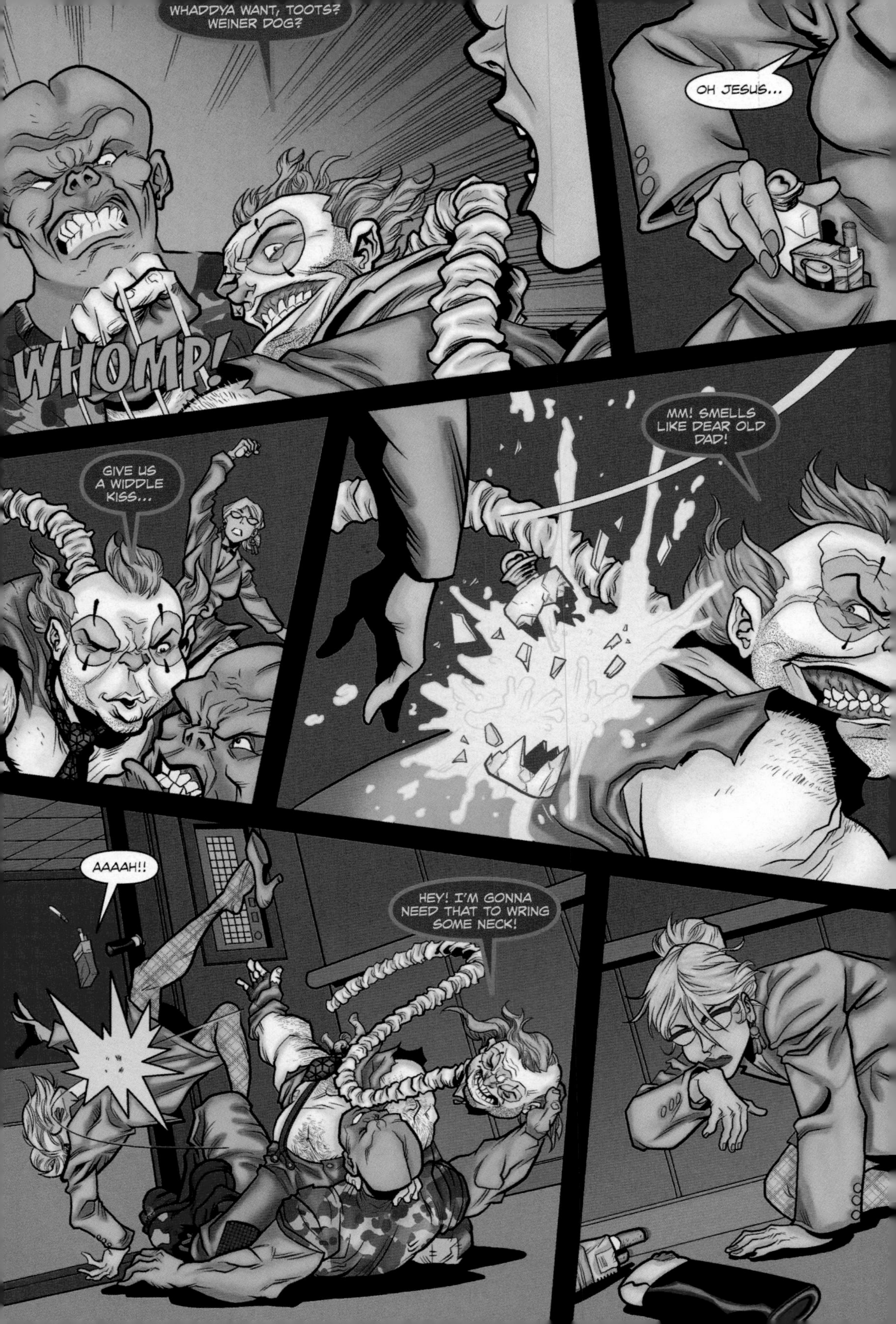
WHADDYA WANT, TOOTS? WEINER DOG?
WHOMP!
OH JESUS...
GIVE US A WIDDLE KISS...
MM! SMELLS LIKE DEAR OLD DAD!
AAAAH!!
HEY! I'M GONNA NEED THAT TO WRING SOME NECK!

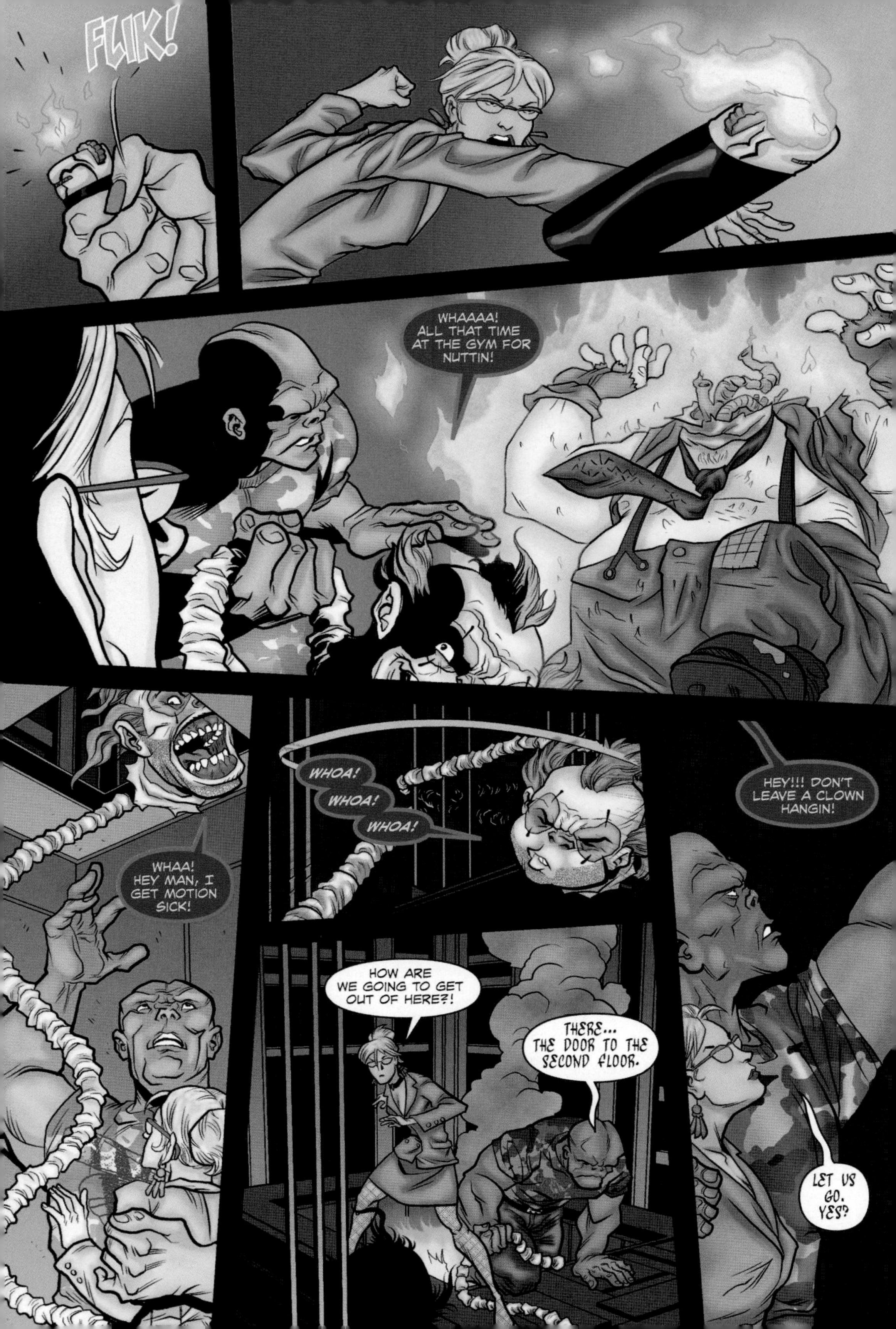
FLIK!
WHAAAA! ALL THAT TIME AT THE GYM FOR NUTTIN!
WHAA! HEY MAN, I GET MOTION SICK!
WHOA!
WHOA!
WHOA!
HEY!!! DON'T LEAVE A CLOWN HANGIN!
HOW ARE WE GOING TO GET OUT OF HERE?!
THERE... THE DOOR TO THE SECOND FLOOR.
LET US GO. YES?

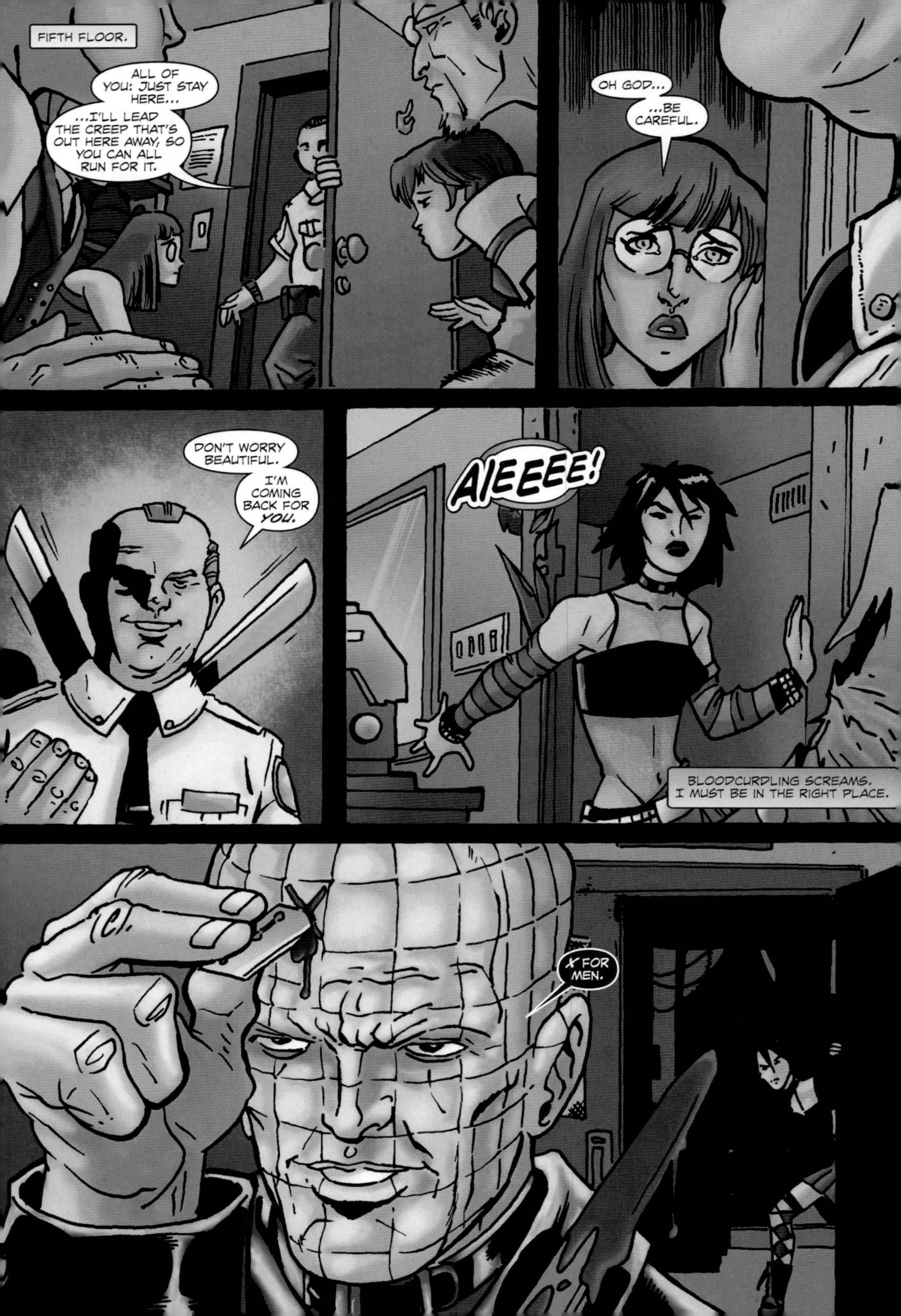
FIFTH FLOOR.
ALL OF YOU: JUST STAY HERE...
...I'LL LEAD THE CREEP THAT'S OUT HERE AWAY, SO YOU CAN ALL RUN FOR IT.
OH GOD...
...BE CAREFUL.
DON'T WORRY BEAUTIFUL.
I'M COMING BACK FOR YOU.
AIEEEE!
BLOODCURDLING SCREAMS. I MUST BE IN THE RIGHT PLACE.
X FOR MEN.

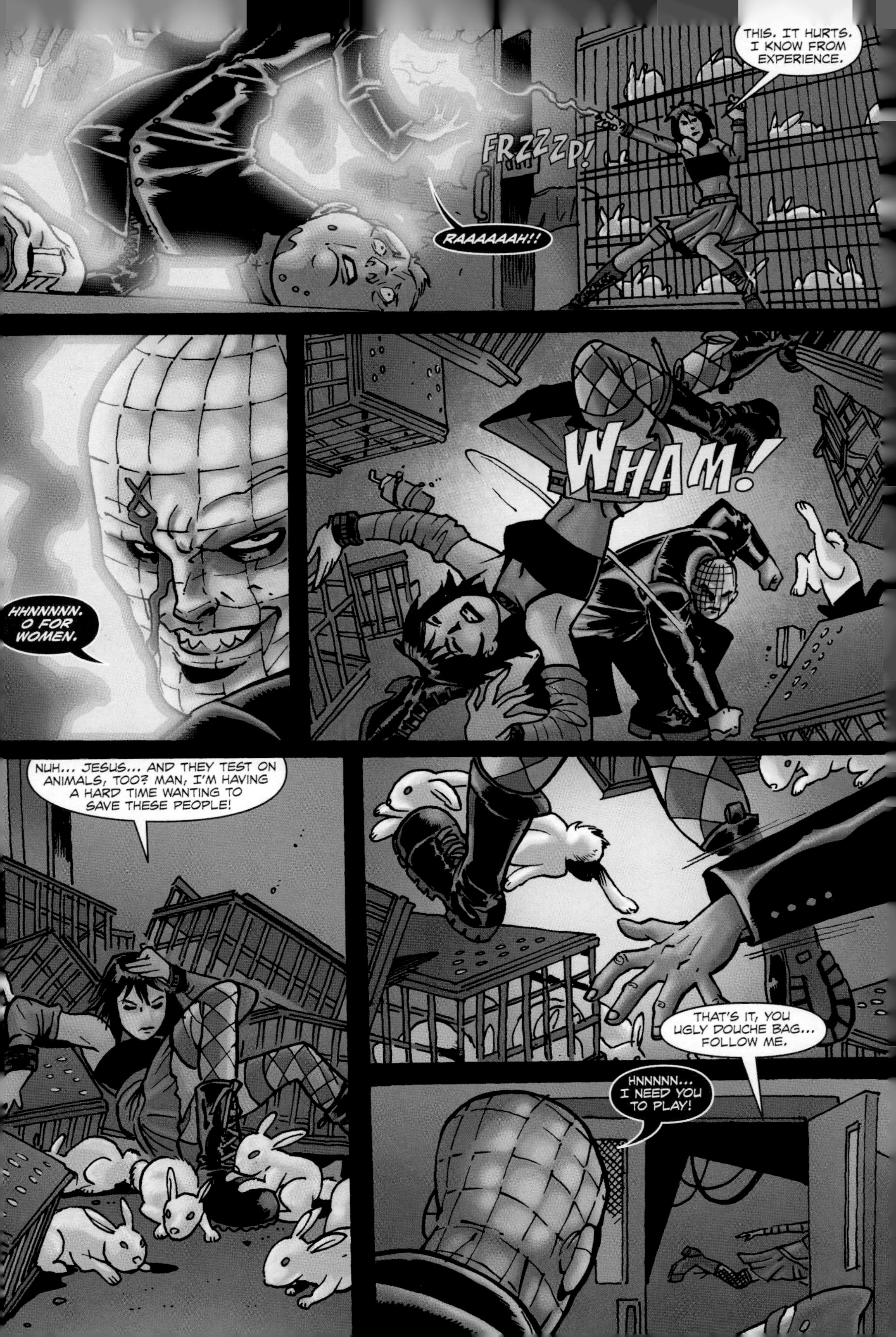
THIS. IT HURTS. I KNOW FROM EXPERIENCE.
FRZZZP!
RAAAAAAH!!
HHNNNNN. O FOR WOMEN.
WHAM!
NUH... JESUS... AND THEY TEST ON ANIMALS, TOO? MAN, I'M HAVING A HARD TIME WANTING TO SAVE THESE PEOPLE!
THAT'S IT, YOU UGLY DOUCHE BAG... FOLLOW ME.
HNNNNN... I NEED YOU TO PLAY!

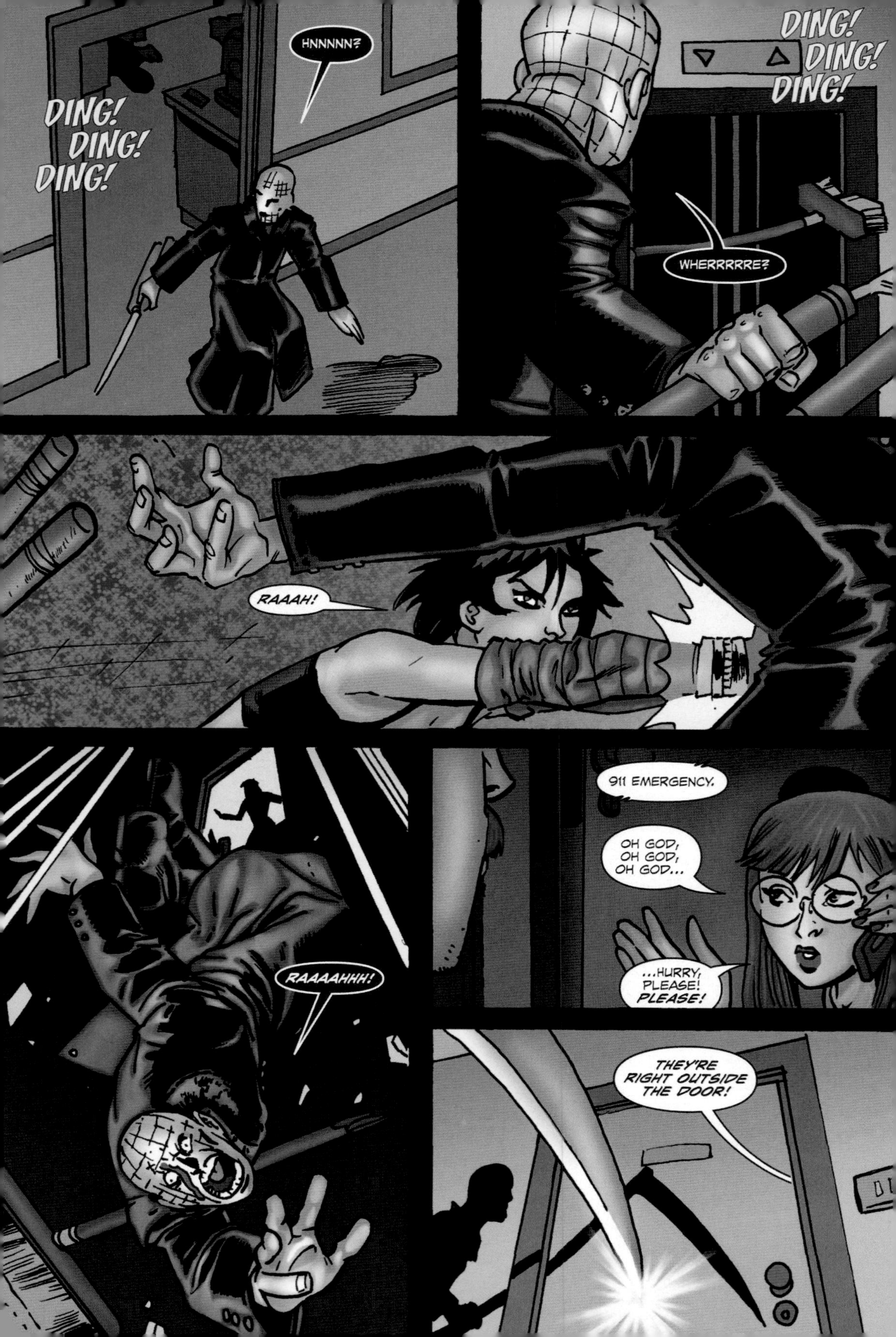
HNNNNN?
DING! DING! DING!
DING! DING! DING!
WHERRRRRE?
RAAAH!
RAAAAHHH!
911 EMERGENCY.
OH GOD, OH GOD, OH GOD...
...HURRY, PLEASE! PLEASE!
THEY'RE RIGHT OUTSIDE THE DOOR!

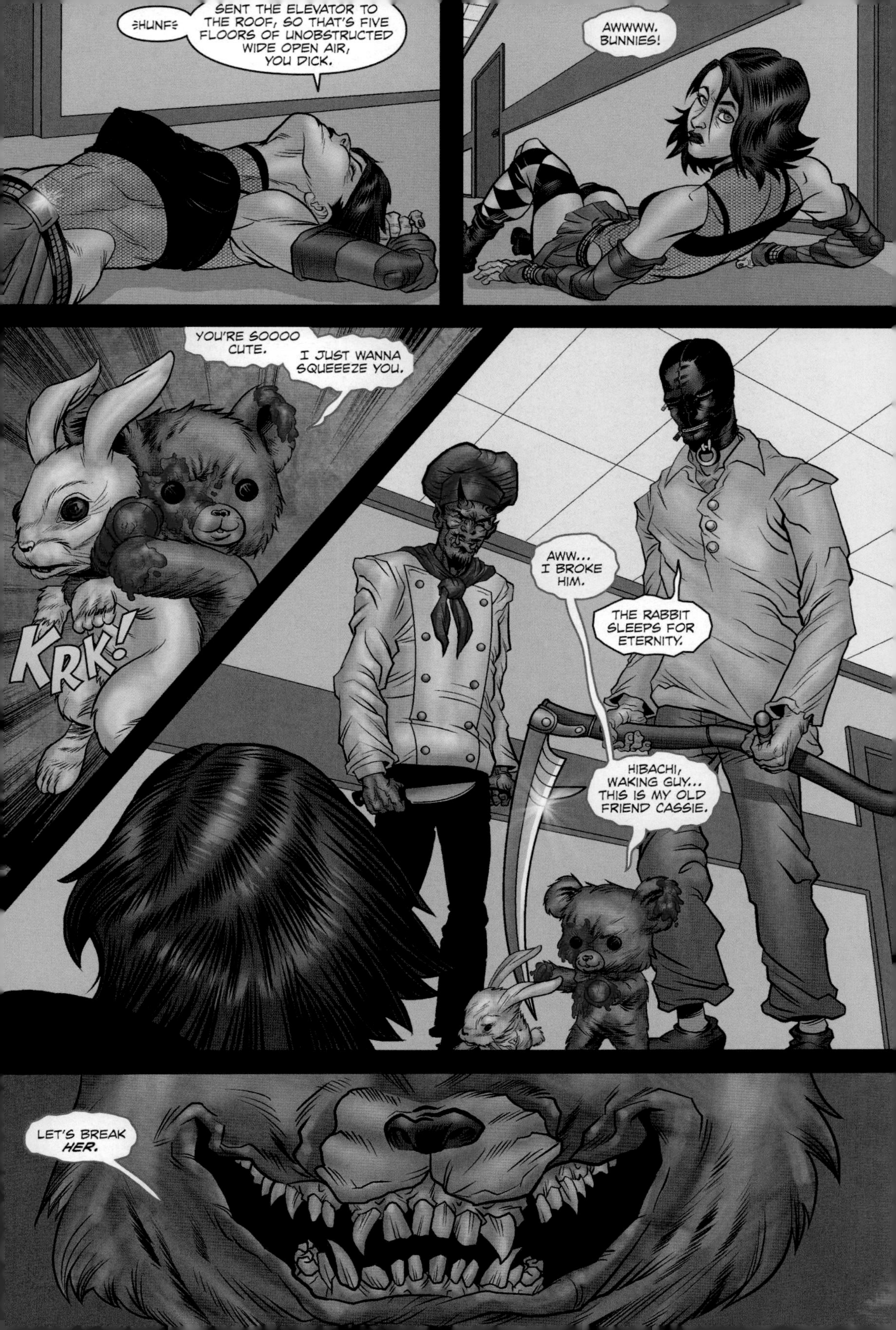

=HUNF=
SENT THE ELEVATOR TO THE ROOF, SO THAT'S FIVE FLOORS OF UNOBSTRUCTED WIDE OPEN AIR, YOU DICK.
AWWWW. BUNNIES!
YOU'RE SOOOO CUTE.
I JUST WANNA SQUEEEZE YOU.
KRK!
AWW... I BROKE HIM.
THE RABBIT SLEEPS FOR ETERNITY.
HIBACHI, WAKING GUY... THIS IS MY OLD FRIEND CASSIE.
LET'S BREAK *HER.*

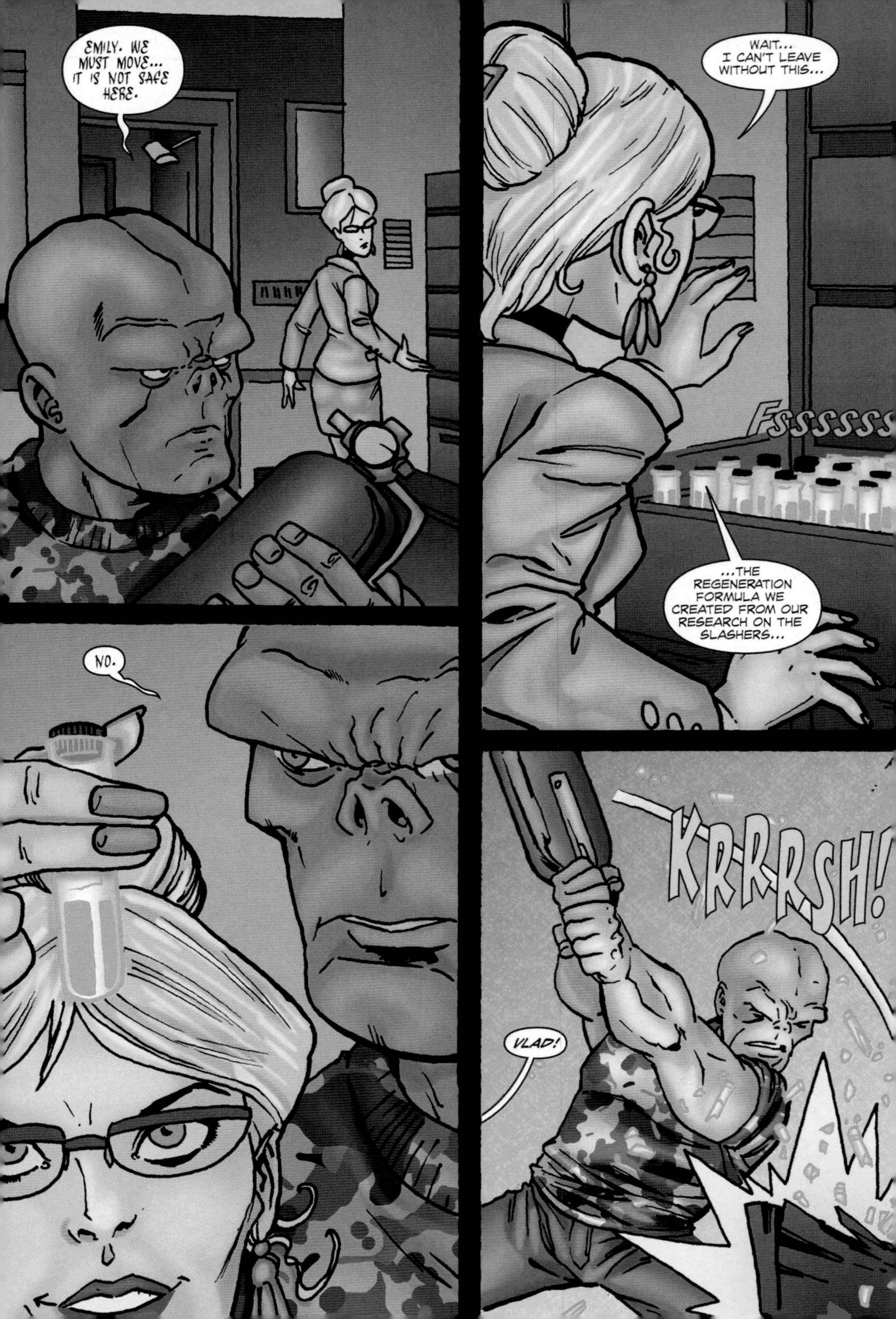
EMILY. WE MUST MOVE... IT IS NOT SAFE HERE.
WAIT... I CAN'T LEAVE WITHOUT THIS...
FSSSSSS
...THE REGENERATION FORMULA WE CREATED FROM OUR RESEARCH ON THE SLASHERS...
NO.
KRRRSH!
VLAD!

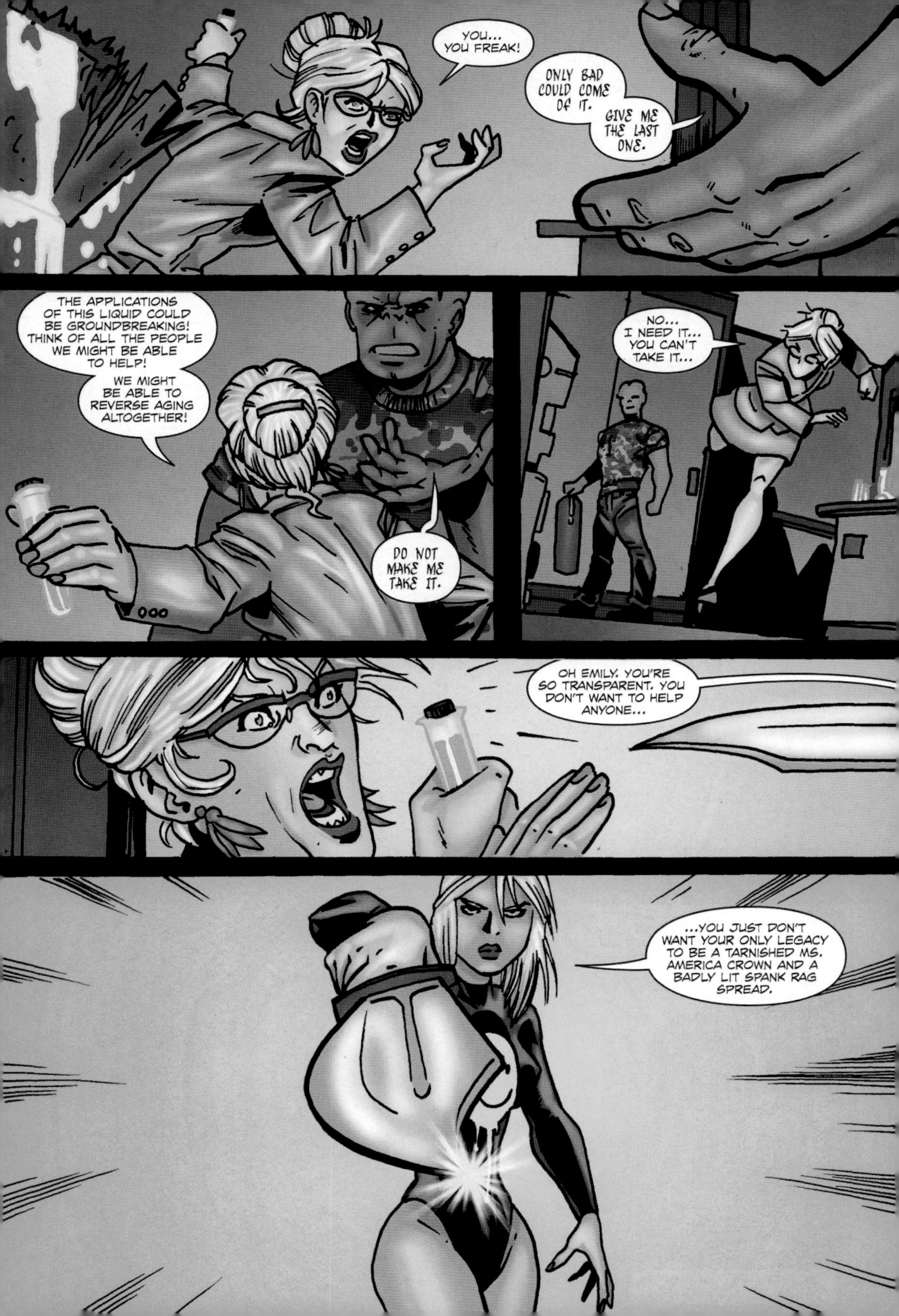

YOU... YOU FREAK!
ONLY BAD COULD COME OF IT.
GIVE ME THE LAST ONE.
THE APPLICATIONS OF THIS LIQUID COULD BE GROUNDBREAKING! THINK OF ALL THE PEOPLE WE MIGHT BE ABLE TO HELP!
WE MIGHT BE ABLE TO REVERSE AGING ALTOGETHER!
DO NOT MAKE ME TAKE IT.
NO... I NEED IT... YOU CAN'T TAKE IT...
OH EMILY. YOU'RE SO TRANSPARENT. YOU DON'T WANT TO HELP ANYONE...
...YOU JUST DON'T WANT YOUR ONLY LEGACY TO BE A TARNISHED MS. AMERICA CROWN AND A BADLY LIT SPANK RAG SPREAD.

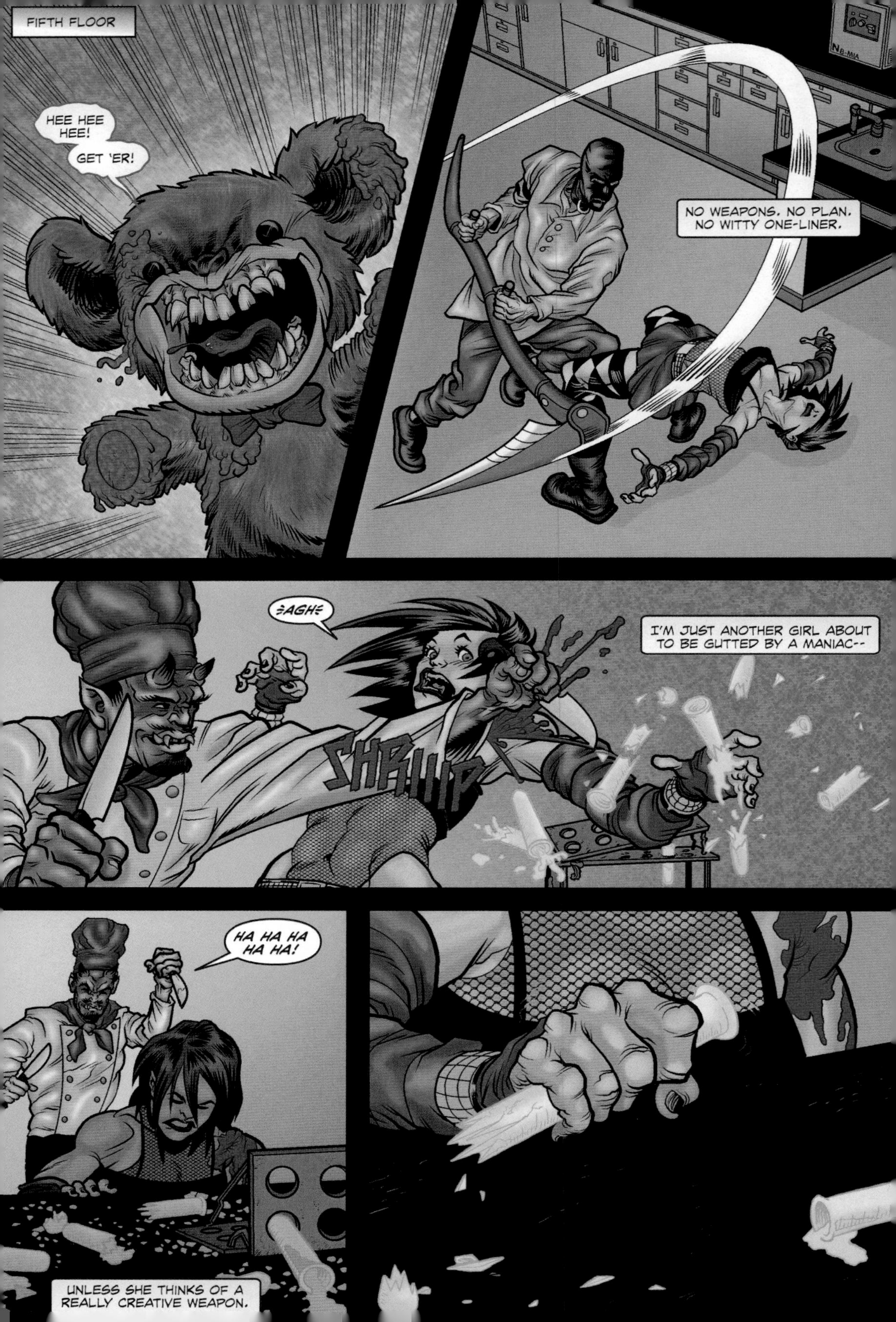
FIFTH FLOOR
HEE HEE HEE!
GET 'ER!
NO WEAPONS. NO PLAN. NO WITTY ONE-LINER.
AGH
I'M JUST ANOTHER GIRL ABOUT TO BE GUTTED BY A MANIAC--
SHRIIIP
HA HA HA HA HA!
UNLESS SHE THINKS OF A REALLY CREATIVE WEAPON.

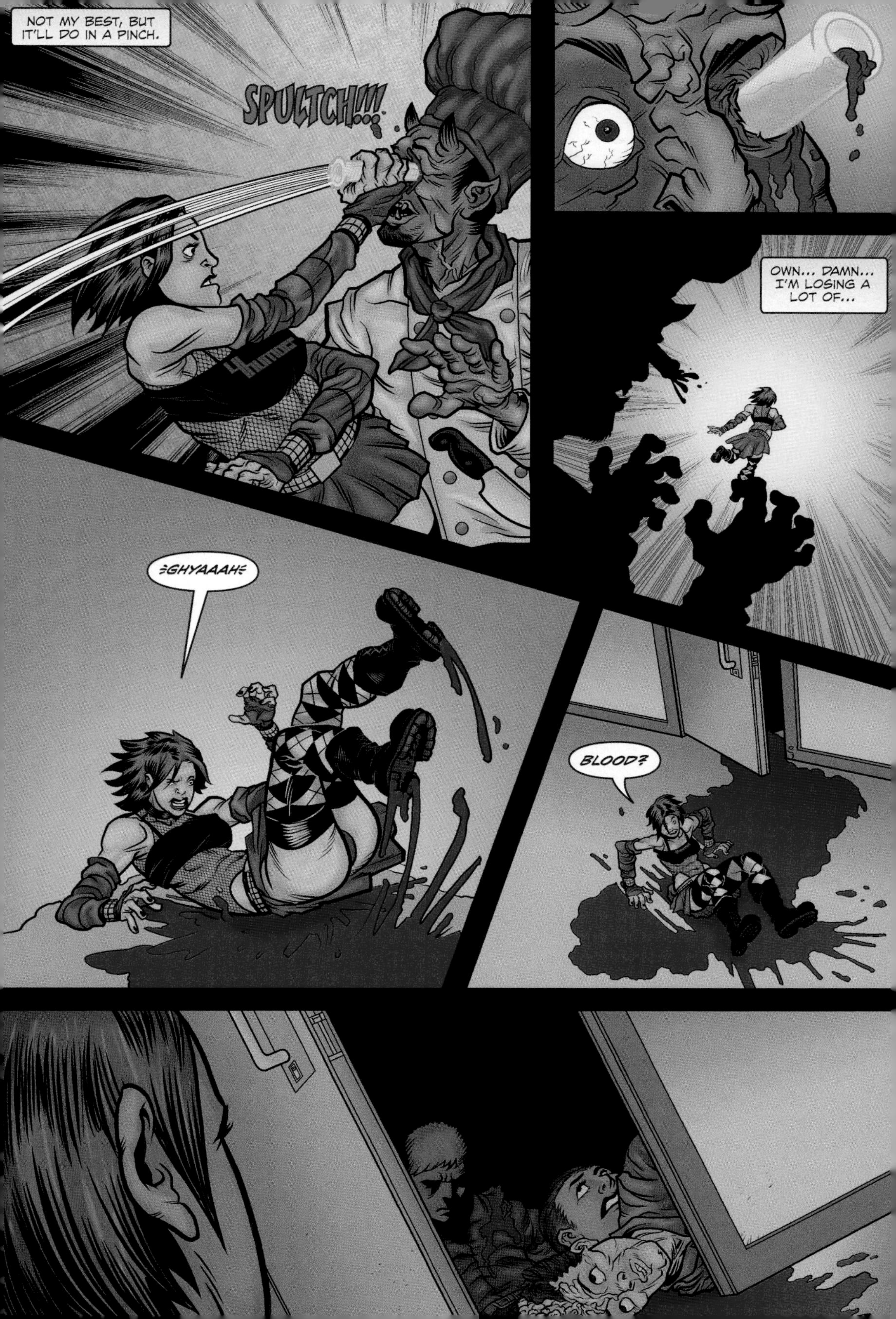
NOT MY BEST, BUT IT'LL DO IN A PINCH.
SPULTCH!!!
OWN... DAMN... I'M LOSING A LOT OF...
GHYAAAH
BLOOD?

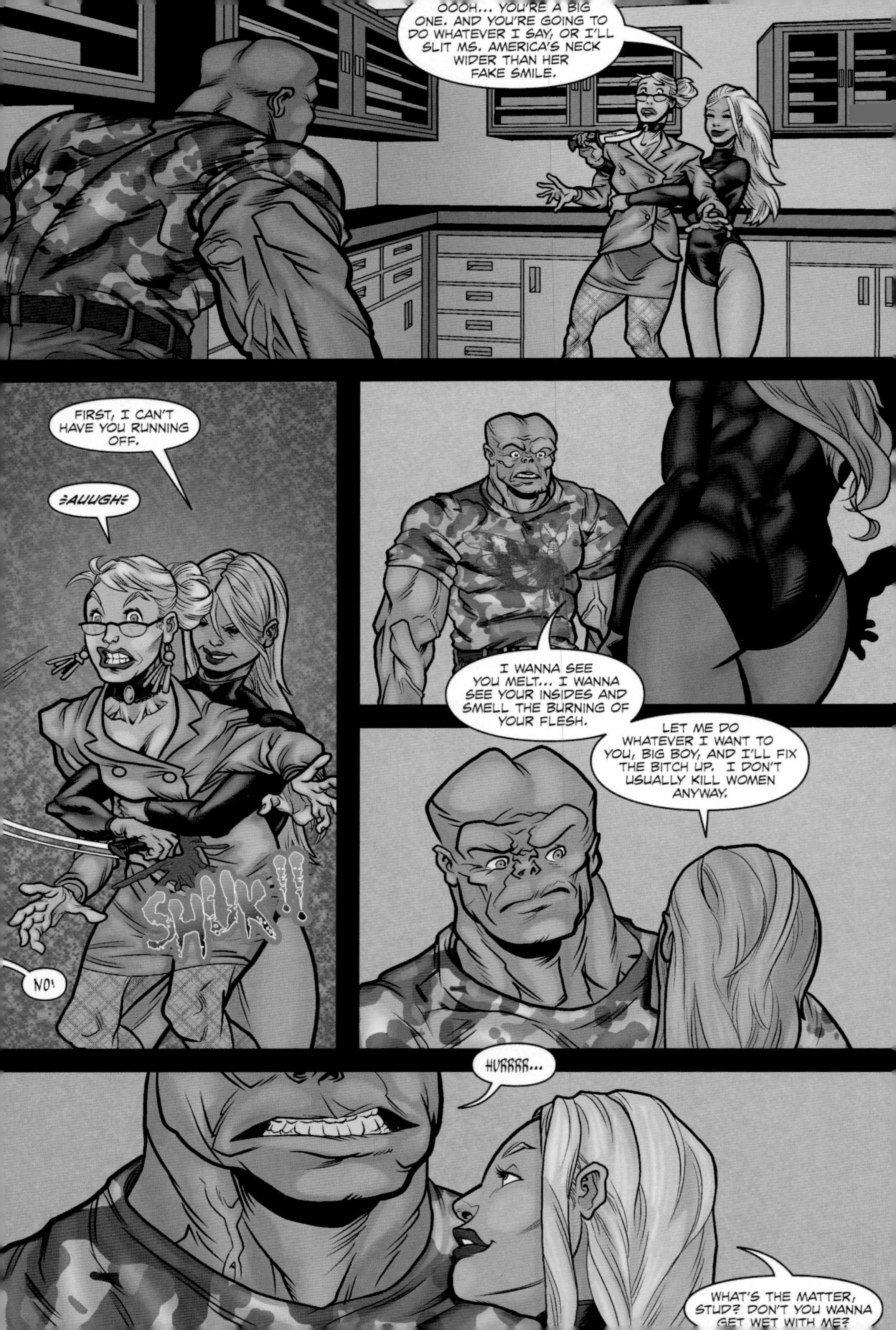
OOOH... YOU'RE A BIG ONE. AND YOU'RE GOING TO DO WHATEVER I SAY, OR I'LL SLIT MS. AMERICA'S NECK WIDER THAN HER FAKE SMILE.
FIRST, I CAN'T HAVE YOU RUNNING OFF.
AUUGH
SHUK!!
NO!
I WANNA SEE YOU MELT... I WANNA SEE YOUR INSIDES AND SMELL THE BURNING OF YOUR FLESH.
LET ME DO WHATEVER I WANT TO YOU, BIG BOY, AND I'LL FIX THE BITCH UP. I DON'T USUALLY KILL WOMEN ANYWAY.
HURRRR...
WHAT'S THE MATTER, STUD? DON'T YOU WANNA GET WET WITH ME?

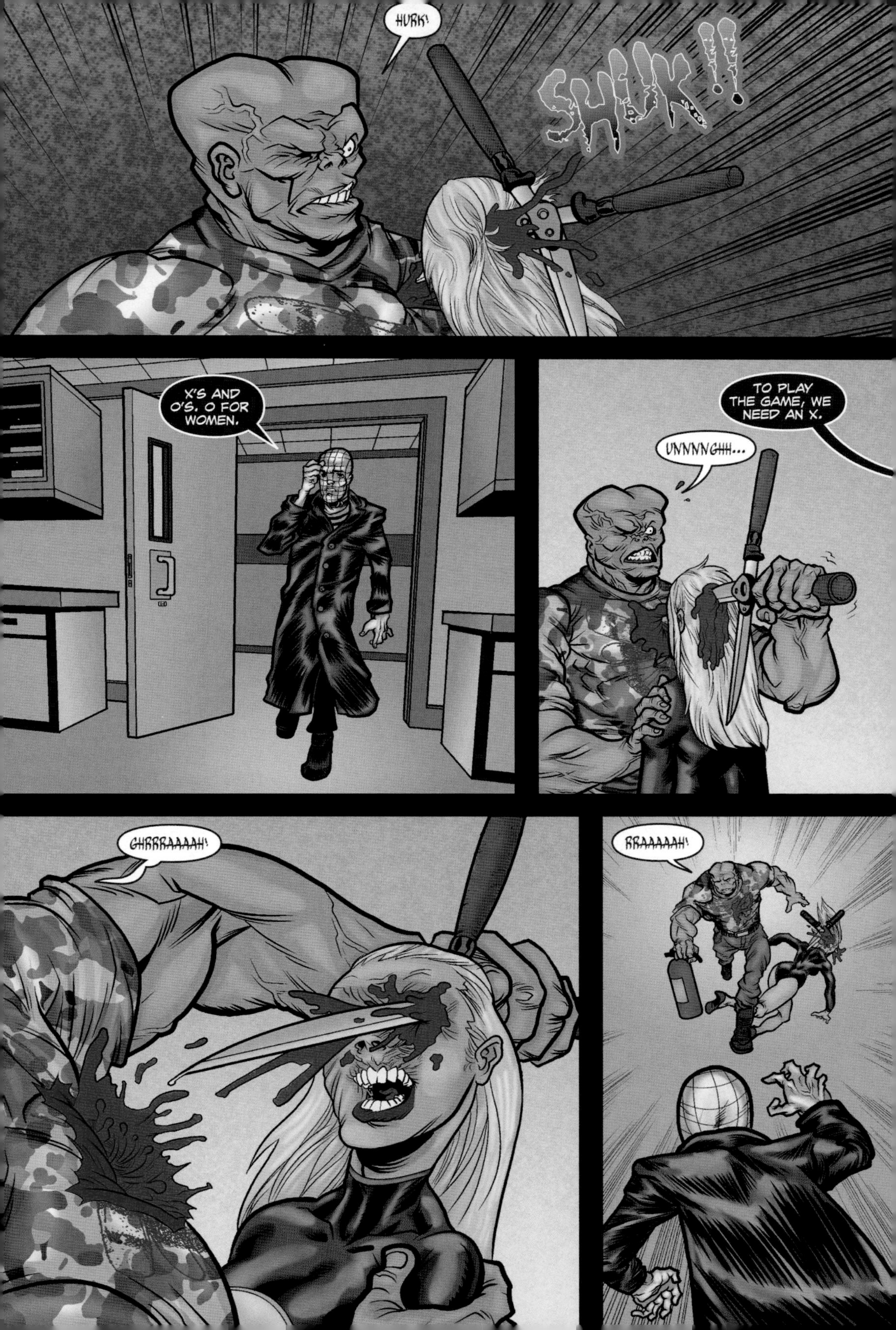
HURK!
SHUK!!
X'S AND O'S. O FOR WOMEN.
TO PLAY THE GAME, WE NEED AN X.
UNNNNGHH...
GHRRRAAAAAH!
RRAAAAAH!

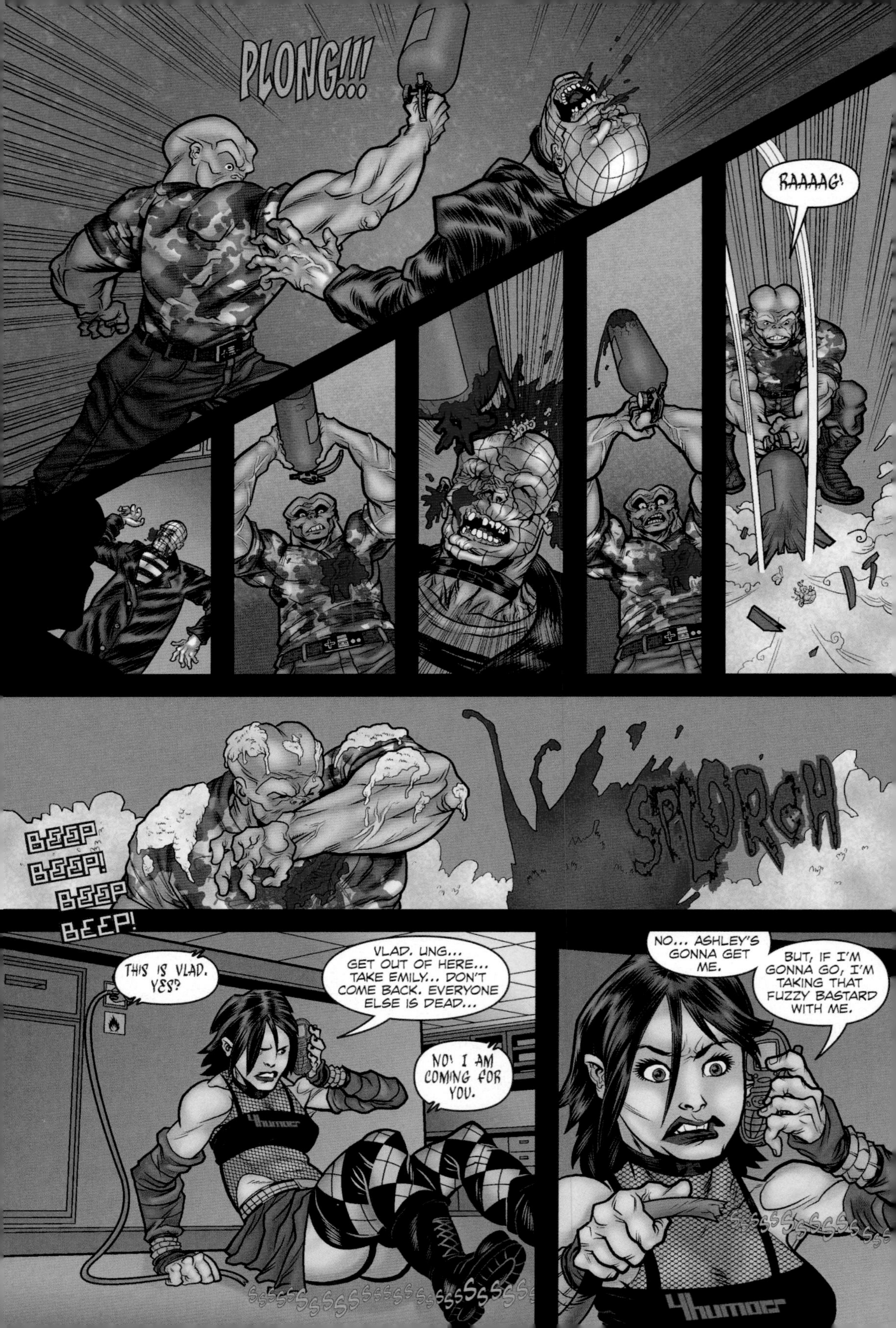
PLONG!!!
RAAAAG!
SPLORCH
BEEP
BEEP!
BEEP
BEEP!
THIS IS VLAD. YES?
VLAD. UNG... GET OUT OF HERE... TAKE EMILY... DON'T COME BACK. EVERYONE ELSE IS DEAD...
NO! I AM COMING FOR YOU.
NO... ASHLEY'S GONNA GET ME.
BUT, IF I'M GONNA GO, I'M TAKING THAT FUZZY BASTARD WITH ME.

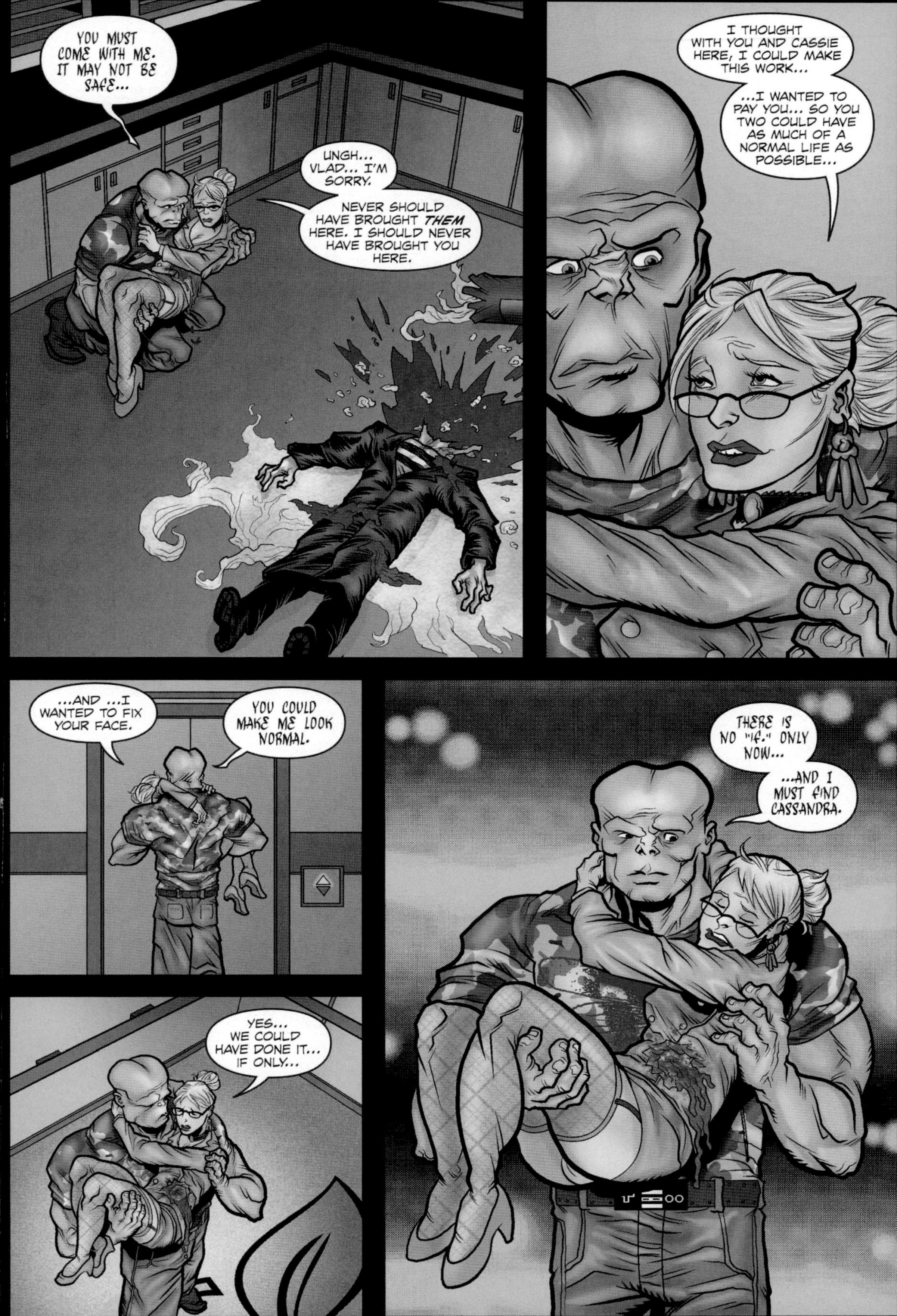
YOU MUST COME WITH ME. IT MAY NOT BE SAFE...
UNGH... VLAD... I'M SORRY.
NEVER SHOULD HAVE BROUGHT *THEM* HERE. I SHOULD NEVER HAVE BROUGHT YOU HERE.
I THOUGHT WITH YOU AND CASSIE HERE, I COULD MAKE THIS WORK...
...I WANTED TO PAY YOU... SO YOU TWO COULD HAVE AS MUCH OF A NORMAL LIFE AS POSSIBLE...
...AND ...I WANTED TO FIX YOUR FACE.
YOU COULD MAKE ME LOOK NORMAL.
YES... WE COULD HAVE DONE IT... IF ONLY...
THERE IS NO "IF." ONLY NOW...
...AND I MUST FIND CASSANDRA.

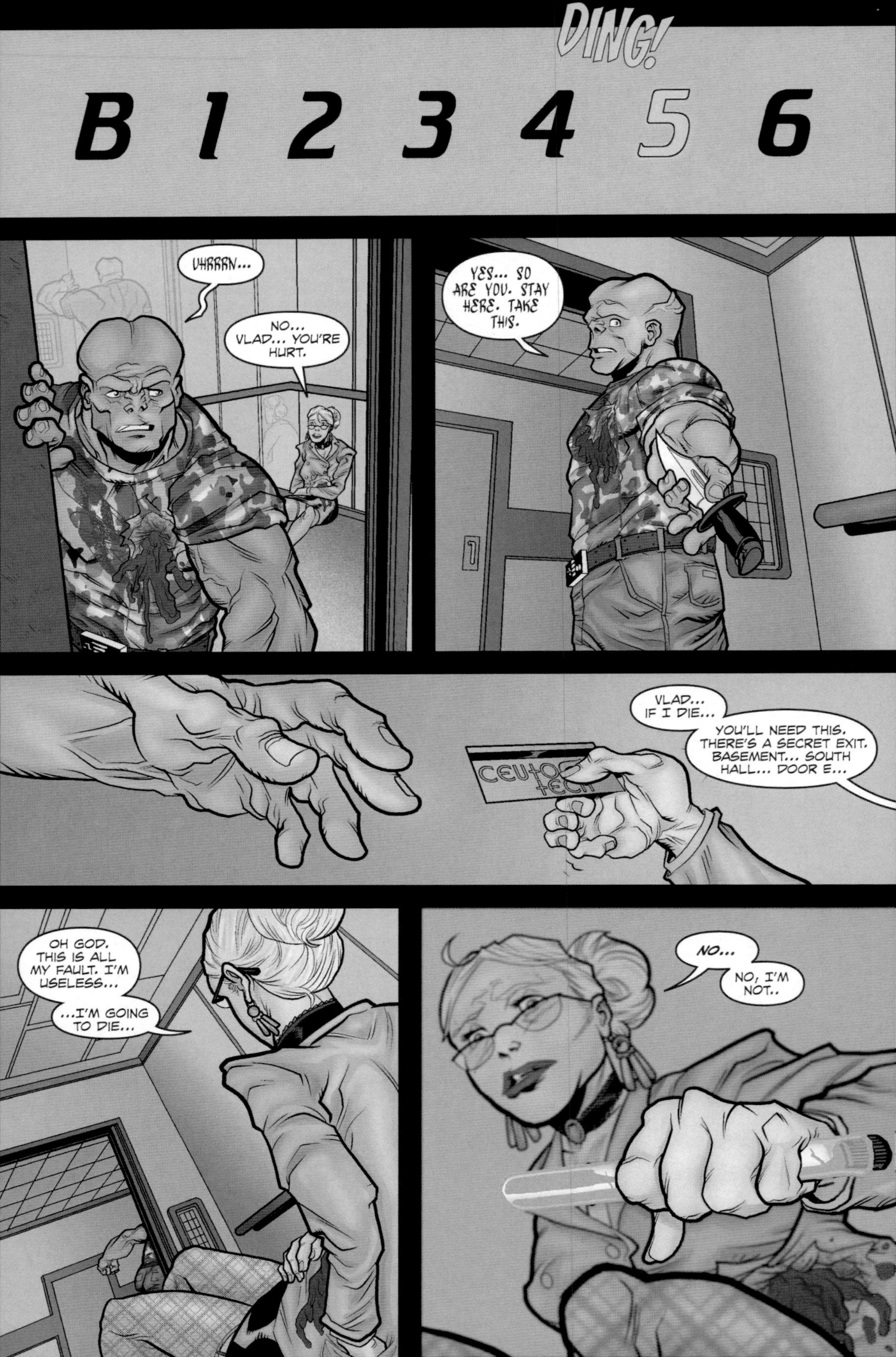
DING!
B 1 2 3 4 5 6
UHRRRN...
NO... VLAD... YOU'RE HURT.
YES... SO ARE YOU. STAY HERE. TAKE THIS.
VLAD... IF I DIE...
YOU'LL NEED THIS. THERE'S A SECRET EXIT. BASEMENT... SOUTH HALL... DOOR E...
OH GOD. THIS IS ALL MY FAULT. I'M USELESS...
...I'M GOING TO DIE...
NO...
NO, I'M NOT..

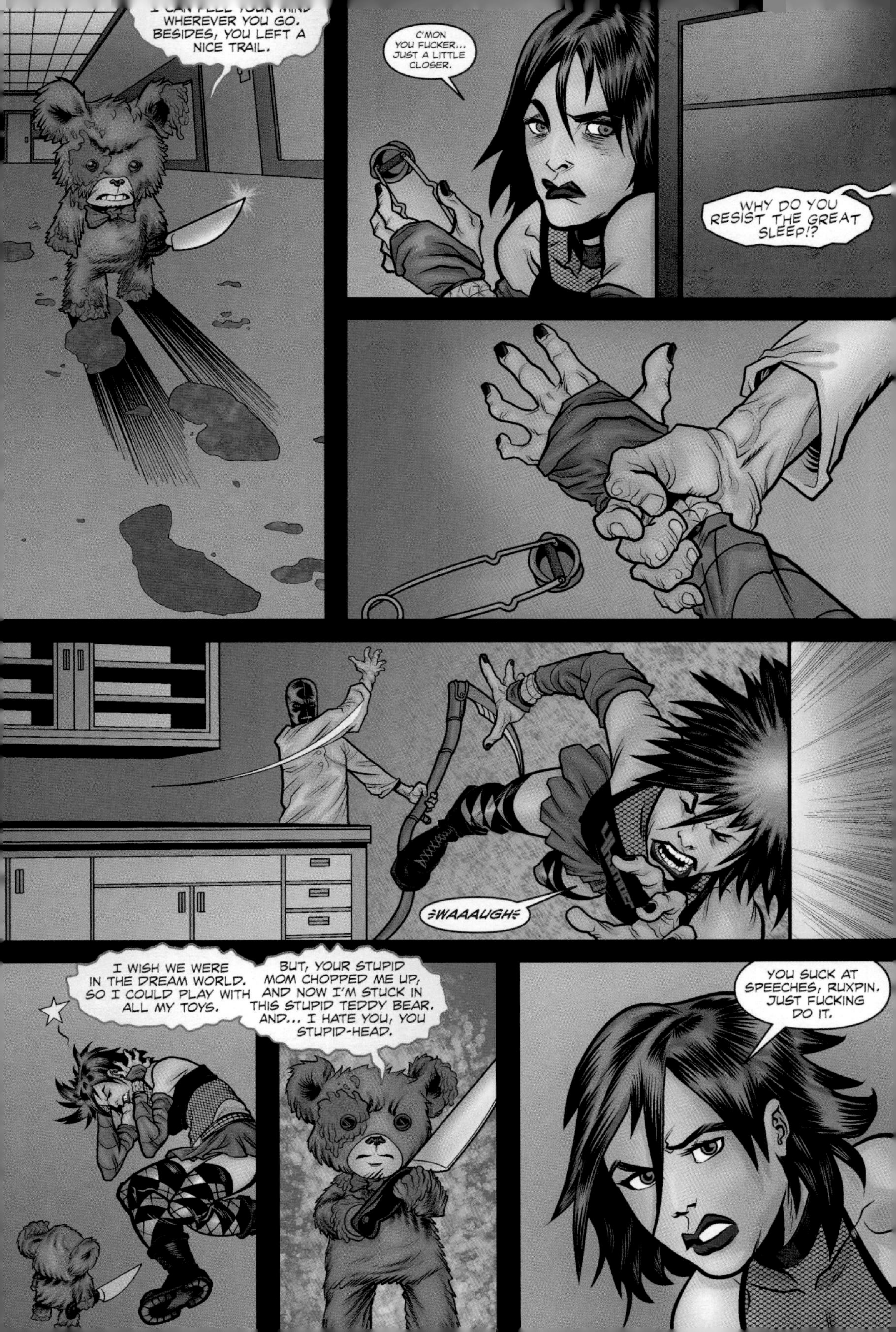

WHEREVER YOU GO. BESIDES, YOU LEFT A NICE TRAIL.
C'MON YOU FUCKER... JUST A LITTLE CLOSER.
WHY DO YOU RESIST THE GREAT SLEEP!?
WAAAUGH
I WISH WE WERE IN THE DREAM WORLD. SO I COULD PLAY WITH ALL MY TOYS.
BUT, YOUR STUPID MOM CHOPPED ME UP, AND NOW I'M STUCK IN THIS STUPID TEDDY BEAR. AND... I HATE YOU, YOU STUPID-HEAD.
YOU SUCK AT SPEECHES, RUXPIN. JUST FUCKING DO IT.

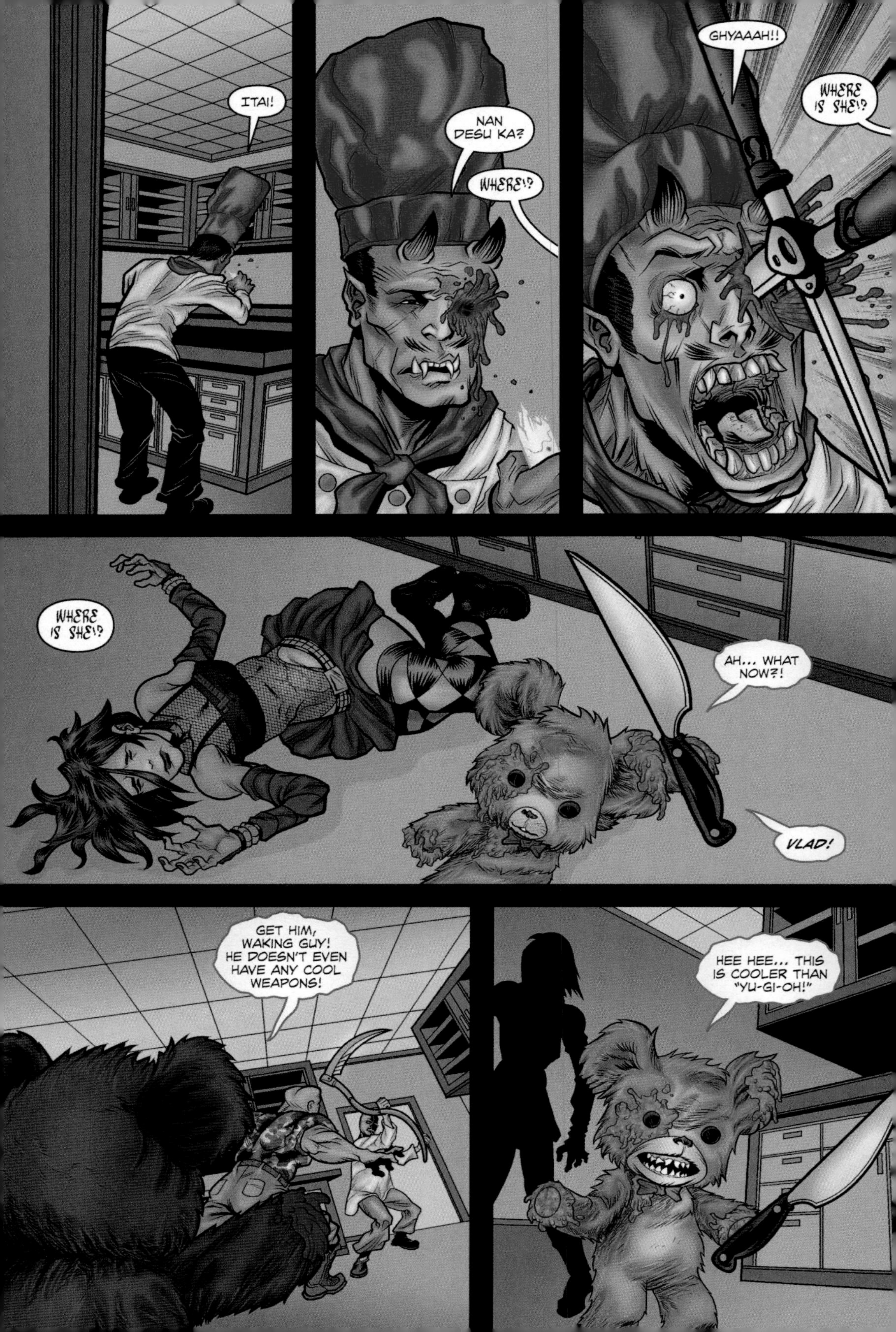
ITAI!
NAN DESU KA?
WHERE!?
GHYAAAH!!
WHERE IS SHE!?
WHERE IS SHE!?
AH... WHAT NOW?!
VLAD!
GET HIM, WAKING GUY! HE DOESN'T EVEN HAVE ANY COOL WEAPONS!
HEE HEE... THIS IS COOLER THAN "YU-GI-OH!"

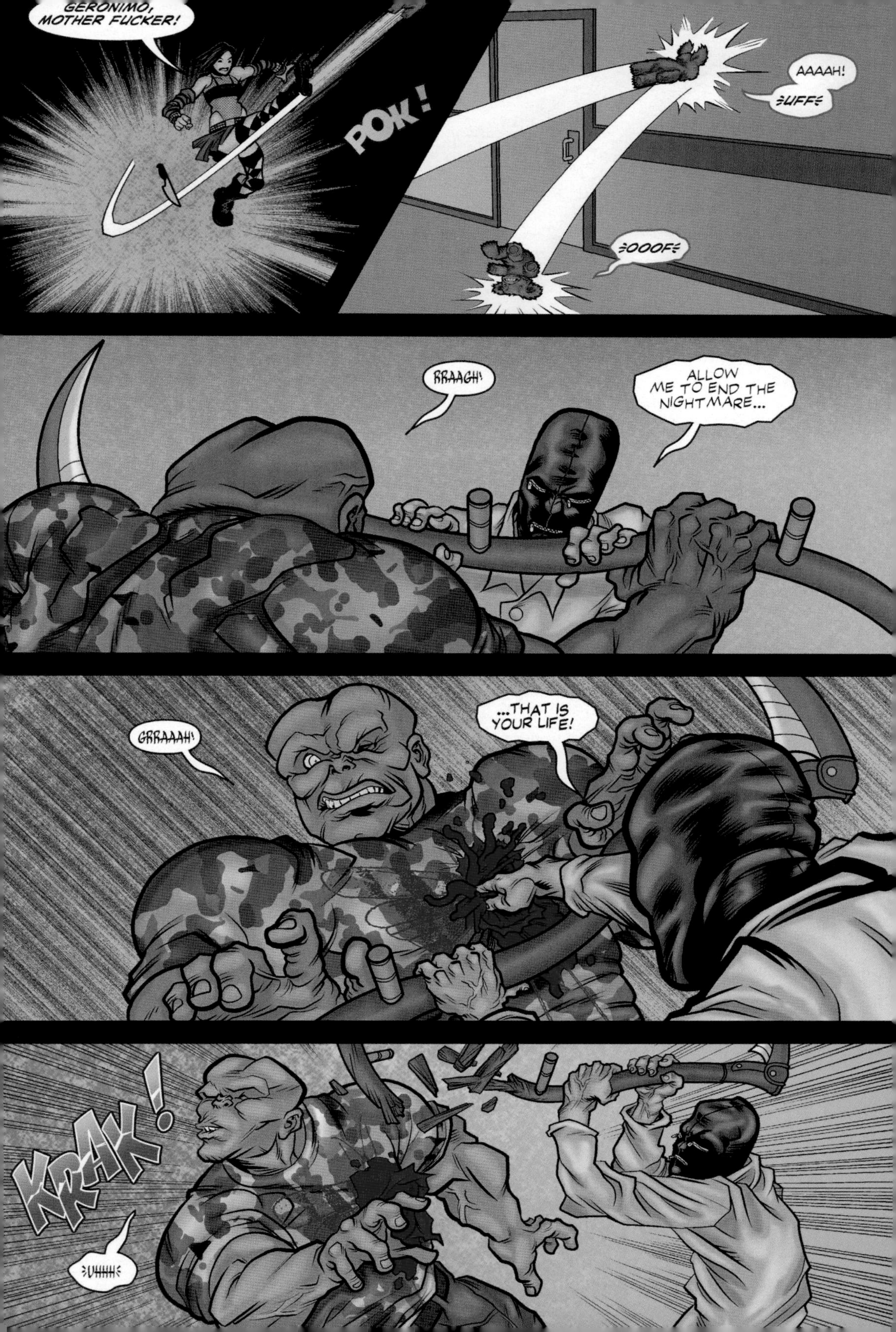

GERONIMO, MOTHER FUCKER!
POK!
AAAAH!
UFF
OOOF
BRAAGH!
ALLOW ME TO END THE NIGHTMARE...
GRRAAAAH!
...THAT IS YOUR LIFE!
KRAK!
UHHH

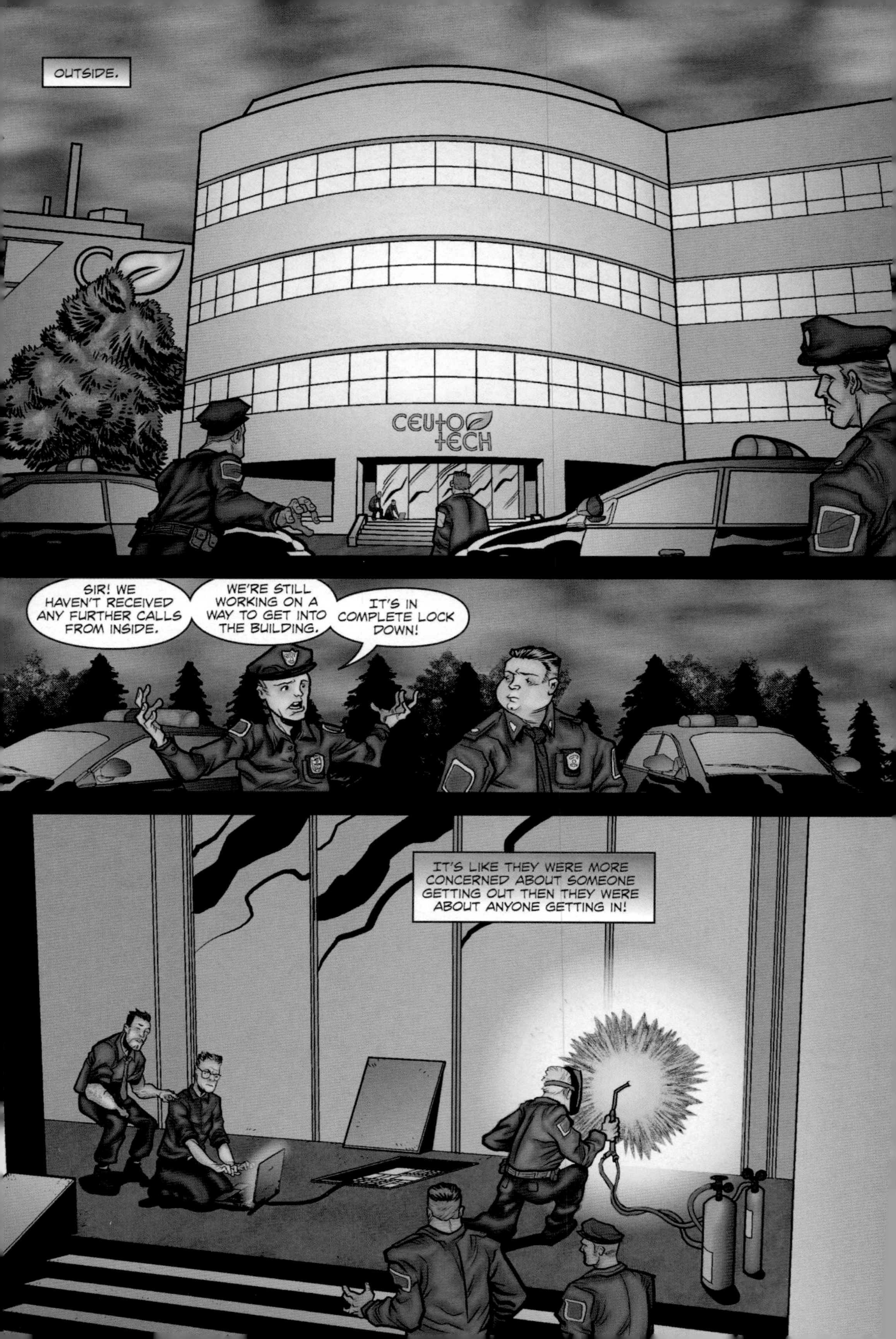

OUTSIDE.
CEUTO TECH
SIR! WE HAVEN'T RECEIVED ANY FURTHER CALLS FROM INSIDE.
WE'RE STILL WORKING ON A WAY TO GET INTO THE BUILDING.
IT'S IN COMPLETE LOCK DOWN!
IT'S LIKE THEY WERE MORE CONCERNED ABOUT SOMEONE GETTING OUT THEN THEY WERE ABOUT ANYONE GETTING IN!

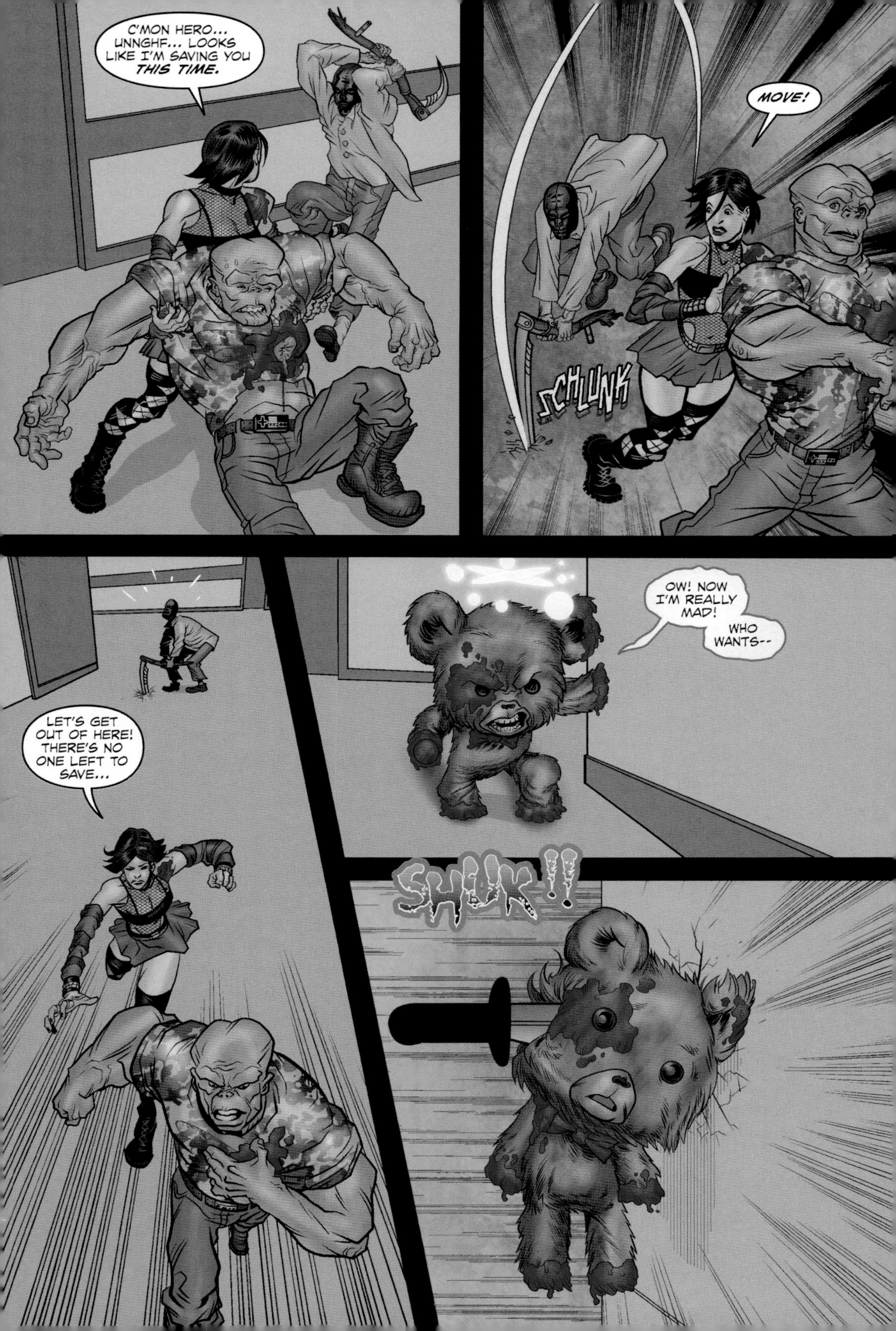
C'MON HERO... UNNGHF... LOOKS LIKE I'M SAVING YOU THIS TIME.
MOVE!
SCHLUNK
LET'S GET OUT OF HERE! THERE'S NO ONE LEFT TO SAVE...
OW! NOW I'M REALLY MAD!
WHO WANTS--
SHUK!!

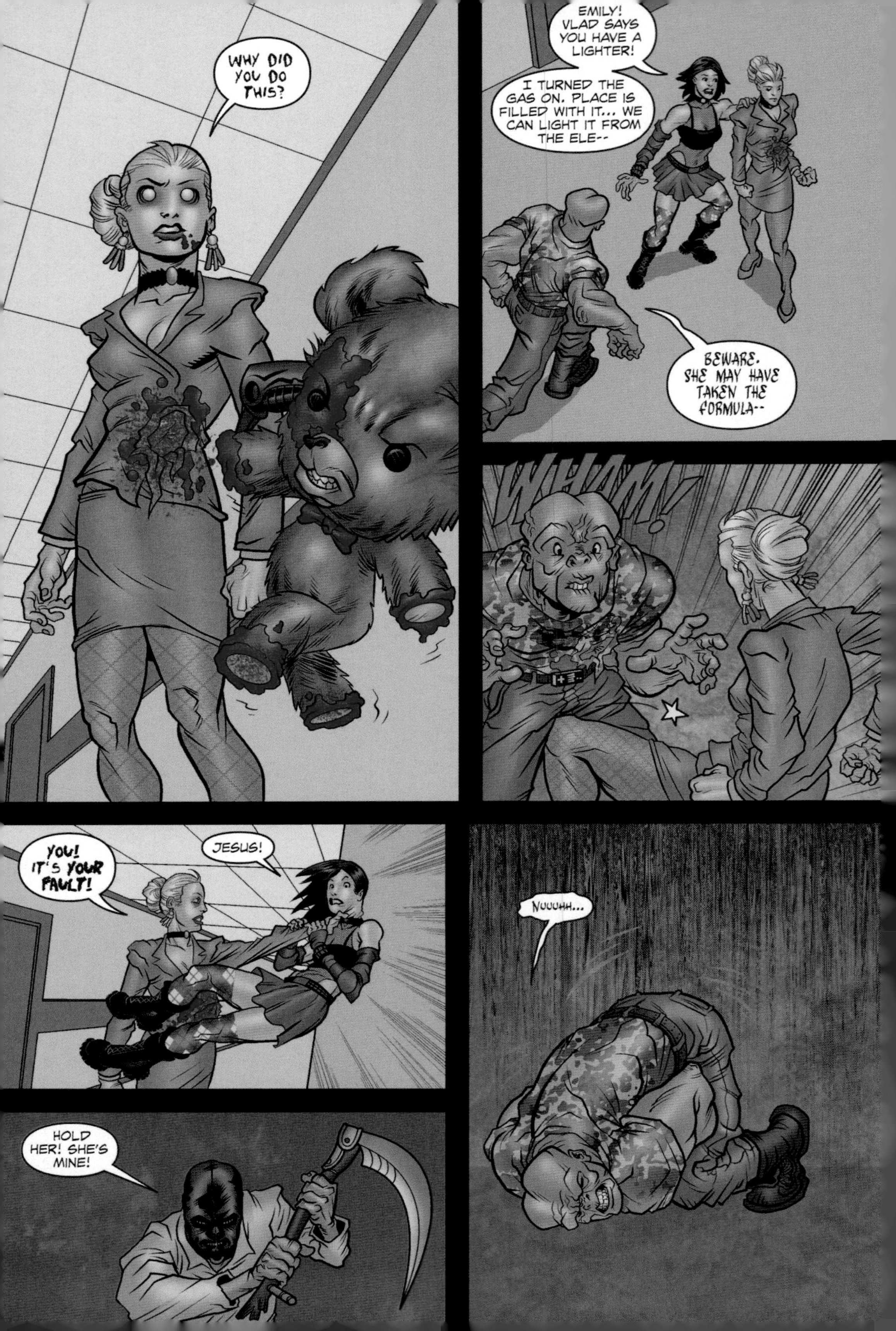
WHY DID YOU DO THIS?
EMILY! VLAD SAYS YOU HAVE A LIGHTER!
I TURNED THE GAS ON. PLACE IS FILLED WITH IT... WE CAN LIGHT IT FROM THE ELE--
BEWARE. SHE MAY HAVE TAKEN THE FORMULA--
WHAM!
YOU! IT'S YOUR FAULT!
JESUS!
HOLD HER! SHE'S MINE!
NUUUHH...

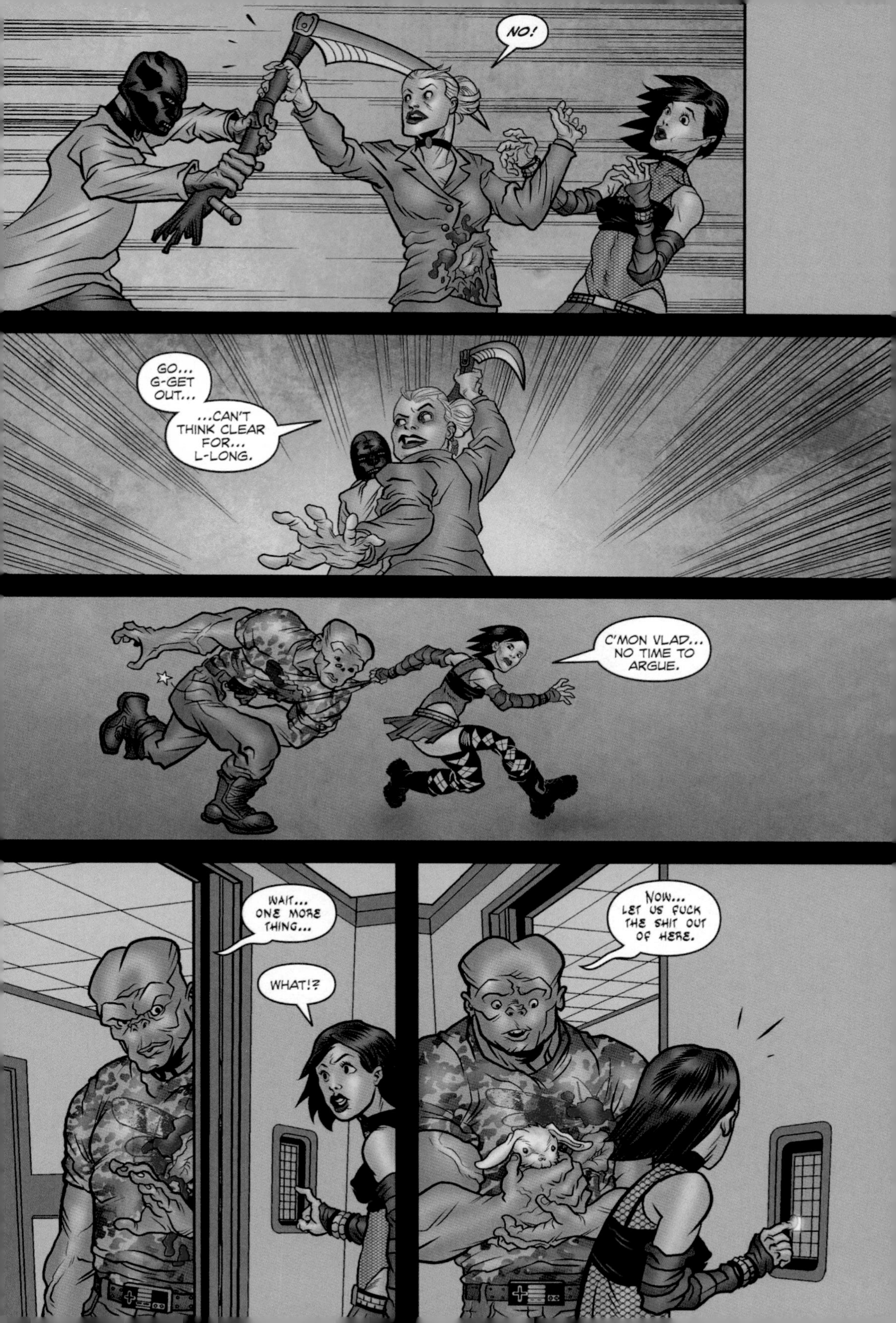
NO!
GO... G-GET OUT...
...CAN'T THINK CLEAR FOR... L-LONG.
C'MON VLAD... NO TIME TO ARGUE.
WAIT... ONE MORE THING...
WHAT!?
NOW... LET US FUCK THE SHIT OUT OF HERE.

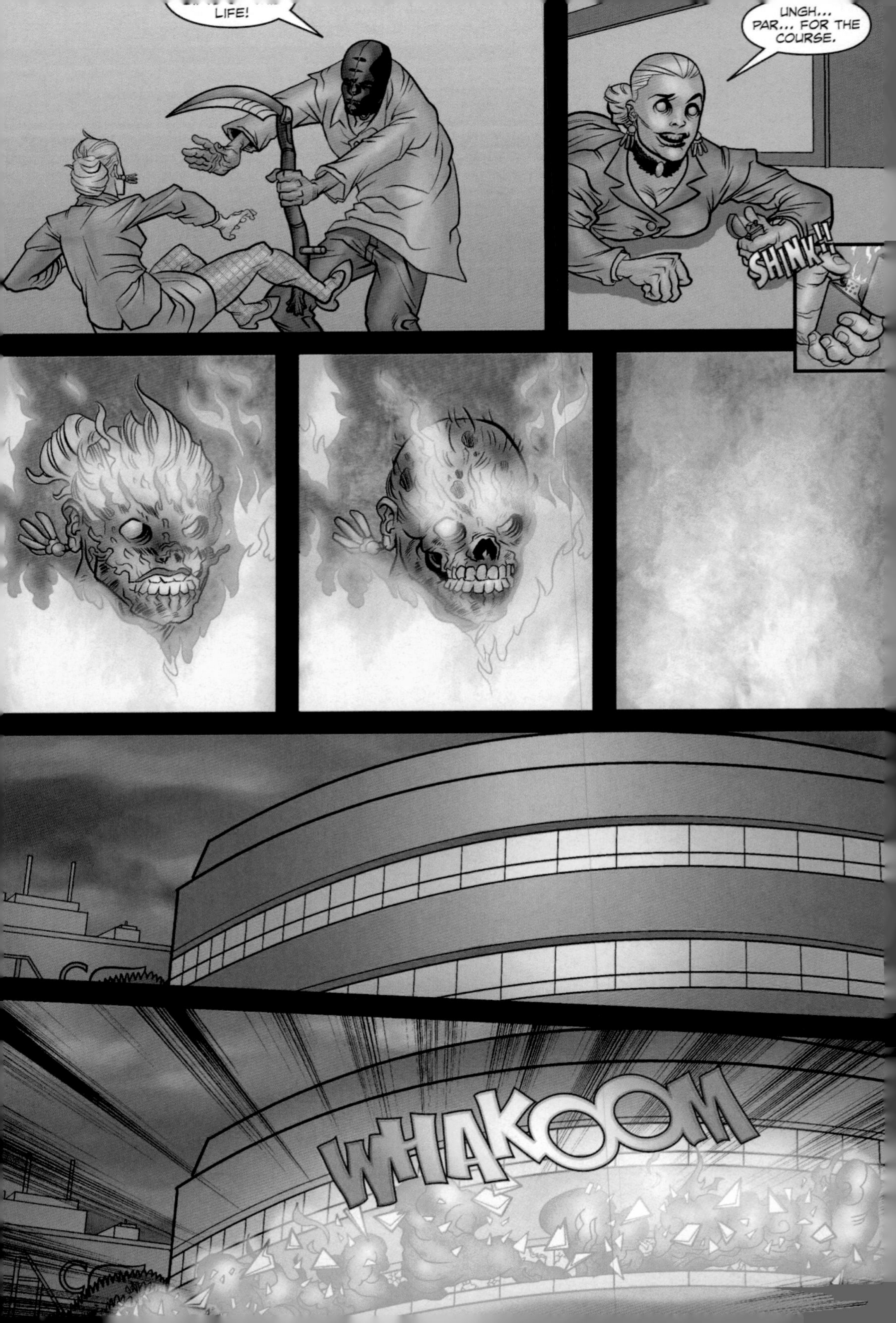
LIFE!
UNGH... PAR... FOR THE COURSE.
SHINK!!
WHAKOOM

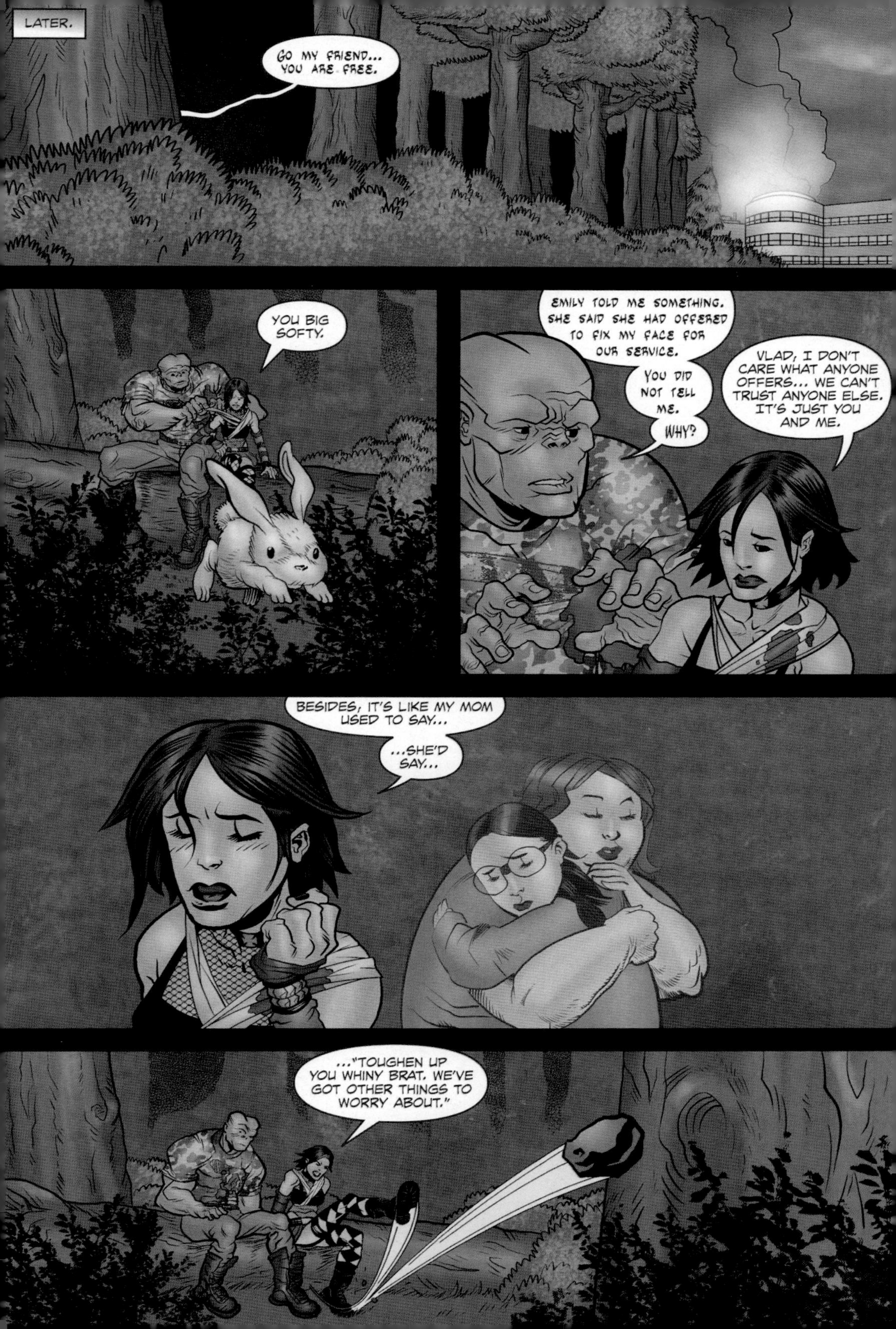
LATER.
GO MY FRIEND... YOU ARE FREE.
YOU BIG SOFTY.
EMILY TOLD ME SOMETHING. SHE SAID SHE HAD OFFERED TO FIX MY FACE FOR OUR SERVICE.
YOU DID NOT TELL ME.
WHY?
VLAD, I DON'T CARE WHAT ANYONE OFFERS... WE CAN'T TRUST ANYONE ELSE. IT'S JUST YOU AND ME.
BESIDES, IT'S LIKE MY MOM USED TO SAY...
...SHE'D SAY...
..."TOUGHEN UP YOU WHINY BRAT. WE'VE GOT OTHER THINGS TO WORRY ABOUT."

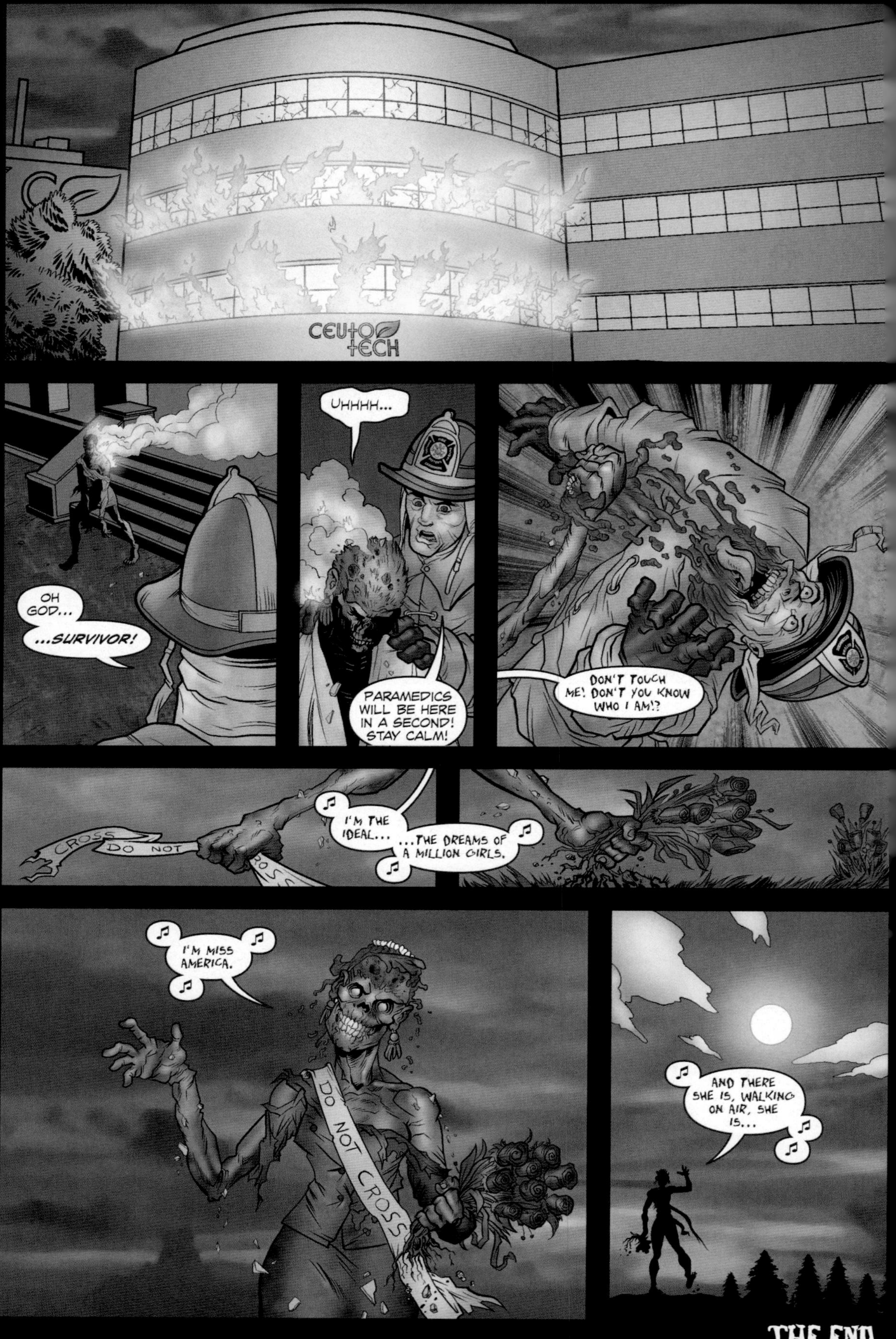
CEUTO TECH
UHHHH...
OH GOD... ...SURVIVOR!
PARAMEDICS WILL BE HERE IN A SECOND! STAY CALM!
DON'T TOUCH ME! DON'T YOU KNOW WHO I AM!?
CROSS DO NOT CROSS
♫ I'M THE IDEAL... ...THE DREAMS OF A MILLION GIRLS. ♫ ♫
♫ I'M MISS AMERICA. ♫ ♫
DO NOT CROSS
♫ AND THERE SHE IS, WALKING ON AIR, SHE IS... ♫ ♫

THE END.

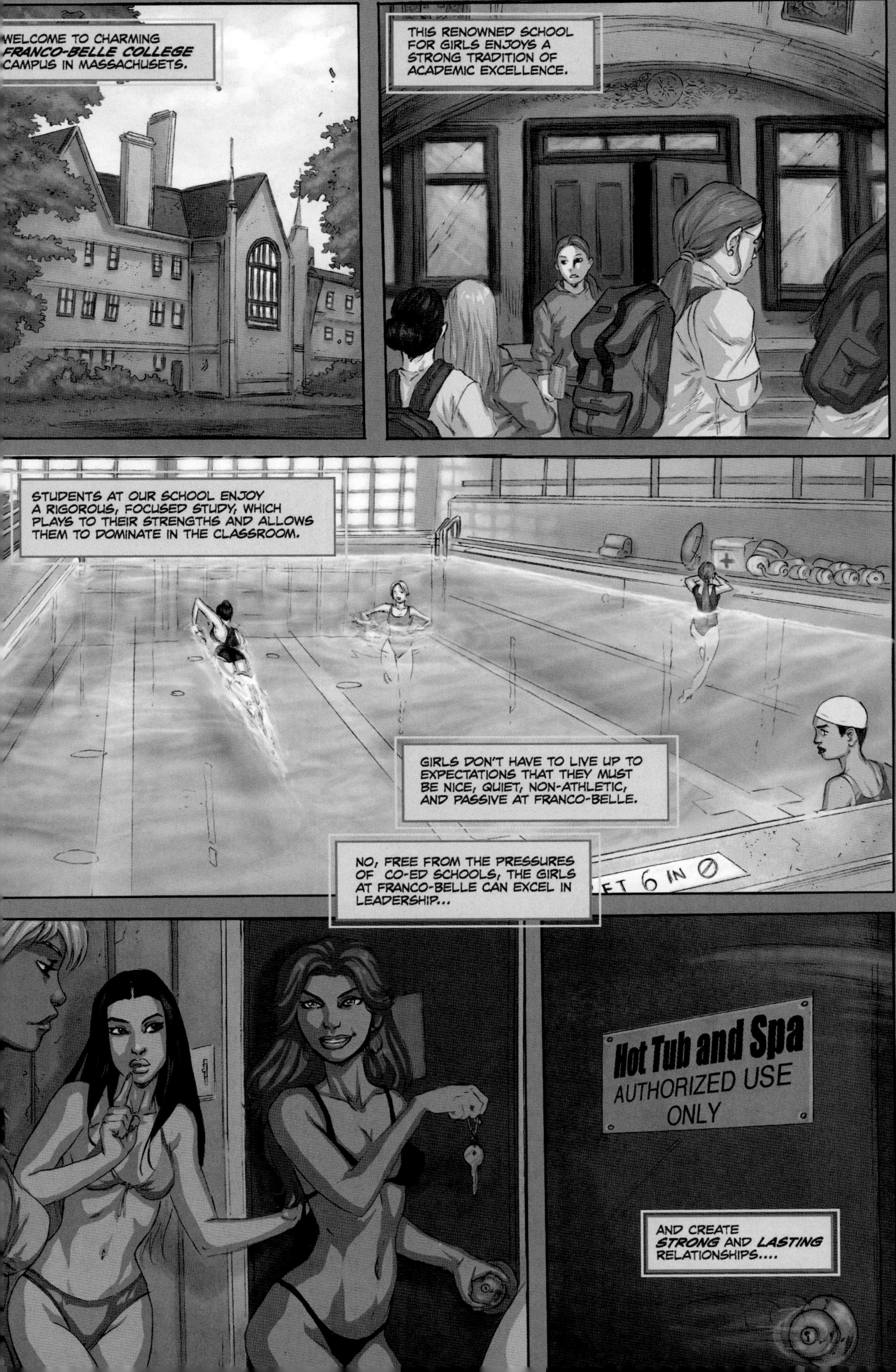
WELCOME TO CHARMING *FRANCO-BELLE COLLEGE* CAMPUS IN MASSACHUSETS.
THIS RENOWNED SCHOOL FOR GIRLS ENJOYS A STRONG TRADITION OF ACADEMIC EXCELLENCE.
STUDENTS AT OUR SCHOOL ENJOY A RIGOROUS, FOCUSED STUDY, WHICH PLAYS TO THEIR STRENGTHS AND ALLOWS THEM TO DOMINATE IN THE CLASSROOM.
GIRLS DON'T HAVE TO LIVE UP TO EXPECTATIONS THAT THEY MUST BE NICE, QUIET, NON-ATHLETIC, AND PASSIVE AT FRANCO-BELLE.
ET 6 IN ⊘
NO, FREE FROM THE PRESSURES OF CO-ED SCHOOLS, THE GIRLS AT FRANCO-BELLE CAN EXCEL IN LEADERSHIP...
Hot Tub and Spa
AUTHORIZED USE ONLY
AND CREATE *STRONG* AND *LASTING* RELATIONSHIPS....

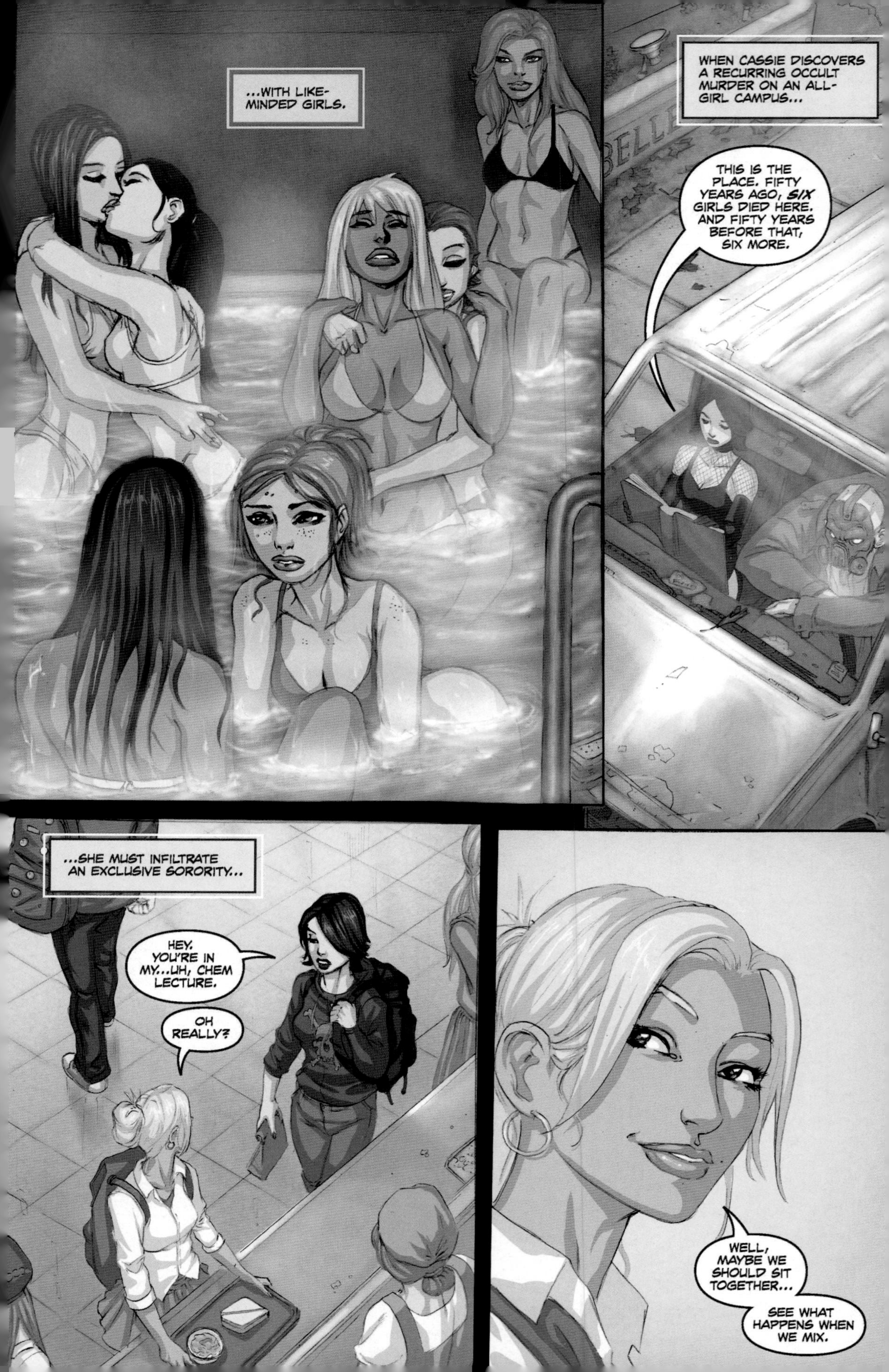
...WITH LIKE-MINDED GIRLS.
WHEN CASSIE DISCOVERS A RECURRING OCCULT MURDER ON AN ALL-GIRL CAMPUS...
THIS IS THE PLACE. FIFTY YEARS AGO, *SIX* GIRLS DIED HERE. AND FIFTY YEARS BEFORE THAT, SIX MORE.
...SHE MUST INFILTRATE AN EXCLUSIVE SORORITY...
HEY. YOU'RE IN MY...UH, CHEM LECTURE.
OH REALLY?
WELL, MAYBE WE SHOULD SIT TOGETHER...
SEE WHAT HAPPENS WHEN WE MIX.

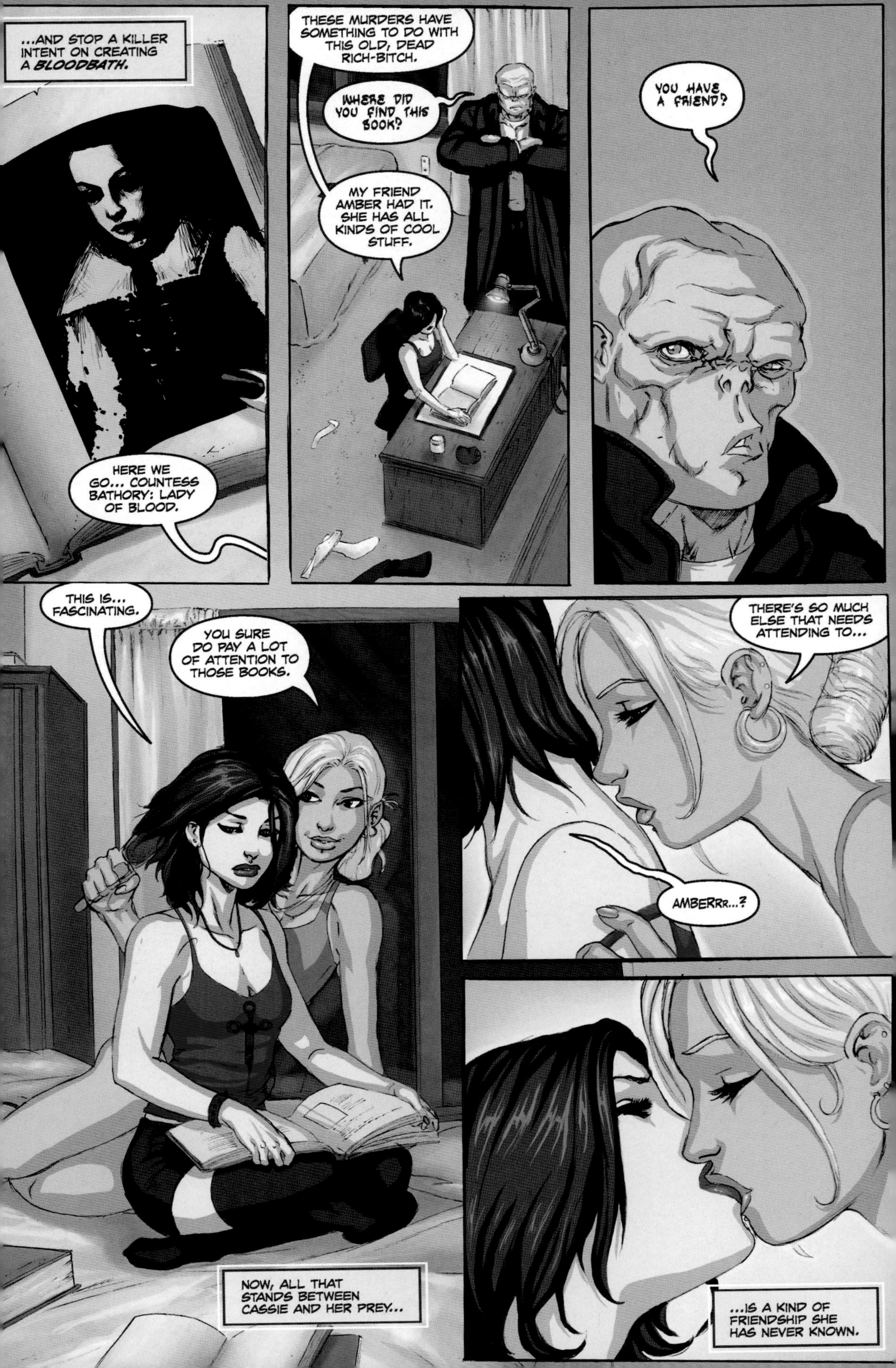
...AND STOP A KILLER INTENT ON CREATING A BLOODBATH.
HERE WE GO... COUNTESS BATHORY: LADY OF BLOOD.
THESE MURDERS HAVE SOMETHING TO DO WITH THIS OLD, DEAD RICH-BITCH.
WHERE DID YOU FIND THIS BOOK?
MY FRIEND AMBER HAD IT. SHE HAS ALL KINDS OF COOL STUFF.
YOU HAVE A FRIEND?
THIS IS... FASCINATING.
YOU SURE DO PAY A LOT OF ATTENTION TO THOSE BOOKS.
NOW, ALL THAT STANDS BETWEEN CASSIE AND HER PREY...
THERE'S SO MUCH ELSE THAT NEEDS ATTENDING TO...
AMBERRR...?
...IS A KIND OF FRIENDSHIP SHE HAS NEVER KNOWN.

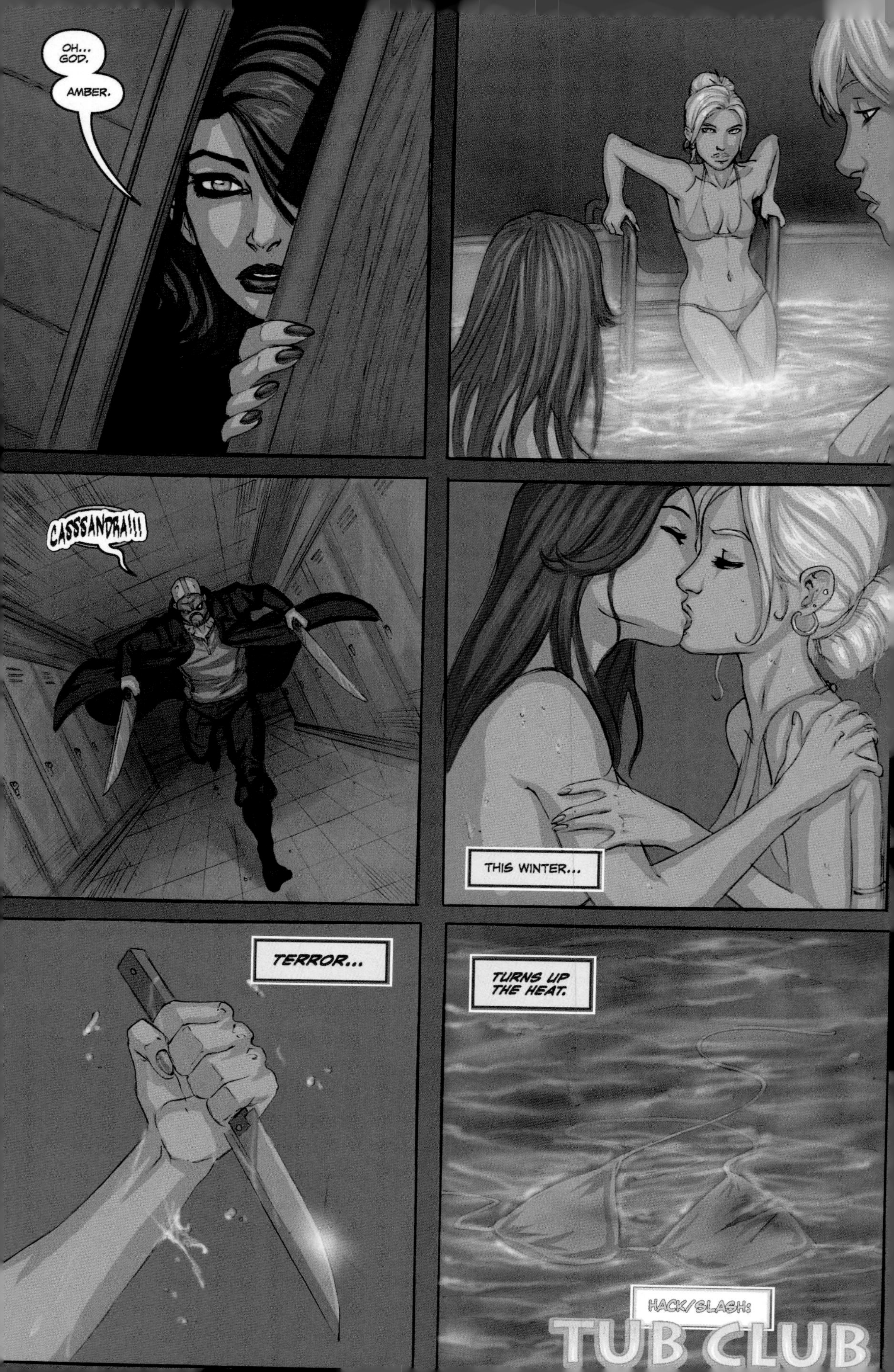
OH... GOD.
AMBER.
CASSSANDRA!!!
THIS WINTER...
TERROR...
TURNS UP THE HEAT.
HACK/SLASH:
TUB CLUB

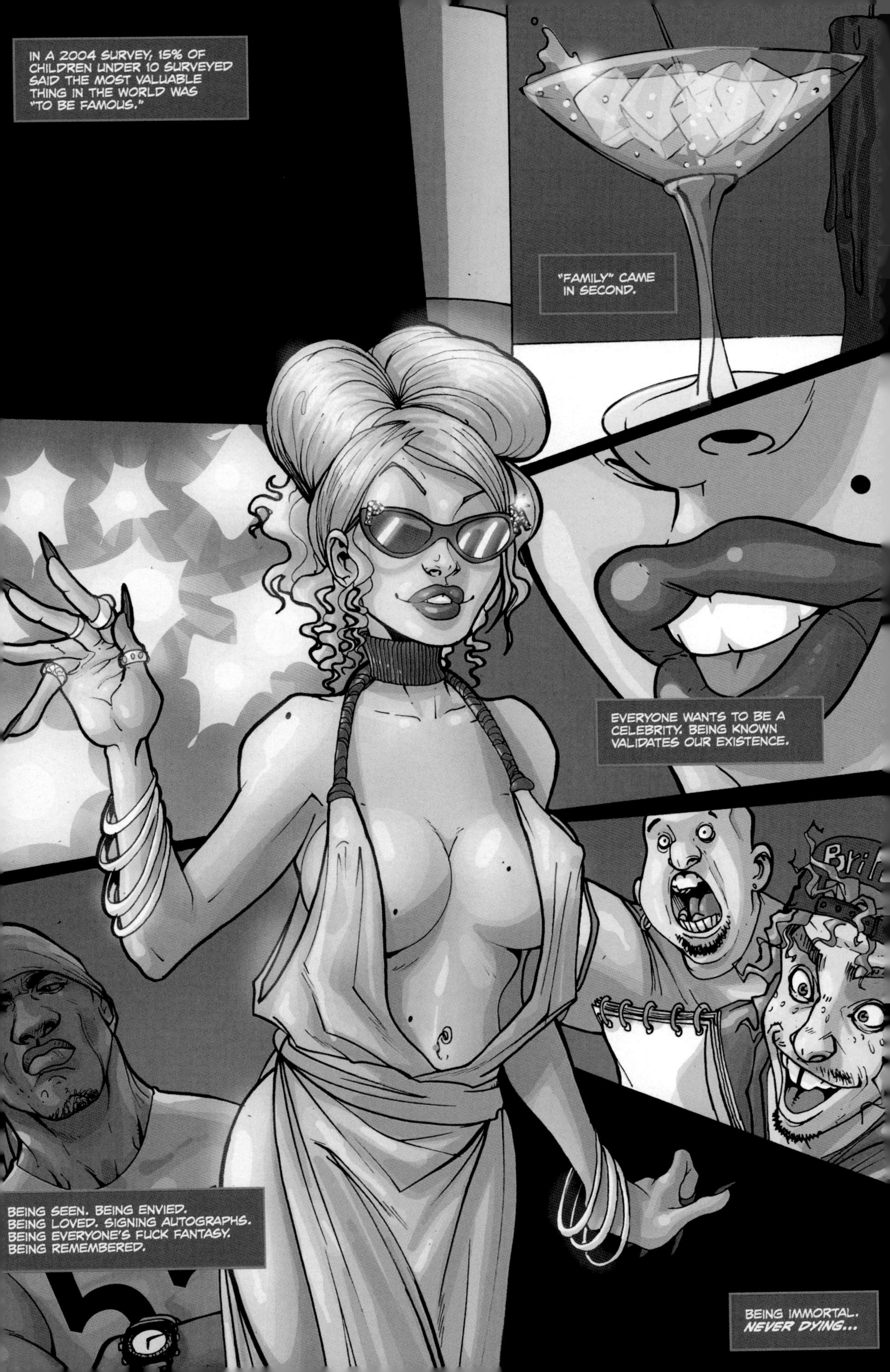
IN A 2004 SURVEY, 15% OF CHILDREN UNDER 10 SURVEYED SAID THE MOST VALUABLE THING IN THE WORLD WAS "TO BE FAMOUS."
"FAMILY" CAME IN SECOND.
EVERYONE WANTS TO BE A CELEBRITY. BEING KNOWN VALIDATES OUR EXISTENCE.
BEING SEEN. BEING ENVIED. BEING LOVED. SIGNING AUTOGRAPHS. BEING EVERYONE'S FUCK FANTASY. BEING REMEMBERED.
BEING IMMORTAL. *NEVER DYING...*

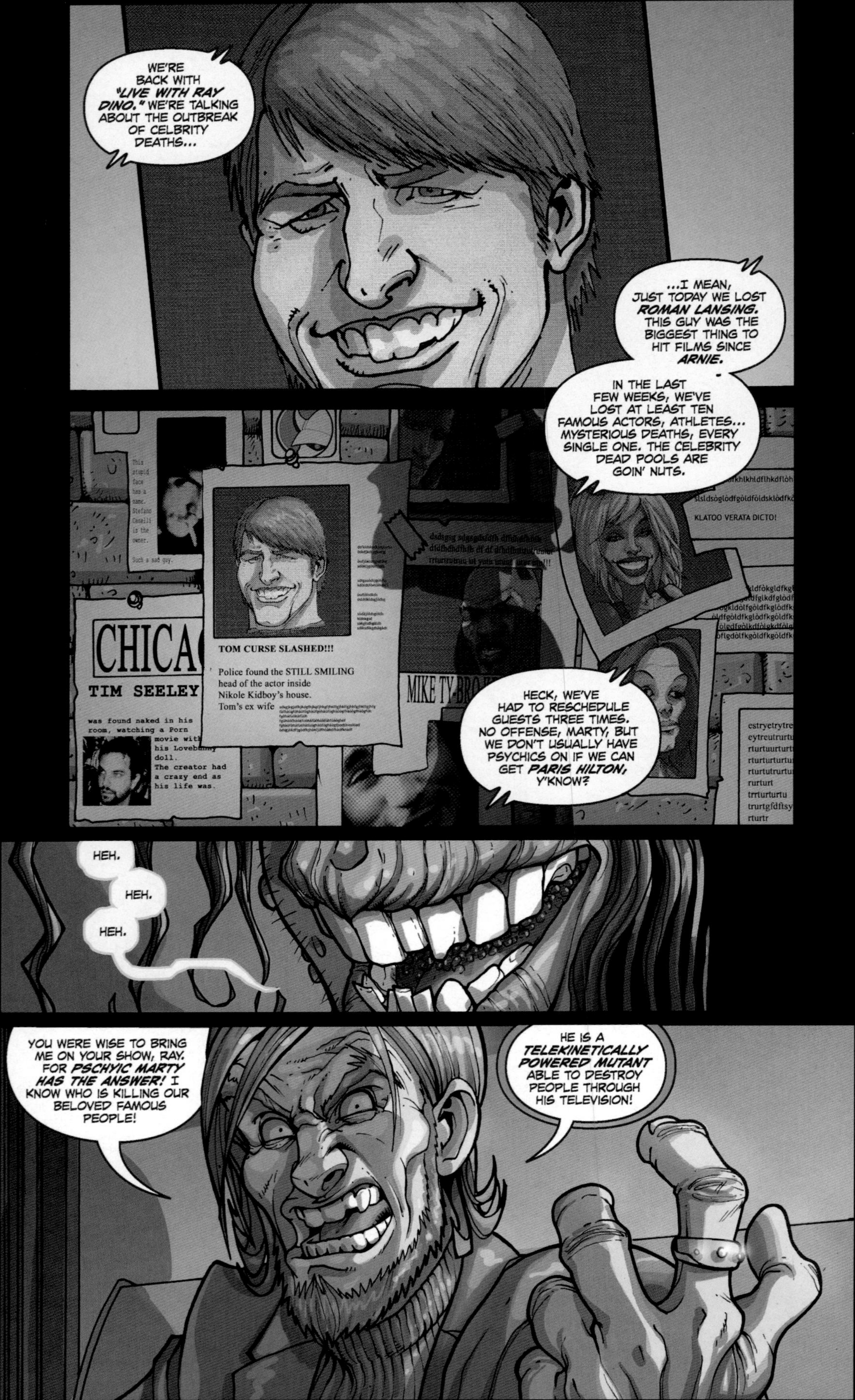
WE'RE BACK WITH "LIVE WITH RAY DINO." WE'RE TALKING ABOUT THE OUTBREAK OF CELBRITY DEATHS...
...I MEAN, JUST TODAY WE LOST ROMAN LANSING. THIS GUY WAS THE BIGGEST THING TO HIT FILMS SINCE ARNIE.
IN THE LAST FEW WEEKS, WE'VE LOST AT LEAST TEN FAMOUS ACTORS, ATHLETES... MYSTERIOUS DEATHS, EVERY SINGLE ONE. THE CELEBRITY DEAD POOLS ARE GOIN' NUTS.
This stupid face has a name. Stefano Caselli is the owner. Such a sad guy.
TOM CURSE SLASHED!!!
Police found the STILL SMILING head of the actor inside Nikole Kidboy's house. Tom's ex wife
CHICAG
TIM SEELEY
was found naked in his room, watching a Porn movie with his Lovebunny doll. The creator had a crazy end as his life was.
KLATOO VERATA DICTO!
MIKE TY-BRO
HECK, WE'VE HAD TO RESCHEDULE GUESTS THREE TIMES. NO OFFENSE, MARTY, BUT WE DON'T USUALLY HAVE PSYCHICS ON IF WE CAN GET PARIS HILTON, Y'KNOW?
HEH.
HEH.
HEH.
YOU WERE WISE TO BRING ME ON YOUR SHOW, RAY. FOR PSCHYIC MARTY HAS THE ANSWER! I KNOW WHO IS KILLING OUR BELOVED FAMOUS PEOPLE!
HE IS A TELEKINETICALLY POWERED MUTANT ABLE TO DESTROY PEOPLE THROUGH HIS TELEVISION!

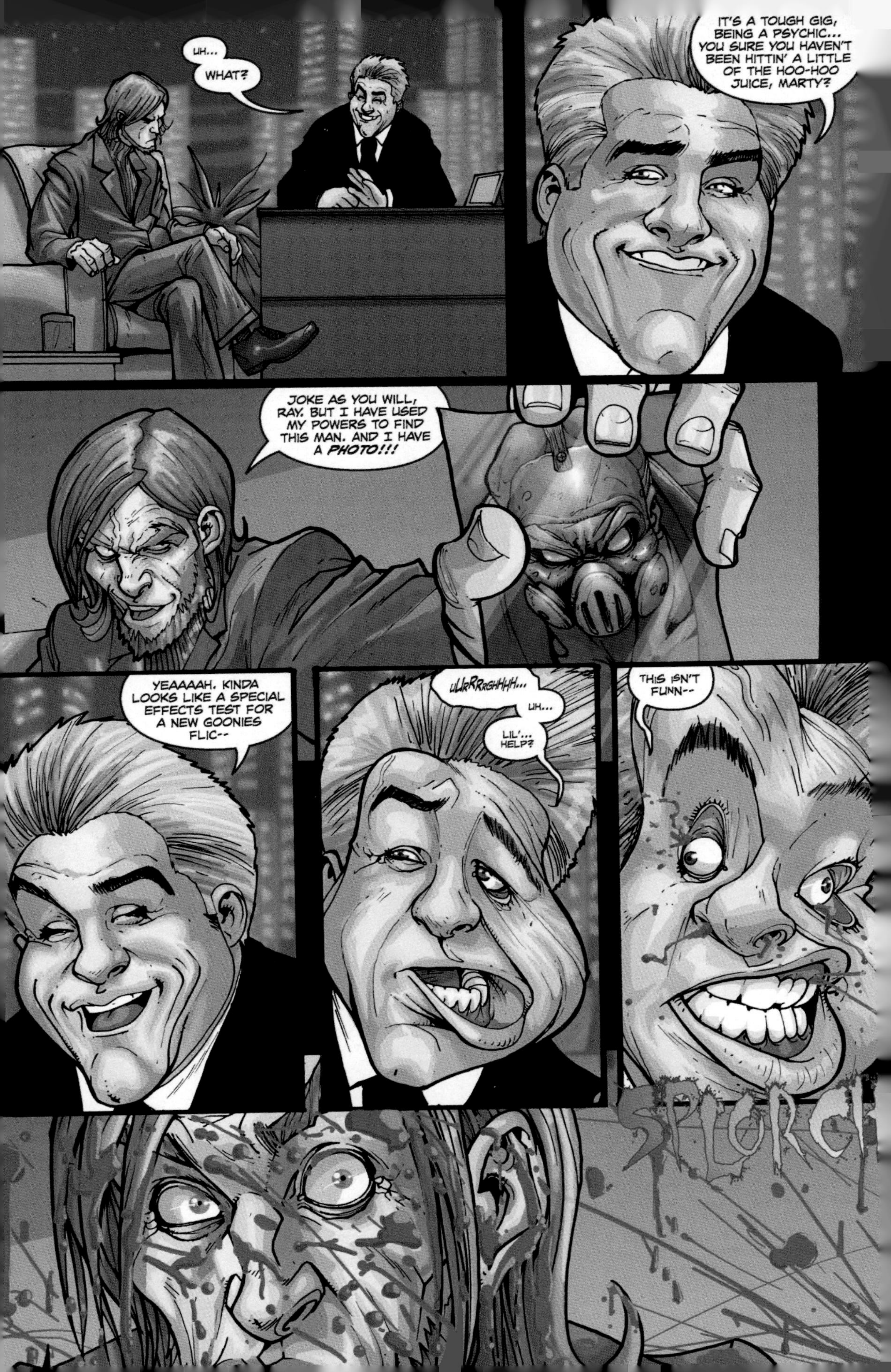
UH...
WHAT?
IT'S A TOUGH GIG, BEING A PSYCHIC... YOU SURE YOU HAVEN'T BEEN HITTIN' A LITTLE OF THE HOO-HOO JUICE, MARTY?
JOKE AS YOU WILL, RAY. BUT I HAVE USED MY POWERS TO FIND THIS MAN. AND I HAVE A PHOTO!!!
YEAAAAH. KINDA LOOKS LIKE A SPECIAL EFFECTS TEST FOR A NEW GOONIES FLIC--
UURRRRGHHHH...
UH...
LIL'... HELP?
THIS ISN'T FUNN--
SPLORCH

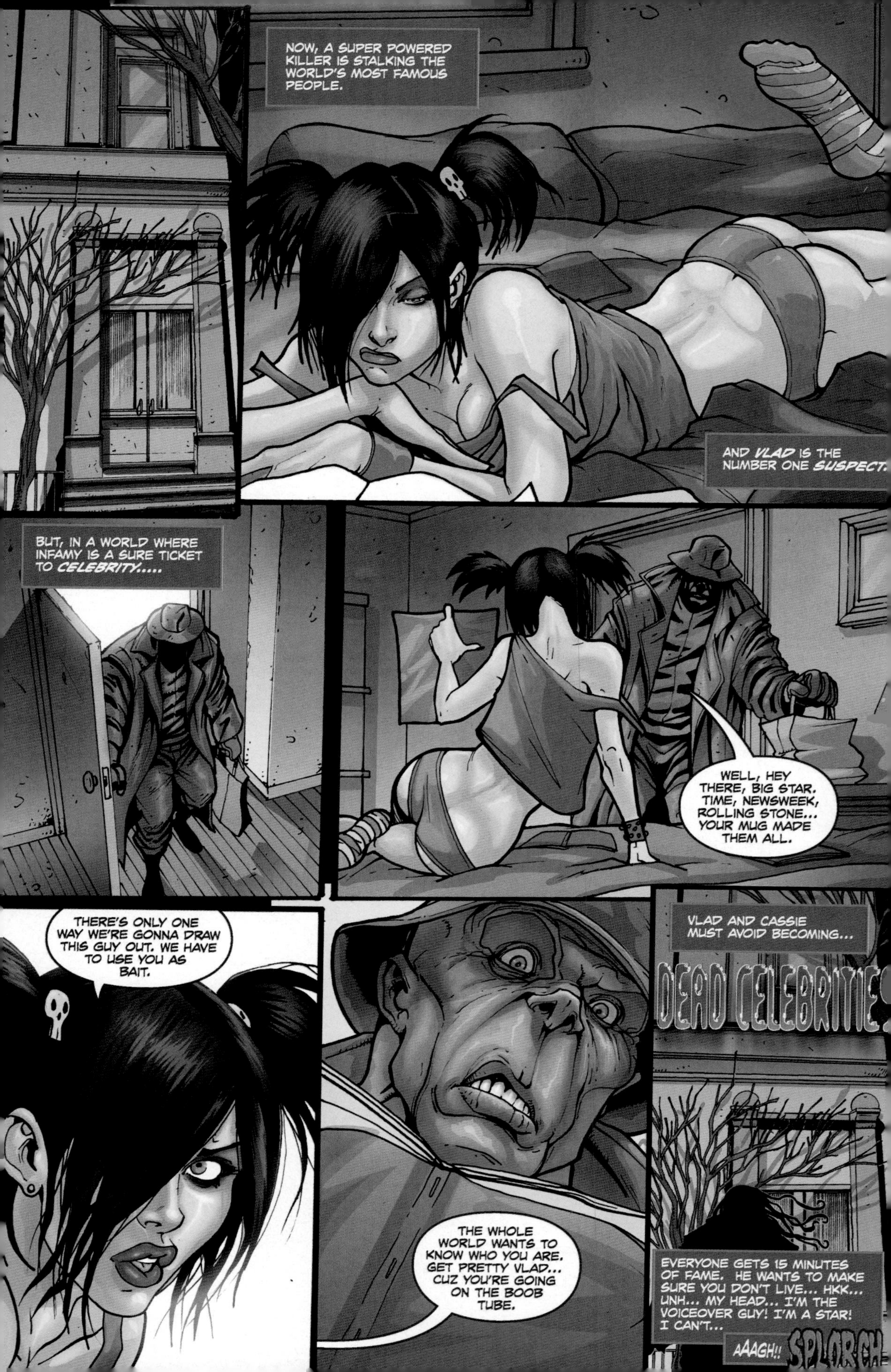
NOW, A SUPER POWERED KILLER IS STALKING THE WORLD'S MOST FAMOUS PEOPLE.
AND VLAD IS THE NUMBER ONE SUSPECT.
BUT, IN A WORLD WHERE INFAMY IS A SURE TICKET TO CELEBRITY.....
WELL, HEY THERE, BIG STAR. TIME, NEWSWEEK, ROLLING STONE... YOUR MUG MADE THEM ALL.
THERE'S ONLY ONE WAY WE'RE GONNA DRAW THIS GUY OUT. WE HAVE TO USE YOU AS BAIT.
THE WHOLE WORLD WANTS TO KNOW WHO YOU ARE. GET PRETTY VLAD... CUZ YOU'RE GOING ON THE BOOB TUBE.
VLAD AND CASSIE MUST AVOID BECOMING...
DEAD CELEBRITIES
EVERYONE GETS 15 MINUTES OF FAME. HE WANTS TO MAKE SURE YOU DON'T LIVE... HKK... UNH... MY HEAD... I'M THE VOICEOVER GUY! I'M A STAR! I CAN'T...
AAAGH!!
SPLORCH

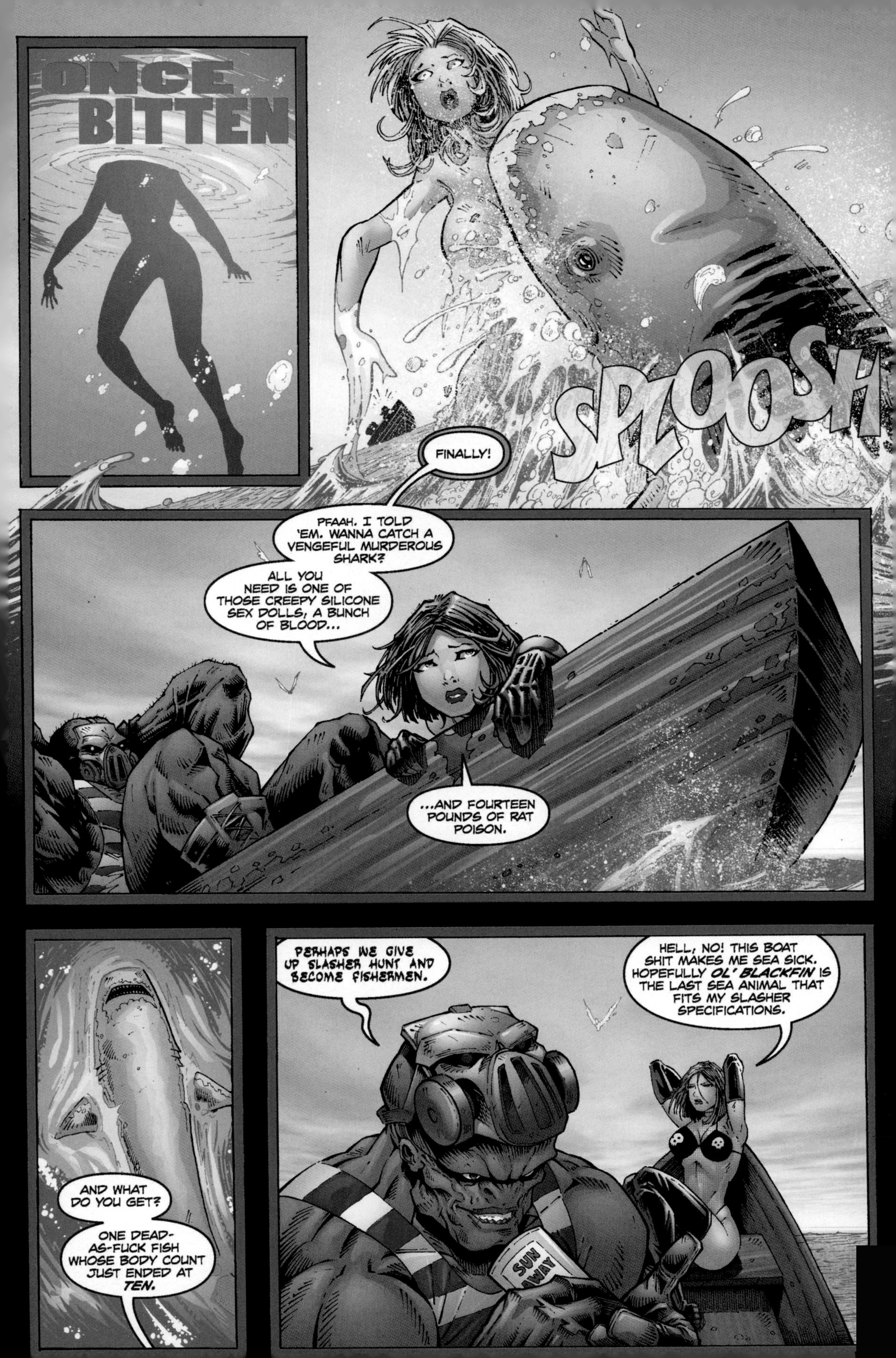
ONCE BITTEN
SPLOOSH
FINALLY!
PFAAH. I TOLD 'EM. WANNA CATCH A VENGEFUL MURDEROUS SHARK?
ALL YOU NEED IS ONE OF THOSE CREEPY SILICONE SEX DOLLS, A BUNCH OF BLOOD...
...AND FOURTEEN POUNDS OF RAT POISON.
AND WHAT DO YOU GET?
ONE DEAD-AS-FUCK FISH WHOSE BODY COUNT JUST ENDED AT *TEN*.
PERHAPS WE GIVE UP SLASHER HUNT AND BECOME FISHERMEN.
HELL, NO! THIS BOAT SHIT MAKES ME SEA SICK. HOPEFULLY *OL' BLACKFIN* IS THE LAST SEA ANIMAL THAT FITS MY SLASHER SPECIFICATIONS.
SUN AWAY

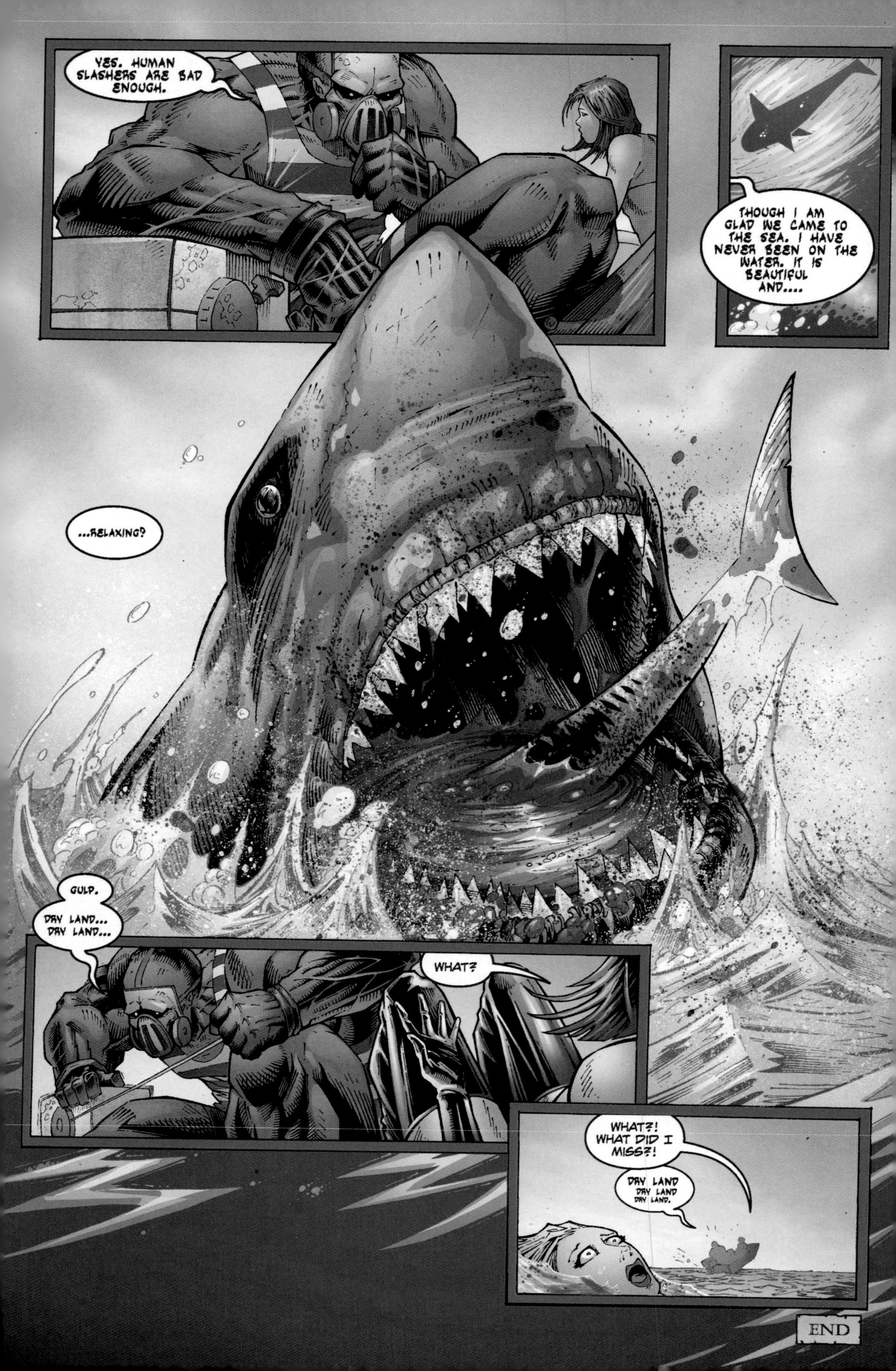
YES. HUMAN SLASHERS ARE BAD ENOUGH.
THOUGH I AM GLAD WE CAME TO THE SEA. I HAVE NEVER BEEN ON THE WATER. IT IS BEAUTIFUL AND....
...RELAXING?
GULP.
DRY LAND... DRY LAND...
WHAT?
WHAT?! WHAT DID I MISS?!
DRY LAND DRY LAND DRY LAND.
END

HACK/SLASH
THE COVERS

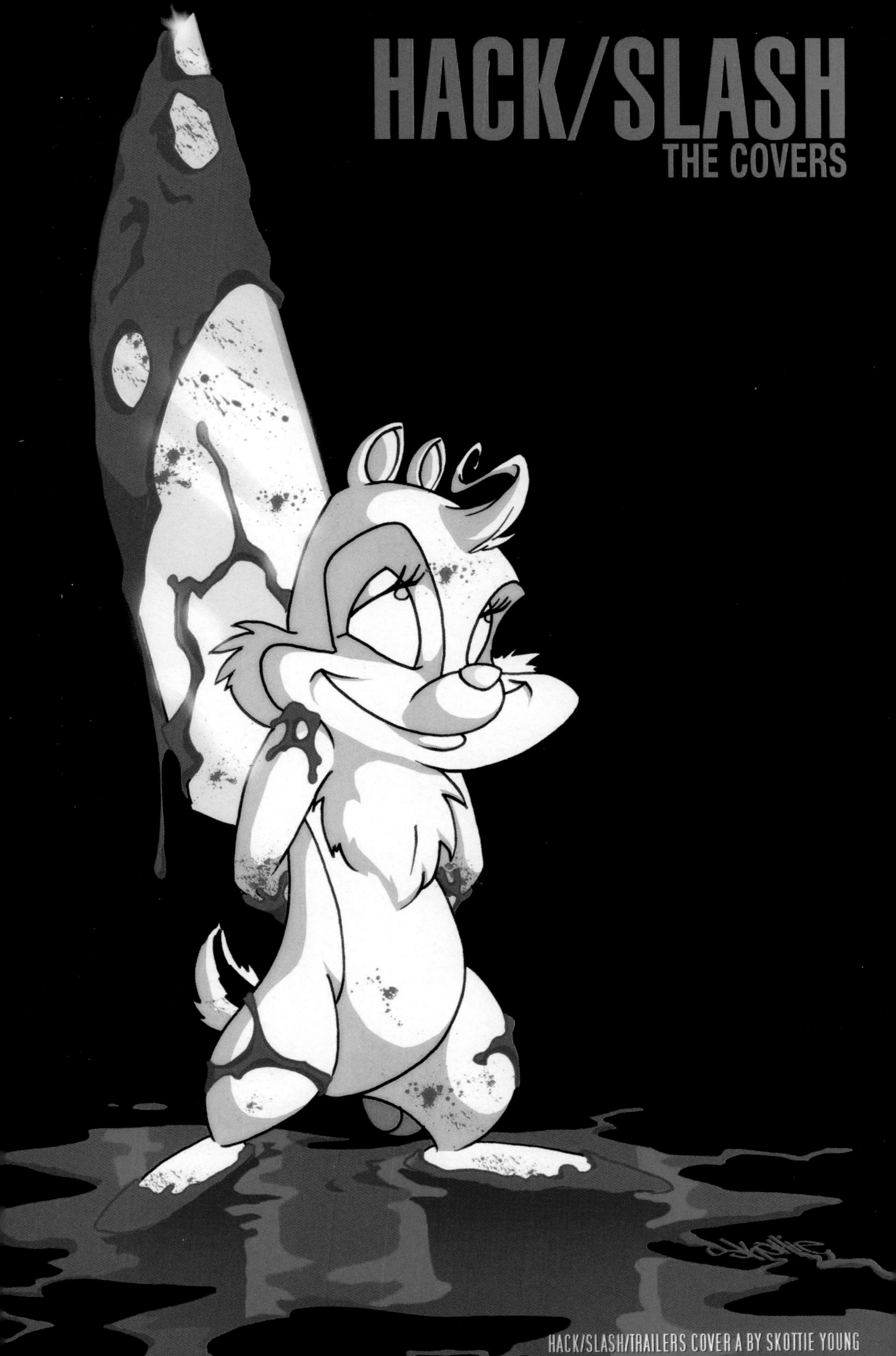

HACK/SLASH/TRAILERS COVER A BY SKOTTIE YOUNG

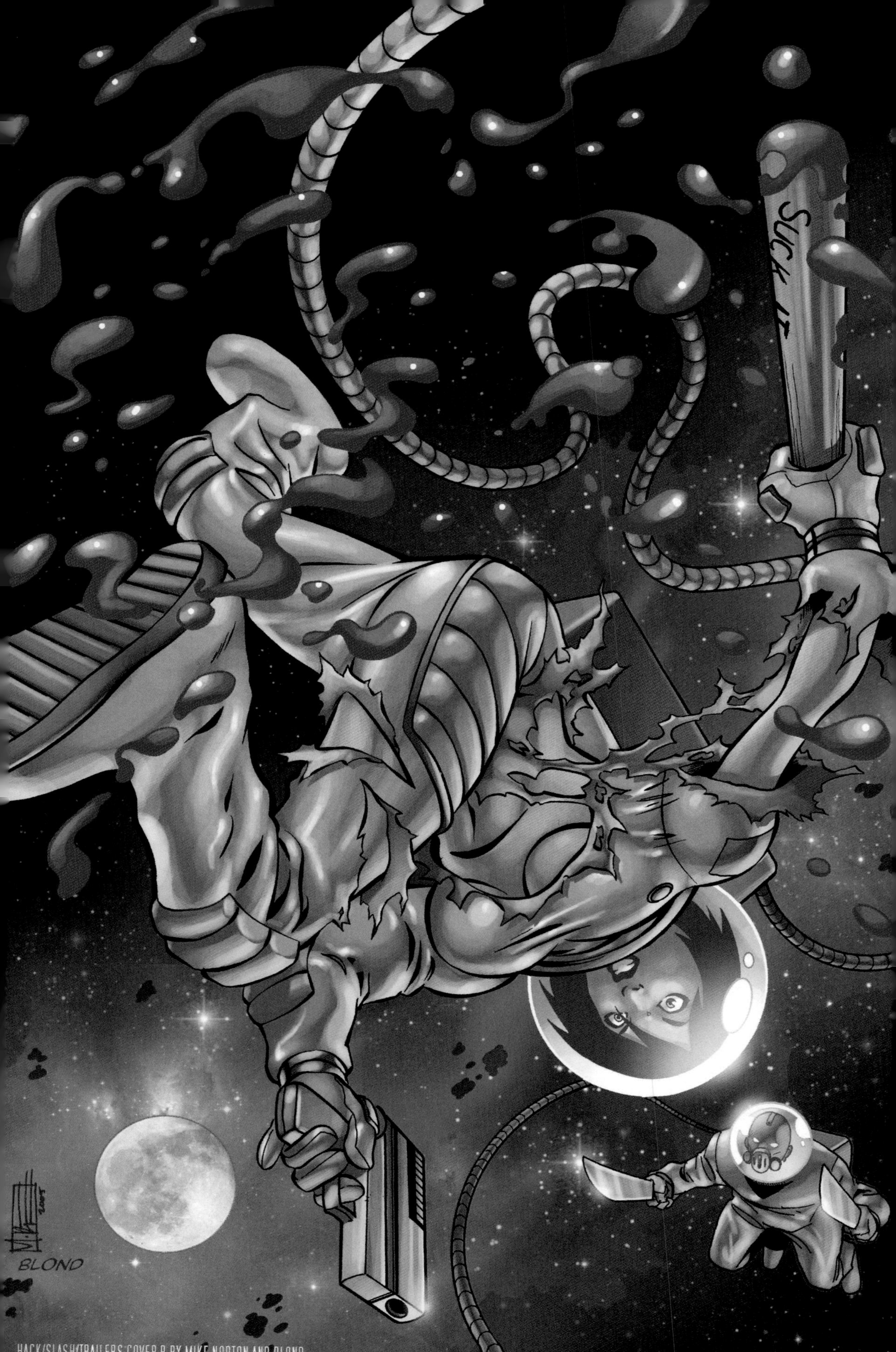
SUCK IT
BLOND

HACK/SLASH/TRAILERS COVER B BY MIKE NORTON AND BLOND

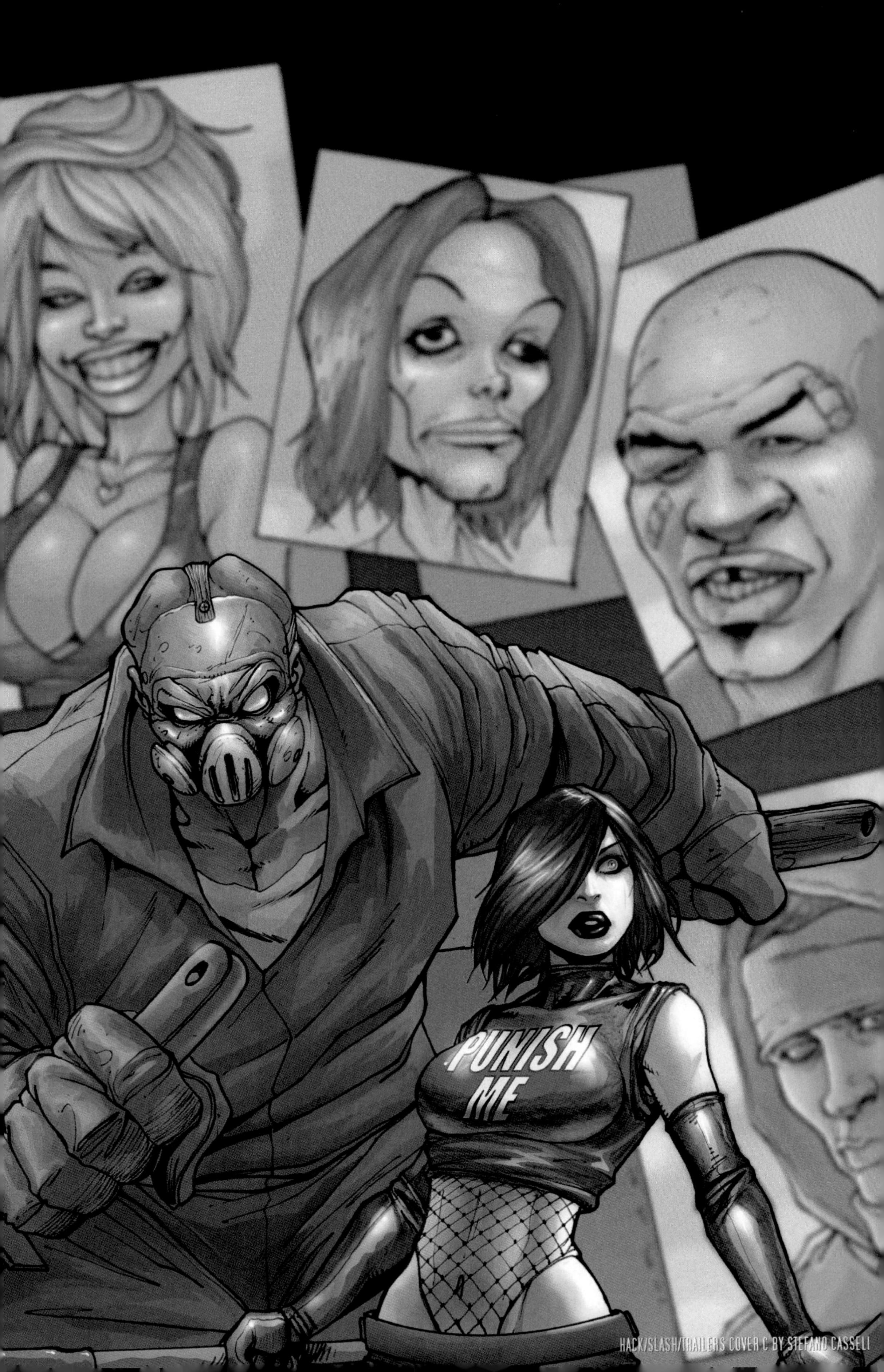
PUNISH
ME

HACK/SLASH/TRAILERS COVER C BY STEFANO CASSELI

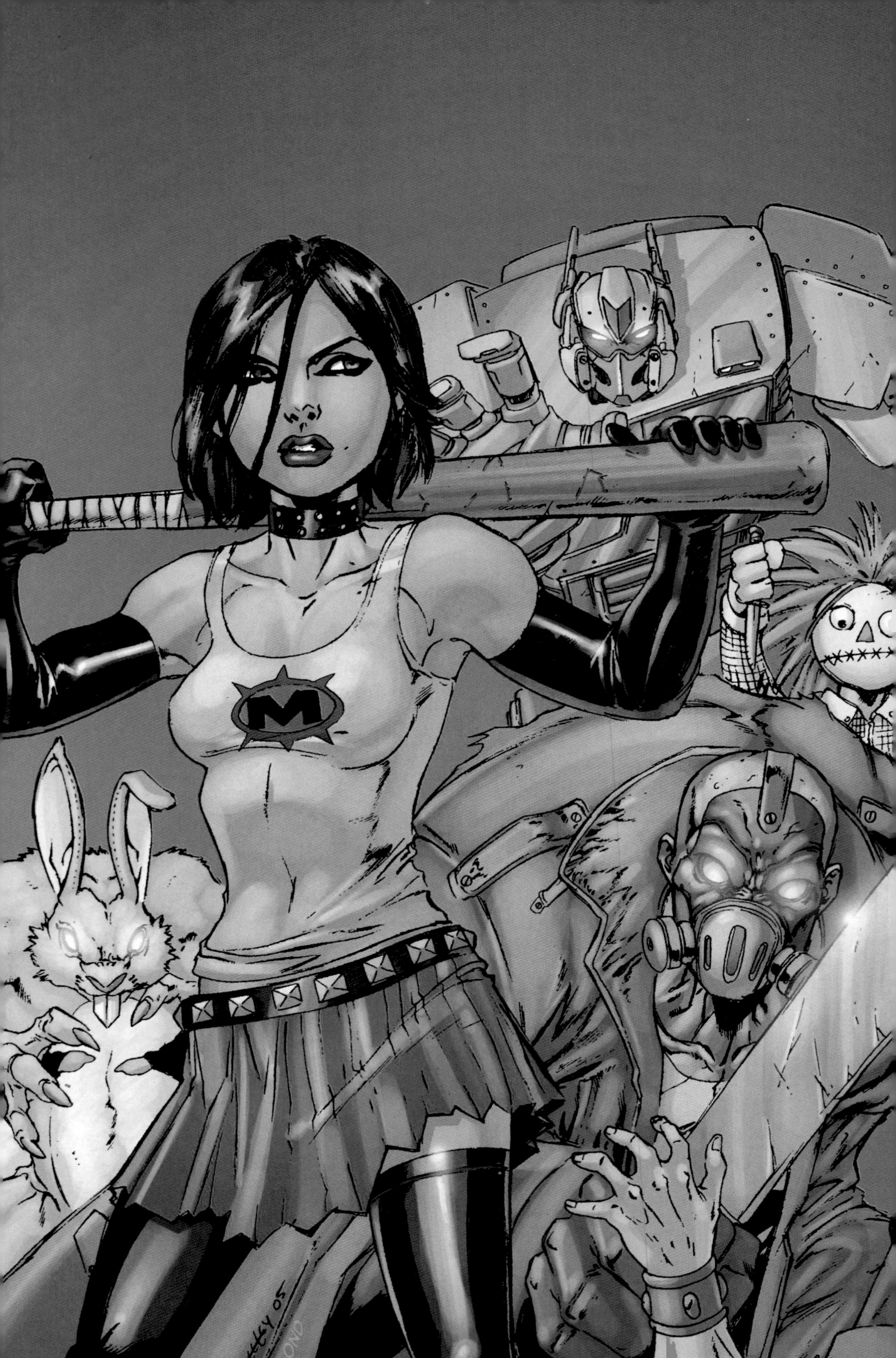

HACK/SLASH/LAND OF THE LOST TOYS ISSUE 2 BY TIM SEELEY

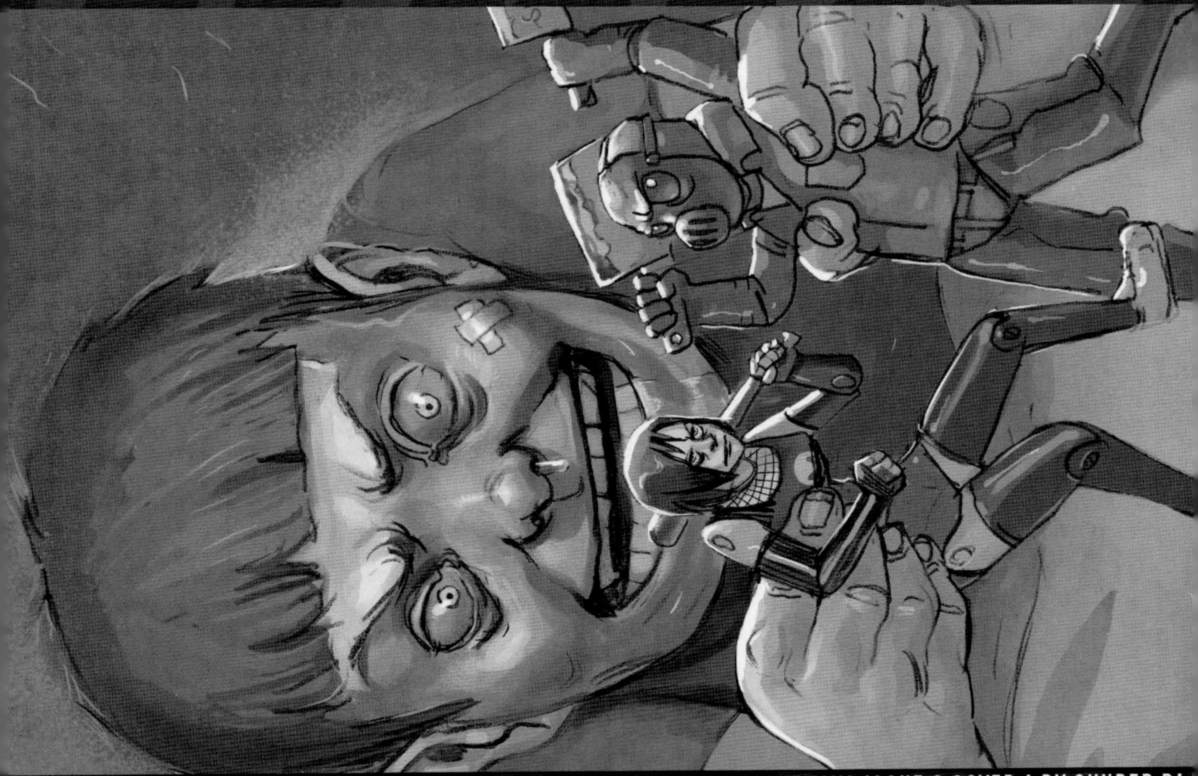

HACK/SLASH/LAND OF THE LOST TOYS ISSUE 3 COVER A BY SUNDER RAJ

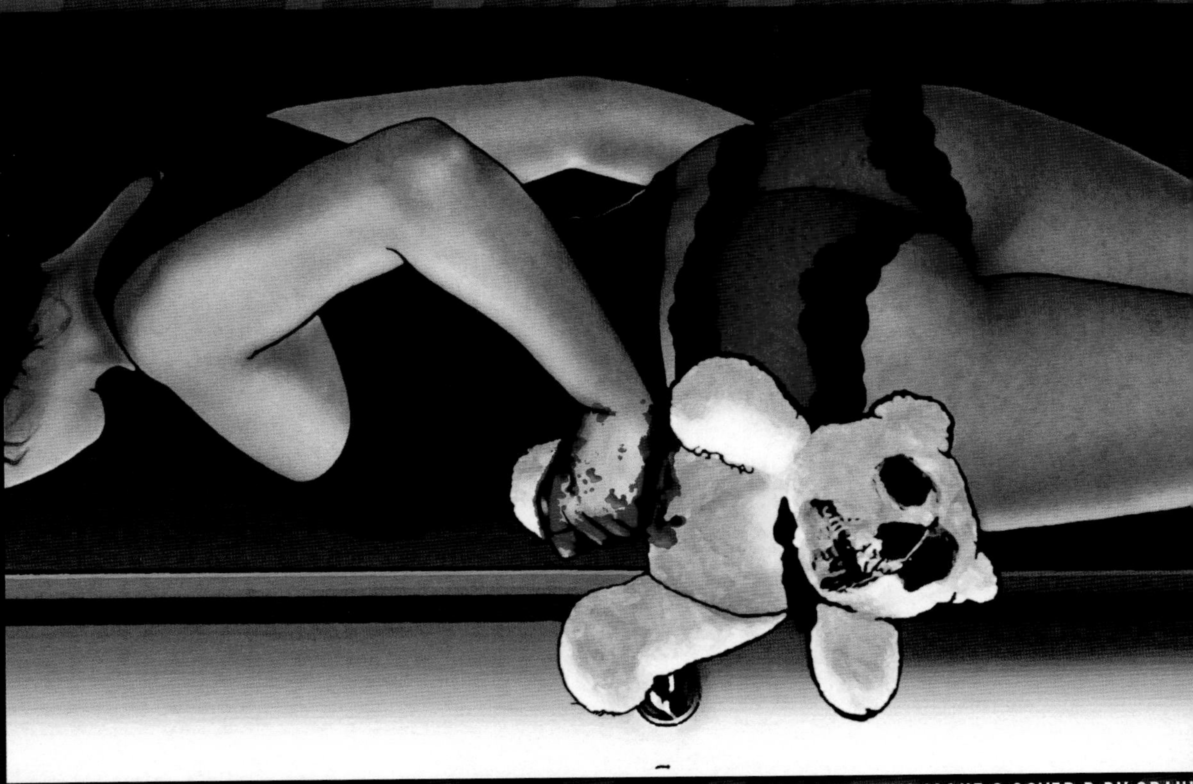

HACK/SLASH/LAND OF THE LOST TOYS ISSUE 3 COVER B BY CRAN

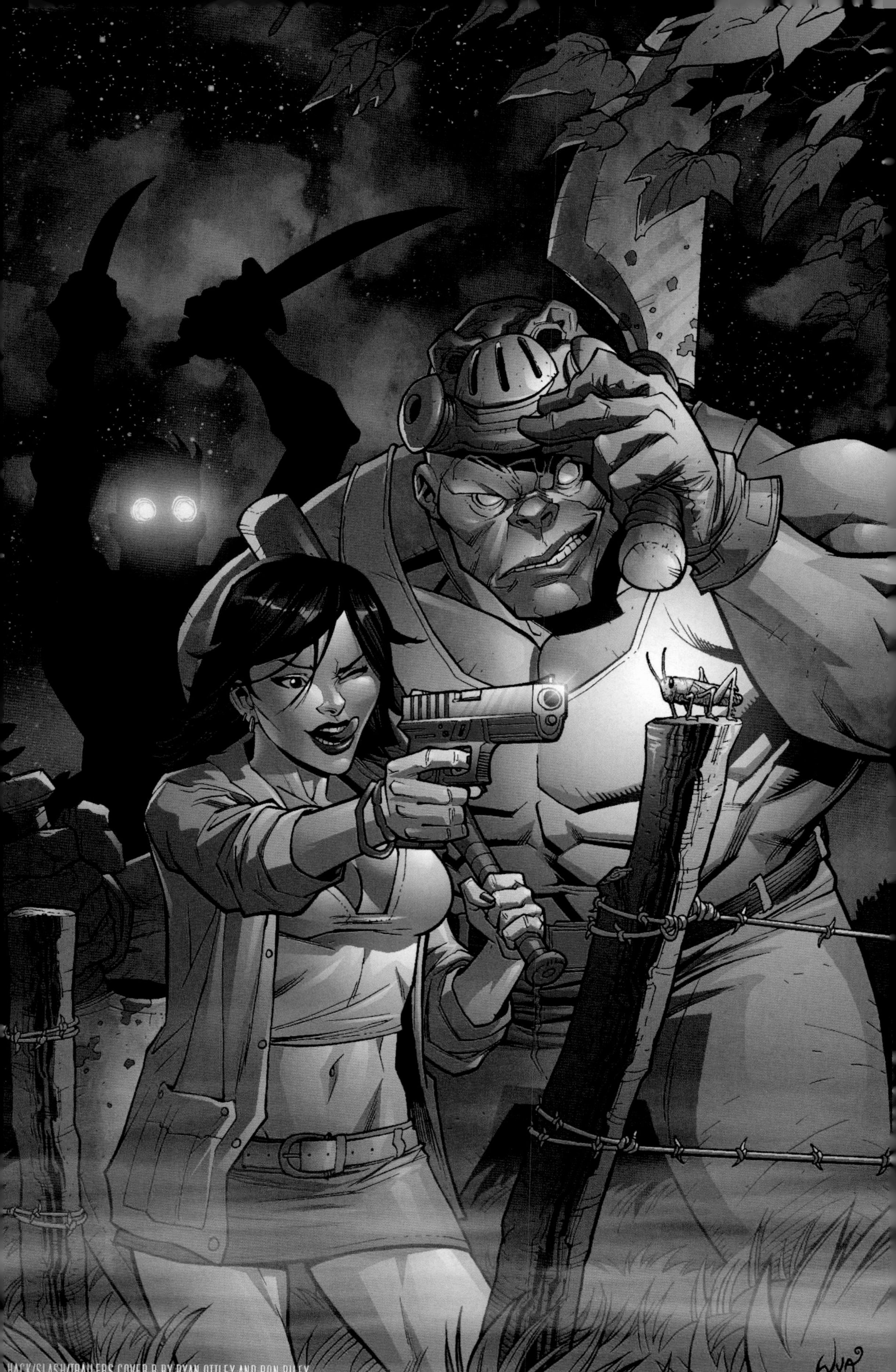

HACK/SLASH/TRAILERS COVER B BY RYAN OTTLEY AND RON RILEY

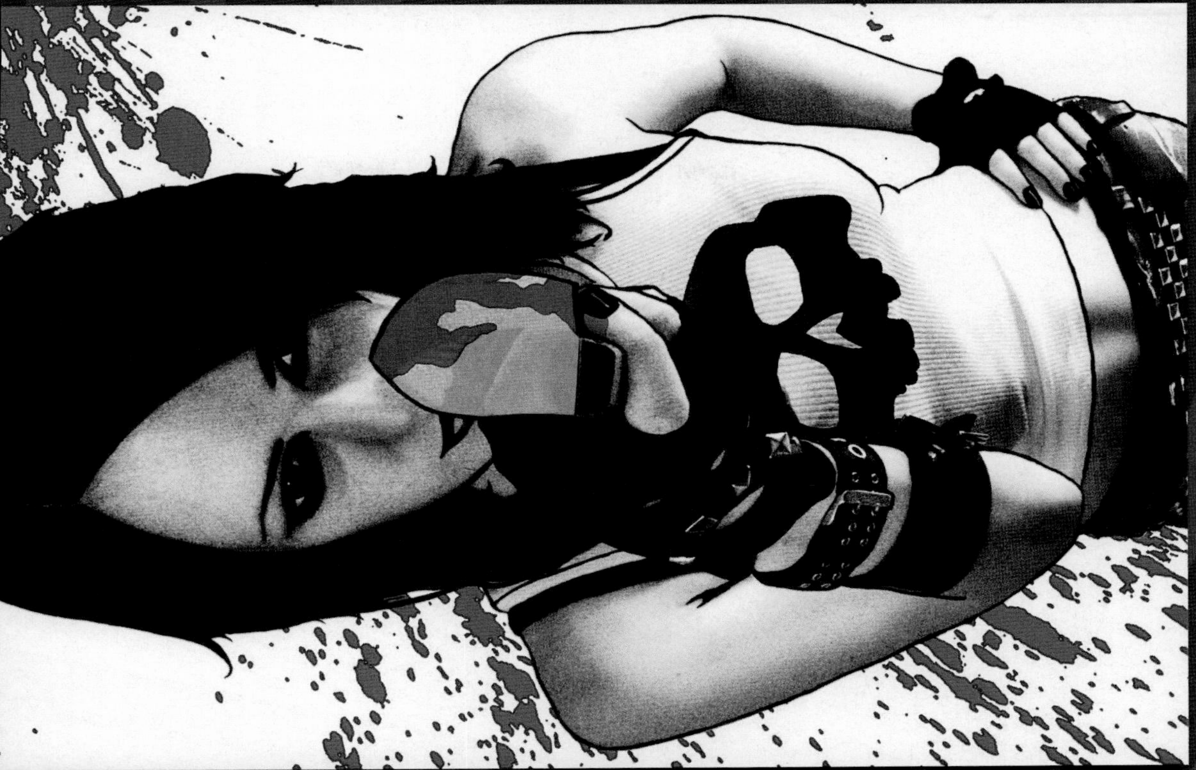

HACK/SLASH/SLICE HARD COVER B BY CRANK!

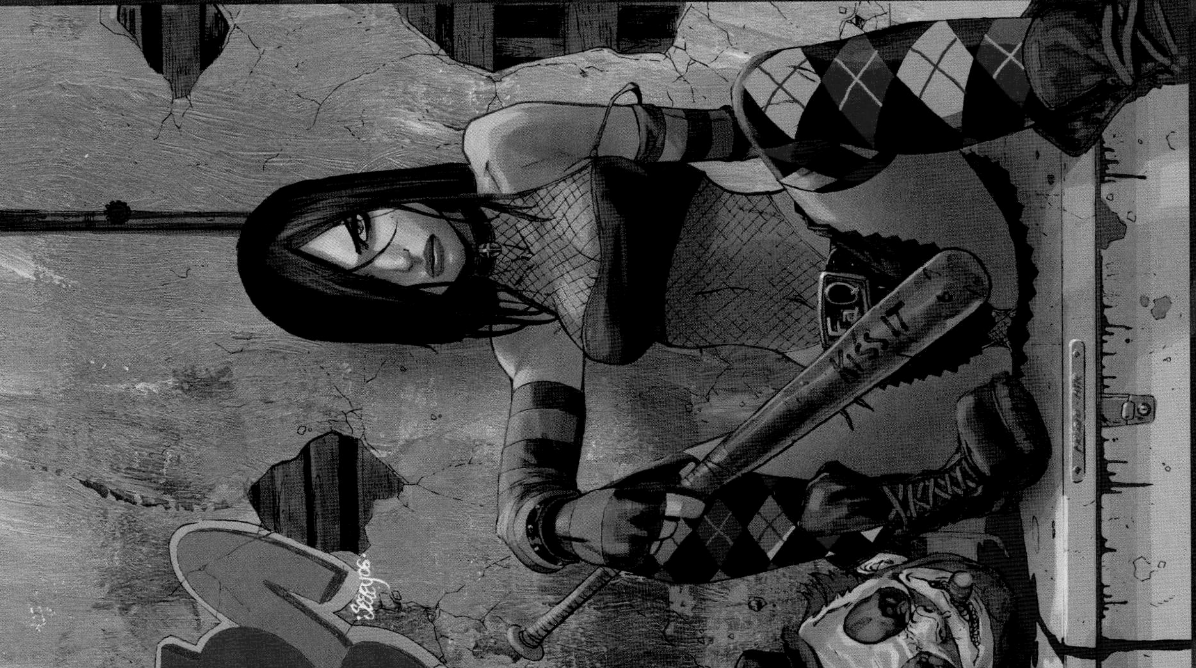

HACK/SLASH/SLICE HARD COVER C BY TIM SEELEY AND SUNDER RAJ

HACK/SLASH PSYCHOFILE

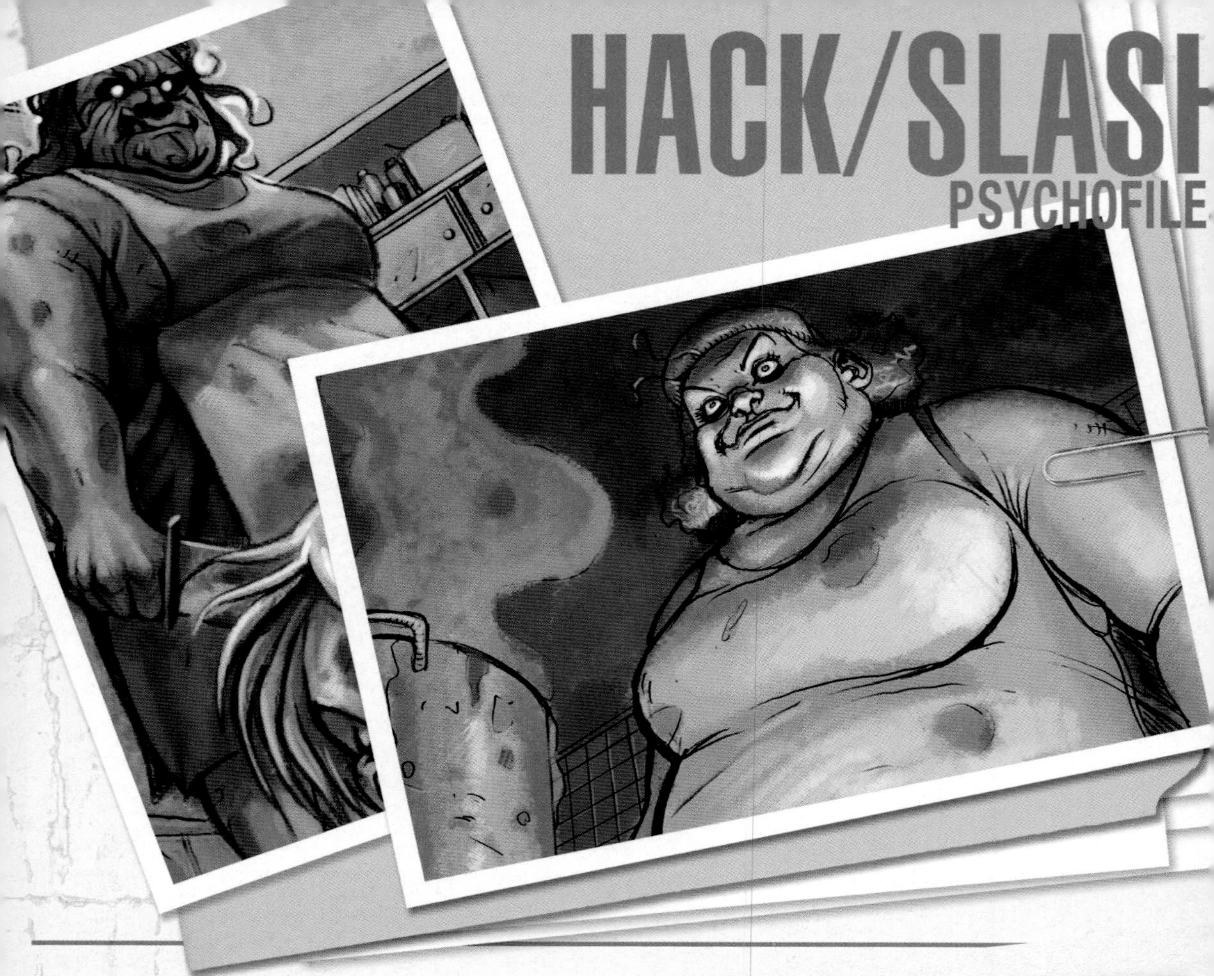

ACID ANGEL

Real Name: Angela Cicero
Death by: Choking
Pre-Slasher Occupation: Real Estate Agent
Slasher type: Vengeful Ghoul

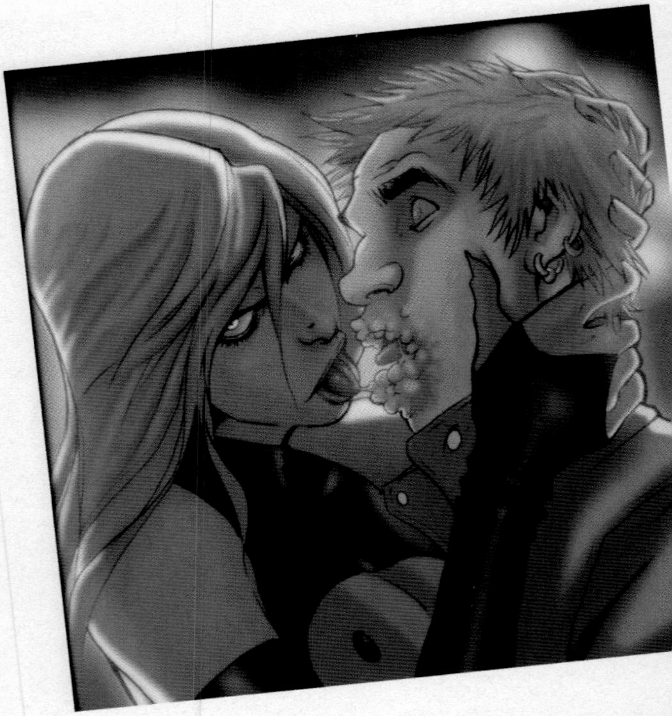

Special abilities: Resistance to damage. Acid generation.

Slasher weapon: Acid

Body Count: 7

The story: Angela Cicero was an urban party girl. She had the looks, the money and the attitude. A new club every night of the week, and a new man to leave behind every morning. Angela had a close, married friend named Michelle, a woman she had known since childhood. Despite the trust placed in her by Michelle, Angela and Michelle's husband were involved in a torrid affair. When Michelle discovered this, she was destoyed, commiting suicide by slitting her wrists in the bath tub. Michelle's husband, overcome with grief and angry at himself replaced Angela's inuslin with hydrochloric acid. The injection killed Angela, but she rose from the grave, intent on continuing her life style, and punishing men.

Cassie's Notes from The Slasher Journal- "So, apparently Slashers don't have to be half rotted nasty lookin' freaks. Bummer."

ASHLEY

eal Name: Ashley Guthrie
eath by: Suffocation with Teddy Bear
e-Slasher Occupation: N/A
asher type: Vengeful Ghoul

ecial abilities: Ashley can control dreams, d is able to create and manipulate "toys" to s bidding within his "dream realm."

asher weapon: Killer toys

dy Count: 10

e story: Ashley Guthrie was a seemingly "born il" child of an affluent family in Ohio. Selfish, d demanding of attention, Ashley did not take ell to having a younger brother, and when forced share a toy, he instead bludgeoned the boy. In ger, Ashley's mother suffocated Ashley with a uffed bear in his sleep. Soon after, Ashley turned to haunt the dreams of other children, ling them as they slept with their favorite toy. assie entered the dream world to stop him, and cceded in destroying him. Or, so she thought. rough unknown means Ashley was able to turn to "life" in the teddy bear he had been suffo-ted with.

assie's Notes from The Slasher Journal- "Once y art teacher talked me into babysitting for his ughter. After about 45 minutes, I was con-nced this kid was Satan incarnate. Ashley uthrie made that kid look like fucking Dolly from amily Circus. People debate the "nurture vs. ture" thing all the time. I've always wanted to lieve a person was a reflection of the world they ew up in..but, Ashley seems to have been bad om the moment the sperm hit the egg."

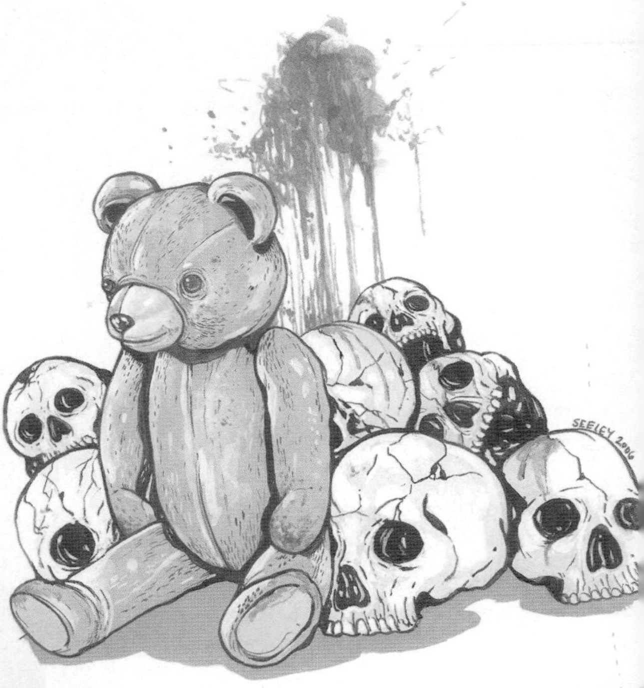

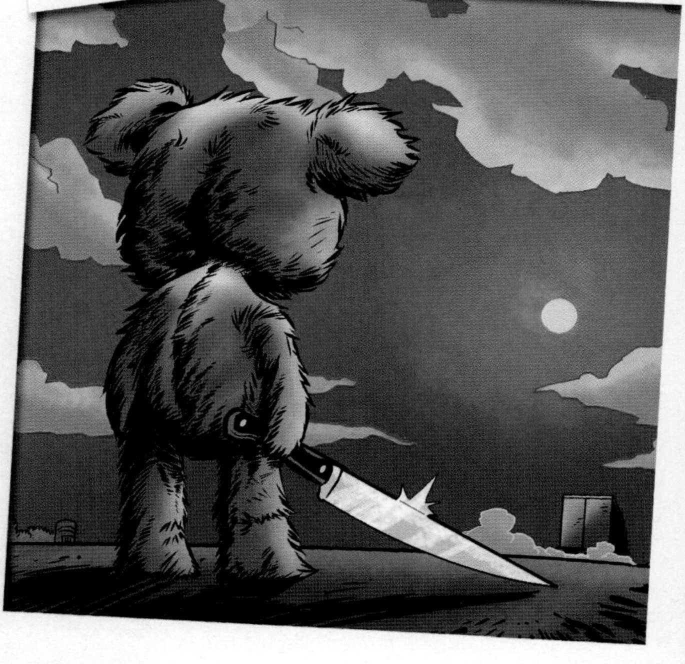

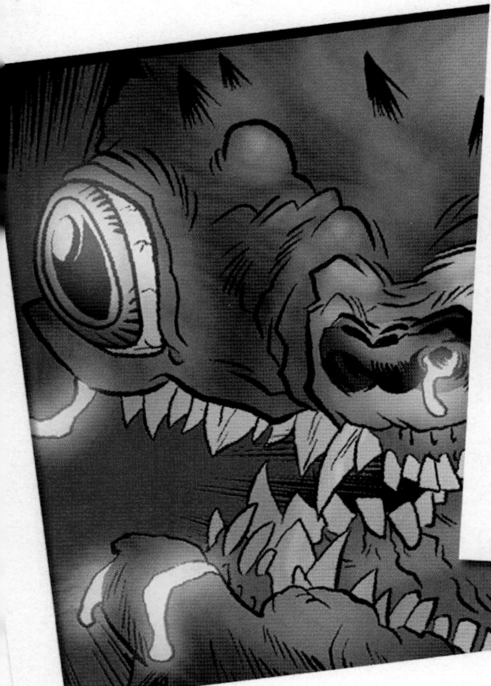

BLACKFIN

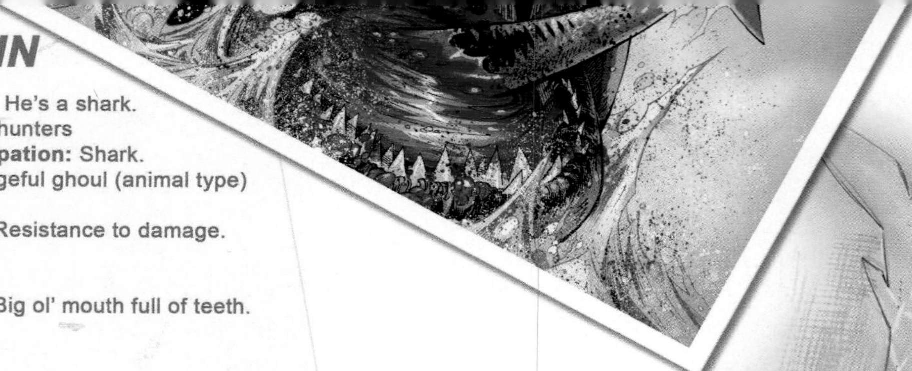

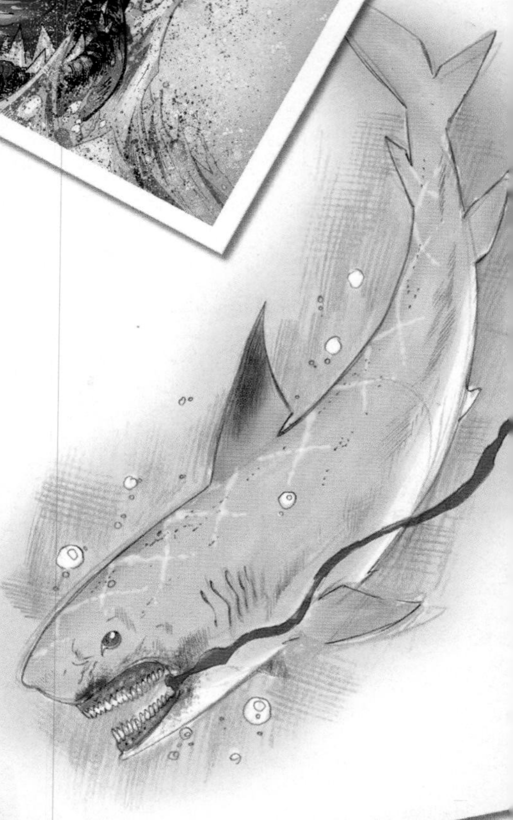

Real Name: None. He's a shark.
Death by: Human hunters
Pre-Slasher Occupation: Shark.
Slasher type: Vengeful ghoul (animal type)

Special abilities: Resistance to damage. Unnatural cunning.

Slasher weapon: Big ol' mouth full of teeth.

Body Count: 16

The story: Blackfin was the name given to a ravenous shark that hunted off the coast of Maine. The shark became poisoned by offshore toxic waste dumping, and during it's illenss it turned to attacking "easier" prey, including beach goers and fishermen. The creature was hunted down and presumably killed, but returned later, more ravenous then ever before.

Cassie's Notes from The Slasher Journal- "This is what I get for wishing for a change of scenery."

HIBACHI DEVIL

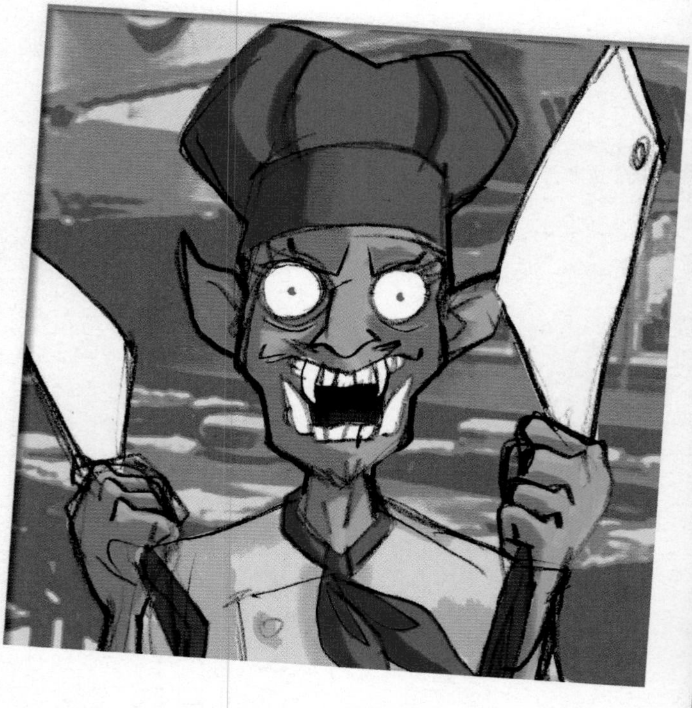

Real Name: Ryu Mafume
Death by: Poison
Pre-Slasher Occupation: Hibachi Chef
Slasher type: Vengeful ghoul

Special abilities: Resistance to damage.

Slasher weapon: Hibachi Knives

Body Count: 8

The story: Junichiro Koizumi was a well known, successful Hibachi Chef at a posh restaurant in Tokyo. His speed with his knives earned him the name Hibachi Devil, which he played up by wearing an Oni mask. Junichiro was known to be an arrogant and selfish man, which further angered his main competitor, Ryu Mafume. Mafume challenged Junichiro to a "cook-off" using selected ingredients. Unbeknownst to Junichiro, Ryu has replaced his tuna with a poisonous fish. When the judges were served they all became ill. Enraged, Junichiro force fed Ryu a lethal amount of the fish. Ryu returned from the dead, killing Junichiro and taking his mask and murdering many, seeking to shame his nemesis.

MORTIMER STRICK

Real Name: Mortimer Strick
Death by: Pulled apart by bulls!
Pre-Slasher Occupation: Rodeo clown
Slasher type: Vengeful ghoul

Special abilities: Resistance to damage. ability to separate and reattach body parts. Each piece retains it's own limited mobility and remains under Mortimer's control.

Body Count: 4

The story: Mortimer Strick was a popular rodeo clown in San Antonio, Texas. Strick also happened to be a serial rapist. When he was caught attacking a cattle hands wife, the man and his freind's reacted by stringing Strick between several bulls and tearing him apart.

WAKING MAN

Real Name: Sam Steiger
Death by: Drug overdose
Pre-Slasher Occupation: Janitor at a Sleep Disorder Clinic
Slasher type: Obsessive Nutjob

Special abilities: Resistance to damage.

Slasher weapon: Scythe

Body Count: 6

The story: Sam Steiger worked as a janitor at a Sleep Disorder Clinic in California. While working overnight, Steiger, a drug abuser, took an experimental sleep drug, hoping to get high. Unfortunately for Steiger, he took 8 times the recommended dosage. Steiger was technically dead for 12 minutes, during which time he had vivid hallucinations involving a world where peace reigned as all of humanity slept. When he was revived, Steiger began a murderous streak, attempting to bring the gift of sleep to the rest of the world.

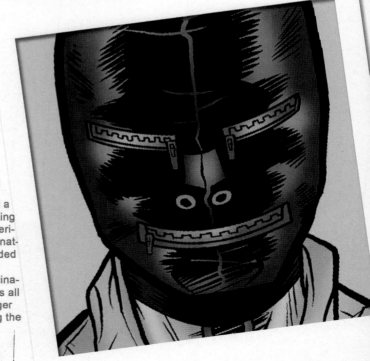

X-O

Real Name: Karl Vox
Death by: Factory accident
Pre-Slasher Occupation: Factory worker
Slasher type: Vengeful ghoul

Special abilities: Resistance to damage.

Slasher Weapon: None

Body Count: 14

The story: Karl Vox worked at a plastic factory in Arizona. A quiet, unobtrusive man, Karl spent his nights cruising highways for victims to play his bizarre "death games" with. Karl was eventually caught, but fled to the factory he worked at. A co-worker stopped him by dropping a heavy metal floor grating on him. He eventually rose to enact vengeance on his former co-workers.

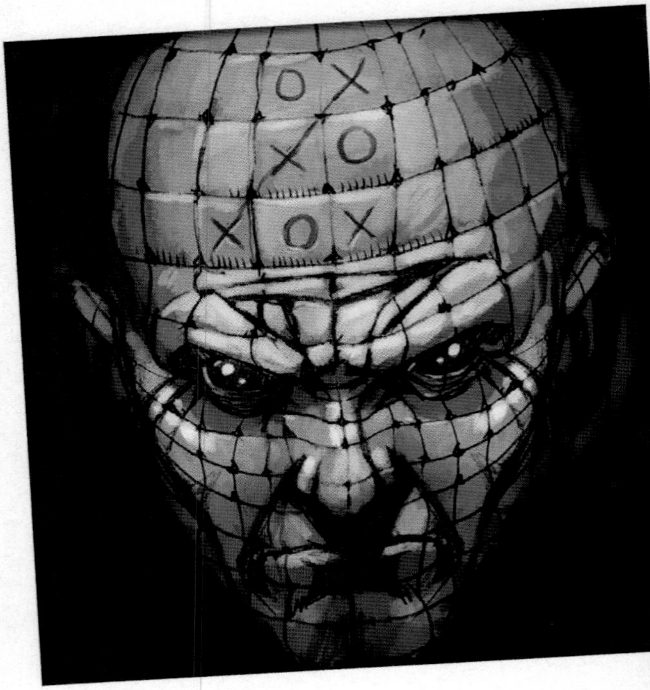

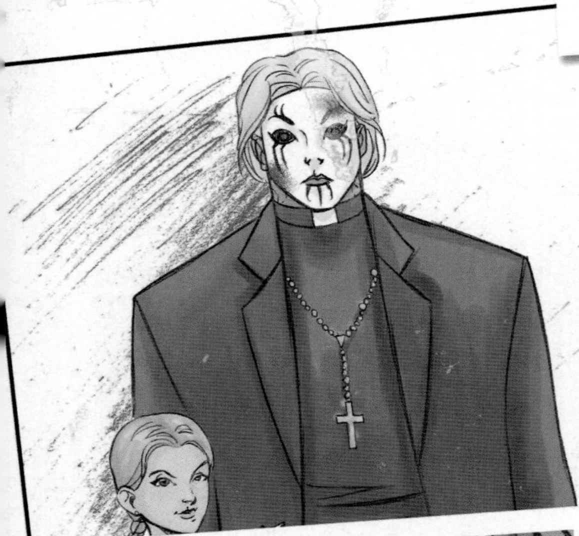

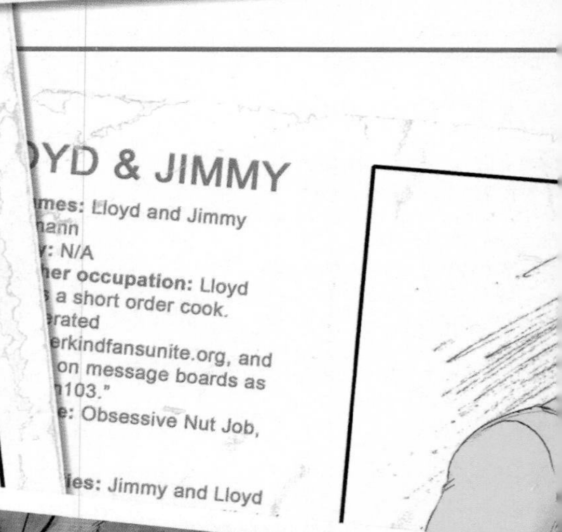
OYD & JIMMY
mes: Lloyd and Jimmy
nann
y: N/A
her occupation: Lloyd
a short order cook.
erated
erkindfansunite.org, and
on message boards as
n103."
e: Obsessive Nut Job,
ies: Jimmy and Lloyd

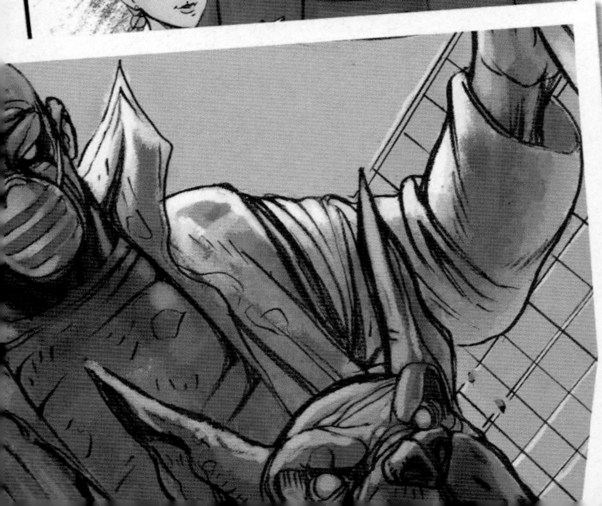

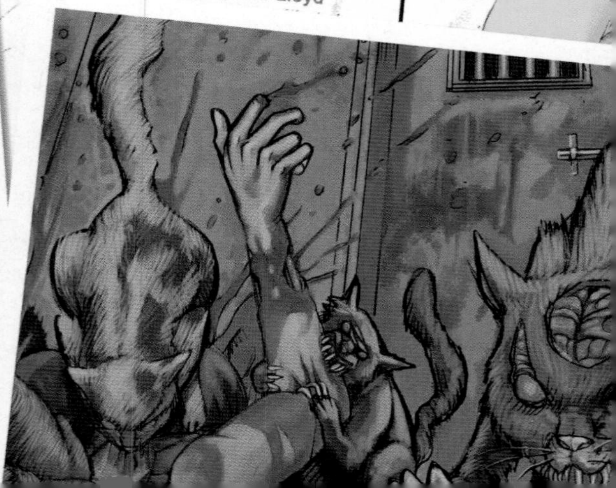

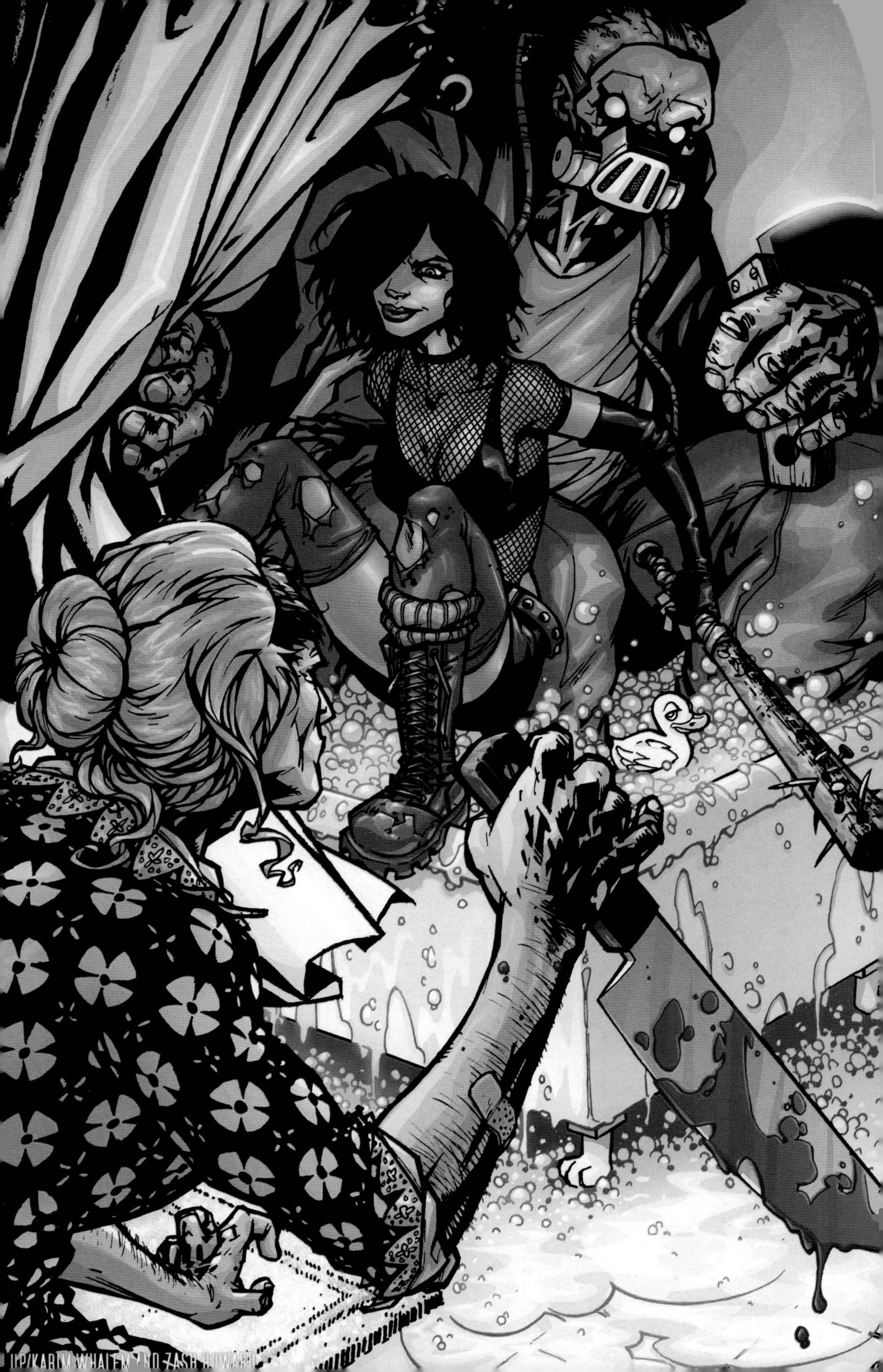

PIN UP/FEDERICA MANFREDI

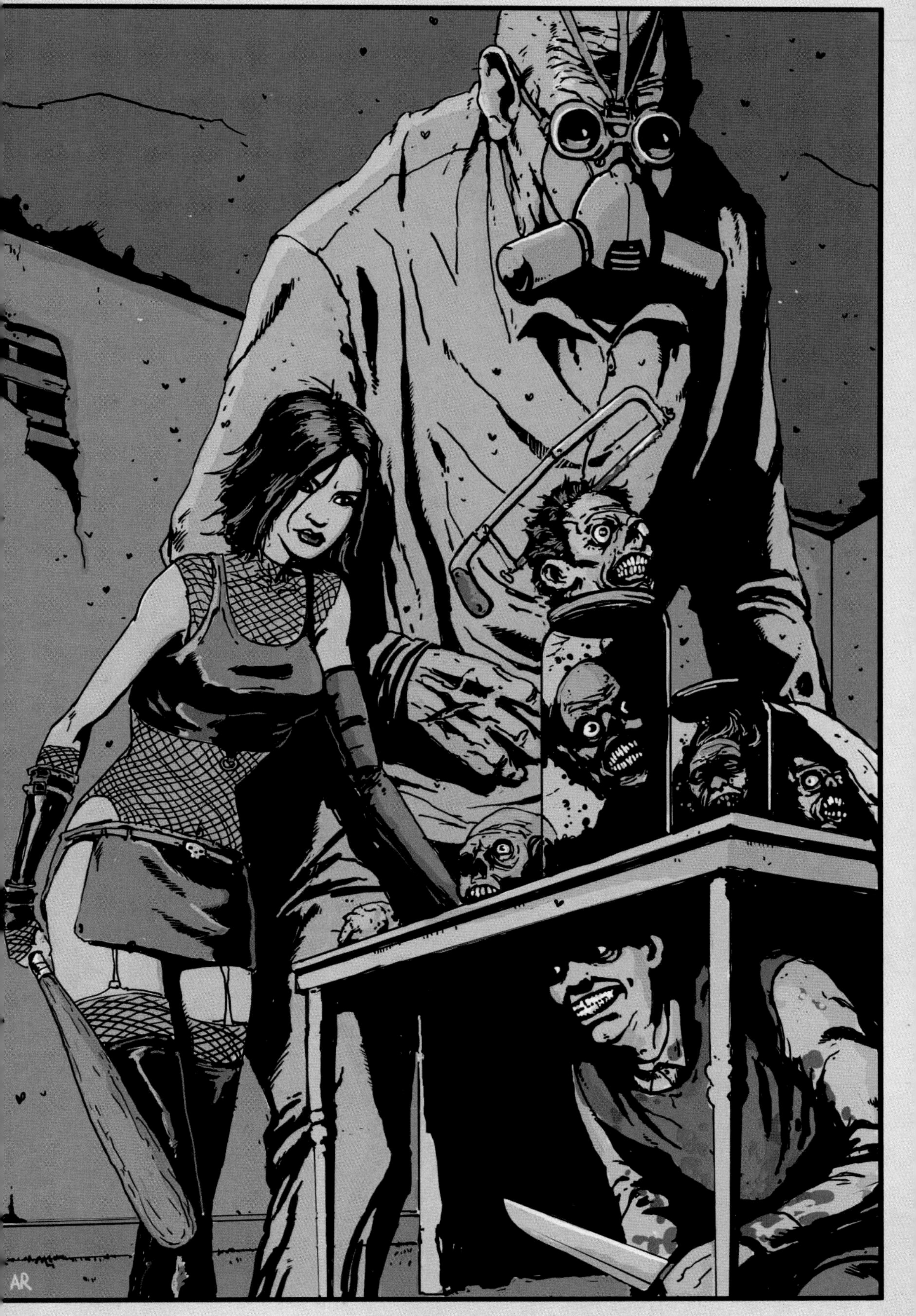
AR

PIN UP/ANDREW RITCHIE

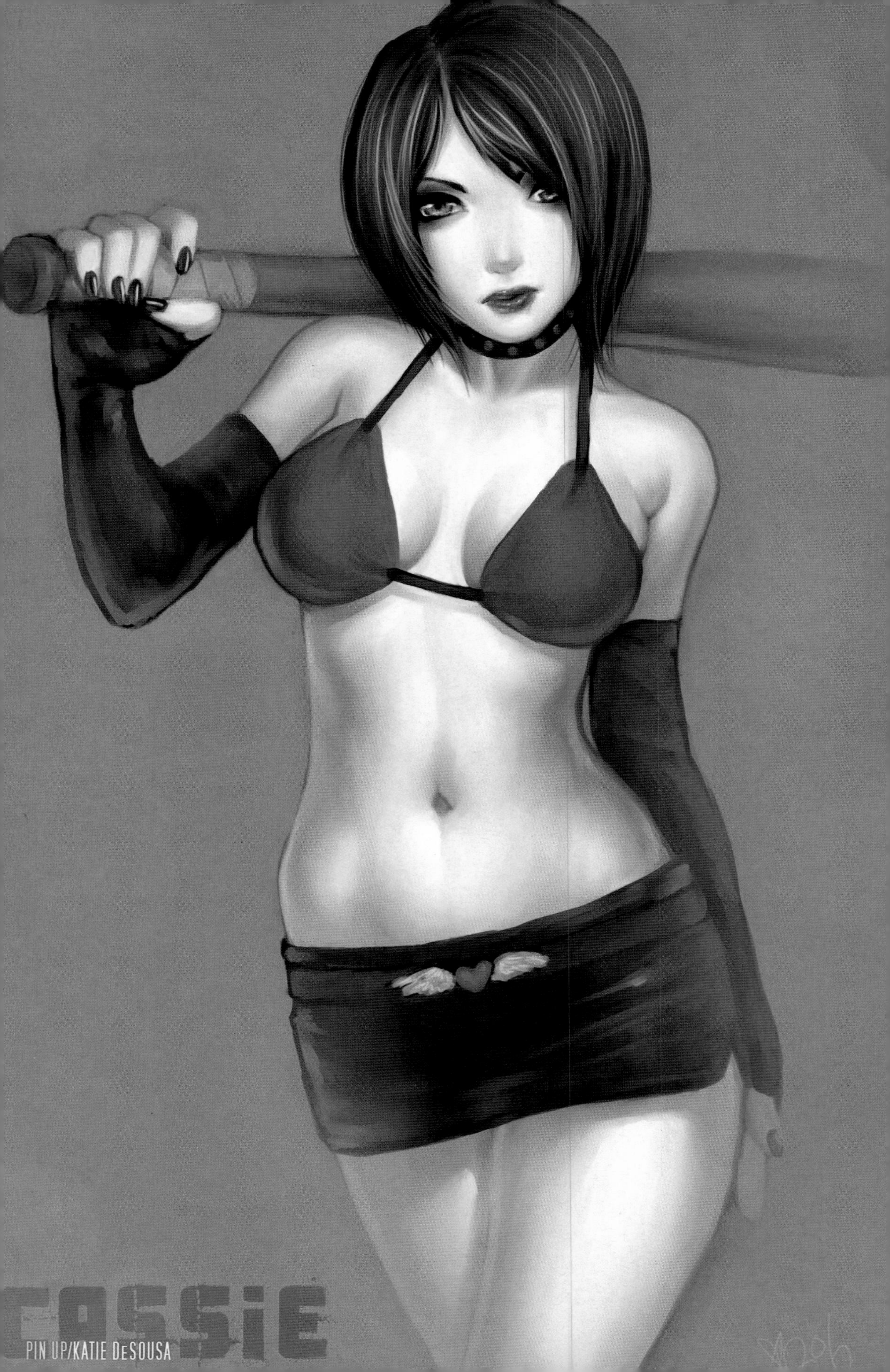
CASSIE
PIN UP/KATIE DeSOUSA